Buffy THE VAMPIRE SLAYER

2

Read how it all began.

BUFFY THE VAMPIRE SLAYER 1

And more Buffy is coming!

BUFFY THE VAMPIRE SLAYER 3

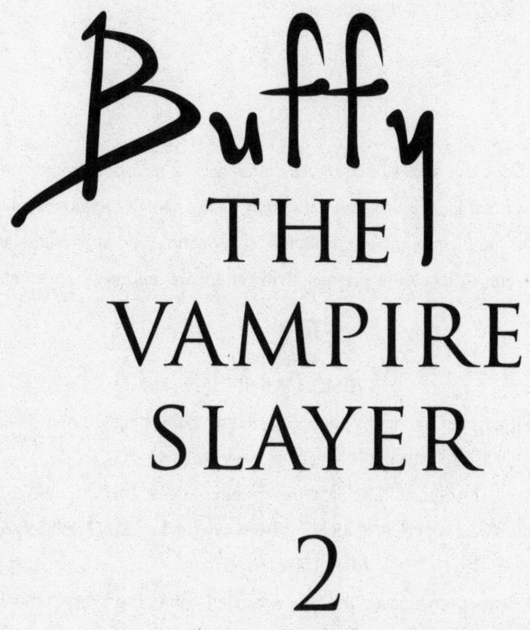

Halloween Rain

Christopher Golden and Nancy Holder

Bad Bargain

Diana G. Gallagher

Afterimage

Pierce Askegren

Based on the hit TV series created by Joss Whedon

Simon Pulse
New York London Toronto Sydney

SIMON PULSE

An imprint of Simon & Schuster Children's Publishing Division

1230 Avenue of the Americas, New York, NY 10020

This Simon Pulse paperback edition August 2010

The text of this book was set in Times.

Manufactured in the United States of America

2 4 6 8 10 9 7 5 3 1

Library of Congress Control Number 2010922983

ISBN 978-1-4424-1210-1

These titles were previously published individually.

Born into a legendary role, Buffy the Vampire Slayer carries the burden of humanity on her shoulders. Her true identity is known only to her Watcher, Giles, her best friends Willow, Xander, Cordelia, and Oz, and her good-hearted vampire boyfriend, Angel. Living in Sunnydale, California, above the Hellmouth, she is a high school student by day and a demon's worst adversary by night. These are her stories.

TABLE OF CONTENTS

Halloween Rain

FOR NANCY, WHO HONORED ME WITH THIS COLLABORATION, AND FOR SARAH MICHELLE GELLAR, WHO MAKES IT ALL LOOK SO EASY.
—C. G.

TO MY BELOVED DAUGHTER, BELLE.
I HOPE YOU'LL GROW UP TO BE AS STRONG AND BRAVE AS BUFFY, AS CLEVER AS WILLOW, AND AS SILLY AS YOUR DAD.
TO CHRIS, MY WONDERFUL COAUTHOR.
YOU'RE THE GREATEST.
—N. H.

No novel is ever completed without a supporting cast and crew. Christopher Golden and Nancy Holder would like to thank the people who helped us with our excellent adventure in Buffy Land, a.k.a. Boca del Infierno. They are: our agents, Lori Perkins and Howard Morhaim; Joss Whedon and everyone connected with our favorite Slayer, Sarah Michelle Gellar; our wonderful families, especially Connie and Wayne; and our Pocket posse, Lisa Clancy, Liz Shiflett, and Helena Santini. A thank-you, also, to Alice Alfonsi, for the jump-start.

And to Isabell Granados from Nancy, *muchas gracias*.

PROLOGUE

It was getting late. In the dim moonlight, the statues atop the gravestones in the Sunnydale Cemetery cast strange shadow-shapes across the dark mounds under which the town's dead lay. How long they might stay buried was in question, of course, since Sunnydale had another name. Early Spanish settlers called it Boca del Infierno. Buffy Summers didn't need to *habla* to translate: She lived in the Hellmouth.

Literally.

The cemetery provided the clearest indication of the town's true nature. Weeping stone angels became laughing devils. Hands clasped in prayer looked like ripping claws. Crosses hung upside down.

Way boring.

Buffy the Vampire Slayer stood just outside the cemetery and scanned the darkness among the gravestones for trouble. She sighed heavily as she leaned her elbows on the cemetery's granite wall. October 30 was almost over. She'd been out on patrol for hours, and she hadn't seen one vampire, one demon, one witch, one anything.

Well, okay, one witch. In gym. But Cordelia didn't count. She wasn't supernaturally evil. She only acted like a broom rider. Buffy understood. Poor Cordelia was cursed with popularity, great clothes, and, no lie, she was a babe. Naturally she had to take her frustrations out on everybody who didn't have it as good as she did.

Buffy supposed she should count her own blessings. She and Giles, her Watcher, had both expected the Halloween season to be the equivalent of finals for her Slayer diploma. All through October she'd trained hard, kept in shape, and sharpened up some very thick and sturdy pieces of wood. She was psyched for slaughter. She was pumped for pounding.

The little things a teenager gets excited about.

But now, standing outside the cemetery, the only monsters she was fighting were major Godzilla yawns. Buffy was so not thrilled. She hadn't seen any extreme vampire action for three weeks. Or much of anything else. Zip. Zilch. Nada. She'd been so bored she'd actually started to study. But that novelty was so over.

Still, no vamp sightings. Wasn't this cause for putting on a happy face?

Ever since she'd found out she was the Chosen One, all she'd wanted was to be a normal teenage girl. Maybe even a cheerleader. To have a honey of a boyfriend, hang out with her friends, and try to graduate from high school while doing as little actual studying as possible.

Instead, her extracurriculars centered around staking vampires, wasting monsters, and trying to keep her friends breathing long enough for them to graduate from high school. Much joy, what a treat. Smart, cute chick in desperate need of a life. But did she try to get a life? No, she wandered around looking for something undead to re-dead.

Pathetic much?

It isn't bad enough I have to pull the night shift, Buffy thought, *but how much more of a waste of time is it to be the Slayer when all the slayees are out of town or something?*

"Yo, dead guys," she called mournfully. Then she shrugged. What the hell. Her mom would tell her not to look a gift horse in the mouth. Good symbolism: Teeth were a big issue in Buffy's life. If you had long, sharp, pointy ones, she killed you.

Not tonight. She was a soldier without a war. All dressed up and no one to destroy. Time to call it a night, she figured. Maybe Willow would come over for some American history tutoring and they could scarf all the Halloween candy Buffy's mom had bought at the store. Or they could curl up with a good gory horror movie, the way Buffy and her mom used to do before Buffy had to burn down the gym at her old high school to kill a bunch of vampires, and they had to move to Sunnydale.

Out of the frying pan, into the mouth of hell.

From deep within the cemetery, a bloodcurdling scream pierced the night. Without hesitation, Buffy vaulted over the cemetery wall. She scanned left and right as she raced in the direction of the scream, dodging broken headstones, bushes, and tree roots. Just in case, she yanked open her shoulder bag and pulled out a stake. Boy Scouts and vampire slayers should always be prepared.

Another scream, this one louder and more frantic.

She ran faster, wondering what she would be going up against. One vampire? Two? A tribe of them? Or something she had never encountered before, a Halloween treat from hell? For half a second, she wished she had an elsewhere to be, but she brushed the thought away. She'd been looking for trouble. Now it had found her. She was the Chosen One, after all.

Another scream—shriek, more like. Now Buffy could tell it was a girl's voice. Screaming.

"Oh, God, stop!" it went on.

Afraid she might be too late, Buffy charged around the nearest headstone.

A blond-haired girl was struggling and kicking on the long, marble slab top of a tomb. A dark figure held both her wrists in his clutches, and he laughed and lowered his head, aiming for her neck. The girl shrieked even louder.

Buffy put one sneaker on top of a headstone and launched herself through the air. She tore the figure off the girl and they tumbled to the ground beside the tomb together. She threw him on his back, wrapped her hands around the stake, took aim, and—

"Stop!" the girl on the tomb screeched in abject terror. "Leave him alone!"

Buffy glanced up at the shadowed face of the girl's attacker. It was John Bartlett, who sat across from her in trig class. And his "victim" was Aphrodesia Kingsbury, his girlfriend.

"What's your *damage*, Buffy?" Aphrodesia yelled as John scrabbled away from Buffy. Aphrodesia threw her arms around him. "Insane much? Are you, like, asylum bound or what?"

Buffy moved away from John, put the stake in her bag as calmly as she could, and cleared her throat. "Sorry," she muttered. "I, ah, thought you were someone else."

She got to her feet. The two kids stared at her. She tried to smile, her face twisted into a grimace of acute humiliation. "Sorry," she said again. "Ah, happy Halloween."

She turned around and squared her shoulders, walking back the way she had come with as much dignity as she could muster.

"What a psycho," Aphrodesia said, and didn't even bother to whisper.

"Way psycho," John replied. "She's a hottie, though."

"Jo-ohn!" Aphrodesia whined.

Buffy could hear them bickering all the way to the cemetery wall. It was that disgustingly sweet bickering people did when they actually had a someone to bicker with. Buffy the Chosen One, the Slayer, the complete moron, went home to concentrate on eating all the frozen yogurt in the house.

After all, tomorrow was another day. And another night. Halloween night, actually.

And there had to be something to keep the Slayer busy on Halloween.

CHAPTER ONE

Buffy hadn't slept well, and as if she weren't tired enough already, the sky was crowded with dark clouds, the air heavy and damp with the threat of rain. It was the kind of day that just made you want to pull the covers over your head and snooze all day. Like a vampire. It was the kind of day when guys and gals too hip to get cancer got all broken up because they couldn't work on their tans.

Actually, sometimes Buffy thought it would be better if tans hadn't become as uncool as smoking. It'd be a lot easier to tell the undead from the brain dead.

Resolved to stay awake in first period, she forced her eyes open wider. Backpack over her shoulder, Buffy marched toward school, a little early as always. Well, not always. She was never even on time at her old school, but she was trying to reform. And besides, when she showed early, she got to hang with Willow and Xander for a few minutes before the whole grand delirium of the school day began.

"Happy Halloween!" Xander cried as he caught up from behind.

Buffy smiled slightly as he fell into step with her. "Xander, isn't Halloween, like, prom night for ghouls? The night when, all over the world, the forces of darkness are set free for their annual block party?"

"Well, yeah, but it's all costumes and parties and trick-or-treat and—," Xander began, but Buffy cut him off.

"And where do we live?" she prodded.

"Okay, I get the point," he surrendered. "But things have been pretty quiet lately, so I figured, why not be a little festive during my used-to-be-favorite-before-I-knew-all-this-stuff-was-real holiday?"

Buffy gave up. "Happy Halloween to you, too, Xander." She winced inside. The last person she'd offered season's greetings to had called her a thundering psycho.

Xander Harris offered her a charming, crooked smile and pushed his somebody-get-me-a-comb hair away from his forehead. It seemed as if he wanted to say something more, but by then they had reached the bench where they met each morning. Willow was already there, her nose in a huge, dusty old book. The title was something about arcane rituals.

Xander peered over her shoulder. "Willow, dear Willow, you used to read such wholesome things." He feigned almost parental disapproval. "Now you've just fallen in with the wrong crowd."

Willow closed her book. "Giles loaned it to me," she said. "Fascinating stuff, actually. Apparently, there was this sixteenth-century alchemist who—and you guys really don't want to hear this, anyway."

Buffy and Xander exchanged innocent looks—Who, us? Not enraptured? But it would be a cold day in a place like, well, here, when they could put anything over on her. She tutored both of them in different subjects, was an Internet commando, and once in a while had to serve as Giles's translator, when the stuffy British librarian forgot he was speaking to people who hadn't spent their entire lives locked up in the Twilight Zone library.

"Happy Halloween, Willow," Buffy said warmly.

"Yeah, trick or treat, *chica*," Xander added.

With her long, straight chestnut hair and sad eyes, Willow Rosenberg was every bit as sweet yet, um, inelegant as her name might suggest. But she and Xander were the best friends Buffy had ever had. They knew everything about her, about her being the Slayer, and they stuck by her. In fact, time and again, Willow and Xander put their lives on the line for her, and for the town.

Buffy was the Chosen One. Slaying was her job. Willow and Xander did all the crazy stuff by choice. As far as Buffy was concerned, her friends were a lot braver than they ever gave themselves credit for.

"I don't know," Willow said as Buffy and Xander sat on the bench on either side of her. "Halloween isn't a big deal anymore. I mean, when we were kids, we got to dress up and go trick-or-treating. Once you're in the double digits, it's so over. I think I'm in mourning for my childhood, and I'm only sixteen."

"Clone that," Buffy said.

"Remember bobbing for apples at those killer Halloween parties your mom used to throw?" Xander asked Willow, and she smiled at him.

The two had known each other their whole lives, and Buffy had only come along this year. But they never made her feel left out, even when they talked about things they'd shared in the past.

"I remember you trying to drown me while I was bobbing for apples," Willow replied, then turned to Buffy. "It's amazing the selective memory guys have."

"Well, you know guys only tease girls when they're trying to get noticed," Buffy said, and raised an eyebrow.

"I noticed him when I was, like, five years old," Willow said under her breath. "I'm waiting for him to notice I noticed."

"I loved those parties," Xander went on, oblivious to Willow's comments. "I always used to win the pumpkin-carving contest. Big fun."

He sighed. "You're right. Halloween sucks now. Even the

horror movies on cable aren't as fun anymore, even since . . ." He hesitated. "Ah, ever since—"

"I know," Buffy said, sighing. "Ever since I came to town. I feel the same way. My mother and I used to watch all the classic fright flicks together and gorge ourselves on popcorn and leftover Halloween candy. Somehow I've lost interest in the movies. Now we just gorge ourselves."

Buffy felt a drop of rain on her arm and was about to mention it when Willow tapped her leg.

"Wicked witch and winged monkey at ten o'clock," she murmured.

Buffy looked up to see Cordelia and her fan club about to pass by. Cordelia paid no attention to them, but Aphrodesia Kingsbury was with her, and Buffy glanced away as the girl spotted her.

"Well, if it isn't my stalker," Aphrodesia sneered. "I told them all about it, Buffy, so don't try to deny your after-hours bipolar wig out to anyone on campus." She glared at her. "Isn't there some kind of medication you're forgetting to take?"

Before Buffy could respond, Xander snapped angrily, "Careful, Miss Twenty-Five-Watt. I wouldn't make Buffy mad if I were you."

"Xander," Buffy hissed, and Willow elbowed him in the stomach.

"Excuse me? Are you threatening me?" Aphrodesia said, zooming in like a heat-seeking missile on Xander. "Because my sister's fiancé is in law school, and, like, he told me he would serve anybody I asked him to."

"You know, I'd love it if he served me. I can't seem to get my own waiter's attention and we don't even have menus yet," Xander mocked. "Good help. Hard to find. So."

"Oh, you people are so . . . *not*," Aphrodesia said, wrinkling her nose as if she'd smelled something nasty. "You two." She nodded toward Xander and Willow. "It's like Cordelia says. You're just run-of-the-mill losers. With a lot of effort, you might actually evolve into primates. But not if you loiter with Buffy. Her weirdness is like some brain-eating virus, and it's seriously infected your chances for a normal social life."

By then, Cordelia and the rest of her crew had moved on, and Aphrodesia spun in a huff to follow.

The three of them were quiet until the others were out of earshot. Then Willow turned to Xander with her eyebrows raised.

"What?" Xander asked.

"Miss Twenty-Five-Watt?"

"Well, Aphrodesia's not very bright," Xander explained. "Twenty-five-watt. Get it?"

"Got it," Buffy and Willow said simultaneously.

"Who writes your stuff?" Buffy asked, and the girls laughed together.

"Well, I thought it was funny," Xander mumbled snippily.

"We're just kidding, Xander," Willow said. "You know we love you."

"Good thing, or you'd both be in deep can't-say-that-on-television," he replied menacingly.

"Witness our trembling," Buffy drawled.

"I have that effect on women," Xander announced.

"So," Willow said, "you guys both coming to the Bronze tonight?"

"The masquerade! Wouldn't miss it!" Xander said excitedly. "I'm going as Indiana Jones."

"Oh, I'm so not surprised," Willow said. "You've dressed in that stupid hat every Halloween since you were nine."

Xander stared at her, horrified, and Buffy stifled a laugh to save him from further embarrassment.

"If adventure has a name, my dear, it's Xander Harris," he said proudly. "Well, actually, it's Harrison Ford, but women confuse the two of us all the time."

They stared at him.

"Okay, it's happened a couple of times . . . once . . . okay, never, but we have kind of the same hair color," Xander explained. "Brown. And my mom thinks I look like him. I suppose you two have a better costume idea for me?"

"I've got one, but I'll tell you later," Willow said cryptically. "It's a surprise for Buffy."

"For me? I'm an extreme no-show tonight," Buffy protested. "It's the Slayer Super Bowl."

Willow and Xander both frowned at her. For once, no snappy retorts. She was almost insulted, but then realized their silence was skeptical comment enough. Both of them knew that she'd been bored out of her mind the past few weeks.

"Okay, I am majorly sorry to have to blink and miss the masquerade, and I know you fun seekers think I'm so wasting my time, but it's Halloween night," Buffy explained. "I mean, so business has been a little slow—"

"Way slow," Willow corrected.

"Way slow," Buffy agreed. "But it's got to pick up tonight."

"You sound like you want it to pick up tonight," Xander said. "I know compared to LA raves, a masquerade is tiny potatoes. But trust us, it's the most fun you can have in this agonizingly lame town."

"Come on, Buffy," Willow pleaded. "At least you can start out at the Bronze. If there's a gory emergency, you can always book."

Buffy thought about it, but not for long. If she didn't start hanging with her friends more, they might adopt a new Slayer as their bud. Or not, since there weren't any others. One in every generation, that was Giles's favorite part of the Big Book of Slayage. But she still liked the idea of a quiet night at the Bronze.

"I'll talk to Giles," Buffy decided. "He still thinks this is all just the calm before the storm."

"Tell him we'll take care of you," Xander suggested.

"Yeah, I'll carry your bag o' holy water and Xander will gas up the Batmobile," Willow said.

As soon as the freedom bell rang, announcing that school was mercifully over for another day, Buffy was up and fighting through the swarm. In the hall, lockers clanged, gossip raged, girls shrieked, and guys laughed. She heard snippets of conversation, mostly about what people were wearing to the masquerade. There was mischief in the air, and a sense that anyone could burst into a fit of the giggles at any time. Halloween was such a kids' holiday.

But it hadn't always been that way. Giles was up on all the wicked history, but Buffy knew enough of it to know Halloween was made up to replace some kind of ancient death ritual or something. She'd have to ask him. Actually, come to think of it, she probably wouldn't have to ask him. Giles didn't usually need to be asked to start lecturing. He just did.

The hall traffic had started to thin. Buffy blew off her locker; she had everything she needed for the weekend in her backpack. Instead, she headed for the library to check in with Giles.

Buffy was passing by the science lab when powerful hands with matted fur and yellow claws flashed out and snagged her by the shoulders. Out of the corner of her eye she saw the open jaws of the werewolf and reacted: a hard elbow to the ribs met with a satisfying grunt from behind. There was a roar in front of her, and Buffy looked up to see a second werewolf approaching. She straight-armed this one with the flat of her hand, knocking him on his butt, leaping high into an aerial roundhouse kick while her brain struggled frantically to send her a message: *Cease. Desist. Remember the cemetery, Buffy?*

Buffy pulled back on the kick and landed ungracefully on her behind. She glanced at the two "werewolves," who she now realized were just big guys in full costume.

"Way to go, Jackie Chan," a short guy with thick glasses and a leaning tower of books cried happily. "Those guys have been defining obnoxious with their bad-hair-scare tactics."

"Uh, sorry," she mumbled to the nearer one, who was trying to get to his knees. The other one was using all the words that were forbidden on sitcoms. "Your costumes are, ah, really there. I guess I'm just a little jumpy."

Buffy looked up in time to see the gathering crowd of vultures part for their queen, Cordelia, and her entourage. Before the other girl swooped down for the attack, Buffy winced and tiredly rolled her eyes.

"Jumpy?" Cordelia parroted. "Just a little psycho, more like. Guys, take note, a major body lingo signal from Buffy here. Don't invade her personal space or she'll go all, like, special forces on you. Or maybe you thought they were real werewolves, huh, Summers?"

"Never know what's going to pop its ugly monster Pez-head up out of hell on Halloween, Cordelia. Witness your sudden arrival," Buffy snapped, then spun and stalked away toward the library. She could almost hear the anger building inside Cordelia Chase.

"Bye-bye, Buffy the walking X-File," Cordelia called after her, followed by a chorus of laughter from kids without the guts to make fun of her to her face.

If she cared about fitting in, if she allowed her feelings to be hurt by someone as deep as the kiddie pool, she might have been upset. But Buffy was so above it all. She was the Slayer. Normal teen angst didn't stack up to fangs at your throat.

Sometimes, it was worse.

Sure, she was the Slayer, but Buffy's face was flushed and she couldn't have forced a smile onto her face with a Neiman Marcus shopping spree. Well, maybe that. She did need black boots. And a few other things.

When she pulled open the door to the library, Buffy was smiling again and thinking cashmere. Winter was coming, after all. Cordelia's tongue was a weapon, but her hack-and-slash approach was clumsy enough that the wounds were never deep.

At a long research table in the library was a stack of moldy old books that could only belong to one man. But despite the presence of titles like *Archaic Druidry*, *Celtic Magick*, and *Shadow Realms*, among many others, their owner was nowhere in sight.

"Giles?" Buffy called.

"Hmm?" a mumbled response came from the library's second-story loft. "Oh, yes, Buffy, up here. Is school over already, or are you cutting class again?"

She looked up at him and realized Giles hadn't even taken his eyes off the racks of books.

"The school is burning down, Giles," she said, trying to raise some reaction. Nothing. "You didn't even hear the bell. What's got you by the nostrils?"

No response.

"Giles?"

"Sorry," he said, distracted. "I'll be down in a moment."

Buffy slid her backpack onto the table. She dropped into a chair, leaned back, and planted her feet on the scarred oak. A quick glance around told her something she'd already known: She and Giles were alone in the library.

Of course they were. Even before Rupert Giles left the staff of the British Museum to become school librarian at Sunnydale High—a career move roughly equivalent to an appointment with Dr. Kevorkian—the library wasn't exactly the place to be seen by people hip enough to look. It was more like a dungeon with books, and barely enough light to read them by.

Still was. Only now, it was *Mission: Impossible* to find the books kids actually needed for class. Giles had brought in his own collection, so very not the kind of reading material parents wanted their college-bound spawn to lay paws on. The librarian had more important things to worry about. He was the Watcher. His job was to prepare the Slayer for her work, to train and educate her, to teach her what she needed to know to keep breathing.

A bit of a stiff, but Giles was all right in Buffy's book. His job was keeping her alive, after all. How bad could the guy be? Call a press conference, though, she actually liked him. He was kind of absentminded, and talked way British—she could hardly understand him at times—but he was cool.

Handsome, too, in that your-dad's-pretty-good-looking-for-an-old-guy kind of way.

Buffy just wished he wouldn't get all overprotective so often. She had a hard enough time getting her mother to let her have a life.

The library door swung open, and Buffy started and spun to face the door. It was only Willow and Xander, though, and she relaxed immediately.

"Not too jumpy, are we?" Xander asked.

"See, that's what I told Cordelia," Buffy said, and smiled.

"We heard," Willow admitted. "Good thing you didn't try beheading those impostor-monsters."

"There's always next time," Buffy replied with a shrug.

Giles came down the stairs behind them, and they all turned to see him fumbling with a tall stack of books in his arms. Buffy held her breath until he reached the bottom, afraid he was going to trip any second. But Giles made it to the table without disaster.

"Ah," he said as he glanced around at them. "You're all here. Excellent. I'm in the middle of an important research project, but I want to give you a bit of preparation for Halloween. Buffy's heard most of this, but as tonight *is* Halloween, I thought perhaps this time she might actually pay attention."

Buffy shot Giles a withering glance, but he went on, totally unwithered. She didn't argue, though. She hadn't really paid attention before.

"Whoa, camel," Xander interrupted. "We've got this masquerade at the Bronze tonight. Didn't Buffy tell you?"

"Tell me?" Giles asked. "Tell me what?"

"I'm off duty tonight," Buffy declared. "It's been way dead in the undead department, boss. I figure it can't hurt to pretend Halloween's just tricks and treats."

"First of all, Buffy, I am not your boss," Giles huffed. "Your mentor, perhaps, if you would do me the honor of considering me such. But not boss. You are the Slayer, and I the Watcher. Secondly, I'm afraid what you propose is impossible."

"She didn't propose," Willow said. "I didn't hear her proposing."

"Definite no proposing," Xander agreed. "More of an announcement. Attention Kmart shoppers, no slaying tonight. That kind of thing."

Giles sighed deeply.

"You must understand, all of you," he began. "The recent lull in supernatural activity, vampiric or otherwise, does not necessarily mean that tonight will be as quiet as we would all wish. To understand, you must understand Halloween itself."

"Here he goes," Buffy said, and rolled her eyes.

"In Celtic times," Giles explained, "the year began in February and lasted until late October. The winter months, during which the land would wither and die, weren't even considered real time, in a sense, but a barren world of shadow and worship of the dark gods, what we call demons, or ancient ones.

"During this dead time, called Samhuinn, the gates between worlds were open; the dead and the living could mingle. There were feasts for the dead, bribes for the evil ones among them, offerings to convince them not to harm the innocent, and rituals to keep them bound.

"Over time, as the faith in such things has waned, the season has shortened so that it now lasts only three days, from today, October thirty-first, to the second of November. But tonight is the night when the Druid priests would hold the ceremony marking the beginning of Samhuinn, and the night when the tribes of the night run free. Without the rituals and offerings to control them, the evil ones are not kept at bay.

"When the English Christians converted the Celts, they changed the names of these days. October thirty-first became All Hallow's Eve, or Hallowe'en," Giles concluded, then took a breath and looked at them expectantly.

The three teens stared back.

"So your point would be what?" Xander asked.

Giles pushed his glasses up his nose and looked at the Slayer. "Buffy?" he asked.

Buffy sighed. "His extreme boredom point would be that whatever happened up until tonight meant as much as a political promise," she explained. "Tonight the dead try to take over the world."

Xander and Willow stared at Buffy, then glanced at Giles before meeting each other's gaze. Finally, Xander said, "Willow, are you pondering what I'm pondering?"

"Yes, Xander. Indeed," Willow replied, then looked at Buffy and Giles as if they'd flunked kindergarten. "Maybe I just haven't been, y'know, paying attention," she said. "But why hasn't this happened before? Okay, since Buffy's been here, things have gotten weirder, but Sunnydale is at the mouth of hell, remember. If Halloween was all that, wouldn't the whole town have been dusted decades ago?"

"Well," Giles replied, "there is that."

"Wait," Buffy said. "You just said since nobody believes in these guys anymore, Halloween keeps shrinking, right?"

"Something like that," Giles admitted.

"I get it," Xander said. "So, this Samhuinn thing is just . . . over, right?"

"*So* over," Buffy agreed. "Which means a quiet night, which means I am going to the masquerade."

Giles began to clear his throat. The stern expression on his face made it clear he was not with Buffy's program at all. She decided quickly that a compromise was in order.

"Okay, plea bargain time," she said. "I'll only stay for a while, and then I'll go out and have a look around. If it's still quiet, I'll go back to the party. If there's slaying to be done, well, I'm the Slayer. Deal?"

"What choice do I have?" Giles moaned. "As you say, you are the Slayer."

"Right," Buffy said happily. "I keep forgetting that part."

"Cool," Xander said. "Just make sure you stay clear of farms and fields, anywhere there's a scarecrow."

Buffy frowned. “Or a tin man or a lion?” she asked.

“It’s raining today, duh!” Xander said, then slapped himself in the forehead. “Duh again! You’re not from around here.”

Buffy looked at Willow. “What flight is he on?” she asked with very mild annoyance.

“It’s a local thing, kind of a bogeyman-type legend,” Willow explained. “According to the stories, there’s dark magick in Halloween rain. If it soaks into a scarecrow, and you trespass on the scarecrow’s territory, it will come to life and give you a stern talking to. No, extreme punishment, really.”

“Odd,” Giles said. “I’ve never even heard such a legend, and yet there are many references to a tie between scarecrows and Samhain.”

“Samhuinn again?” Xander asked.

“Not quite the same thing,” Giles explained. “Samhuinn is the season or the night of ritual itself. Samhain is the spirit of Hallowe’en, the king of the dead souls who haunted the land of the living on that night. Apparently, he was one of the demons, one of the ancient ones who inhabited this world before the birth of humanity, and he was sort of adopted by the Celts as one of their gods.”

“So he’s a foster demon, really,” Xander joked.

“Not a laughing matter,” Giles said, turning to the stack of books he’d brought down. “Samhain is one of the most evil creatures ever to walk the earth. Vicious and cunning. I really ought to look into this . . .”

The Watcher's word trailed off as he lost himself in his books again.

Buffy, Xander, and Willow waited for a few seconds, to see if Giles would continue. He didn't. The books had possessed him again, and the rest of them had become invisible.

Finally, Buffy shrugged.

"So, see you tonight," she said to Willow and Xander. "Watch out for wet scarecrows."

"It's no joke, Buffy," Xander said.

"Who's joking?" Buffy asked.

CHAPTER TWO

When Buffy bounced down the last couple of stairs toward the living room, she could hear the popcorn drum solo coming from the microwave. The smell started her craving salt, butter, and those little unpopped kernels she always gagged on. Her mom sat in the living room watching *Fright Night* on Showtime. Buffy smiled. Mom had no idea she was watching what amounted to Slayer training videos.

After she'd gone into the kitchen and dumped the popcorn into a large bowl, Buffy went in to see her mother. She slid the bowl onto the coffee table and stood and watched the movie for a moment.

"Sit down, honey," her mother said without looking up.

"After this, they're going to show *Burnt Offerings.* Now that's a creepy one."

"Uh, I'd really love to, Mom, but I'm supposed to meet Willow and Xander down at the Bronze. There's a masquerade tonight," Buffy said quickly.

Her mother had glanced up as she spoke, and Buffy could see the surprise and then disappointment in her eyes as Joyce Summers saw that her daughter was in costume and then realized what that meant. Then the disappointment evaporated.

"That's great, Buffy," Joyce said. "I guess I can't complain when you hang out with that Willow. She's a nice girl. I'd like to know more about this boy Xander, though."

"*So* nothing there, Mom," Buffy said, rolling her eyes. "Sorry to dash your hopes against the rocks of my singleness, but he's just a friend."

"Well, I'm sure your singleness will be in jeopardy once you show up at the Bronze in that costume," her mother replied with a mixture of teasing and disapproval. "It's a bit . . . abbreviated."

Of course her mother had no idea that this year, Buffy had dressed for function and not form: in her knee-high boots, black shorts, and red silk blouse tied in a knot, the Chosen One could leap, kick, gouge, run, and skewer with the greatest of ease. Add a patch over one eye—yo, ho, ho and a bottle of root beer. If anybody asked, she was captain of the H.M.S. *Hellmouth.* The very model of a modern Slayer general.

"I'm a pirate queen, Mom," Buffy explained. "Like Anne Bonny. They all dressed like this."

"I don't know about that," her mother commented. "Just please be careful. You don't want to attract the wrong kind of attention."

Of course not, Buffy thought. No slavering sixteen-year-old boys, just slavering, long-fanged vampires.

Major sigh.

Her mother had offered to drive her to the Bronze, but Buffy just couldn't accept. If there was trouble, it would be easier for her to handle knowing her mom was safe at home where no uninvited vampires could cross their threshold. Not to mention that when your reputation needed CPR, you might as well show up in a hearse as have your parents drive you somewhere.

Still, she knew it was no joy for her mom to be alone in a new town on a nostalgic night, and Buffy was sorry.

Things were quiet on the walk. Buffy scanned the area through her clear plastic umbrella, seeing nothing but glowing pumpkin faces on porches, the moon shrouded by clouds, and her own shadow splashed across buildings like a billboard: *Here she is! The Slayer, all alone!* But no one was checking the classifieds, not a single vampire or demon, and definitely no walking scarecrows. Come to think of it, she couldn't remember if she'd ever seen a scarecrow in Sunnydale. There were some fields by the cemetery, but she couldn't recall any straw men hanging around. It would be a long detour to the Bronze just to go over there and cross them off her sightseeing list. Another time, she thought.

By the time Buffy got to the Bronze, the rain had slowed but not stopped. She paid the cover to the masked hunchback at the door and joined the rest of the crowd streaming inside.

Xander and Willow had been right: On Halloween night, the Bronze was clearly the place to be if you were too old to beg for candy from strangers. Sunken cheek by devil tail, the club was jammed with dozens of witches, Frankenstein monsters and Count Draculas, four zombies, three mad scientists, two white-sheeted ghosts, and a hanged man in a pear tree.

Everyone was a little damp from the rain, and through the Bronze wafted a fragrance that could only be called eau de wet dog. Makeup was running, frizzed-out Bride of Frankenstein hair was sagging, and costumes were clinging conspicuously to people who possessed any conspicuosities to be clung to. Hey, not everybody at sixteen looked like Wonderbra Woman.

Speaking of possessed, Cordelia was in the corner putting the hex on some honey wearing a buckskin shirt, chaps, and moccasins. Cordelia was working overtime for tepee time in a very slinky, clingy Morticia Addams unoriginal complemented by her black hair and matching lips, nails, and soul. She had put a lot of time and no doubt somebody else's effort into the Spider-Woman motif.

As Buffy looked on, Cordelia and the victim of her

attentions were interrupted by a tall, dark stranger. He wore a white half-face Phantom of the Opera mask and a long cloak, and Buffy thought that with his high cheekbones and shoulder-length, blue-black hair he looked Native American. The Phantom sneered something at the guy dressed up as an Indian. It looked as though the costume had pissed the Phantom off, because he got in threateningly close—Listerine close—and sneered something at the object of Cordelia's affections.

The costumed Indian backed off as if the Phantom were for real. Buffy watched him scramble away, obviously wigged. Then she stared in disgust as Cordelia shamelessly smiled at the Phantom, laid a hand on his biceps, and started chatting him up, herding him toward the bar.

"Major harlot," Buffy muttered under her breath, then turned to scan the rest of the masquerade.

Cardboard skeletons hung from the ceiling of the Bronze, and each table was decorated with a black candle inside a grinning plastic jack-o'-lantern. Drinks spewing dry ice were lined up on tables and along the balcony railing. A fog machine churned out graveyard mist. The cover band jammed out a harsh version of Michael Jackson's "Thriller." Everybody was hopping at the zombie jamboree.

Willow and Xander weren't there yet. Buffy was less than eager to wait by herself. She was fast becoming the school psycho, just as she had been back at Hemery High in Los Angeles. She'd totally been there, had so done that. Giles would never savvy why she thought it was so not fair. All Superman had to do was put on a pair of glasses and act clumsy at his day job. He never had to contend with the evil forces of high school while trying to save the world.

"Buffy," Willow said behind her. Finally. "Hi."

Wedging herself against a couple of jock types dressed as girls, Buffy twisted herself around in a tight half circle to face Willow. Xander stood beside her. Buffy blinked.

Willow and Xander were wearing suits.

Xander's hair was slicked back. He was a new Xander, a Bizarro-world Xander, too young to be a yuppie and too clean-cut to be himself.

Willow was in a baggy dark blue suit with a skirt that hung down to her low heels. Oddly, her hair gleamed with a henna wash, and it looked pretty good. But as if to cancel out the color's cool factor, she had tied it back with a severe tortoise-shell clip.

"Accountants. How unique," Buffy said brightly. "I wish I'd thought of that. I could be scoring major babe points as we speak."

Willow frowned. "No, Buffy. Not accountants."

Xander looked dashed. "Scully and Mulder. *The X-Files*." He flashed her a badge that read Sunnydale Junior Policeman and muttered, "FBI. You're under arrest for killing dead guys."

Buffy laughed. "It's perfect! I'm not exhibiting much originality, I fear. Just a pirate queen." She posed. "You two slap the cuffs on and I'll run 'em through."

"Oh, you look totally . . . seaworthy," Xander gushed.

Willow added, "I thought you might dress up like a vampire. You know, as a joke."

"Too self-referential. Besides, if I screwed up the uniform I might piss 'em off."

"Off-pissing of vampires. You'd never want to do that." Willow touched her hair a little shyly. "So, how do I look as a redhead?"

"A hottie," Buffy assured her. "Maybe you should keep it."

Xander looked confused as he glanced at Willow. "You did something to your hair?"

Willow and Buffy treaded glances and looked back at him. Willow looked philosophical and said, "No, Xander. I've always had bright red hair."

"It, um, looks nice." He flushed and said to Buffy, "Well, I was hoping we'd finally get to see your secret Slayer costume."

Buffy shrugged. "Oh, I was going to wear it, but it's so hard to accessorize a skintight leotard. As I'm sure you know, Xander."

Xander threw back his head. "Yeah, but I had to hang up my cape. I was always getting typecast as a lovable, decent guy girls were safe around. Not that I'm not," he added quickly. Reconsidered. "Or that I am."

A contemporary man, Buffy thought, *Xander seems totally confused about the acceptable male aggression level.*

"I am what I am," Willow said, "and that's all what I am."

Buffy nodded. It must be nice to be able to say that.

Ten times fast.

She gestured at the stage, bobbed her head in time to the backbeat. "The band is called?"

Willow smiled. "Children of the Night, believe it or not."

Buffy grinned and continued to rock with the rhythm. "What music they make," she said happily.

Xander kept glancing at Willow's hair, and now he piped up, as if he had finally made all the connections. "Willow," he said exuberantly. "Hair. Red. Red is good. Fire engines are red. Porsches are red."

"So is blood," said a deep, not-good voice.

Buffy's mouth dropped open. Shoulder to shoulder, hip to hip, a cold-flesh-and-congealed-blood vampire bumped into her as he carried a cup across the club.

"All right. Hold it right there and let's take it outside," Buffy said between gritted teeth, grabbing his arm.

"Please." He took a step backward, shaking her off.

A plague victim groused, "Ouch. That's my foot, dude."

The vampire ignored him. These days, most people who still said "dude" got ignored.

"This is sacred Samhuinn, the night all demons run free," the vampire said.

"He read the same book as Rupert," Xander commented.

"A very sacred, holy night," the vampire continued, "when we rest while the others hunt."

"We being the fat cats?" Buffy jibed. "The ones who've ordered in?"

"The vampires." He said the word with dignity and pride, the way an armchair quarterback might say "MVP" or Cordelia might say "holder of a platinum charge card."

"What? You sucky boys have the night off? No preying or slaying?" Buffy cocked her head and put her hand on the zipper of her Slayer's bag, which was sitting on a bar stool. In case he was hungry, she had a nice juicy stake just waiting for him. "But if this is a scared—sacred—holy night, shouldn't you be doing that whole praying thing in some church? Like, down in the tunnels with Big Daddy?"

"You mock us." The vampire narrowed his eyes. "You know that if it hadn't been for that earthquake, my master would not be trapped inside that buried church." He was speaking of his leader, the Master vampire who had emigrated to America with the thought of making it big, like so many others in the brave New World. He came to the Hellmouth for the purpose of opening a dimensional portal that would release a Pandora's box of evils into the world . . . including his followers.

That was a tricky business in itself; add in a major earthquake that tumbled him into a church and scattered the portal into pieces, and you have one very not-so-happy monster.

"Were it not for the unforeseen shaking of the earth, he would be aboveground with us, here, now. We'd rule this place."

"The Bronze?" She looked around the room and spotted another fanged wonder. Another. Another. Once you noticed them, they stuck out like Waldo. The place was a regular Fangoria. "And you're here why? To measure for curtains?"

He flashed his nasty overbite at her and said, dead seriously, "We're here to have fun, the same as you."

"My idea of fun doesn't include ripping people's throats open and drinking their blood." Buffy opened the zipper of the bag and put her fingers around her cross, which she had taken off because it didn't go with her costume.

Stupid much?

The vampire offered her an evil smile. He lifted up a plastic cup. "You should try it sometime."

Willow covered her mouth. "There's human blood in there? Oh, God, I'm going to be sick."

Buffy raised her chin. "Anyone I know?"

"Just a snack." The vampire made a show of tipping back the cup and taking a good, long swallow. "Mmm. A fine bouquet. Young. Fresh. Innocent."

"So it's not Cordelia." Her hand hidden inside the bag, Buffy gripped the stake and glared at the vampire. "If we were alone—"

"But we're not." He set the cup on the table next to the pumpkin candle and dabbed at his lips with his fingertips. "Truly. We're simply here for the celebration. I propose we call a truce."

"Which you'll break the first chance you get." Buffy took a step toward him. This time he did not back up.

"We won't break it," he said confidently. "You have my assurance."

"I'm supposed to stake our lives on your word?"

"Pun intended," Willow added, stepping up behind Buffy, then taking a very courageous step to the left, slightly away from her.

The vampire's smile was a cry for dental coverage with all major medical plans. "Tonight you can make fools of yourselves. Tomorrow night, we'll kill you."

"And my little dog, too?" Buffy sneered at him. "Don't count on it."

The vampire touched his cheap-hussy fingernail to his forehead in a kind of salute. "Oh, but we do. We count on it very much."

"Well, I'm counting now. As in, hike-taking is your best bet for surviving the night. Ten, nine, eight, seven, six—"

"Don't threaten me," the vampire said angrily. "Or I'll—"

"Hurt me?" Buffy flung at him. "Rip me to pieces? So much for your word."

The vampire growled and stomped away.

"Yeah, and don't come back." Xander doubled his fists.

"Have a Zen moment, Xander. I'm the Slayer. You, not so much."

Buffy patted his arm, touched by how her friends rallied to her defense. She was once again perplexed by the complex rules of high school life, where kids like these were outcasts while the cruelly hip had licenses to crush.

"We'll hope for the best, okay?" she said. "Try to have fun."

Xander lit up. "My wish is your command, O slaying one. Care to dance?"

Willow gave her a half-crooked smile and a shrug: Go ahead.

Buffy had picked up the vampire's cup and was looking into it. "There's nothing in this cup," she said. "He was toying with us."

"Buffy?" Xander pumped his arms in a vaguely disco manner. "Um, dancing?"

"You have got to be kidding," Buffy said slowly as she stared at a couple across the room.

"Gee. No also works," Xander said, hurt.

"What? Oh, Xander, I didn't mean you," Buffy said. She pointed. "That's Jean-Luc Picard, the foreign exchange student." Actually, his name was Jean-Pierre Goddard, but no one got out of high school without a nickname. "And look who he's with."

"You've never been into the gossip thing before," Xander said.

"I'm looking," Willow announced. "Nothing I see is taking my breath away."

"He's with a vampire chick," Buffy announced, taking off her eye patch. Without turning her head, she felt for, and found, her Slayer satchel. "Looks like they're headed for the storage basement."

Indeed, the vamp chick, truly beautiful in a skimpy Cleopatra costume, had him by the nose—or rather, the hand—and she was letting her hips do the walking as the couple edged through the crowd. The look on Jean-Pierre's face spoke of the hope that he was going where no French foreign exchange student had gone before, and it wasn't to take inventory of how many black plastic cups the Bronze had on hand for the masquerade.

"How do you know she's a vampire?" Willow asked, with true curiosity. "I can't tell."

"Yeah, you wouldn't want to make a mistake and mess up a beautiful moment," Xander said.

Buffy shrugged. "Giles has been teaching me. There are a few clues. She's very pale. Her way of walking indicates she's a predator."

"Well, so is Cordelia, and if we staked her, we'd get in *mucho* big trouble," Xander pointed out.

"Or a medal," Willow said. She shivered. "What are you going to do, Buffy?"

"Mess up a beautiful moment. Hopefully, it won't be too messy."

"We'll come with," Xander announced.

"No way. You stay up here. Monitor the sitch. Make sure no one else follows." Buffy took a breath. Halloween was heating up after all. "For all I know, this is a plan to get me down there."

"Then don't go," Willow said nervously. "He's a big boy. He'll be able to fight her off."

Buffy grinned at Willow. "You know I can't do that. I have a solemn responsibility." She raised her chin and affected a British accent. "I and I alone, in all my generation, am the Slayah."

"Pip, pip," Xander said sourly. "Some girls will do anything to avoid dancing with me."

"Not all girls," Willow murmured.

"Yeah, well, enough of them."

"Dancing would be good," Buffy said. "You guys could funk 'n' roll over to the top of the basement stairs and stand guard."

"Well, if you put it that way, I guess sacrifices have to be made," Willow said. She firmly took Xander's hand and led him into the gyrating cast of thousands.

Buffy worked around the perimeter, muttering halfhearted excuse me's as she kept her gaze solidly on the storage door. It closed behind Jean-Pierre. She hurried, getting some protests as she bumped drink cups and stepped on toes. Couldn't be helped.

When she reached the door, she held her satchel between her knees and fastened her cross around her neck. In this crowd, flashing it sooner would be like flashing a sheriff's badge: Okay, ya lousy vampires, there's gonna be trouble. She wondered if all the really cool fangy people there knew the Slayer was in their midst. If there were wanted posters of her. If the Master did an orientation for new vampires that included a manila folder labeled Buffy Summers, Slayer. Dossier. Bloodshot eyes only.

Buffy opened the door.

The stairs went down at a sharp angle. Overhead, a bare lightbulb hanging from the canted ceiling had burned out . . .

or been smashed. She couldn't do anything about that unless she wanted to announce her approach. Same thing with turning on the hefty black flashlight in her bag.

She took the steps one at a time, moving as silently as fog.

Down she went, listening to her own heartbeat. Sparing a worry for her friends, even a thought for the French kid she'd never spoken to but was risking her life to protect.

Farther down.

There was the mildew smell of standing water mixed with the smell of dirt and perfume.

She heard low laughter.

Candlelight glowed against the wall as she reached the foot of the stairs. There was soft music playing. She reached the corner, paused for a heartbeat, then three. Finally, she poked her head out and saw four or five couples cuddling on some old couches draped with bedspreads. She hesitated. If she hadn't seen the vampire girl leading Jean-Pierre into the basement, this would be her cue to mutter, "Sorry," and tiptoe back upstairs. But she knew that something funky was going on. Something unnatural. Evil.

Then she heard the whimpering.

And the slurping.

Buffy turned on her flashlight and held it high above her head.

Five vampires, five human victims pinned beneath them. The vamps raised their faces and hissed at her. One of them was the fang-boy who had offered her a truce. Blood glittered on his lips.

"We meet again, Obi-Wan," Buffy said to him, reaching into her Slayer's bag. She brought out a cross and a stake. "Let's rumble."

"Get her!" the lying vampire shouted, and they moved toward her as one, a wall of living darkness.

Upstairs, the door slammed.

CHAPTER THREE

Willow glanced at the door to the Bronze's basement. Buffy had gone down there after some vamp tramp several minutes earlier and hadn't reappeared. "Maybe we should go after her," she suggested.

Xander pressed his lips together as he considered it. He raised his eyebrows. "She did tell us to stay here," he said. "You know how cranky Buffy gets when we ignore the Slayer's apprentice guidelines."

"She just worries about us, Xander," Willow said. "Buffy's all souped up with Slayer superpowers or something. We're just normal."

"Bite your tongue!" Xander scolded.

"Whatever," Willow said. "You know what I mean. Sometimes we can help, sometimes we're a handicap. Vampires don't spot you points for having your friends along. How many times did Superman almost die because he had Jimmy and Lois to worry about?"

"Wait, am I Lois or am I Jimmy?" Xander asked.

Willow glared at him.

"All right," Xander surrendered. "I get it. But is this one of the times we can help or one of the times we'd be cramping her style?"

They looked at each other, then turned and stared at the door.

"That's the big question," Willow admitted.

Silence reigned for a sprinkling of seconds. Outside, the wind had suddenly died down. They glanced at each other again, and Willow opened her mouth to say something but changed her mind.

"What?" Xander asked.

"Nothing."

"Something. What?" Xander prodded. "Come on."

"I think we should go after her," Willow suggested. "She could be in real trouble. If we don't look out for her, nobody else will. They all think she's psycho anyway."

"Right," Xander grumbled as he pushed off from his stool and headed for the basement door with Willow in tow.

A second later their path was blocked. Willow thought the blond guy in the cowboy getup was a total honey. He had these sideburns that were very out of date but made him look steamy anyway. His eyes were a cold blue like nothing Willow had ever seen.

"Want to dance?" he asked, and Willow had to look around to make sure he was talking to her.

She grinned. So wide it hurt. Willow was about to say "Why not?" when she caught sight of the girl next to the smoking blond guy. She was dressed Old West trampy, a saloon girl to go along with Blue Eyes's cowboy outfit. Long red hair usually only found on TV. Eyes like chocolate. Eyes only for Xander. Willow liked Xander; Willow did not like the way this girl was looking at Xander, or the way Xander was looking back. For a moment, Blue Eyes was forgotten as Willow tried to think of something witty to say to distract Xander from this girl.

The girl was wearing chunky Mary Janes, which were *way* over. Too dramatically unhip even for someone as I-don't-care-about-hip as Willow. Guy with sideburns. Girl with Mary Janes.

"Xander," Willow said, and whacked him on the arm.

"Yeah," he answered, but didn't look away from the red-head.

"Xander," she said again. "I think this pair is a little too old for us."

"What?" he asked, turning to stare at her as if she were a psychonaut, somewhere in mental space.

Willow grabbed his arm, stood on tiptoe to whisper in his ear. "They're dead, you moron."

As Xander and Willow turned to examine the pair who'd started to hit on them, the two vampires grinned widely. Willow was sort of proud of herself, and relieved, at the same time that she was pretty wigged out. Maybe Buffy's undead radar was starting to rub off, or at least some of her fashion sense.

"Well?" said Blue Eyes, staring at Willow as if she were filet mignon. "Do you want to dance, or not?"

"That'd be option number two: not."

"Yeah, clone that for me," Xander agreed. "Sorry."

Xander and Willow began to move away, but almost as soon as they turned, the vampires slid up next to them. Blue Eyes grabbed Willow's arm tight enough to cut off circulation, and she could see that Red had done the same to Xander.

"We're all leaving now," Blue Eyes whispered to her. "Together. Out the front door. Scream, and we'll kill you here and now."

"Or later," Willow suggested nervously. "Later would be a big improvement on that idea. We could meet back here in, say, an hour, and you can exhibit your homicidal tendencies then, okay? That would be way better for us."

"Shutting up would be better for you," Red hissed at her as she strong-armed Xander toward the door.

"Okay, extreme time out here," Xander said loudly, drawing attention.

Red spun him around and practically spat in his face. "Another word and you're dead. We do not bluff."

"Okay," he muttered. "I can totally see that, but you two

are making such a ginormous goof here, and I thought I'd help you out before you ended up on the end of a stake."

"Mistake," Willow agreed, hoping Xander knew what he was doing. "Huge. Fatal. Hope your insurance is all paid up."

Blue Eyes held her wrist so tight Willow gritted her teeth waiting to hear the snapping of bones. It didn't happen. Oh, joy. All her limbs would remain intact until Blue Eyes sucked her dry.

"What are you two bloodbags talking about?" Blue Eyes demanded.

"Well," Xander said, still quietly, not wanting to rush headlong toward death, apparently. "See, it's like this. You both seem like nice bloodsucking fiends, and you," he indicated Red, "are better looking than any girl who's ever even spoken to me."

Red actually looked pleased.

"But, sad to say, we're with the Slayer," Xander went on. "And she's forbidden us to hang with you guys."

Blue Eyes and Red looked as if they'd each been slapped.

"The Slayer?" Red whispered.

"That's right," Xander continued. "So, y'know, I don't think you want to get all fang-ugly on us, right? Maybe if you scurry off right now, the Chosen One will spare your nasty selves until tomorrow night."

Blue Eyes and Red stared at them for several seconds, then exchanged an anxious glance.

"You have not seen the last of us," Blue Eyes vowed before

the pair of vampires drifted off into the masquerade crowd.

"Promises, promises," Xander said, sighing.

"You behave now," Willow called after them. "Don't bite anyone I wouldn't bite."

She stood beside Xander and watched until the two Old West–costumed vampires were lost from sight.

"Well," Xander said, "that was interesting."

"Quite," Willow replied. "Good job, Xander." She wiped her forehead. She didn't know about Xander, but she'd been really sweating. "Maybe we should wait for Buffy after all?"

"Waiting." Xander nodded eagerly. "Original concept. Tremendous idea."

In the basement of the Bronze, Buffy stood her ground as five vampires—three guys and two girls—got up off the costumed teenagers they'd been using as unwilling blood donors. She glanced over at the victims and was relieved to see that, though either unconscious or way disoriented, they all seemed to be breathing.

Thank God for small respiratory favors.

"You've come at a bad time, Slayer," hissed the vampire with whom she'd agreed to a truce not half an hour before.

"I know, I know, you would've baked a cake. Well, I'm way sorry to interrupt the suckfest," Buffy sneered, "but haven't you leeches ever heard of the Red Cross?"

"Cold, lifeless blood," one of the vamp chicks growled. "We do not ask for our food, the warmth and life, we *take* it!"

"Take it?" Buffy chuckled. "You couldn't take a hint, never mind get a clue or buy a vowel."

The female vampire's face morphed into the typical extreme ugliness of her kind—like a Klingon burn victim with fangs. She roared and launched herself across the basement at Buffy. The Slayer waved her thick cross in front of her, and the other four vamps stayed back. Still, the first continued to rush forward.

"I don't believe in your God, Slayer!" the thing roared.

Buffy had the stake in her left hand and the cross in her right. When the vampire was almost on her, she ducked under its outstretched arms and slammed a hard uppercut to its gut, not bothering to use the stake for the moment. The vampire was stopped short, bent slightly, and Buffy brought her boot up into its face, knocking it over on its back. She straddled the fang-girl and sat down on her chest, all the time keeping the four other vamps in her peripheral vision. They were afraid of something—her or the cross, it didn't matter. Keeping them back was the key.

"Doesn't matter if you believe in God," Buffy said grimly as the groggy vampire began to struggle to rise. "He believes in you."

She slammed the cross down on the vampire's face, and it burst into flame. Two of the other vamps shrieked. Buffy staked the fang-girl in the heart, and she exploded into blood-scented ashes.

"Better get the dustpan," she muttered as she stood and stared at the other four.

"Slayer," the liar began, glancing nervously at the crucifix in her hand, "perhaps we could discuss a truce again."

"Yeah, y'know, we could talk about that," Buffy began reasonably. "We could, maybe, have peace negotiations and . . . well . . . why not?"

The vampires stared at her.

"Really?" the liar asked.

"No." Buffy smiled. "Not really."

The liar began to growl, majorly pissed off at Buffy's mockery of him. The others began to creep forward, eyes on the cross.

"Oh, I'm sorry," Buffy said innocently. "If this thing is giving you guys a wiggins, I'll just put it aside until we're through."

To the obvious astonishment of the undead, Buffy threw the cross on the cement about halfway between them. It clattered to the ground and stayed there.

"Now, unless you guys have some major elsewhere to be, why don't we fast forward to the juicy bits so I can return to my loitering amongst the tragically hip?" Buffy asked, switching the stake to her right hand.

A smile spread across the liar's face.

"Destroy her!" he shouted.

The four vamps rushed her together. Buffy crouched and then launched herself high in the air—higher than a normal teenage girl would have been able to jump, but then, as Buffy often said, normal was overrated. She grabbed hold of the thick copper cold-water pipe running across the ceiling of the basement, swung her legs, and tucked her head into a somersault. She spun in the air and landed on her feet, facing the backs of the four vampires.

They turned quickly to face her, but she'd thrown off the focus of their attack. Buffy leaped again, into a high roundhouse kick that nearly snapped the neck of a fang-boy. He spun into another vampire and Buffy went after them. She grabbed the vamp she'd kicked around the neck, choking him, and used him as a shield as she rammed the stake into the other's chest. Even as the vamp disintegrated, she staked the creature she'd kicked, and it disintegrated too.

"No more shield, no more games," the liar on her right sneered, and Buffy spun to face him. The only other surviving vampire, a fang-girl, was behind her now, but she could almost sense the undead thing's presence. Maybe her vampire radar was actually starting to work? Or it could just have been the glare from the vamp chick's screamingly tacky fashion sense.

"Maybe this is, like, Scrabble for you," Buffy snapped. "To me it's more like pest control."

"Vermin," the liar snarled.

"That is so my point," Buffy replied . . .

. . . then backed up a step and used both hands to plunge the stake under her left armpit right into the fang-girl who'd been about to rip her throat out from behind.

"Liar, liar," Buffy chided, and brought the stake in front of her again.

She was gaining a reputation as the Slayer. The creatures of darkness were wary of her. Buffy knew it would help her, give her an edge, to have them fear her. But she couldn't afford to get all celebrity arrogant about it. There were no paparazzi for Slayers. If she let it go to her head, she'd be over, a ridiculous punchline. She'd be dead.

The liar might be nervous around her, but that didn't mean he wasn't deadly.

They circled each other as if they were acting out that fine drama known as professional wrestling. The liar ran his tongue across his bloodstained fangs.

"Y'know, they've got this way cool new invention called Crest," Buffy taunted him. "Give it a try. I'll bet you'd have a killer smile."

"That is the last time you'll mock me, Slayer," the liar declared.

"For once, you're right," Buffy agreed.

The liar lashed out at her. Buffy blocked with her left arm and slashed the tip of the stake across the vampire's face. The spilling of his own blood seemed to madden the creature, and he thundered toward her. The liar was too large, too powerful, for her to escape his grasp. He wrapped his arms around her and squeezed the breath out of her. Buffy knew her ribs were on the endangered list. She still had the stake, but couldn't get at his heart from the front and couldn't reach it from the back. A stab at the head or shoulder might distract him. . . .

She slammed the stake into the back of the vampire's

neck. He howled in pain and dropped her. Buffy scrambled back, picking up the fallen stake, and rose to her feet just as the furious vampire came after her again. There was no reason in its eyes now, only bloodlust and rage. It came after her.

Buffy ran.

But she didn't run far. Four long strides took her to the basement wall. The liar was breathing clammy air at her back, reaching for her. She didn't even slow as she leaped up, planted her feet on the wall, and did a backflip over him. The liar slammed into the wall, hard. She heard things cracking inside him.

When he turned to pursue her, Buffy staked him right through the heart.

On her way out of the basement, she picked up the cross and returned it to her bag along with the stake. The five victims in the corner were still alive, still breathing. She had checked to see that none of them had lost too much blood. Soon, they'd wake up in an extremely bad temper, probably assuming somebody had added a nasty something to their drinks.

At the top of the stairs, Buffy glanced over her shoulder into the darkness. Her heart had already slowed, but she felt wound up, energized.

"Beats spinning by a mile," she muttered to herself.

Then she rejoined the party.

Giles stared out one of the library windows at the neighborhood that surrounded Sunnydale High School. He'd been working all afternoon and into the evening and still hadn't come up with anything to substantiate his anxiety. Ever since Willow and Xander had told Buffy of the local legend concerning scarecrows and Halloween rain, he had been bothered by a feeling that he had read something similar somewhere. Some connection between Samhain, the spirit of Halloween, and scarecrows.

Every half hour or so, he would get up from his musty books and wander to the window. It had rained all day and through the early evening. Finally, the rain had begun to taper off. It was almost stopped now, but the hour had grown too late for children whose parents had kept them home due to the weather to set off on their Halloween candy-scavenging journey.

Still, there had been quite a number of children whose parents had not kept them home. Giles had seen them moving along out on the street and the side roads, in soaked costumes or with umbrellas, and he had come to a shocking realization. The neighborhood had followed through, no matter that it was unintentional, on the observance of Samhuinn, honoring the creatures of darkness. The rituals may have changed, but the offerings, the respect for supernatural power and the land of the dead, those had remained.

Samhain still had power.

Which bothered Giles quite a bit. There had been very little slaying for Buffy to do the past few weeks. He prayed she would not let her guard down because of this false sense of safety. It might prove a fatal error.

Now he walked back across the library. He imagined that he was probably the only person who would dare spend time in the place alone. It had been dark enough before he had begun to bring in his private collection. But with the evil bound within the volumes on the school library's shelves, the books themselves seemed to absorb any additional light that was brought into the room.

Giles sat down in a hard wooden chair and closed the book he'd been glancing through before taking a break. He scanned the table, noting which volumes he'd looked through already. At the far edge of the study table, a stack of thin volumes caught his eye: They were Watchers' journals. He kept his own Watcher's journal, a record of Buffy's exploits. But these were the chronicles of past Slayers.

"Hmm," he muttered to himself. "Perhaps."

Giles slid the tower of journals toward him, lifted the first from the stack, and began to read.

"Well, that was refreshing," Buffy said as she joined Willow and Xander in loitering orbit around the coffee bar. "I don't even need a caffeine fix."

"Buffy. Caffeine. Putting the fire out with gasoline," Xander mused. "Certain things are just so not a good idea."

"I assume that means we don't have any more sharp-toothed trouble to look forward to?" Willow asked.

Buffy smiled, glanced around the Bronze, and noticed at least half a dozen others who were probably vampires. Still, as long as she could keep an eye on them and they weren't misbehaving, she was determined to enjoy herself. The Slayer had been called upon to do her duty, and she had done it. The other vampires appeared not to know what had gone on downstairs, or else they didn't care that five of their kind had been destroyed. After all, they were not the most warmhearted bunch.

"I'm glad you told me the assistant manager shut the basement door. Otherwise I might assume there was some kind of major plot to dust me. I think we'll be okay now," Buffy replied hopefully.

Apparently sensing Buffy's uncertainty, Willow sighed and raised her eyebrows.

"You must be a little rusty, huh?" she asked, changing the subject. "I mean, what with things having been so quiet until now. I assume the French kid, Jean-Pierre, is still alive."

"He'll be pretty light-headed from loss of blood, but he'll live," Buffy replied. "So will the others. And actually, I didn't feel rusty at all. Just . . . pumped."

"Pumped," Xander repeated, then shook his head in disbelief.

"Others?" Willow asked. "How many people were down there?"

"Five people, five vampires," Buffy replied. "Kind of like the buddy system, you know? Everybody pick a partner with fangs."

"Five?" Xander said, disturbed. "Next time, we are definitely part of the fangface posse."

"It was fine," Buffy insisted. "I was fine." It was true, too.

"Okay, whatever you say." Xander's eyes widened. "But how about wearing my jacket? You've got, like, blood, all over your blouse. Red is very in now, or so my many fashion-conscious friends tell me, but I think it clashes with the pirate queen motif . . . or goes too well. Just wear this."

As Xander slid his jacket off, Buffy glanced down at the blood on her blouse and made a totally grossed-out face. She thanked Xander distractedly as she put the jacket on.

"Much better," Willow said.

Now it was time to start researching what kind of strategies were necessary to have a social life.

Buffy bobbed to the music of Children of the Night, practically humming along even though she didn't understand a word. Major Halloween grunge points for wearing costumes and for effort, but the band was years late and too musically challenged to be anything but a Seattle-schooled garage and cover band.

Sad commentary. They were the best band Buffy had seen at the Bronze. Then again, it was Sunnydale, after all. Boca del Infierno. If there was a rock 'n' roll heaven, they'd have a hell of a band. But rock 'n' roll hell was listening to mediocre covers of mediocre music, and that's what you got here in the Bad Place.

Still, Buffy was up. So up, the quality of the music was about three thousand miles from the point. The drought was over, it was raining vampires, hallelujah! She would gladly have swayed to Motörhead, if that was all she could get by way of tunes.

Xander and Willow gossiped, and Buffy chimed in when she had something particularly juicy to add or if she wanted more details. Gossip without the gory details was like black-and-white horror movies, all bark and no bite.

CHAPTER FOUR

Xander had zeroed in on a hottie none of them knew—but to whom Buffy had given a yes-this-chick's-alive stamp of approval—and moved in to ask for a dance. Or the somebody's-dad-had-too-much-to-drink-Hustle that passed for dancing where Xander was concerned.

To Buffy and Willow's severe nonsurprise, the girl had blown him off.

"I just don't get women," Xander sighed as he pulled up a stool.

Buffy and Willow glared at him.

"Not you guys," he backpedaled. "I mean, you're not, like,

women women. You're my buds, not catty females who . . . you're not into that girlie stuff, that . . . You two are the ultimate women of the millennium. Feminist ideal. Women. Great. Men. Root of all evil. Cordelia, shallow witch. Buffy and Willow . . . not." Xander swallowed, eyes wide, and glanced at Buffy and Willow hopefully. "Just didn't want you guys—uh, girls, to get the wrong idea."

"Wrong idea," Buffy repeated, eyebrows raised. "Of course not."

She glanced at Willow, nodded, and they each reached out and grabbed hold of one of Xander's ears.

"Oowwwww!" he howled.

"That was an almost-save, Xander," Willow told him. "But close only counts in—"

"Horseshoes and hand grenades," Xander finished. "I know, I know, now let go, okay? You know I love you guys."

The girls let go and Xander rubbed his ears, felt them, possibly trying to be certain they were still attached.

"Well, Buffy," Willow said. "You've saved Halloween, right? And the vampires who hit on Xander and me have Jimmy Hoffa'd, so maybe we can actually hang out and enjoy the rest of the masquerade."

"Aye-aye to that," pirate queen Buffy agreed. "I've had my share of Halloween tricks."

"It is so time for the treats," Xander said.

"Let's find some chocolate," Willow added eagerly.

Buffy laughed. They began to move toward the snack bar

when the door slammed open and Mr. O'Leary blew into the Bronze.

Glenn O'Leary was the town psycho. Well, besides Buffy, of course. But he'd been at it much longer than she had, and had greater celebrity because it wasn't just the high school kids who thought he was a few fries short of a Happy Meal. The whole town thought he was damaged merchandise.

Inside the Bronze, raving like a street-corner preacher with a heavy Irish accent, he was very convincing as a nut job.

"They've come back for us!" Mr. O'Leary shouted. "The dead are risin' from their graves, diggin' out from the earth, wet with Halloween rain. They're comin' for us all!"

"So much for treats," Buffy said miserably.

Long, heavy sigh.

As the band thrashed on, the strange man dropped his hands to his sides and looked defeated. "They're risin', sure as I'm an O'Leary," he insisted, looking bewildered as the kids lost interest and drifted away.

He approached the next person who came near him, who wasn't a person at all but a vampire, and took his arm. The vampire, whose costume was apparently the leather jacket and hair gel that made him look like John Travolta in *Grease*, stopped and regarded Mr. O'Leary with amusement.

"What's that you say, Grandpa?" the vampire asked, egging the old man on.

"Risin'! The dead risin' up out o' their graves!"

"You haven't lived around here very long, have you?" the vampire asked, taunting the old man.

Fang-boy looked around and preened as some nearby partyers chuckled and applauded. He actually looked like a normal, sarcastic American guy for a second or two. Hmm, maybe it was a simple self-esteem problem that compelled them to murder human beings. With some positive reinforcement, perhaps they could be made useful members of society. Like Cordelia.

"Don't mock me, me boyo," the old man said. "I barely escaped with me life to come and warn you! I've lived here in Sunnydale for near twenty years."

"Then you should know that around here the dead are always rising from their graves," the vampire sneered. "It's dead folks that put Sunnydale on the map."

"I told you not to mock me!" Mr. O'Leary cried. "I seen it meself, with me own two eyes! Clawin' and crawlin' up out o' their graves, shamblin' around the cemetery in search o' somethin', and I don't want to know what it is!"

The vampire brushed Mr. O'Leary off and wandered away. The rest of the masqueraders just did their best to uncomfortably ignore the crazy old man. Buffy was sad for Glenn O'Leary. They were kind of kindred spirits. Sunnydale did its best to ignore her the same way it did him—ignore her, and the evils that she saved their bacon from almost every night.

"I so don't want to even bring this up," Buffy said, "but

have you guys considered the majorly depressing possibility that the old guy isn't as follow-my-nose Froot Loopy as the rest of the town has an aching desire to believe?"

Willow and Xander exchanged a glance, looked at Buffy, then back at each other.

"Xander, know what I truly hate?" Willow asked.

"In fact, yes," Xander said. He took a deep breath, and they turned back to look at Buffy again. "You hate when Buffy's right," he said. "Which I know, because I'm right there with you. Hate that. Totally."

"Because when Buffy's right it usually means blood, death, maybe some recreational flesh-eating," Willow said, and raised an eyebrow as she stared at Buffy.

"Fine!" Buffy sniffed. "If you guys want, I could just leave you in the dark on all this. Next time there's some demonic force or serial-killing ape monster on the loose, you'll be off the James Bond, eyes-only, need-to-know list. Aren't you thrilled!"

"Not so fast," Xander said nervously. "Darkness not good. Nobody said anything about—y'know, we're the Slayerettes, right?"

"You're our beacon of light in the darkness," Willow said, wide eyed and with as much sincerity as she could manufacture on a moment's notice. "And you're right, of course. The rest of the town is psycho. Nobody sees anything, or will talk about it. They all want to pretend Sunnydale is as sunny as Sunnybrook Farm."

"Which is where?" Xander asked, looking at Willow strangely.

"In a book," Buffy replied, shaking her head. "Where you might think about sticking your nose once in a while."

"You've never read *Rebecca of Sunnybrook Farm*?" Willow asked, horrified.

"Sounds like a girl book," Xander said, then fumbled, "about a girl. A book about a girl. Named Rebecca."

"Anyway, you're right about the major denial that's happening here," Willow went on. "Doesn't it strike you as odd that with all the strangeness that goes on, we don't rate a Scully-and-Mulder moment or two?"

"Will, I hate to break it to you," Buffy said with a little wink, "but those guys are just pretend."

Willow gave her head a shake. "You know what I mean. Giles always has me looking online through the newspapers for information about the Hellmouth. The stories are all there—gruesome deaths, missing persons reports, maximum weirdness all over the place—but nobody connects the dots."

"Because nobody wants to," Buffy said, understanding. Xander and Willow nodded. She looked again at the raving Irishman. "Maybe it's time for the Slayer to have a chat with Mr. O'Leary."

"They're comin' out o' the ground o' Sunnydale Cemetery!" the old man shouted.

"Hey, Mr. O'Leary," said an older man, maybe about thirty-five or forty, wearing nicely pressed jeans, a Grateful

Dead T-shirt, and a ponytail. He firmly took Mr. O'Leary by the arm and steered him toward the coffee bar. "Why don't you sit down and I'll make you a nice cup of Irish coffee."

Willow gestured at the man in the T-shirt. "That's Nick Daniels. He's the assistant manager of the Bronze." She lowered her voice. "He was a student of Mr. O'Leary's a long time ago. A lot of people in this room were his students." She sighed. "He was fired about ten years ago."

"Coffee!" Mr. O'Leary cried. "Isn't anyone listening to me?"

Buffy murmured, "I am," and looked at her two pals. "Looks like I'm on duty again." She slid off her chair. "Watch my bag for me, okay?"

Xander looked excited. "Okay," said. "And can we rummage through it?"

Buffy shrugged. "Sure, Xander. It's not as if I'll lose my membership in the secret society of vampire slayers if mere mortals take a gander at the tools of the trade." She gave him a halfhearted smile, envying his status as a perpetual spectator. "Enjoy."

As Buffy turned to go, she heard Xander say to Willow, "Poor woman. No wonder she's not dating. Can you imagine her getting to sit through an entire movie?"

"So you wouldn't want to go the movies with Buffy?" Willow asked.

"You kidding?" he said quickly. "I'd sit through the Meg Ryan chick flick marathon with Buffy."

As she walked off, Buffy heard Willow sigh, and she

wanted to smack Xander. Willow and Xander went together like Shaggy and Scooby, vampires and stakes, studying and passing. Why couldn't that blind guy see it?

". . . zombies," Mr. O'Leary was saying to Nick Daniels as the assistant manager sprayed whipped cream on top of a cup of coffee. Daniels picked up a chocolate shaker and looked questioningly at Mr. O'Leary. "Are you daft, man? What do I care for sugar sprinkles and cream at a time like this?"

"Mr. O'Leary?" Buffy began, coming up behind him.

Mr. O'Leary swiveled on his stool and looked at her. Looked again, harder. His lips parted.

Something passed between them, some strange connection like a very mild electric current. He seemed to feel it too, for he pulled away from her slightly. Without looking away from her, he picked up his coffee cup and took a sip. His hand shook.

"Who are you?" he asked slowly.

"My name is Buffy," she began. "Buffy Summers. I was, ah, curious about what you were saying." Nick Daniels leaned on the counter, clearly without plans to move along and do some other assistant-manager type of thing. "About the graveyard."

He took another sip of coffee and turned his gaze toward Daniels. "Nick, boy," he said kindly, "would you be making my friend Buffy Summers here a drink with that fancy machine o' yours?"

Daniels looked at Buffy. "May I have a latte?" she asked, quickly adding, "Decaf? Nonfat milk?"

"Sure." Daniels looked concerned, as if by going to use the espresso machine, he would leave her vulnerable and helpless. If only he knew. But go he did, and Buffy inwardly sighed with relief.

"Now," Buffy said, climbing up on the stool beside Mr. O'Leary. She folded her hands and put them on the bar. "Please. Tell me."

"And why would you be wanting to know, miss?" Mr. O'Leary asked carefully.

She shrugged. "I'm a curious sort of girl."

"That y'are, lass," he replied. "But of what sort, I'm uncertain."

"Give me dish," she urged. "I mean, please tell me what you saw."

He stared downward and whispered something. She leaned in. *Now* he mumbled.

"The dead are risin'. They are coming up from their graves to destroy the living."

"Um, could you be more specific?" she asked. "That covers an awful lot of territory."

He frowned. "Who *are* you?"

"Someone who believes you," she said softly. "Mr. O'Leary, these dead people. What kind of dead people are they?"

He looked as if he might cry. "Do you know how long I've been thought insane? My teaching job—" He swallowed hard. "Everything lost. But it's all true."

Buffy covered his hand. "I know, Mr. O'Leary."

They looked at each other without speaking. A single tear ran down his cheek.

"My country's folktales speak of heroes. This place is in desperate need of one."

"I know that, too." She gave his hand a little squeeze. "Please, Mr. O'Leary, tell me before Mr. Daniels comes back with my coffee."

"Zombies, they are," he said in a rush. "Do you know of Samhuinn?"

"Yes, a little." She wished she'd paid better attention to Giles's lecture. It occurred to her that she often wished that. She just wasn't used to doing the listening thing.

"The dark time of year, when the pumpkin king reigns."

"The pumpkin king?" Confused, she scratched her cheek. "I'm not tracking. What about the zombies?"

"He holds dominion over all." Mr. O'Leary's voice began to rise. "Creatures awaken to do his bidding. Werewolves. Zombies. Demons. They strike like warriors to thin our ranks while he searches for the one."

Buffy was silent while she processed that. Then she said, "The one." She blinked. Uh-oh. "Would that one be called the, um, Slayer?"

He looked at her blankly. "That's a name I've not heard."

"Oh." She brightened slightly. "Good. I mean, oh, how interesting."

"Interesting?" He stared at her for a moment just as Mr. Daniels put her mug on the bar. Then Mr. O'Leary threw his coffee cup to the floor. It smashed and coffee and whipped cream flew everywhere. "You're just as thick as the rest of 'em! I didn't come here to tell stories. I came for help against the forces of evil."

"What's going on here?" a woman's voice asked pleasantly. She was thirtysomething, but barely showed it. Her name badge read Claire Bellamy, Manager. Nick Daniels came out from around the bar and joined her.

"I thought you understood me," Mr. O'Leary shouted, pointing at Buffy. "That you were going to do something!"

Daniels and Bellamy looked at Buffy. Though she felt bad doing it, she moved her shoulders and said, "I don't know what he's talking about."

"You, you—" Mr. O'Leary sputtered. Then, at the top of his lungs, he bellowed, "You little liar!"

Heads turned. Buffy cleared her throat, trying to hint that they would get more accomplished if he'd be a little sly about it.

"Okay, Mr. O'Leary," Claire Bellamy said. "I'm going to have to ask you to leave. Nick, a hand?"

Mr. O'Leary raised a finger at Buffy as the manager and assistant manager shuffled him firmly toward the exit. "If more die, it's on your head, Buffy Summers!"

"Could you say that into the PA system, please?" Buffy said under her breath. "There may be a few people who didn't hear that." Not to mention a vampire or two.

From their perches, Xander and Willow made *oh, great* expressions. Buffy pointed to herself and then to the door.

The two jumped down and joined her. Xander said, "Buffy Summers, you little liar person, what are you going to do now?"

"Well, I don't suppose I'm going to Disney World," Buffy said glumly. "I guess I'm going to the graveyard."

She reached out her hand for her Slayer's bag, which Xander was carrying. He had her box of matches in his hand, and she knew he was dying to ask her what she used them for. If she told him they were for just in case, like to light a candle, she knew he would be disappointed.

At that moment, thunder shook the Bronze. The lights flicked off and the band wound down like a tired battery-operated toy. The only light in the place was from the candles in the grinning pumpkins on the tables. The faces above them—both human and vampire—looked eerie and skeletal.

"Wow, cool," Xander said. He cleared his throat. "I mean, oh, what a drag."

The lights flicked back on. Everybody cheered.

Buffy looked down at her elbow and said, "Anybody want a nonfat decaf latte?"

"This time we're going with you," Willow insisted.

Xander nodded. "We don't want you to get your brains eaten by zombies."

Willow added, "You might be outnumbered. I mean, really outnumbered, if there are, like, a kabillion of them and only one of you."

"I'm the Slayer, guys."

"These are zombies, not horrible demons or ultrastrong

vampires," Willow said reasonably. "I think civilians are allowed to kill them, like a citizen's arrest, y'know." She looked a little nervous. "I mean, don't they just stumble around real slow?"

"Stumbling's what I've heard," Xander agreed. "They do that sort of mummy-stumble thing." He puffed out his chest. "Most definitely can I run faster than a speeding zombie. Hey, I won third place in the fifty-yard dash at camp the summer before sixth grade."

Willow smiled patiently at him, then turned to Buffy. "There, you see? Proof positive of our suitability for the mission."

Buffy wasn't convinced. She said, "If Giles says it's okay, you can come." Figuring that he'd most likely say no, especially once she told him the bit about the dark lord. "I need to call him anyway and see if he has any fun facts and helpful tips on how to deal with zombies that I didn't get from watching *Dawn of the Dead*."

Xander shuddered. "I loved that movie the first time I saw it. I never dreamed I'd be in one of the sequels."

Buffy smiled ironically. "Stick with me, baby. I'll make you a star." She pointed to the door that led to the alley where there was better cell reception. Although all of Sunnydale was spotty when it came to technology.

Special Agents Harris and Rosenberg flanked Buffy as they worked their way through the Bronze. Then Buffy pushed open the door just as a zombie stumbled in.

She drew back her arm and was about to smash its face in when it said, "If you're going to use the phone, there's, like, no signal."

"What?" Buffy said. She tried her phone as Xander and Willow looked on.

"It doesn't work."

"I'll ask to use the Bronze's private line," Xander suggested and dashed off, leaving Willow and Buffy alone.

"Poor Mr. O'Leary," Willow said. "Nobody believes him."

"Clone that thought," Buffy said, thinking of the tears in Mr. O'Leary's eyes. She felt as if she had betrayed him. But what else could she have done? "I wonder if I'll end up like that, Willow. You know, Giles refuses to tell me the average Slayer life span. You notice how it's always one *girl* in every generation? Not one middle-aged matron in every generation? One bridge-playing—"

"—Harley-riding," Willow threw in.

Buffy blinked. "I don't own a Harley."

"You don't play bridge, either."

Xander poked his head in. "Their phone's out too. Word on the street is that all the lines and cell towers went down in the storm."

"Oh, well," Willow said unhappily.

"Oh, well, nothing," Buffy shot back. "I want you two to go to Giles and see if he can dig anything up about zombies." She snapped her fingers. "Oh yeah, and about the pumpkin king."

"Tim Burton flick. *Nightmare Before Christmas*," Xander supplied helpfully. "He wants to be Santa Claus."

Buffy looked at Willow. Willow said, "I'll ask him about the pumpkin king."

"And the dark lord, too," Buffy said, wrinkling her nose. There were too many big-shot bad guys interrupting her good times.

"I'm not certain I'm liking this split-up maneuver," Xander said. "In the movies, the kids split up and then the dude with the chain saw shows up."

Buffy said, "Hmm." What she was thinking was, maybe the term "dude" wasn't so over after all. When she realized Xander thought she was reconsidering her insistence that he and Willow go to Giles, she shook her head. "Xander, I need his input."

"Let's all three go, then," Xander said.

"I need to go now. Who knows what's going on over there? Besides, I'm worried about Mr. O'Leary. He might try to save the world all by himself."

"Saving the world all by oneself. Sound like anyone we know, Agent Rosenberg?" Xander said in his best David Duchovny voice.

"Indeed, Agent Harris," Willow replied. "But as much as I hate to admit it, Buffy has a point. I'm thinking we should be obedient little Slayerettes."

Xander scrunched up his face. "That's your thought?"

"Yes. The thought that I have," Willow said.

"Okay." Buffy clapped her hands. "Synchronize your watches. Let's hit the streets."

"Jolly Roger, Captain." Xander saluted. Then he got serious and said, "Don't do anything I wouldn't do."

Buffy grinned. "Can't think of anything offhand, Xander, but okay."

The three of them hurried out of the Bronze and out into the Halloween night together. Buffy hoped they were more Three Musketeers than Three Stooges. If they were the Stooges, she didn't think Larry and Curly were going to survive the night.

CHAPTER FIVE

In the silence of the library, Giles sat and pored through the many volumes of Watchers' journals. The exploits of the Slayers of the past made for some horrifying and exciting reading, but he had no time to be fascinated by any of it. As the night wore on, he found that instead of being relieved that he hadn't heard from Buffy, he became more and more concerned. He couldn't shake the feeling that something was going to happen, or was happening even now.

It had to do with Halloween, with Samhuinn, the season of the dead. And with that local legend about scarecrows and Halloween rain. Of that he was certain. But though he had been equally certain that he'd once read references to Samhain, the demonic spirit of Halloween, in connection with scarecrows, he hadn't yet come across any mention of either thing.

Disgusted and in a hurry, Giles had resorted to something he despised: skimming. Now his eyes whipped across journal pages and he looked for any references to the Druids, the Celts, scarecrows, Samhuinn, or Samhain.

Nothing. Or, as he'd heard Buffy say many times, "no joy."

Giles pushed up his glasses and rubbed his eyes. He was tired, but he hadn't begun to drift off yet. That was something, at least. He had to stay awake. Buffy's life might depend upon it.

On the other hand, and this was a thought he'd kept avoiding because his instincts screamed otherwise, it was possible that he was wrong. It was possible that any connection between local legends and ancient Halloween demons was just in his head, and Buffy wasn't in any real danger. That Sunnydale was not going to be overrun by the minions of the Halloween king.

Slowly, Giles became aware of a certain anxiety, a feeling of dread that had snuck up on him. He tried to pinpoint the source of this feeling, to identify it. Then he did. There was a warmth on his back, that feeling he'd always gotten when someone was staring at him. Watching him. Sizing him up, maybe for a next meal.

He turned, narrowing his eyes and peering at the doorway and the darkened hall beyond. Giles blinked twice, trying to focus, but there was nothing there to focus on. Nobody watching him. Watching the Watcher. A shiver ran through him, just a little excess energy he'd stored while concentrating so hard on his research. At least, that's what he was going to tell himself.

Rupert Giles was not a nervous person by nature, not anxiety prone or jumpy at all, in fact. He'd prided himself on that. It had served him well as a Watcher, and in all the years of study he'd had to prepare for that role. He was simply not easily spooked.

Somewhere in the school, down the hall a way, a door closed. Just short of a slam, it was, but loud enough for Giles to hear it. Giles glanced around at the door again.

Curiosity got the better of him and he rose from his chair and strode across the gloomy library to the door. He poked his head out into the hallway and looked in both directions. The hall was empty. If he'd been asked, he would have thought the school was empty. Now, however, it seemed as though he was not alone.

"Just the custodian," he assured himself as he returned to his chair and began skimming journals again.

A sudden thought gave him pause. He'd been sure the custodian had already left for the evening.

Giles brushed the thought aside. He'd spent many a late night in the library without incident. In truth, while most people were deeply disturbed by being alone in a place that was usually populated—a school, or office, for example—Giles preferred it.

Easier to concentrate, he'd always felt. No jumping at shadows for him.

Suddenly, his eyes fell upon the word Samhain in the journal he'd been reading. He scanned back to the beginning of that entry and began to read.

"Mr. Giles?"

"Aaah!" Giles cried out, and leaped to his feet, knocking the chair onto the floor with a *clack* as he spun to see who had spoken to him.

Wayne Jones, the white-haired custodian, stood in the doorway to the library with a broom in his hand, frowning at Giles's reaction.

"Ah, Mr. Jones," Giles said, trying to calm his pounding heart and cover his embarrassment. "You startled me."

"Sorry about that, Mr. Giles," the older man said in his gravelly voice. "I see you're burning the midnight oil as usual. I just wanted to tell you I was locking up, make sure you had your keys and see if there was anything you needed me to do in here before I go."

"Hmm? Oh, no, thank you," Giles said. "Have a good evening, Mr. Jones."

"You, too, Mr. Giles," Jones said. "Sorry again about frightening you."

"Frightening . . ." Giles said absently, rubbing the back of his neck, as he often did when he found a subject of conversation uncomfortable. "Not at all. I'm just a bit on edge, actually. You go on, I'll be all right."

"See you tomorrow," the custodian said as he started off down the hall again.

"Yes, yes," Giles said, turning back to the journal once more.

He'd found a reference to Samhain in the Watcher's journal referring to the exploits of a Slayer named Erin Randall, an Irish girl who'd lived in the seventeenth century. The Watcher, Timothy Cassidy, had been very fond of the girl, and if Giles's memory served, Erin had been the Slayer for only a short time before her death. She'd died violently, as most Slayers did in the end. But in her short term as the Chosen One, she had faced a horde of demons, monsters, and vampires. Even the Tatzelwurm, which she had destroyed.

"I ought to have known it would be you," Giles whispered to himself. "Who else could have faced Samhain and lived?"

Giles paused then, upset by the question. Could Buffy battle Samhain and survive? It wasn't even certain that Samhain was here, in Sunnydale, but Giles suspected that if the spirit of Halloween, the demon king of ancient Druidic rituals, was going to settle anywhere, it would be the Hellmouth.

He pushed his concern away. Buffy had become quite accomplished as the Slayer in a very short time. What she lacked in her studies, she more than made up for through determination, physical skill, and sheer courage. If Buffy couldn't stop Samhain, Giles suspected the Halloween king couldn't be stopped. Somehow, the thought did little to comfort him.

"Ah, here we are," he muttered as he found the journal entry and began to read.

The Randall lass is but a wee slip of a girl [the Watcher Cassidy had written], yet now she must face one of the most powerful demons born of the time before man. The Vikings and the French paid their respects to this demonic spirit, the lord of the night, whom the dead and the creatures of darkness all obey.

Let me amend my words to this: that they did obey him in the days of old. Through the lifting of the veils of superstition and ignorance, the dark lord, Samhain, has lost much of his power. 'Tis a good thing, for otherwise my young lady would not dare hope to defeat him.

Aye, once 'pon a time, the Celts, the ancient people of my own land, green Ireland, did hide away from Samhain and his followers for all the long winter months. That was the dead time, called Samhuinn, called thus after the old demon himself. Feasts there were, for the dead. Candles burned all of a night to keep the dead away, and offerings bought lives for another day. The folk carved pumpkins to represent the dread lord of the winter, and Samhain rejoiced. He reigned supreme as the pumpkin king, the spirit of the dead time.

The dark lord, some called him.

But power cannot stay forever, and the time of the Druid priests came to an end. Through the grace of God, the heathen Celts became Christian Irish, and the season of the dead began to wither like unto a tree denied lifesaving water. Soon, Samhuinn was a three-day festival, a holiday, and the old faith was gone. Hallowe'en had taken its place.

The pumpkin king was enraged, but could do nothing. He would survive, of course. He had been there before the Celts, before humanity, and he would remain. But he was weakened. Samhain could enter the world only through a vessel built in his image. There must be a little faith, at the least, for him to return.

Jack-o'-lanterns, carved pumpkins, would serve him as hosts, even if their makers did not know they were following the ancient rituals. Jack-o'-lanterns are the eyes of Samhain, the eyes of the king of Hallowe'en. He can see everything that they see, but he cannot act, for he himself has no form.

There is only one form the old demon may use to walk the earth now. Many farmers, too foolish to realize what they have done, have provided Samhain with host bodies by making scarecrows for their fields and using carved pumpkins for the scarecrows' heads.

Last night, All Hallow's Eve, the dead walked

the countryside, the werewolves and ghouls, ghosts and goblins along with them. And they had their king to lead them. My lady the Slayer, Erin Randall, was kept busy through the night by various creatures of darkness, and she was forewarned by them that the pumpkin king had set his sights on her, that tonight he planned to take her life.

I have provided Erin with garlic and angelica for her protection, with signs and sigils which she may draw in the ground to trap the demon—a feat which may also be accomplished with a ring of fire—and I have given her a weapon of my own making which may, I pray, destroy the host vessel. Mayhap this will return Samhain to the netherworld, where he resides the rest of the year. Or perhaps it will destroy the pumpkin king forever.

Giles studied the markings on the page, the symbols and designs which, when drawn in a circle in the dirt, would apparently trap Samhain, as in a sacred circle. He memorized the parts used to make the ancient Slayer's weapon. Then he moved on, to read about Erin Randall's battle with Samhain. According to Cassidy's journal, Samhain had managed to disarm the girl, so the weapon was never used. She had, instead, found a way to destroy the scarecrow host body, thus banishing Samhain for another year. This part was a bit vague: Cassidy had been interrupted while writing and hadn't filled in all the blanks.

The pumpkin king must have been furious, Giles thought, and he wondered what had happened the next year. He flipped pages until he came to the following Halloween's entry. The last entry, as it turned out. For the following year, Samhain killed Erin Randall.

Giles closed the book, turned, and stared at the moonlight shining through the library window.

"Buffy," he whispered to himself.

He stood quickly, picked up a canvas bag, and began to gather items he knew he would need. Then he hurried out of the library.

Xander and Willow were tired. They'd made good time, and the high school was definitely within walking distance, but it wasn't a short walk. All the while, they'd been glancing over their shoulders, expecting trouble to come leaping out at them at any moment. Despite what Buffy had hoped, Halloween night was turning out to be pretty horrible. Xander himself had hoped for some quality time with Buffy—and Willow, too, of course. No such luck. At this point, he figured he'd have to be dead to spend any real time with the Slayin' babe of his dreams.

And as romantic as he'd always considered himself, that was really not an option.

He and Willow stepped onto the campus lawn and started across toward the front of the school. As they passed by the bench where they met every morning, there was a sudden snapping sound behind them, and they both turned and stared up into a nearby tree.

"Not good," Xander said.

"We're just jumpy, is all," Willow said, offering some of her famous rationalization. One of the reasons she had been Xander's best friend since kindergarten. "What with the night we're having, we'd have to be extreme morons not to be a little nervous."

"Right," Xander agreed. "A little nervous."

Somewhere off in the dark, they could hear a high, child-like laugh.

"Ignore it, Xander," Willow said. "Let's move."

They picked up their pace, heading for the front steps of the school.

"There's nothing to be afraid of," Willow insisted. "Right? I mean, what do we have to fear?"

Xander glared at her out of the corner of his eye, even as he walked faster.

"Oh, I don't know," he muttered. "How about zombies and werewolves and vamps?"

"Oh my," Willow gasped.

Xander rolled his eyes. "What is it with you and the *Wizard of Oz* references? Zombies and werewolves and vamps, oh my. Zombies and werewolves and—"

"Vamps," Willow finished, and whacked him in the chest.

Finally Xander realized that her "Oh my" hadn't been a film reference, but an actual gasp of oh-boy-we're-in-trouble-now astonishment. He followed her gaze and saw that they weren't alone. They really had been followed.

"Well, well, what have we here?" sneered the blond-haired fang-boy Willow had nicknamed Blue Eyes.

"Miss me, baby?" asked his sidekick, the vamp chick they'd dubbed Red, batting her long lashes at Xander.

"Like a hole in the head," Xander grumbled. "Or two in the neck. One hundred people surveyed, top five answers on the board. Number one answer is no. Definitely no."

The vampires began to move across the grass toward them.

"We've been following you," Blue Eyes growled. "The Slayer isn't around now to protect you. You're just another pair of bloodbags, just meat. Let's see if you're as brave without the Chosen One to protect you."

"Bravery is extremely overrated," Willow said. She reached out and gripped Xander's hand.

"Absolutely," Xander agreed nervously as the vampires split apart, moving to trap him and Willow between them. "There are so many ways to respond to danger that are more constructive than bravery."

"Name one," Red sneered through perfect pouty lips that almost distracted Xander from the danger.

"Oh, I don't know," he mumbled. "Well, then, there's running!"

Dragging Willow along, Xander bolted for the school. A second later, she passed him and he let go of her hand. The vampires roared and ran in pursuit. The stairs were just ahead, but he knew they weren't going to make it.

"Willow!" he shouted. "Open the door!"

Xander reached behind his back, under the white shirttail that had been hanging down over his pants. He yanked a cross from his belt and stopped short, turned, and lifted the cross to face the vampires.

"Xander!" Willow cried in alarm behind him. Then he heard her begin to bang on the door, screaming for Giles.

Blue Eyes and Red hissed as they stumbled to a halt on the lawn. The vampires were taken off guard, but Xander knew that in a second they'd be moving in on him again like social-climbing sophomores after Cordelia. Holding the cross behind him, he stumbled toward the stairs.

"What in the world?" Giles's voice came from behind him, and Xander knew that was his cue.

Fast as he could manage, he loped up the stairs, pushing through the double doors past Willow and Giles. As they slammed the doors, Blue Eyes and Red were pounding up the steps. Giles and Willow hurried, but Red got a hand inside and reached her clawed fingers toward Willow's face. The doors were crushing her arm, but the vampire kept coming. Blue Eyes slammed against the door, trying to force it open.

"Denied!" Xander shouted, and slapped the cross down on Red's bare arm.

The vamp chick howled in agony and withdrew, but in a heartbeat, Blue Eyes was there, propping open the door with his foot.

"Xander!" Willow shouted.

The cross was still gripped in his hand. Xander hurled it at Blue Eyes's forehead. It struck him there, and he fell back as if the Hulk had popped him one, the flesh of his face smoking.

Willow and Giles were finally able to get the doors closed. Xander rammed the bolts on the top and bottom of the doors into their respective holes, then stood, breathing heavily, as the vampires began to slam against the doors from outside.

"Either I'm having a heart attack or a supermodel has agreed to be my bride," Xander huffed, and turned to face Willow and Giles, who stared at him grimly.

"Not that I'm not happy that you produced that cross from thin air," Willow said, "but have you been carrying that around all night?"

Xander looked away. "Not exactly. When I was rifling through Buffy's Slayer bag, I kind of borrowed it. I figured it might come in handy, and she had another one."

He shrugged.

"Well," Giles sniffed, "I, for one, am pleased with your sudden burst of kleptomania. Without it, we might be dead now."

"Thanks," Xander said. "I think."

"So what now?" Willow asked.

"We do seem to be in a bit of a pickle," Giles commented.

"Enough with the condiments," Xander began, but Giles interrupted.

"I'm sorry, Xander, but we've no time for the usual banter. It seems your story about pumpkin-headed scarecrows and

Halloween rain may be true after all. I suspect that Samhain, the demon spirit who once ruled Halloween, may be out to destroy Buffy. Your appearance here tells me it hasn't been a quiet night."

"Only if you call vampires and zombies a quiet night," Willow said.

"Which may have been sent after Buffy by Samhain himself," Giles muttered, almost to himself. "We've got to get out of here. It seems our Slayer may have gotten herself into serious trouble."

"Maybe you haven't noticed, Giles," Xander replied. "But we're in a bit more than kinda sorta trouble ourselves, here. Any ideas how we're going to get to Buffy to warn her about the Halloween demon guy?"

Giles pushed his glasses up the bridge of his nose, raised his eyebrows, and smiled thinly. "Well," he said, "we're just going to have to slay those vampires outside, now aren't we?"

CHAPTER SIX

When zombies rose, they scrabbled like rats as they clawed their way out of their graves. You'd almost think they were suffocating below the earth and needed the fresh air, the way they struggled.

At least, that was one Slayer's opinion as she sat on top of the locked wrought-iron entrance gates of the Sunnydale Cemetery. Gray hands coated with slime and crawling with earthworms shot out of the ground and searched for something, anything, to grab on to—a bush, a headstone, another zombie—to pull the rest of the zombie out.

Make that *most* of the rest of the zombie.

Sometimes things were left behind in the effort, like an

arm or a leg or a face. But that didn't seem to matter as they got free of the grave and started doing their zombie thing.

Of all the forces of evil Buffy had to fight, zombies were probably the grossest. No way was she delighted to go in there and mess with them.

But when zombies rose, they were hungry.

For human brains.

They would do just about anything for a bite or two.

The walking dead smelled dinner, and its name was Buffy.

They must have smelled the rest of Sunnydale, too, because about a dozen of them had clumped into a mosh pit at the stone wall, and they were pushing to get the heck out of the cemetery and cruise for munchies. The wall so far had not given way. But farther down, a second bunch was pushing on another section. Several small stones had chipped out of the cement grout and clattered to the sidewalk on the other side.

Beneath her perch atop the gates, fifteen or twenty shambling corpses, in different stages of decay, surged against the iron bars. The chain that held the gates closed screeched, as did the iron hinges. It wouldn't be long before one or the other gave way and the zombies would be out on the streets of Sunnydale.

Buffy tried not to look at them. The dead faces, some just bare skulls with tufts of skin and hair here and there, gaped up at her. There was a moaning coming from the dead that gave her a major wiggins, a shiver all through her. It was like putting her ear to a seashell, only much worse. She couldn't tell if it was their voices, or just the wind whistling through their exposed bones and skulls. That sound was worse than Cordelia's whining, and even more likely to drive her crazy.

"Okay, you guys have killer harmonies. But could you please *shut up*!"

The zombies didn't respond at all, just continued to moan and stare. Some of them were staring without eyes, and Buffy so did not want to know what they were seeing.

She glanced out over the cemetery as more zombies clawed out of their graves. There were an awful lot of them. Sunnydale seemed like such a small town, but this was one major zombie square dance. If one fell, the others walked right over it. Do-si-do, whoops, smush. Buffy made a face. No doubt about it. Zombies were gross, and they were rude.

The newcomers moved to join the others at the dead folks jamboree, and the walls began to bulge with the pressure. The gate hinges and chains screeched even louder, close to snapping. They were going to get out. Buffy wrinkled her nose. Zombies, meet Slayer. Slayer, stop zombies from feasting on the neighbors.

"I am definitely going to need a bath after this," she muttered, and leaped over the heads of her fan club, smack into the middle of the cemetery. Since almost everybody was pushing against the walls, Buffy could warm up with the stragglers and the newly risen who didn't know what the heck was going on.

Yeah, like any of them had a clue.

As if she did. These spooky ooky guys were rising why?

The zombie closest to her wheeled around and came for her, arms stretched forward like a classic sleepwalker. Its eyes were huge and blank. Its jaws opened and shut. But the fact that it had eyes and a jaw meant the guy hadn't been dead too long, so he'd be stronger than the others. Buffy jumped into the air and launched a hard kick at its face. Whiplash: The thing did a one-eighty and keeled right over.

Another zombie approached from behind. She shot her leg out and back, crushing the zombie's ribs, and sent it flying backward. She nailed another with a fist to the top of its head and it crumpled again.

"Eeuu," she said. Her knuckles were covered with mold and spiderwebs. Absently she wiped them on her blouse.

Besides being disgusting, zombies were pretty easy to stop. Problems started only when there were a whole lot of them. Like, say, a whole cemetery full. With three quick kicks, Buffy took down as many zombies. She picked up a broken headstone and smashed in their skulls.

Now the silent majority had begun to realize something tasty was in their midst. Their heads rose. They looked like dogs sniffing the air or high school boys at the Bronze. They started to turn.

They began to advance on her.

"Giles," Buffy said under her breath, "this would be a good time to show up with some special zombie-stopping gear or spells or something." To the zombies, she bellowed—loud enough to startle, if not wake, the dead—"Simon says go back in your graves."

They kept coming. Some wore ragged shrouds, others had on rotting business suits and dresses. One was dressed like a clown, and that one gave her the wiggins worst of all.

"Yo, zombie guys, pay attention," she said, smashing her fist into the chest of one without looking at it, kicking at another, flipping backward over a third. "When it's Simon says, that means you have to do what I say. Let's be more direct. The Slayer says, die, like, forever."

Still more zombies stumbled toward her. She whirled in a circle, completely surrounded. She heard the click of their jaws opening and shutting. The moaning continued, grew louder now, and really started to bother her. She could feel it in her bones, an ache, a rattle, a weariness. The moans were this extreme wall of sadness, and if that's how being dead made you feel, Buffy figured it was even worse than high school.

Her heart was pounding. She had this mental picture of them overtaking her, cracking her skull open like a coconut, and eating her brains. There were just too many of them. Besides, a lot of the ones she managed to mangle got back up.

"Hey, look, my brains aren't that special, okay?" she said, half-pleading. "I'm flunking history. You don't want them."

A zombie woman in the tatters of a wedding dress grabbed her arm. Buffy fought it off just as another zombie, this one in the remnants of a tuxedo, grabbed her other arm. She threw that one off too.

"Have you two met before?" she asked as the zombies collided with each other and fell to the ground. "Like, at the altar?"

Then the clown trudged toward her. Its orange fright wig sat askew on its head, and pieces of gray hair escaped from beneath it. Beneath caked and moldering white clown makeup and a huge, gaping grin, the face was vaguely familiar. There was something about it that reminded her of someone.

It came closer. And closer.

Someone she had seen recently . . .

It opened wide.

The hair stood up on the back of Buffy's neck.

"Mr. O'Leary?" she cried at the zombie clown as she backed up into the arms of another zombie, who began to squeeze her around the middle, hard enough to push the breath out of her lungs.

"I'm comin', darlin' girl!" a man's voice cried.

As the zombie clown lurched toward her and grabbed her around the throat, Mr. O'Leary—as alive as she was, and probably for just as long—dropped down from the cemetery wall and barreled toward her.

"Oh, no," Buffy groaned breathlessly. "Mr. O'Leary, get out of here."

"'Tis a good thing I decided to come back. I'll save you!" he shouted, pushing a zombie from his path.

About a third of the zombies, smelling fresh meat, headed for him. The clown zombie kept strangling Buffy as he tried to get his mouth around the side of her head for that first dainty chomp.

"Giles," she said through gritted teeth, "now's a good time."

Or not.

"Okay, Giles, the plan is?" Xander asked anxiously as the female vampire Willow and Xander had been calling Red body-slammed the double entry doors of Sunnydale High School for an estimated one hundred and first time.

Thus far the vampires had not been able to enter, which made Giles suspect they could not. Perhaps it was because they hadn't been invited over the threshold. On the other hand, it was clear that Red was alone now. Her partner, whom Willow and Xander had referred to as Blue Eyes, had stopped pounding on the door, and they hadn't heard him shouting for a minute or two.

In addition, Giles was not certain Blue Eyes and Red were alone or if they were all barred from entrance into the school. At any moment, one could come crashing through the doors. In fact, they might already be sneaking down the corridors, intent upon ambushing the three humans.

The time for research was over, Giles knew. The time for action was upon him. Things like this had never occurred back in London. He'd been rather excited to discover he was to be the Watcher of the Slayer. Oh, the misspent enthusiasms of the innocent. Or the ignorant.

"We're coming for you," Red cooed. "You most of all, Xander."

"She knows my name," Xander blurted, obviously even more terrified than before.

Willow, at Giles's side, said with mock concern, "Oh, dear. Now she can look you up."

"We're unlisted," Xander said, as if the thought afforded him some measure of relief.

Giles had been holding the journal of Timothy Cassidy. Now he put the book beside the crossbow he had planned to bring to Buffy, gathered the two teenagers closer, and dropped his voice to a whisper.

"Right," he began. "It appears these two at least cannot come inside without an invitation. This is what we'll do. We'll uncover all the windows in the library. Then we'll lure them in and seal them up. When the sun rises, we'll let it do our work for us."

"Solar-powered death-dealing," Xander said, nodding. "Cool. Lure them in how?"

"Seal them up how?" Willow added.

Both the youngsters looked at him with trusting, inquisitive expressions. After all, one might suppose the Watcher would have instant answers to questions such as these.

In which case, one would be sadly mistaken.

"Yes, well, I've been mulling that over." He pushed up his

glasses again and gave a thought to Buffy. He was very worried about her. Each moment he wasted dithering in indecision was a moment that could cost her life.

"All right." He nodded at them reassuringly and picked up a canvas sack full of supplies. "I've some things in here that vampires aren't fond of—garlic bulbs, crosses, holy water. Along with some other items I've collected for Buffy." He opened the sack and showed them four pieces of wood like broken tree branches with the bark still on. "To kill Samhain, the Slayer must—"

"Uh, Giles? No offense, but just in case, can we go into that later?" Xander asked.

"Xander, be polite," Willow said, poking the boy in the ribs.

"I said 'no offense,'" Xander murmured defensively.

"None taken, I assure you." Giles cleared his throat as he handed Willow the sack. He hesitated a moment as he worked on his plan. Willow and Xander traded worried glances. Giles's sense of responsibility weighed on him ever more heavily.

"You two go to the library and tear the draperies off the windows, then put a cross on each one. We'll just have to hope they either don't notice what you're doing, or don't care. Then we'll get them into the library, block their way out with garlic and holy water, and in the morning, the sun will rise and"—he snapped his fingers—"two dead vampires."

"Neato keeno." Xander snapped his fingers in response. "Will, let's go."

"Wait." Willow frowned at Giles. "How are we going to get them into the library?"

Giles nodded. "Right. I shall invite them in and allow them to chase me. You two hide. Once we're in the library, I'll get out somehow, and then you two scatter the garlic and water over the threshold before they can follow."

Willow shook her head. "I was with you—sort of—until the 'somehow' part."

Xander crossed him arms. "Yes. 'Somehow' is the part where I also feel challenged about moving forward. Also, the part where they chase you."

"Well, all right, then, have you a better plan?" Giles looked at each of them in turn. "In that case, we'll go with mine."

"But, Giles," Willow said anxiously, "you're the Watcher. Buffy needs you. If you die, she'll probably get killed."

"But if one of *us* dies," Xander went on, "she'll totally feel bad." He raised his hand. "I say we vote on Giles's plan. See, Giles, we live in a democracy," he added. "We vote on stuff."

"To my knowledge, the pursuit of the vampires is not part of your Constitution," Giles countered.

"Neither is pursuit by the vampires," Willow said firmly.

"Or for the vampires." Xander nodded wisely.

Giles blinked. There were times when he appreciated the rather esoteric babble of the average American adolescent, and if pressed, he would have to admit that he found Xander Harris and Willow Rosenberg to be above average in many respects. Studying not being one of them in Xander's case, however, but that was beside the point. He found their strong sense of loyalty to each other and to the Slayer most admirable, and he was touched by their concern for his welfare.

However, returning to the notion of babbling, he was beginning to feel cast adrift in this conversation. In short, they were losing him, and he was just about to inform them of that fact, when they both nodded at him.

"We don't like it, but we'll do it your way," Willow said.

"Oh," Giles said, surprised. "Good."

"If you promise to take a cross and holy water," Willow added. She shrugged uncertainly. "I guess if you have garlic with you, they might not follow you."

He looked at them and said, "And I assume each of you will carry a cross on your person?"

"We're armed and loaded for bear," Xander assured him as he took a cross out of the sack and held it up for inspection. "Whatever that means. Watch as I exhibit my ignorance."

"It's a hunting reference," Willow observed, also holding up a cross. "Bears. Rifles. Bullets."

"Okay. Cool. Ignorance resolved. But I move on," Xander said. "I get the part where vampires can't come into your house if you don't invite them in. But that's, like, your house. Your territory. What about public buildings? Like, um, schools?"

Willow looked worried. "I can't remember. Have we ever seen a vampire at the movies? Or in a grocery store?"

The three looked at one another.

Further discussion was curtailed by the shattering of a window somewhere inside the school.

"Not the answer I was looking for," Willow said anxiously. Her eyes widened. "Giles?"

"Run," Giles said, fishing in his pocket for his keys. "I shall detain them for as long as I can."

Xander grabbed her hand. "Giles, if you are . . . *way* detained, what do we tell Buffy?"

"Take the crossbow," Giles began, then realized there wasn't enough time to go through everything. "The Watcher's journal," he said, handing the volume to Willow. "Timothy Cassidy's. Be sure to take that with you too."

Footsteps pounded down the corridor.

"For God's sake, run!" Giles shouted.

The two dashed around a corner and disappeared.

"Xan-der," came the teasing whisper of Red, the vampire female who'd set her sights on the young man.

Giles began to run too.

In the direction of the voice.

"No, no!" Mr. O'Leary shouted. "Sean!"

He jumped on the back of the clown zombie and pounded on its head and arms, trying to stop it from strangling Buffy. "It's me own dead brother!"

That explained why the clown looked so familiar, Buffy realized as she started to lose consciousness from lack of air. She'd thought it was Mr. O'Leary himself, somehow, as impossible as that would have been. Or maybe she thought she recognized the clown from one of those childhood nightmares called magic shows at kiddie birthday parties. She hated them.

Clowns wigged her . . .

. . . and ventriloquist's dummies . . .

. . . and dying . . .

. . . and raisins . . . raisin bran . . . something about raisin brain.

Raisin brains . . .

. . . risin' brains . . .

"No!" she shouted, gathering her strength as Mr. O'Leary managed to damage his brother enough for Buffy to break his grasp. She tucked in her head and collapsed to the ground. She heaved in huge gasps of air, fighting against blacking out, and kicked backward, shattering the knee of the zombie who'd had her around the waist. In front of her, Mr. O'Leary tumbled to the ground with the walking, clown-suited corpse of his brother.

Mr. O'Leary was pinned beneath the flailing clown zombie.

Buffy leaped to her feet and started kicking zombie parts as fast and hard as she could.

"This is—I mean, was—your brother?" she asked, horrified.

Mr. O'Leary rolled from beneath the clown and struggled to get to his feet. "Alas, dead these sixteen years. I'll tell you this. He was not buried in a clown costume. Someone has done this out of spite."

"This must be hard for you," she said, huffing. She yanked Mr. O'Leary up and slammed her fist into another zombie who attempted to grab on to the man. "Now, please, get out of here," she said.

"I'll stay and fight with you," he insisted.

"Go to the school. Ask Mr. Giles, the librarian, to come as fast as he can." She thought of Willow and Xander. Surely, if they'd made it to the library, they'd be here with Giles by now. "He can help."

"I'll not be leaving you here alone!" Mr. O'Leary insisted.

Suddenly, he cried out, grabbed at his chest, and fell to the ground. The zombies swarmed over Buffy, and she thrashed at them, breaking free. But it was getting harder and harder to move.

The Slayer was getting tired.

CHAPTER SEVEN

As Giles ran toward the voice of the female vampire, her companion, fully attired in a cowboy costume, jumped out from around a corner.

"Howdy, pardner," he said to Giles, who halted immediately, whirled around, and ran toward the library as fast as he could.

It was not fast enough.

Blue Eyes was upon him, jumping on Giles's back as if he were a horse. He kicked at Giles's sides and yelled, "Yee-ha!"

Taking his cue from his training sessions with the Slayer, Giles tucked in his head and leaned forward. The vampire flew over his head and sprawled on the ground.

"I can't take you anywhere," Red drawled at Blue Eyes in mock disgust.

Giles threw himself against the wall and held out his cross, brandishing it from side to side as the female vampire slowed to a walk and smiled at Giles. Blue Eyes got up and moved in on him from the opposite direction.

"You don't need that, Deputy," Red said sweetly. "Just put it down."

"Stay back." Giles reached in his pocket and uncapped the holy water. He wasn't certain how to play this out. This was what the Americans charmingly called a Mexican standoff. Each of the three of them had a weapon, and as long as none of them made the first move, they were stuck here indefinitely. But if he ran again, they would surely overtake him.

As Giles watched in horror, the two vampires transformed into the hideous creatures they truly were, the faces they wore when the hunger was upon them. They licked their fangs and swiped their clawed hands menacingly at him, hissing. Giles swallowed hard and stood his ground. The Slayer faced such danger daily; he could do no less when called upon to save her.

"You're the little Slayer's Watcher," Red said. "The Master has promised a reward for your heart. We'll make you die slowly. Painfully."

"We should take him to the Master alive," Blue Eyes cut in, averting his eyes as Giles tilted the cross slightly in his direction. "Our reward will be even greater."

"I'm sorry to disappoint you, but neither of you is going anywhere," Giles said.

Red's laughter seemed to echo down the corridor. "Your arm will tire soon," she said.

She began to sit down on the floor when Xander called, "Yo, Giles! Do we have any books on interior decorating?" It was the cue that they had finished pulling down the curtains and adorning the windows with crosses.

Red's hideous face broke into an enormous smile. "My dear Xander must be in the library."

"With my girlfriend," Blue Eyes agreed, grinning.

They looked at Giles, who made his eyes move left, away from the library, as a ruse.

"It's this way," Blue Eyes said, pointing left, skirting around Giles and joining Red. "We'll take the kids by surprise and come back for him."

They loped down the corridor in the wrong direction, as Giles had planned, the two laughing horribly. Giles took off toward the library.

"Xander! Willow! I'm coming!" he shouted, and behind him, the vampires called out to each other and turned to give chase. Giles redoubled his efforts, running as fast as he could, and flew toward the open library door. Blue Eyes and Red were perhaps three or four feet behind him. Giles sailed over the threshold and was immediately yanked to one side by Xander.

The vampires passed over the threshold.

Willow darted from the other side of the door and tossed open vials of holy water at them, holding a cross in her hand. Their faces began to smoke as they howled in pain and covered their eyes.

Xander pulled Giles out of the library and tossed a pair of crosses behind them. Willow hopped over them, sprinkling the floor and doors with holy water.

"We'll get you for this!" Red cried, lowering her hands to her sides. Her face was a smoking mess; she looked as if she was wearing a Halloween fright mask that had melted. She started toward them and screamed as her foot came down on a cross.

Willow pulled the double doors shut with the vampires hissing at her, then wrapped strands of garlic bulbs around the door handles. Similar strands were on the inside handles as well.

"Let's go," Giles said, and he, Xander, and Willow raced down the corridors and passages of Sunnydale High. Giles hoped that the trap had worked, but now was not the time to verify it. At the least, they had bought themselves some time.

He hoped they had bought Buffy time as well.

They reached the front doors, his books, and the crossbow. Willow still held the canvas sack. Wonderful girl. She had kept her head.

Xander pushed open the door and said, "What if there are more of them out here?"

"Ever the optimist," Willow retorted. "I'm holding the

bag; why don't you make yourself useful and grab the crossbow?"

"Don't we need arrows?" Xander asked as he hefted the weapon.

"They take bolts. Which there are. It's all right," Willow replied.

They gathered up the supplies and raced out of the school and down the stone steps.

Buffy gritted her teeth, wishing for anything that could drown out the way depressing, emo moaning of the zombies. Mr. O'Leary was dead. Buffy knew that just from looking at him. And it wasn't from any zombie attack. The poor old guy had just up and died. The cardiac police had come along and cuffed him. Heart attack city.

Not that she was in any position to do anything about it.

As she defended herself, several of the zombies latched on to Mr. O'Leary's corpse. She tried to protect it—him—but saving her own bacon was hard enough. The Slayer looked away; she didn't want to see what would happen to the old man's corpse when the dead guys got their choppers going.

A zombie grabbed her shoulder, and as she spun to crush its face, she saw what they'd done with Mr. O'Leary. Nothing like what she expected. He'd been hung up in a large pepper tree in the center of the cemetery, where he dangled like a horrible scarecrow. Scarecrow. Coincidence, or nasty inspiration?

She'd no idea, but had to assume they only liked really-truly-alive folks. As a fellow dead guy, Mr. O'Leary didn't meet their culinary needs and was tossed out like garbage. She only hoped the sweetly crazy old man didn't rise again.

Buffy didn't want to have to fight him.

She turned away. Buffy didn't want to see any more.

The zombie moaning started up again, and the shambling dead began to crawl to their feet once more. Buffy glanced quickly around and realized that there were still dozens upon dozens of them moving. Hungry. Not good. She had to destroy their brains to kill them, if the movie rules applied. And she just couldn't concentrate that much with so many bony fingers clawing at her.

And that noise! It was enough to make that happy mailman on Mr. Rogers go postal!

Giles hadn't arrived. Willow and Xander might be dead for all Buffy knew. She wanted to get out of the cemetery, find them, make sure they were all right. Then they could all come back, Giles could find some anti-zombie spells in one of his smelly books, and they could gorge on whatever Halloween candy was left at her house.

"Nice fantasy, Summers," she whispered to herself. She had to get out of there first.

Buffy turned and started for the gates, slamming her open palm into the nose of a nearby zombie, sending bone splinters into its brain. It fell over a headstone and didn't move again, and she figured if she could pull that maneuver on all of them, she'd be in good shape. Problem was, when they started to move in, she didn't have time to aim.

And they *were* moving in. In fact . . .

There were so many hungry zombies stacked up at the walls and in front of the gates that Buffy just couldn't see how she was going to get out without shutting them all down. Which could take, oh, the rest of her life. However long that was.

"Look, folks," she said nervously, growing truly frightened now as they closed in on her, a wall of dead flesh and bone. "It's been a heck of a fiesta, y'know? But, really, I turn into a pumpkin at midnight."

Buffy pulled the broken nose trick on two more zombies, then elbowed another in the chest. The dead man's chest collapsed, and the stink from the corpse almost made her throw up.

Being the Slayer didn't mean that Buffy wasn't afraid of the things she faced. Only that she was confident in her ability to overcome them. Most of the time. But when that confidence failed, she was still a sixteen-year-old girl who wanted very much to keep breathing.

She glanced around nervously and noticed something odd at the rear of the cemetery. Something that hadn't seemed significant before because it didn't threaten her life. While the sides and front of the cemetery had high walls, the back was bordered by farmland. The only thing separating the graveyard from the fields beyond was a three-foot-high stone wall that looked as if it had been there since man discovered fire. Or at least the gas grill.

The reason she hadn't noticed it was because there weren't any zombies back there. None. Zero. Nada. Now, sure, the more residential sections of Sunnydale had more people, which to the headsuckers meant more brains to eat. But she couldn't believe none of them had realized they could just step over that wall and be out of the cemetery.

Not that it mattered. What mattered was it was a way out. Not too many zombies between Buffy and the field.

"I'll be back," she said in her gruffest Terminator voice. Then she ripped an arm from a particularly decrepit-looking zombie and used it to shatter the skulls of two others. Then she was bounding from grave marker to tombstone to the roof of a crypt. She held on to the wings of a carved marble angel and looked toward the low stone wall again. Not far away. Not too many zombies.

No problem.

Buffy dropped down to the ground again, and immediately bony fingers began reaching for her. The moaning had reached a fever pitch, as if they knew she was going to escape them. A part of her wanted to slow, to surrender, to ease their pain. That's how much of a downer their vocals were.

Instead, she kicked, punched, and elbowed her way toward the field. A high, spinning kick actually beheaded one of the zombies, and Buffy was psyched to see that she only had another thirty yards or so to go.

Twenty.

Ten.

Dead fingers twined in her hair, yanking her backward off her feet. Zombies came down on top of her, jaws clacking as they tried to bite into her. The moaning became too much.

Buffy closed her eyes, a tear beginning to form.

Too much.

Her heart raced. Then a fire exploded in her gut and roared its way up into her throat to blast out of her as a scream.

"Noooooooo!" she cried, and surged upward with incredible strength. Zombies went flying like bowling pins, save for one or two that she shook off as she turned to run, wide eyed and terrified, for the stone wall.

Then she was there. Buffy dove over the wall, rolled into a somersault, and sprang to her feet again. She felt something in her hair and batted at it: the remains of dead flesh torn from fingers as she struggled against a dead man's grip. Buffy pulled the flesh away, then wiped her hand on her pants in disgust. She panted, trying to catch her breath, then glanced around to see which way would be best for her escape. The zombies would be after her . . .

Zombies. After her.

Not.

They weren't coming after her at all. It gave her the wiggins, but they just stood there on the other side of the stone wall and moaned, staring at her out of withered eyes like raisins—there, she knew there was a reason she didn't like raisins!—or empty sockets.

"Okay!" Buffy said, confused but pleased. "You guys and gals just hang out here, and I'll go find someone who will know how we can lullaby you all back to death."

She looked at them one last time, shivered off the wiggins that was creeping up on her, and turned to walk along next to the wall. If she circled around the cemetery, she'd get back to the street. Then she'd have a long walk to school to find Giles.

Once more, she worried for Willow and Xander.

Buffy had an odd sensation, a familiar one. In fact, she'd felt it earlier that same night. As if she was being watched. As if some Peeping Tom was checking her out in the girls' locker room. As if someone was sneaking up on her . . .

The Slayer spun, ready to attack, poised to take on any zombies that had finally come over the wall for her.

There was nobody there.

Buffy took a deep breath, let it out, and wrote off her jitters as the result of a very long, majorly tiring Halloween night. Somewhere off in Sunnydale, the church bells began to toll midnight.

"Great," she muttered. "The witching hour has begun. As if this night hasn't been enough of a drag."

She began to turn, to start for the street again, but something caught her eye in the moonlight. Up the hill, a cross jutted from the ground, silhouetted in the moonlight. Not a cross, she realized, but a post with a bar nailed near the top.

Her stomach sank and churned and burned. Then went deathly cold. Every muscle in Buffy's body tensed, as true, rabid fear coursed through her. There had been a scarecrow on that post earlier, she was certain. She had seen it from outside the cemetery. But now . . . Where had it gone? Where could it have gone?

It had rained all day, Halloween rain. And Willow and Xander had warned her about Halloween rain and scarecrows, and not trespassing on the fields they watched over.

Sure, reason enough for a serious wiggins, but not for the fear she felt now. Horrible. Terror like nothing she'd ever known. It was almost enough to make her want to curl up in a ball there in the field. It wasn't natural. It was some kind of . . .

". . . magick," she whispered.

But it didn't matter. She was terrified. So much so that she didn't want to walk all the way along the cemetery to get to the street. She was willing, even happy, to make a beeline right through the zombie-shambling-room-only cemetery to get away from this field. Besides, she just realized that she had left her Slayer's bag somewhere in the cemetery.

Buffy launched herself toward the zombies, toward the stone wall—and slammed into something hard and unyielding. She smacked her forehead against it, had the breath knocked out of her, and was thrown back to the ground.

Now she knew why the zombies weren't coming into the field. They couldn't. And whatever was keeping them out was now keeping her in. She was trapped. Her breathing sped up, her terror growing by the instant.

Somewhere up the hill, she heard a low, hissing voice. *Please, maybe it's only the wind!*

It called to her.

"*Ssslayer!*"

CHAPTER EIGHT

Willow stared out the passenger window of the Giles-mobile as they raced toward the cemetery. Xander, in the back, scanned through the rear window. Somewhere in the distance thunder rumbled, and the air seemed to fill with moisture again.

Willow shivered, chilled through to her bones. The rain had stopped, but now she wondered if it wasn't going to start all over again. Still, the chill she felt wasn't from the weather, but the horrible fear and dread that was creeping over her.

"I don't think it was an act of nature that interfered with cell reception," Giles observed as he stepped on the gas.

Willow stirred and shivered harder. "I'm thinking supernature," she agreed as she glanced in the rearview mirror. "Something didn't want Buffy to contact you."

Nervously she played with the frayed edge of Giles's canvas bag o' tricks.

"You know," Willow said hopefully, "one of the vampires at the Bronze told Buffy they had the night off. I wonder if that's true. We haven't come across anything diabolical since we three left the school."

Maybe it was all over because Buffy had killed the pumpkin king, Samhain. Maybe Halloween was over forever.

Xander looked away from the window long enough to drawl, "Yeah, well, he's the same vampire she dusted for unauthorized snacking not five minutes later. And don't forget our own private posse, Will. Those being the escapees of the dude ranch from hell who wanted to corral us three."

"Roy Rogers and Dale Evans," Giles observed. Willow and Xander looked at him blankly. "Popular American cowpeople. I was referring to your Red and Blue Eyes, and their Halloween, um, getups."

"Cowpeople?" Willow quickly covered her mouth, but she knew Giles saw her quick grin. It amazed her that she could grin at a time like this, but that's what hanging with Buffy did for—or to—you. You developed a strange sense of humor to keep from going bonkers when confronted by horrors you thought existed only in movies. It was kind of like surviving high school. At least, that was how it was for her.

"Hey, I know about those cowpeople," Xander piped up. "They had a horse named Trigger that they stuffed after he died."

"Okay, that's gross," Willow said, thinking uncomfortably of the many pets she had had in her life. She couldn't imagine keeping them around like strange dead trophies. Willow cast Giles a sidelong glance. "Were these people in one of your dusty demon books for mummifying their pony?"

Giles shook his head. "No. They were quite famous, in their day. Which clearly is not your day. As for the stuffing, they put the horse in their museum, I believe." He pushed up his glasses. "They had a famous theme song. It began, 'Happy trails to you . . .'"

Giles stopped, apparently distracted.

"He trailed off," Willow said. "Don't abandon us now, Giles, we were just reveling in your magnificent tenor."

Giles sniffed, stared out past the windshield. "Let me tell you what we must do to help the Slayer. To begin . . ."

"He trailed off again," Xander said.

"What's wrong, Giles?" Willow asked, peering at him as he put a foot on the brake.

"Mr. Rupert, sir?" Xander queried.

Wordlessly, Giles raised a hand and pointed through the windshield.

The wrought-iron entrance to the cemetery rose like a strange flower in the moonlit sky. A broken tree drooped behind it.

From the tree hung a human body.

"No," Willow groaned. "It can't be." She swallowed down her terror and wrenched open the car door.

"Willow, wait," Giles called, but she was out of the car before he had completely stopped it. She stumbled, kept running. Her chest was so tight she could hardly move. Certainly, she had been afraid for Buffy before, but it had never really sunk in that Buffy might actually be killed. That they could go on with their lives minus the best friend she had ever had. That the forces of evil might win.

How could she go on without Buffy? How could any of them go on knowing that the Slayer had . . . had lost?

"Buffy," she cried, and ran through the open gates.

She stumbled to a stop and burst into quick tears of relief. It wasn't Buffy. It was Mr. O'Leary.

Or what was left of him.

Willow stared at his corpse a moment, then tore her gaze away. Priorities.

"Buffy?" Willow called.

By the time she got hold of herself, Giles and Xander had caught up with her. Giles carried his sack and Xander had the crossbow. Both of them stared up at the dead man.

"Oh my God," Xander said. His face was chalk white.

"It gets worse," Willow said, and tugged on Xander's hand.

"I hate worse," Xander grumbled, and turned to peer into the darkness across the cemetery where Willow was pointing. "What, are the headstones moving?"

"Those aren't headstones," Giles said. "Those are zombies. The walking dead."

Suddenly, as if someone had given the zombies their cue, they began to moan. It was a horrible, starving, desperate sound that hit Willow like a fist. She staggered under the grief and despair, almost unable to remain standing. There were dozens of them, maybe hundreds, all making the same awful noise.

They were crowded together at the far end of the cemetery. Willow was relieved to see that they didn't even seem aware that she, Giles, and Xander were nearby.

Then it was as if they had heard her thoughts. A cluster off to the right pivoted slowly to look at the newly arrived alive people. Some of the dead guys began to stumble toward them. The rest were like a writhing, rotten wall of flesh as they stood facing outward, lined up against the back wall as they stared and moaned.

"Isn't that Mr. Flutie?" Willow asked, first staring and then purposely turning away from the half-chewed-up corpse shambling toward them.

"They're stuck in here," Xander shouted, covering his ears. "It must be bumming them out. That's why they're moaning."

"No. They've gotten out at the back," Giles shouted, pointing, but Willow was too short to see whatever it was he saw. "They're grouping along the perimeter of that field."

"Field?" Willow and Xander cried at the same time.

"But they're not going in," Giles mused. "Odd."

"Is there a scarecrow? Do you see a scarecrow?" Willow demanded anxiously.

"I don't see one," Giles said loudly after a minute. "But clearly they can't go into the field."

Xander tapped Willow on the shoulder. "What?" she asked, craning to see. "Is there one? Xander?"

He tapped her again.

"Xander, just tell me."

She began to turn, then realized Xander was standing slightly in front of her to the right. He couldn't be tapping her shoulder. She whirled around.

A zombie with one eye lunged at her. It grabbed her arm and pulled her toward itself; its mouth opened wide and a worm slithered out.

"Willow!" Giles shouted. He yanked her away and swung the sack at the zombie's head.

As the three looked on, the sack crushed the zombie's skull and it sank to the ground.

"Back up," Giles ordered as three more zombies lurched toward them.

The zombies split up, one coming for each of them. The undead buddy system.

Xander said, "Okay, the plan is modified to?"

"Oh, dear," Giles said. "Back up."

"We need a plan B, Giles," Willow cried.

"That *is* plan B!" Giles said in frustration.

Somehow, in the short time the three had spent inside the

cemetery gates, zombies had completely surrounded them. Over their awful groans came a strangely soft but audible hiss.

"Sssslayer."

The sound made the hair stand up on Willow's neck. It spoke of pure evil and hatred and death.

"It came from the field," Xander said into her ear as he darted a glance over his shoulder toward the back of the cemetery.

One of the zombies swiped at Willow. She jumped back, then spun around to see that more of the zombies who had been standing along the back wall were turning in the direction of those present and accounted for with living, pulsing brains.

"Buffy might be in that field," Xander went on. "Will, it's been raining, and Buffy may be in a field."

Then Xander made a face. He said, "Um, incoming info fact: The bar has just been raised on the possibility of Buffy's presence in that field."

He pointed at something.

"Why do you think that she—," Willow began, then saw Buffy's Slayer's bag next to a headstone near the wall.

"Isn't it great to have twenty-twenty?" Xander asked, not happily.

Willow bellowed, "Giles, we have to get to her."

"Getting to her. There's plan B," Xander agreed as he dogged his zombie dance partner. "But a notion here. Getting to her alive with our brains still in our heads is even better. And the way we do that is?"

No answer.

"Come on, Giles!" Willow said frantically. "It's shambling room only in here."

"There are too many of them for us to fight," Giles observed, swinging at his zombie. His fist connected and the zombie tumbled to the ground. Its legs and feet still moved as if it were walking. "We've got to fend them off until I can figure something out."

"What?" Willow made a fist and grimaced as a zombie in moldy black priest's garb stumbled in her direction. Its mouth opened and closed, making its jaw do the Rice Krispies snap-crackle-pop. There was nothing in its sightless gaze to suggest it had a mind, and that made it all the more frightening. Vampires and werewolves could be talked to, possibly outwitted. But these witless wonders would keep coming until they were physically stopped. And the Three Musketeers did not have the physics to make that happen.

"Buffy!" Willow called as loudly as she could. Her voice shook. "Buffy, we're coming as soon as we can!"

"Buffy!"

It was Willow's voice. Coming from the cemetery. Where the zombies were. Not good.

"Willow, are you okay?" Buffy shouted back. "Is Giles with you? Is Xander okay?"

"There are so many of them!" Willow called. "We're trying to get to you. We found your Slayer's bag and Giles has some things he thinks will help you!"

"No, stay away!" Buffy ordered her, waving her hands in case they could see her. "I can't get to you, but stay out of here."

Buffy pushed against the invisible barrier, way wigged. Hordes of moaning zombies pushed on the other side. If it should give way when she didn't expect it, she'd be a nice midnight snack. The zombie equivalent of raiding the fridge. But what was happening to her friends?

"Get out of there!" she cried frantically.

"We can't. We've been boxed in," Willow said.

Then Willow screamed.

"Willow? Willow! Xander? Giles?" Buffy threw herself at the barrier. She had been terrified moments earlier by the voice she had heard, by the presence she had felt there in the field with her. Now that terror was overwhelmed by her fear for her friends. She kicked and pounded, getting nowhere. All she heard was moaning.

Then Giles said loudly, "Buffy, stay where you are. I'm working on the problem."

"Which one?" she called. "The barrier, or the zombies, or—"

"Ssslayer."

The single word sizzled across the back of Buffy's neck like a piece of dry ice. She began shivering so hard she thought she might be sick. She couldn't explain it, but there was something in that voice that frightened her more than any horror she had ever faced.

"Ssslayer, come."

Buffy whirled around and scanned the horizon. To the left was the rise of the hill and the empty cross shape that had once held a scarecrow. To her right, the ground was dotted with rows of trees. Then the hill fell away into a valley, and there was a box shape at the bottom. A building of some sort.

Black clouds began to tumble one over the other, threatening to cover the pale moon. Buffy had the distinct feeling she was being watched, by someone besides her peanut gallery of reanimated corpses. She swallowed down the knot in her throat and glanced from side to side. She could hardly breathe.

"Sorry, I'll pass on that invite," she called out as firmly as she could, but her voice shook.

The answer was a low, cruel laugh that seemed to slither up toward her from the valley. She peered into the night. The field was gloomy and dark, and the ground was soaked from the earlier rains.

There were pumpkins everywhere. She was in a pumpkin field.

Xander and Willow had warned her not to walk in any fields. By coming in here, she had set them up for chowtime and landed herself in a trap.

"Come, or they die."

She could think of nothing to say. No clever retort sprang to mind. No silly remark. It was as if everything was sliding away from her and she was balancing at the edge of a cliff. She took a step forward and tripped over something stretched across the earth. Before she could catch herself, she fell to her hands and knees into thick mud and tangles of vines.

The sense of being watched grew even stronger. As she lifted her head, the vines between her fingers seemed to tighten. She peered down at the earth.

A small, round pumpkin swiveled as she moved her head. She blinked, lurched forward, raised her fist, and crashed it down on the pumpkin. It caved in and began to roll down the hill.

Laughter filled Buffy's ears, low and cunning and eager.

"Come."

"Willow, can you hear me?" Buffy called, ignoring the voice.

There was no answer.

Then Buffy realized she no longer heard the moaning of the zombies. She heard nothing but her heartbeat. Struggling, she got to her feet.

"Giles?" she called.

No answer. The voice had told her, essentially, to follow the bouncing pumpkin. Down into a valley. Where she couldn't see a thing. Instead, she turned left and started climbing the hill.

Suddenly, like huge plumes of smoke, more clouds raced across the moon. They were gigantic, more like a thick web than clouds, and before she realized what was happening, Buffy was plunged into complete blackness.

She took a breath and kept walking. She thought of her Slayer's bag back in the cemetery, and all the goodies it contained—stakes, matches, candles—and realized that she was basically defenseless except for her strength and her reflexes. At least the others might be able to make use of the things in her bag, she thought. At least they weren't as defenseless as she was.

"So *not* defenseless," she muttered. "I'm the Slayer."

Something crackled behind her. She whirled around in an attack stance. She could see nothing. She moved her hands in front of herself, to each side, waved them behind herself. She felt nothing.

A bolt of lightning cracked across the sky, lighting up the field.

A dozen pumpkins were fanned in a semicircle behind her. She didn't know if they had actually moved or if they had lain in the field that way, but she slammed as many as she could down the hill as the light faded.

Another crack of lightning spiked through the blackness.

Buffy spun to face the hill.

At the crest, in the brilliance, a figure loomed. The way he stood, the flash of light gave her just a glimpse of his body, his head still blanketed by darkness. He wore overalls and a dark, ragged shirt. His hands were on his hips and his feet were encased in cast-off work boots. His hands were made of straw.

She took a step backward.

Lightning cracked a third time.

She saw his face.

She opened her mouth to scream, but no sound would come out.

His head was a huge, rotting pumpkin. Green flame licked out of jagged carved eyes, which shifted and squinted as he looked down on her. A nightmare jack-o'-lantern, the pumpkin head leered at her, hideous and savage. Its mouth—lined with horrible fangs—was pulled into a broad smile so wide it disappeared around the sides of the blistered gourd.

It belched sickly green fire from its mouth and carved nostrils; flames shot from its eyes and glowed beneath the orange, uneven skin, casting shadows over its face as it cocked its head, regarding her. Its eyes stared at her, almost spinning. It began to slaver and drool, jagged rows of teeth flashing and slashing as it opened and closed its mouth like a mindless zombie. Licking its chops.

But it—he—was far from mindless. Cunning and hatred were etched clearly on his face as if someone had carved them there.

He lifted his arms from his sides as if mimicking being hung above the field. Blood dripped from their razor edges.

Blood, black in the green firelight, streamed from his mouth.

He threw back his head and whispered, *"Happy Halloween."* Though the sound was a whisper, it echoed over the field.

"Off to see the Wizard," Buffy muttered, and began to back up.

CHAPTER NINE

As Buffy backed away from the hideous pumpkin-headed scarecrow, she found herself thinking simply, *This is it. This is when the Slayer crashes and burns.*

How else to explain the complete and total horror that had seized her and throttled her like the scarecrow's blood-drenched hand around her throat? She couldn't stop staring at him. She couldn't turn her back on him and run, though all her Slayer's training—and her own personal wish to keep living—told her that that was exactly what she must do. Some misfiring instinct for self-preservation insisted that she not take her gaze off him, not for a second. To look away was to die.

But if she didn't get moving, that was exactly what was going to happen.

The pumpkins behind Buffy began to laugh.

Something nudged her boot. She kicked at it without looking.

It bit her through the leather.

"Ow!" she cried involuntarily.

The pumpkin-headed scarecrow looked down on her.

"Do you think that hurt?" he demanded. *"That is nothing compared to the pain you will feel when I rip out your beating heart."*

Buffy swallowed hard. She wanted to say, "Samhain, I presume," to sound smart and unafraid, but all that came out was his name. "Samhain."

"Slayer."

Samhain extended his arm toward her and beckoned for her to approach. It was not difficult to stand her ground. She was paralyzed.

Something else bit her, harder this time. By pure reflex, she kicked at it but did not dare take her eyes away from Samhain.

"Come to me now," Samhain said. *"Join the revel of all the fears of the timeless hours. Of witches and ghouls and demons, of death and pain and dying and the forever blackness you call the Dark Place. Lay your life at my feet and I will give you relief from the soul-killing terror that you feel."*

"I don't feel anything," she insisted weakly.

Samhain smiled, and his head was almost sliced in two by his own fanglike teeth. Blood streamed from his mouth and splattered on the ground.

"You feel everything," he said. *"Every fear you have ever had. Remember when you were very little, and the pile of clothes in the corner looked like the bogeyman? Remember how you were certain that your dolls were watching you? That they moved when you looked away? Remember your clothes closet, and how the door would open slowly in the night?"* Samhain smiled. *"Remember the nightmare helplessness you felt then?"*

Cold dread washed over her. She did remember.

"My handiwork," he said proudly. *"A monster under your bed. Someone following you home. Someone waiting in the hallway with a knife. I command the fears of your kind. I conjure them up. I smother you with them like a pillow over your face. I make hearts stop. I make Slayers die."*

Buffy shook herself hard as buckets of fear splashed over her. She was trembling violently. She was so afraid. Afraid to move, to breathe.

Afraid to die.

"You will not stop me, girl," Samhain crowed.

Buffy raised her chin. Those fears were no longer childhood nightmares. They were part of her daily life. There really were monsters lying in wait for her. In her reality, evil creatures did live inside dolls and creep under her bed and rise from the dead to wound her and kill her. As afraid of them as she had been, and still was, she faced them and fought them.

And defeated them.

She was the Slayer.

She looked at Samhain with narrowed eyes and said, "Oh, but I will stop you, Mr. Pumpkin Eater. You're not the king of all fear, just of this one night. And frankly, you're not that much of a king at all. I didn't vote for you."

Samhain shook with fury. The flames shot out of his eyes and mouth and a horrible growl rumbled in his chest, making the earth shake.

"Enough!" he shouted.

Samhain threw open his arms. The skies cracked open and rain poured down.

There was intense, incredible pain at her ankles.

She glanced down. The pumpkins had advanced on her. They were slicing through her boots with jack-o'-lantern teeth. Buffy tried to shake them off, then looked up to see Samhain spring at her like a huge wolf.

Buffy shouted and dropped to the ground. Samhain arced over her head. She whirled around and fell into a battle stance, then smashed her right foot into his midsection as hard as she could.

It was like kicking iron. She fell onto her back, the wind knocked out of her, sheer terror knocked into her. It had been a mistake to touch him. He was evil in solid form. He was the power of fear incarnate.

She had never been more afraid in her life.

As he flung himself at her, she skirted around him and began flying down the hill. She had to get out of here, get away. There was no way to kill fear. And even if there were, she was not going to be the one to do it.

Her Slaying days were over. She had just resigned.

She wanted to live.

The rain came down in torrents. She slid and fell a dozen times in the pitch-black, her only light the glowing head of Samhain as he bolted after her. Her hands were bleeding and slick with mud, which the rain sluiced off as she ran for all she was worth.

To her right was the cemetery; she saw some flickering lights and wondered if that was Giles, Willow, and Xander with her Slayer's equipment. She wondered if she would ever see them again.

"You cannot outrun me. You cannot outfight me," Samhain growled after her. She felt icy breath on her neck and ran until she thought her heart might burst.

I make hearts stop, he had said. He had not lied.

Incredibly, huge pumpkins flung themselves at her, pummeling her. Though she realized it must be Samhain's power somehow, it still seemed as though the pumpkins had an evil of their own and moved by their own will. But that couldn't be. It just couldn't!

Within seconds she was bruised and aching and soaked to the bone. Unable to see the pumpkins, she raised her arms to protect her face and continued her run.

She ran into the rows of trees, and thought at first that pumpkins were leaping from them. But they were apple trees, and she was hitting the apples as she ran.

"You cannot defeat me," Samhain added.

"I know, I know, I get it, okay? Class dismissed," Buffy whispered, and kept going.

The ground leveled off; she realized she was at the bottom of the valley. There'd been a building down there. As she stared wildly into the blackness, terrified that at any moment he would catch her, the lightning flashed again.

Dead ahead was the building. It was a barn.

For a moment, her hopes were raised as she instinctively ran toward shelter. Then she realized that he was herding her into it. Once inside, she would be trapped.

She liked to think he would be trapped too.

But at the last moment, she veered off and ran to the side of the barn. By then the lightning burst had faded, and she was running in torrential rain and utter darkness again.

Behind her, Samhain said, *"I can see you, Slayer. I see every move you make. There's nowhere to hide from the Dark King of Samhuinn."*

Something whipped her knees. After about a minute, she was wading through a field of tall vegetation that brushed around her hips. She glanced over her shoulder.

The glowing ball of Samhain's head was perhaps twenty yards away.

She wondered if he really could see her.

"Help me, someone, please," she whispered, and dropped to her stomach in the tall plants. She lay as still as death and clenched her jaw. The scent of grass rose around her.

And then the scent of the grave, as his heavy footfalls smashed into the tall grass.

"Sssslayer," he called. *"I'm coming for you now."*

She remained unmoving as the rain washed over her. Her mind raced. She had to figure out how to stay alive until morning, or destroy Samhain, or both.

His footsteps shook the ground.

A small furry something with tiny paws and a very long tail crawled over the backs of her hands. She didn't flinch, didn't move a muscle.

He came closer.

And closer.

Without breathing, she waited.

"I will destroy you tonight," he said.

Buffy swallowed hard. Tears streamed down her face. She was afraid, deathly afraid. She couldn't even think, she was so terrified.

As soon as she could no longer hear his footsteps, she got up and blindly ran back toward the orchard. She had no plan, no thought, except to get away from him.

In the cemetery, in the pouring rain, the zombies had surrounded Xander, Willow, and Giles. Xander looked at Willow, who was doing a much better Slayerette job of pounding them than he would have expected, she being, er, a nonguy. But that was so sexist of him.

"Giles, plan C would be good now," he said anxiously as he kicked a zombie in the shins and pushed it hard. It tottered backward and fell into the mud. But it would be back. Oh, it would be back. These things took a licking and kept on ticking.

Flashlight in hand, Giles had been trying for some time to get one of his books out of his canvas sack to look for a spell or something to redead the undead. But the zombies kept coming too fast for him to complete the mission. He, Willow, and Xander could do only so much damage to the opposition.

Could anyone around here spell Alamo?

"Look!" Willow cried, pointing. "There's a little space between them. If we can get to the top of that crypt—"

Xander glanced in the direction of her outstretched finger and pushed her to the side as a zombie tried to chomp down on it. He smacked the zombie in the face with the crossbow. It slipped on the wet grass and crashed to the earth.

"Thanks," Willow said. "Look, see how we've mowed down a path?"

He did see. Somehow, the three of them had thinned the zombies in a fairly clear line from where they stood now to a standing crypt, which Giles had once told him was also called a vault. If they could vault onto it, maybe Giles would have enough time to save the day.

That is, if Giles could find the secret ingredients in his magickal recipe file.

"Should we go for it?" Xander asked Giles, rubbing his hands together in anticipation.

"Yes," Giles said. He turned off the flashlight and put it in his sack. The weak moonlight made his face look as gray as a zombie's, a majorly upsetting visual. "Willow, take Buffy's Slayer's bag. I'll carry my sack. Xander, get the crossbow."

Xander put the crossbow under his arm. Then he bent low and cried, "One, two, three, hike!" He barreled in front of Willow and began knocking zombies over like a line-backer. He was afraid of falling, but he was more afraid of being dinner.

"We're right behind you, Xander," Willow said.

Xander got to the vault, kicking a zombie out of his way as Willow joined him. Giles brought up the rear. He threw his sack onto the top of the vault. Xander and Willow did the same.

Then Giles laced his fingers together and stooped. His hair was plastered to his head. He said, "Willow, go first."

She put her foot into his interlaced fingers. Xander held her around the waist. She turned her head and seemed about to say something to him, then looked at him through the buckets of rain for a few seconds and sighed.

She said, "Go."

Giles and Xander hoisted her up. She grabbed on to the stone overhang of the vault's roof and shinnied the rest of the way up and onto the top.

"Xander, go next," Giles ordered.

"No, you go," Xander insisted. When Giles hesitated, Xander said, "You're the only one who can stop these guys permanently."

"Xander, do not argue with me. I'm your school librarian," Giles said, as if that carried any weight.

"Oooh, the voice of authority speaks," Xander said.

Giles rolled his eyes. "As the Watcher, then."

The zombies began to close in. Xander knew it was a waste of time—in more ways than one—to argue with the man. He smacked a zombie in a nice green dress, then realized the shimmering green color of the dress was slime. He put his foot in Giles's handhold and pushed himself to the top of the vault. Then he rolled onto his stomach and held out his hands for Giles.

A zombie dressed in a policeman's uniform grabbed Giles around the neck. Willow shouted, "No!"

Xander found a broken stone angel resting on its side and wound up for the pitch. He hurled it at the zombie formerly known as cop, connecting with its head. The zombie collapsed to the ground, and Giles climbed up the slippery side of the vault, until Willow and Xander grabbed his hands.

"Heave, heave!" Xander shouted.

"Xander, how can you keep joking at a time like this?" Willow demanded.

"Because if I don't, I'll be visiting Screamland," he confessed, and they hoisted Giles the rest of the way.

"I shall never understand the humor of the American adolescent. Or the American adult, for that matter," Giles said, scrabbling to grab his sack. He pulled out the journal of Timothy Cassidy and began paging, squeezing under the small overhang of the vault to shelter the book from the rain.

"Um, Giles, shouldn't you look through *Magickal Realms* for an antizombie reversomatic spell?" Willow queried, looking nervously at Xander. Xander nodded at her.

"Will's right," he said. "Isn't she?"

"Here's my thinking," Giles said as he searched through the book. "Samhain is considered the spirit of Halloween, the king of the dead souls who haunt the land of the living. What are zombies but dead souls? His minions? His slaves?"

"One man's perspective," Xander said slowly. "And the correct thing to do with that input is?"

"Mr. Cassidy has written down a spell to deny the power of Samhain over the dead." He kept paging. "Ah, yes, here it is. He calls it the 'Hymn of Orpheus.'" Giles paused and cocked his head. "I rather like that. Orpheus, of course, being the man who—"

"Please, Giles, just do it!" Xander said.

"Yes, yes, of course." Giles cleared his throat and read: "'King of the Dead, your sway over these forsaken ones is now ended. Begone, animating spirit which moveth limbs most justly frozen!'"

He made a strange sign in the air.

Xander whispered, "Behold the mark of Zorro!"

Willow smacked his arm.

"'Begone, animating demon which setteth upon these souls hungers most unnatural.'"

The zombies began to gasp.

"'Release them from their torment and return their souls to God!'"

They stopped moving.

They stared at one another with eyes that blinked once, twice . . .

Xander distinctly heard one of them murmur, "Glenn, my brother."

And then they fell to the ground and crumbled into dust.

Xander blinked and leaned over the edge of the vault. Willow joined him. Xander put his arm around Giles. "Strong work, Englishman," he murmured.

Giles didn't answer.

Xander and Willow turned to see that he had gotten a stick out of his canvas sack. Giles said, "I believe there are matches in the Slayer's bag, are there not?"

"There areth," Xander said. He picked up Buffy's bag and rummaged through it. "Behold, that which lighteth."

"Giles, what are you doing?" Willow asked.

"Right," Giles said as Xander found the matches and tossed them to him. "Here."

He handed each of them a bulb of garlic and a few plant leaves. "These are garlic and angelica. Garlic I know you're familiar with. Angelica's quite another matter. It's also called henbane, insane root, fetid nightshade, even poison tobacco, which I find to be a redundant term if there ever was one."

"Yeah, okay, and it's repetitive, too," Xander said, trying to hurry Giles up.

"Highly poisonous," Giles went on. "Extremely. It's said the Egyptians used it to assassinate unpopular pharaohs."

Xander looked uncertainly down at his hand. "And we are doing what with it?"

Giles gestured to the four sticks. "Smear it and the garlic over the tip of the yew ward."

"Smear? Ward? Um, this looks like a stick," Xander said.

"A ward is something that protects you from evil," Willow said quietly as she took the supplies from Giles.

Xander caught Willow's wrist. "I thought that was a warden. And I thought you just told us this stuff will kill us in fifteen minutes."

"No, we're fine," Giles said distractedly. "Xander, please, just do as I ask this one time."

Miffed, Xander took the garlic and angelica as well and, imitating Giles, began to rub them all over the sticks. "And we are doing this why?"

"According to Cassidy," Giles said, tapping the journal, "we need to coat these with candle wax and light them to illuminate our dark way, and then we need the juice of an apple to remind us of the sins of mankind, to preserve our relationship with good," he went on as if he were reciting a grocery list. "These will protect us from Samhain. I hope," he added under his breath. "It worked for Timothy Cassidy."

"The juice from an apple?" Willow said slowly.

"Right." Giles smelled his hand. "Has a pungent odor, wouldn't you say?"

"I would say," Xander said breathily. "Okay, Teach, let's review the material. Now that the zombies are history, and we busy bees are smearing stinky poison stuff on tree branches, and Buffy is on a field trip with the big demon on campus, we are not getting in the car and driving the long, possibly safer, way to the other side of the field, are we?"

Giles looked surprised. "But, Xander, that's an excellent suggestion. Why would we not?"

Willow smiled sadly at Xander. "Because we know, since we both grew up here, that there's an apple orchard not far from where we stand." She gestured with her head toward the field. "Right over there."

"Oh, good," Giles said excitedly. "Then we must go. We can complete our wards with the apples from the trees."

"Except there's a barrier there, isn't there?" Willow asked.

"We'll see, won't we?" Giles replied. "First, let's drip the candle wax onto the wards." He gestured toward Buffy's Slayer's bag, which Willow had by her side. "I believe there are candles among Buffy's equipment."

There were. A match flared in the darkness and cast yellow shadows on Giles's face. Xander watched as Giles pulled out a candle and began to mumble things in his Ghostbuster language of choice, which was Latin.

The stink of sulfur cut the scent of the plants as Giles

began to drip the wax onto the sticks. He finished coating the first one and handed it to Willow. He coated another one and gave it to Xander, then made the other two.

"Waxing our wards," Xander said. "Oh, to be in Malibu, waxing our boards."

As soon as all four were coated, Giles hopped off the vault and hurried to the wall. Without a moment's hesitation, he crossed from the wall into the field.

"We are permitted," he said.

Xander looked at Willow. "Much joy," he whispered. "Samhain is letting us in."

"It *is* much joy. We have to save Buffy," Willow said urgently.

"That'll be a first." Xander smiled at her. "Us saving her. Don't worry, Will. You know I'm in on any crazy prank that has to do with Halloween and a violent demise of my person."

She squeezed his hand. "My hero," she said, and he almost believed that she meant it.

He got down off the vault. Willow scrambled down after him.

"After you, m'dear," he said, bowing low, and she carried the Slayer's satchel toward the wall, climbed onto it, and hopped into the field.

"We're here," she said nervously.

"Let me light your wards," Giles said. "They'll offer partial protection until we make it to the orchard."

Then he set theirs on fire. Magick kept them lit despite the pouring rain.

"We must hurry. Samhain will detect our presence. And as we aren't fully protected . . ." Giles trailed off, looking uncomfortable, then shrugged.

"What?" Xander asked anxiously.

"Nothing," Giles said.

"There's a rift in the Force," Willow said, staring at Giles. "You think Buffy's—you aren't sure this is going to work."

Giles looked at both of them very seriously. "That's correct. I'm not sure. I can't ask you to risk your lives without telling you that. We may fail."

Willow and Xander were silent for a moment. Then Willow raised her chin and said, "Lead on, Macduff."

"And McDonald's, too," Xander said, nodding. "Let's hit those happy trails."

The rain did not let up as they hurried into the orchard. "Smear all the wards with the juice of apples," Giles said. "I have sigils to draw."

"Squiggles?" Willow repeated.

"Sacred symbols," Giles said. "They'll—"

He stopped speaking as something crashed, shrieking, into the orchard. The three froze and stared at one another.

Willow said hopefully, "Buffy?"

CHAPTER TEN

The rain came down even harder. The field was already saturated from the earlier storm, and the ground was muddy. Buffy knew she should be careful. She might turn an ankle, even break something, if she didn't slow down.

She didn't slow down.

A broken ankle held no fear for her, not after looking into the flaming eyes of the pumpkin king, the spirit of Halloween. It was as if Samhain was fear itself. Being near him gave her the most monster wiggins in history. All she wanted to do was escape.

Her ragged, bloodstained blouse and black shorts were soaked. Her now-ragged boots punched the muddy ground, splashing when there was a puddle to splash in. Maybe someone else would have fallen, but Buffy was the Slayer. The Slayer was agile. Buffy was—

On her butt in mud. Covered with it. Wanting desperately to make a joke, a snide comment, a wry observation.

No. Nada. Nyet.

There was nothing funny. She didn't even have time to be humiliated by her fall. She got to her knees and glanced back down the hill toward the barn.

"Oh, God, keep him away," she whispered, terrified, though her fear had diminished slightly as she moved up the hill.

In the darkness in front of the barn, she couldn't make out his body at all, couldn't see his shape. But she could see the face. The green flame spurting from the eyes and mouth of his rotting pumpkin head. She had to fight the urge to throw up.

Buffy stood quickly and started up the hill again. She didn't go any slower, but she stared at the ground in front of her, trying to watch her step.

Then she was in the orchard, darting through the trees, arms up to keep branches from whipping her in the face. She squinted, trying to see through the darkness ahead, and realized she'd have to go through the pumpkin patch again. Still, pumpkins she was sure she could handle. Leap over them or outrun them. They couldn't do her any real damage.

But there was that magickal barrier still to be dealt with.

She couldn't keep evading Samhain until dawn. And who was to say he'd even be gone at dawn? It wasn't as if he were a vampire.

Buffy crashed through the orchard, not caring about the noise she was making. She didn't even turn around to see if Samhain was chasing her now. Even if she could see the demon through the trees, she didn't want to. Ever again.

"Sssslayer," his voice whispered nearby, playfully.

She started, eyes darting side to side in search of him. But it was a trick. He was still behind her. But in pursuit, she was sure. He would never let her out of the field alive.

Branches snapped and apples thumped to the ground as she ran on. Her lungs sucked air in greedily, and her breath came in ragged gasps. Then she heard another soft voice.

"Buffy?"

Stunned, she stared up the hill through the trees. The night was pitch-black, and the rain whipped through the trees, a staccato patter on the leaves. But even through night and rain and orchard, she could see three burning points of light ahead. White-orange flame, not green.

Not Samhain.

"Willow?" she cried. "Xander? Giles?"

"Buffy?" A different voice this time. Giles.

Then she burst from the orchard on the hill and saw them, just a few yards off to the right. They looked almost comical to her, soaked with rain, hair plastered to their heads and faces, holding the thinnest, wimpiest looking torches she'd ever seen. She might have smiled. But she couldn't, for their presence only added to her nausea.

"No, no, no!" she shouted. "I told you guys not to come in here! Majorly bad move, people. Now move it! He's right behind me!"

As if on cue, they heard a crashing through the orchard. Still far down the hill, but they only had a minute or two before Samhain caught up to them.

"He?" Giles asked, obviously unnerved. "Then I was right? It's—"

"Samhain, yeah, and he's very strong, very scary, very unhappy with the Slayer and anybody who happens to be her bud," Buffy said. "So move it."

"We're not going anywhere," Xander said. "Even if we weren't all trapped in here, which we are, which is bad, we're not running out on you."

"Right," Willow agreed.

"Hear, hear," Giles concurred.

The crashing through the orchard grew louder.

"How are those torches burning in the rain?" she asked.

"Magick," Giles replied. "We've got a great deal of magick to do, I'm afraid. You see, in all this chaos, I have come up with a plan."

"Plan? Good. Go. Quick. Talk. Speak," Buffy babbled, taking a terrified glance over her shoulder.

"These yew sticks are specially treated. They're wards, which will protect us from the dead and from the spirit of

Halloween, but unless we want to beat him to death with them, they won't really harm him," Giles said.

"Good. Then we can just sit around until morning," Buffy said happily.

"They'll burn out before then," Giles said apologetically. "We've got to destroy his physical form to stop him. At the very least. The Watcher Cassidy wrote that Erin Randall used fire for that purpose. Which means we've got to trap Samhain and burn the scarecrow inside which he has taken up residence. There are symbols we can use to trap him, but we don't have time for a circle of them, and there's still the matter of the burning."

"Sssslayer! I'm coming for you and for your friends. I haven't eaten a Watcher's heart in four hundred years," Samhain whispered on the wind, his voice echoing in the hiss of the rainstorm.

"Oh my," Giles murmured worriedly, and pushed his glasses up.

Buffy grabbed her Slayer's bag from Xander, glanced once at the canvas sack that Giles had brought, then rummaged through her bag until she came up with what she'd been searching for.

"A weapon?" Willow asked hopefully.

"Absolutely. Lilac Breeze," Buffy replied, holding up a tube of lipstick.

"You keep your lipstick in your Slayer's bag?" Giles asked, appalled.

"Well," Xander said, jumping to her defense, "a fashionable Slayer has to be prepared for anything. Right, Buffy?"

"So right. Giles, show me these symbols," Buffy said.

Giles held up a thin book. On the cover were the words *The Journal of Timothy Cassidy, Watcher*. He opened it and showed her a page of crudely etched designs. Sigils, Giles said they were.

Buffy hefted her bag, slung it over her shoulder, and looked up. The crashing in the orchard had stopped.

"There's a barn down there," she said softly. "Maybe it's too wet to burn, I don't know. But I'll bet it's full of nice, dry, fire-lovin' hay."

Giles's eyes lit up. In that moment, they connected as Watcher and Slayer. Mutual respect, parallel thoughts. She could tell he knew exactly what she was going to suggest.

Which was good, because that was the moment Samhain chose to make his grand entrance.

The spirit of Halloween erupted from the orchard, razor-straw fingers reaching for Buffy's throat, pumpkin fangs gnashing for her blood. She leaped out of the way as Willow shrieked in horror, and Buffy knew that they were all experiencing the same terror that was lancing through her. It was as if she were being electrocuted with fear.

"Buffy!" Xander called, and she glanced up in time to see him throw her crossbow toward her.

Even as she caught it, Buffy knew it wouldn't do much more than buy her time, but time was exactly what she needed.

"Ah, Ssslayer," Samhain said as Giles, Willow, and Xander held up the weird ward sticks with the white burning wax on their tips. *"Your friends have come prepared. Well done, Watcher. I see not everyone has forgotten me."*

"For Timothy Cassidy and Erin Randall, we'll all see you destroyed, pumpkin king!" Giles roared bravely.

Buffy was proud of him.

Samhain was not psyched.

"How dare you call me that! I am no mere gourd, I am the demon lord of all fear, of Samhuinn, of Halloween itself!" Samhain barked angrily. *"Your little sticks will not burn for long. Then I'll taste all your hearts."*

The rotted face turned to stare at Buffy with flaming green eyes.

"But you, Slayer, have no protection," those snapping pumpkin jaws whispered.

"Hello," Buffy said, pushing away her fear for the sake of her friends. "Blind much?" she asked. She lifted the crossbow and fired a bolt right through the rotten pumpkin forehead. It passed all the way through Samhain's head and left a gouting hole of fire behind.

The dark lord of Halloween grunted and took two steps backward before lifting his hurting, burning head. Buffy paid no attention. The moment she'd fired on him, Buffy tossed the crossbow on the ground near Xander—obviously it wasn't going to stop him—and crashed back through the orchard.

"Tag, you're it!" she called mockingly to Samhain.

"I'll be back for you when the fire burns low, Watcher. You and your friends," Buffy heard Samhain threaten.

Then he thundered after her.

Buffy only hoped that she could beat him to the barn a second time. She realized that even one hundred years earlier, when the horrors of real life had not yet begun to overshadow the horrors of legend and superstition, she would have probably been dead already. But this Samhain was far weaker even than he'd been the last time he'd faced a Slayer.

"Just keep telling yourself that," she grunted as her boots splattered mud to either side.

It seemed only seconds before she burst from the orchard farther down the hill and began to sprint through the rain. She prayed, really prayed, that she would not slip again. This time, a fall would mean her death, and the deaths of the others as well.

"Sssslayer!" Samhain hissed behind her. *"The chase is becoming tiresome."*

The barn loomed ahead, huge sliding doors wide open. Buffy didn't even slow this time, just barreled straight inside and headed for the ladder that went up to the hayloft above. She scrambled up to the loft as fast as she could, then turned and pulled the ladder up after her. If not for the prodigious strength that her calling as Slayer gave her, she would never have been able to do it.

She ducked into the hay just as Samhain came in after her.

"I ssssee you, girl," he hissed. *"This time, I see you, hiding there in the hay. My eyes are everywhere on this night."*

Buffy spun and saw it. On the sill of the huge window from which hay was lowered on pulley and cable, the window that looked down on the orchard and the field, sat a carved jack-o'-lantern.

It didn't move. Not this one. But it stared at her.

Then it said, *"I seeeee you!"* in Samhain's voice.

Buffy felt the fear creeping up on her again, spreading through her entire body. She was freezing up with terror, and she couldn't afford that. There was a sudden shudder beneath her, and she heard scratching and sliding and knew that Samhain was climbing the post at the center of the loft, climbing to reach her. To eat her heart. To slay a Slayer.

"No!" Buffy screamed.

She jumped up, ran to the window, and kicked the pumpkin, caving in its face as it tumbled out of the barn. She glanced at the big entry doors and saw that Giles had arrived there. Willow and Xander stood behind him, holding the flaming wards. Buffy thought she could smell apples and garlic, a weird combination, especially considering her fear and the strong smell of the hay. But it wasn't the worst thing that had ever happened to her.

That was climbing up to the loft.

Giles was using one of her vampire stakes to draw in the dirt entry of the barn, sealing the massive doors with powerful magickal symbols. Buffy remembered the designs from the journal very well, had memorized them for one specific reason.

She reached into her pocket and pulled out her Lilac

Breeze lipstick. Her favorite, at least this week, but it would go to a good cause. Namely, saving all their lives. She pulled off the top of the tube and started to draw on the windowsill, re-creating the symbols as best she could remember.

"Now, Slayer," the king of Halloween whispered behind her. *"You've nowhere left to run. Turn and face me."*

Buffy turned, dropping the lipstick. Last stop, everybody off.

"I'm assuming you know your face is on fire," she said, her throat dry, voice cracking with fear. "But were you aware that so is the barn?"

The horrid, sickening, burning smile dripped blood as it grew wider. She was certain that he would merely laugh at her, then step forward and tear her head from her neck with those razor straw hands. But the flames were rising up the walls of the barn now—Willow and Xander had done their job—and the roar of the fire was clearly audible.

Samhain turned to see the barn ablaze.

"Watcher!" Samhain screamed. *"You're next!"*

Buffy shuddered almost uncontrollably at his booming voice, the fear infecting her. It came off him in waves. Her hands shook, her teeth chattered, and she winced and shrank away from him, even though he hadn't come any nearer.

"That's it," Buffy whispered. "I'm outta here."

She turned and stepped onto the windowsill, careful not to smear the lipstick symbol, and with Samhain roaring furiously behind her, Buffy leaped out into the air, forty feet above the ground.

Anyone else would have been killed, or at least have had numerous shattered bones. Sometimes being the Slayer had its advantages.

"Uhnnffff!" she grunted as she hit the mud and rolled.

Willow was there next to her a moment later, and Giles stood above her, offering a hand to help her up. Xander was a few yards away, still working his way around the barn with his yew ward, or torch, or whatever. She didn't know how Giles had come up with the things, but she was glad he had. Otherwise they'd be dead now.

"Sssslayer!" Samhain screamed from the window above. His rage was obvious. He was trapped, about to be burned to nothing along with the old barn.

"It isn't over! I'll be back next year, and I won't give you any warning next time. No games. Just your death! Year after year until I've tasted your lifeblood, eaten your heart and soul!"

Buffy shivered, turned to Giles, and hugged him. Willow put her hands over her ears.

"She's not listening to you, Great Pumpkin!" Xander shouted. "You are so toast!"

"Over," Willow agreed, and looked at Buffy.

Buffy frowned.

"I don't like that look," Willow said. "I know that look."

"Giles?" Buffy said. "What's he talking about? I thought if we torched him, he'd, y'know . . . scarecrow, fire? As in, finito completo?"

Giles sighed, reached two fingers under his glasses to rub the smoke from his eyes.

"I'm afraid not, Buffy. He's telling the truth. Unless we can trap the spirit, the actual demon Samhain, into that scarecrow body, destroying it will only stop him for this year. He'll be free to come at you again someday," Giles explained apologetically. "But we'll be better prepared next time. We hadn't any idea what we were facing, but now that we do, we will be ready. And one must remember that he gets weaker as the years pass and faith in his power withers."

Buffy stared at Giles. Then she glanced up at the window of the burning barn, where the green flames of the laughing pumpkin mouth were still blazing, mocking her. Threatening gleefully.

"We are not pressing pause," she said, determined. "We are pushing the stop button."

The Slayer held out her hand. "Xander, give me your Swiss Army knife."

Xander pulled the requested multipurpose and much-valued, had-it-since-third-grade knife from his pocket and reluctantly handed it over.

"Giles, give me the ward thingy," Buffy demanded, and held out her other hand.

"What are you going to do?" Giles asked.

"If this magick is a ward, a kind of barrier for him, do you think it'll trap him in that scarecrow body, kind of pin him in there?" she asked.

"Well, there is a certain logic to that, but there's no way to know. You're just guessing!" Giles snapped. Clearly he was grasping her plan. And not liking it, because blazing infernos and really pissed-off demons were not healthy for Slayers and other living things.

"Uh, Buffy, going back in there would be an extreme lock-me-up-for-my-own-good, okay? Just wanted to get that straight," Xander babbled.

"Buffy," Willow said quietly. "Please don't."

They didn't want her to do it. Buffy didn't want to do it either. The fear was still there. Samhain wasn't gone yet, the scarecrow body not destroyed. Her stomach churned and she chewed her lip, fighting off the terror.

The yew stick was thin enough, but too long. She sawed the back end of it off, then used the knife to whittle a point on the wax-coated burning end. Her fingers got a little singed, but the magickal flame did not go out.

"How much time do I have before this thing is useless?" she asked. "How will I know?'

Giles shrugged. "When the fire goes out, you'll know," he said. "I'm sorry I can't do better than that."

Buffy finished whittling, stared hard at Giles. "You've done great, Giles. Saved my life. A lot of lives, probably. I wanted to run away tonight. I did run away. I let you down—"

"Never—," Giles began, but Buffy went on.

"I'm not going to run again. Not ever," she vowed. "I'm the Slayer. No matter what. You've never told me how long you expect me to live, but you have told me I have a duty. I'm going to honor that, Giles."

Buffy picked up the crossbow, which Xander had carried down from the orchard, and slotted the sharpened yew stick into the weapon. It was larger than the bolts the crossbow usually took, and not totally straight, but it would do.

It had to.

She turned and marched into the burning barn. When the others called after her, she pretended not to hear.

Samhain stood, burning, at the edge of the hayloft and looked down at her with fury. The entire loft was in flames and would probably come crashing down any second. It didn't matter. The demon had to be destroyed forever. She wasn't even certain that her plan would work. But she had to try.

"I knew you'd come back," Samhain roared, his voice penetrating the deafening crackle of the inferno around them. *"No true Slayer could walk away from this final confrontation. That's why Erin Randall died centuries ago, and why you will die now!"*

Screeching, trailing fire, parts of his scarecrow body dropping to the floor of the barn, Samhain launched himself from the hayloft. Straw claws lashed at Buffy.

Buffy tried to get the crossbow up in time, but she was too slow. The smoke was heavy, her eyes were tearing, and Samhain dropped in front of her, slashing her face and arms with razor-sharp straw fingers. She dropped the crossbow.

Blood ran from the cuts on her forehead. She didn't know how deep they were, but she didn't want to know just now. There was blood on her arms as well. The Slayer ignored them.

She retreated a way across the barn, and Samhain gave chase. He was burning, falling apart, and he had little time in which he could still use his body to destroy her. The problem was, Buffy had exactly the same amount of time in which to destroy him before he was freed by his own destruction, freed to return in another year.

"Ssssad in a way, to see you die. But that's the wonderful thing about Slayers," Samhain hissed. *"There's always a Chosen One."*

"That's right," Buffy sneered. "Crunch all you want, we'll make more."

He lunged at her. Buffy sidestepped the raking claws; she kicked at the arm and it separated from Samhain's body at the elbow. Flaming straw and clothing landed at her feet.

The pumpkin king hissed and went for her again, green flame within the pumpkin head, green fire burning inside the orange. Buffy dropped to her hands and kicked at his scarecrow knee. With the crackling pop of a blazing log, the knee buckled, burning embers flying.

Buffy had hoped Samhain would fall. He did not. The pumpkin that was his face blackened and bubbled. One half of his head was caved in, green flame diminishing.

"You're fast, little girl," the demon sneered. *"Destroy this*

body, die here in the barn with me, burned alive. I'll still come back."

Buffy stared at him, the fear threatening to overwhelm her again. She pushed it away, determined. The loft crashed down and she turned her eyes away, held up a hand to block the burning wood and hay that flew into the air.

Samhain came for her then, dragging his ruined leg, but still fast. Buffy was faster. She leaped over him as he dove for her, flipped in the air, and landed in a crouch right next to her crossbow, which was hidden from his view by a piece of charred wood.

The pumpkin king, the demon lord of Samhuinn, roared with pleasure and the pain of his burning host form. But he was triumphant. He would return. And to kill Buffy, all he had to do was keep her inside the barn. She could hear the burning beams above begin to crack and buckle.

"Die with me, Slayer," he whispered.

"Ever the romantic," Buffy snarled, and aimed the crossbow at the scarecrow's chest.

The remaining pumpkin eye widened as Samhain saw the magickal flame that still burned at the end of her crossbow bolt, saw the white candle wax, and knew what it was she had planned.

"Trick or treat," Buffy said grimly.

She pulled the trigger; the bolt flew impossibly straight and true and embedded itself in Samhain's chest.

"Nooooooo!" the demon screamed, and grabbed for

the end of the shaft with his remaining claw, but could not remove it.

She heard the screeching of the ceiling giving way and ran for the open doors. Just as the whole inferno collapsed in on itself, she dove over the symbol Giles had etched in the dirt, rolling to safety, choking on the smoke she'd inhaled, soot on her face.

Buffy lay on the ground, staring at the fire, listening to the king of Halloween scream in fury and pain. Giles, Xander, and Willow helped her to her feet, and she leaned on them as they moved a safer distance from the burning barn.

"Whoa, pyromania," Xander said in an awed voice.

"I'm not sure how we shall explain this to the owner of this place," Giles said.

"Wait, uh-uh," Buffy replied, and grabbed Giles and Willow by the hand, dragging them away. Xander followed.

"Buffy, what are you doing?" Giles asked. "We cannot simply leave."

"Sure we can!" Buffy said, then went into another fit of coughs.

"Can," Xander agreed.

"Have to," Willow added.

"I've been branded an arsonist once already, Giles," Buffy snapped. "That's why my mom and I moved here to the Hellmouth, remember? I'd rather avoid another police investigation."

"Absolutely," Willow agreed. "I mean, you live in the mouth

of hell. If you got caught again, I'd hate to think where you'd end up next time."

"Indeed," Giles remarked thoughtfully, then turned to Buffy.

"Well, Miss Summers," he said, "I suppose you've learned a lesson this evening, yes? Perhaps you'll think twice in the future before complaining about a lull in the Slaying business."

They all stared at him.

Buffy was the first to laugh.

It felt good.

Bad Bargain

With gratitude and affection for
Mary Piccin,
sister, friend, and critter charmer

CHAPTER ONE

"Are the boxes still in the car?" Buffy looked past her mother toward the driveway.

"Was I supposed to get takeout?" Joyce Summers walked into the house and kicked off her shoes. "Sorry, Buffy, but I spent all day unpacking canvases for the Joel Shavin show next week, and—"

"Not worried about dinner, Mom." Buffy closed the front door and turned with an accusing stare. "Worried about donations—"

Joyce set her shoes on the stairs, then straightened suddenly. "For the school rummage sale."

"Right!" Buffy forced a bright smile. The students at Sunnydale High were raising money to send the marching band to the California state competition. If the band did well, Principal Snyder had promised to hold another fund-raiser next year to pay for new uniforms. Her mother's well-to-do gallery customers had agreed to contribute collectibles and other items of value. "Did your clients forget?"

"No, everyone brought everything in, just as they promised." Joyce smiled weakly. "*I* forgot to bring it all home."

"But we're setting up *tonight*." Buffy tried not to look anxious.

Buffy's mom was paying closer attention to Buffy's comings and goings lately, and the scrutiny was wrecking her Slayer and social lives. If her mother caught her going out or Angel coming in her bedroom window, she'd be grounded until she graduated. Giving up her gorgeous, good-guy vampire boyfriend was not part of the new and improved, more responsible Buffy package. Tonight, however, she had a good excuse for leaving the house, and she didn't want to waste it.

"I'm sure Ms. Calendar won't mind if I bring the boxes in tomorrow morning," Joyce countered.

"Probably not, but I still have to go help tonight. It's extra credit," Buffy quickly added.

"Extra credit for what?" Joyce asked as she headed toward the kitchen.

"For doing our civic duty." Flashing another smile, Buffy waited. She really had volunteered to unpack, price, and arrange sale items in the cafeteria. “It’ll look great on my transcript when I apply for college.”

Joyce stopped suddenly and looked back. “When did you start worrying about getting into college? Not that I’m complaining.”

“It can’t hurt to think ahead, right? Covering all my bases just in case—before it’s too late to rack up those extracurricular points.”

Joyce stared at her, obviously skeptical and not buying the academic ambitions ruse. She sighed as she continued down the hall. “If only . . .”

“Okay, all my friends will be there.” Realizing she had overplayed her hand, Buffy tried a modified version of the truth. Willow and Xander *were* all her friends. Giles and Angel had their own individual categories: Watcher and vampire boyfriend.

“What about dinner?” Joyce filled the teakettle with water and set it on the stove.

“Had a sandwich, not hungry.”

Joyce relented with a hopeful smile. “All right, go. But try not to be too late.”

Buffy promised as she bolted out the back door.

Always vigilant, Buffy was tuned to every movement and sound on the street. Sunnydale swarmed with evils that preyed on the innocent and wouldn’t run from a fight with the Vampire Slayer. Staying alert and primed to react wasn’t a strain. It had become second nature.

The typical teenage aspects of her life were much more complicated, mostly because her mother didn't know she had been empowered by mysterious forces to kill vampires and other monster meanies. Mostly she saved the world—or at the very least a hapless victim—almost every week, sometimes more often. She had died once, but only for a couple of minutes, and Xander had brought her back. All things considered, sneaking out, neglecting her schoolwork, and spacing on her chores only *seemed* irresponsible.

Buffy broke into an effortless jog, eager to get to the school. She wasn't particularly rah-rah for the marching band, but the rummage sale reminded her of similar events at Hemery High, when she was just a popular cheerleader without a destiny or a rap sheet. She wanted to spend one lousy weekend pretending to be normal.

Xander scanned the rows of tables lined up end-to-end in the cafeteria. Taped to each table was a neatly printed sign designating a sale category: clothes, household, hardware and tools, auto, furniture, knickknacks, books, and miscellaneous junk. Cheerleaders, football players, and the marching band were pricing and arranging merchandise the students had collected over the past two weeks. Extra credit hounds and goof-offs looking to skip Friday classes had also volunteered.

Jenny Calendar—computer teacher, practicing pagan, and faculty adviser—supervised the setup from the checkout table by the door. Collectibles, quality jewelry, antiques, and other expensive donations were on the next tables over. Cordelia Chase was in charge of the pricey display. Harmony Kendall, the ditzy blonde of the Sunnydale in-crowd, hovered nearby, basking in Cordelia's aristocratic aura.

Xander was also checking out Cordelia and her luscious lips. His sly smile froze as he cast a guilty glance at Willow. She would never forgive his clandestine make-out affair with Cordelia, who had taunted them with caustic put-downs since kindergarten. Not noticing his wandering eye, Willow continued to expound on the inevitability of global decline, the topic of her civics essay, while she scribbled *$3.00* on a strip of stickers. Xander looked at her blankly.

"What?" Willow blinked. "Dead dinosaurs aren't a renewable energy source, Xander. One of these days the whole world will be running on empty."

"But not today." Xander handed her a folded muscle shirt and scanned the room again. There was no sign of Buffy. With anyone else, parental interference was the logical explanation for a no-show. But Buffy had probably been attacked and detained by a demon. Sunnydale vampires and other dreaded beasties had no respect for her non-Slayer obligations.

Or her mysterious surge of school spirit, Xander thought. He didn't know why Buffy wanted Willow and him to participate in the rummage sale, but he was pretty sure it wasn't to sell junk and hand-me-downs to bargain hunters. Whatever the reason, he'd find out when she arrived.

Devon MacLeish and Daniel "Oz" Osbourne, members

of the local band Dingoes Ate My Baby, were sorting CDs and old vinyl albums. They had plugged in a 1970s stereo turntable someone had donated, and a scratchy recording of *The Wall* by Pink Floyd was playing.

Jonathan Levenson and Andrew Wells had staked out toys and comics. Xander had never had a complete conversation with either of the shy, practically invisible boys, even though he had gone through grade school and junior high with them. Their odd looks and personality quirks would have fueled relentless ridicule if anyone popular knew they existed. Noting their furtive looks, Xander assumed they were stashing action figures and other media items for themselves. They were hard-core science-fiction collectors, but Ms. Calendar was enforcing Principal Snyder's latest law: No one could buy anything until the sale opened at noon tomorrow.

Xander wasn't remotely tempted to break that rule. All the men's shirts were priced at an affordable three bucks, but he hadn't come across anything in khaki or camouflage. The persistent preference for all things military was an aftereffect of being transformed into a soldier on Halloween. He pulled a wrinkled, cotton button-down from the cardboard box, folded it, and held it out.

"Too bad we can't just use magick." Willow slapped a price sticker on the shirt and dropped it on the appropriate stack. "But there's probably all kinds of hidden moral implications."

"For what?" Xander's attention snapped back to Willow.

"Using magick to ensure world peace or cure all the sick people. Would that be so wrong?" Willow's eyes sparkled with enthusiasm. "Think of it! No more commercials begging for money to feed starving millions! No more depressing educational TV programs."

"Programs that we don't have to watch if we don't want to," Xander said, folding another shirt. "Besides, we could have all that without using magick. It's called science."

"Oh yeah, that." Willow peeled off another sticker.

"Put enough money and power behind anything, and it'll get done," Xander added. "That's how we got to the moon."

"Then it's too bad we don't just do it."

"Yeah," Xander agreed, "but the people with the power and money don't *have* any problems they can't solve."

The last item in the box was a silky, iridescent green. Xander held up the cloth and stretched it out. "Why would someone donate glow-in-the-dark boxer shorts?"

"Good choice, Xander." Cordelia paused in the aisle behind him. "Only a loser would wear those."

"I wasn't going to buy them," Xander shot back, flustered. Cordelia held him with a dark-eyed stare, daring him to spill their tawdry secret. She knew he wouldn't. The instant their relationship came out of the utility closet, it would be over.

"Why not? No one but you would ever see them." Smiling smugly, Cordelia lifted the shoe box in her hand. "Got any jewelry or interesting trinkets?"

"Sorry." Willow shrugged. "Just shirts and shorts."

Xander tried to look annoyed as Cordelia sauntered away. He didn't expect life to be fair, but sometimes he wished it wasn't so weird.

"How much are we charging for shorts?" Willow asked.

"Three dollars." Xander handed her the green boxers and picked up the empty box. "If you're tired of sorting clothes, I can look for something more interesting."

"No, clothes are good." Willow dangled a long strip of stickers. "I've got all these three-dollar price tags."

"They won't go to waste. Every dad in town donated classic shirts nobody else wants either." Xander took a couple of steps, then looked back. "Should we be worried about Buffy? Because she's late, I mean."

"If she was late to slay or late for a date, I'd worry," Willow said, "but she's just late for school."

Xander frowned. "Except she wanted this extracurricular gig and talked us into it."

"It's still school." Setting the marker and stickers aside, Willow began to sort the shirts by size.

Xander hurried outside the cafeteria and down the corridor. The access doors to the basement were usually locked, but since the rummage sale donations were stored there, the door by the cafeteria was propped open. At the bottom of the stairs, Xander started to heave the cardboard box into a corner with the other empties. Then he noticed a short, thin high school boy pawing through boxes that hadn't been unpacked yet.

Although most of the sale items had been moved upstairs,

several boxes were still stacked along the wall or piled on tables. The floor was littered with clothes and books the boy had dumped during his frantic search.

"Looking for something?" Xander asked tensely.

The teenager spun to face him, poised to bolt at the slightest provocation.

Xander relaxed the instant he recognized the culprit: Michael Czajak, another miserable misfit.

A quiet kid with slicked-back hair and tormented eyes, Michael rarely talked to anyone. At the beginning of the school year, he had started wearing black T-shirts—no logo—and jeans. It was hard to tell if he was trying to hide any trace of personality or displaying his true dark colors. The boy was so introverted and strange that he made Jonathan and Andrew look like hunks with an acceptable modicum of cool. "Spooky" was the first word that came to mind as Xander stared him down.

"The sale doesn't start until tomorrow, Michael."

"My mom, she—" Michael paused, clearing his throat. "She cleaned my room—"

"Don't tell me. She donated one of your prized possessions to the rummage sale," Xander guessed.

Michael nodded.

Xander felt sorry for him. Having personal space invaded by a neat freak, suspicious, or just plain curious mom was every teenager's nightmare. Something usually turned up missing, beginning with privacy and almost always including treasured or forbidden possessions. His parents didn't care what deep dark secrets he kept from them, but he played it safe and never wrote anything down.

"A journal? Videos?" Xander guessed.

"A medallion," Michael said.

After several silent seconds, Xander realized that Michael wouldn't elaborate without prodding. "Can you describe it? So I'll know it if I see it."

"It's a sunburst, gold with red and green stones on a gold chain."

Xander frowned. "You might have to check with Cordelia. She's the boss of the good stuff."

Michael looked stricken at the mention of Cordelia's name. That wasn't an uncommon reaction among those who preferred being ignored to being a victim of Cordelia's verbal barbs.

"But Cordelia doesn't wear anything fake," Xander added. "So if it's just cheap costume jewelry—"

"That's what my mom thought." Michael's tone betrayed the hurt and contempt teenagers often felt for adults who didn't understand them. "It's priceless, but the amulet only protects me—"

"From what?"

Michael hesitated, then sighed as though he had already said too much and had nothing more to lose. "Supernatural evils. Sunnydale is overrun with them."

"Does it work?" Xander blurted out. Everyone in the

Slayer-know could use a heavy-duty protection charm, but Giles had never suggested making one. Since the Watcher wouldn't want them harmed, he had assumed there was no magick powerful enough to protect them from the superthings Buffy had been chosen to fight.

"I haven't vanished or burst into flames," Michael answered. A defiant gleam shone in his dark eyes.

The other boy's defensive attitude reminded Xander that he had to mask his interest. The residents of Sunnydale rarely—if ever—spoke of the many disappearances, deaths, and other incidents of magickal mayhem that plagued the town. Only a privileged few knew that Buffy Summers was the Vampire Slayer, and they were sworn to keep her secret. Appearing to be as deaf and blind to the weirdness as everyone else was the surest way to do that.

"Neither have I," Xander retorted, flipping his hands palms up, then over again. "Still here, no burns."

Taking the flippant remark as a put-down, Michael turned his back and resumed rummaging.

Xander didn't like slinging insults at tongue-tied nerds, but it had the desired effect. Tossing the empty box, he picked up another box of clothes and turned toward the stairs. He heard Michael muttering, but the boy's back was to him and he couldn't make out the words.

Probably cursing me out for thinking he's a fool. The funny thing was, whether the amulet was effective or not, Xander knew that Michael was smart to take precautions.

"Looks like you're working hard, Xander." Ms. Calendar paused halfway down the stairs to look in his box. "More clothes."

"And even more clothes," Xander said, glancing back.

The computer teacher scanned the unpacked boxes. "I had no idea we had this much left to unpack."

"I just hope most of it sells so we don't have to pack it all back up again," Xander said.

"That would be nice." Ms. Calendar focused on Michael. "Let's go, Mr. Czajak!"

Michael's head snapped around. "I—I have to find something."

"Sorry, Michael," Ms. Calendar said, "but you know the rules. Nobody can buy anything until we open for business tomorrow."

"But my mom—"

Ms. Calendar silenced him with a raised hand. "Grab a box and take it upstairs."

Michael lifted a box.

Xander caught his eye, but he didn't correct Ms. Calendar's mistaken assumption that Michael was a volunteer. He didn't care if Michael pretended to work while he looked for his missing charm.

Principal Snyder hovered by the door, lying in wait for Ms. Calendar. A small, balding, disagreeable man, he blocked her way as she tried to exit. "How late are you and these kids going to be here?"

Xander and Michael waited on the stairs behind her.

"Another hour or so. We can come back early tomorrow morning to finish up." The teacher waved the boys into the corridor and rolled her eyes as Snyder locked the basement access door behind them.

Buffy gasped, shocked. For five dollars, the soft leather skirt was a bargain she couldn't pass up. Pulling the must-have item off the stack, she continued down the clothes aisle to the men's section, where Willow was arranging shirts.

"Where are you stashing stuff, Willow?" Buffy glanced around to make sure no one else was listening.

"Stuff to buy tomorrow that they won't let us buy today?" Willow asked pointedly.

"Well, yeah." Buffy was *not* going to feel guilty. Saving money was one way to prove to her mom that she had changed her irresponsible ways. However, the bottom line of being budget conscious was having a wardrobe that became progressively more dated with each passing day. "I can't be the only early shopper here tonight."

"Hardly!" Willow laughed. "Everybody's doing it, except me. But that's only because I haven't found anything worth getting in trouble for."

"But if you had something, where would you put it?" Buffy bent over to look under the table.

"Well, I wouldn't put it in a box under a table," Willow said with certainty. "That's the first place Ms. Calendar would look. Half the stuff people are hiding will be back on the tables by morning."

"Good point." Buffy clutched the skirt tighter.

"So if I found a men's shirt I wanted, I'd put it in women's slacks or sweaters or something." Willow tugged the skirt until Buffy let go. "And I'd hide a skirt in a stack of men's shirts."

"You're sure?" Buffy frowned.

"Would you look for chic leather in piles of plaid?" Willow held Buffy's gaze for a knowing moment, then slipped the folded skirt between cotton knits. "Don't worry, Buffy. Nobody cool enough to know that skirt is worth a lot more than five dollars is going to get anywhere near this old-guy stuff."

"I hope you're right." Buffy tried to look busy and innocent when Ms. Calendar walked into the cafeteria behind Xander and Michael Czajak. The teacher and Michael turned in opposite directions down different aisles. Xander kept coming toward them.

"Hey, Buffy. Are you having fun yet?" Xander dropped the box on the table.

"I didn't volunteer to have fun, Xander." Buffy peered at the tangle of clothes in the box and wrinkled her nose.

"All slay and no school project makes Buffy . . ." Xander looked at her expectantly.

"Really annoyed," Buffy said. Then she realized Xander wasn't trying to be difficult, and softened her tone. "I just want to spend a couple of days battling bargain hunters and not you-know-whats."

"For real?" Xander didn't look convinced. "We're not doing this to avert some diabolical threat?"

"Other than enduring Cordelia's disdain at the checkout table because we're buying cast-off clothes? In a word, no."

"I like the extra credit part," Willow said.

Buffy smiled. Extra credit couldn't boost the redheaded whiz kid's GPA past the 4.0 she already had.

"Okay, so the no-class thing is a plus, and I never miss a chance to score Slayer points, but . . ." Xander lowered his voice. "Look, I don't want to burst the wishful-thinking Buffy bubble, but the you-know-whats don't have a charity exemption."

Buffy leaned closer. Xander was right, and she appreciated his honesty, but there was a critical fact he had overlooked. "A tired Slayer is a dead Slayer."

"Point taken. Not literally," Xander replied.

"Looks like Michael's in trouble," Willow said.

"For what?" Buffy followed Willow's gaze across the room.

The box Michael Czajak had brought up from the basement sat untouched. He had been caught looking through "miscellaneous junk" that had already been sorted and priced.

"I warned you once, Michael," Ms. Calendar said sharply.

Michael cringed.

"Isn't she taking Principal Snyder's no-early-student-shopping rule a little too seriously?" Buffy asked.

"Yeah," Xander agreed, "especially since he's just trying to find something that belongs to him. His mom cleaned his room."

"Bummer," Willow said as the teacher pointed Michael toward the door. Embarrassed by the public reprimand, the boy fled.

"No fair." Buffy frowned. Since Michael seemed to value his status as a nonentity, she had never tried to get to know him. However, her Slayer soul was sensitive to any injustice. Invasion of privacy wasn't trivial, but parental concern always trumped a kid's territorial rights. Ever since her mother had moved her diary—a narrowly averted catastrophe Angel had observed from her bedroom closet—she had kept her room Mom-proof clean.

Willow turned to Xander. "What did he lose? If we find it, we can stash it for him."

"Gold medallion on a gold chain with red and green stones," Xander said. "It's an amulet."

"As in magickal?" Willow asked, her interest moving beyond sympathy for Michael's plight.

Xander shrugged. "Michael thinks so. He says it protects him from Sunnydale's evil element."

"Is he just guessing or has it been field tested?" Buffy asked.

"If Michael had a close encounter with a demon and he's still around to talk about it, then maybe the charm works," Willow muttered thoughtfully, more to herself than her friends.

"If charms could protect people from the big bads, my job would be a lot easier," Buffy said.

"And safer," Xander added. "Which raises the question:

If there's a protection charm that works, why is Giles holding out on us?"

"He's not." Willow's brow knit with consternation. "He wouldn't. . . . Would he?"

"Probably not, but someone should find out." Xander snapped a finger toward Buffy.

"I'll ask." Buffy tossed Xander a shirt from the box. "In the meantime, it's fold and stack, not stake and dust."

"I guess playing merchandise mart beats hanging out in the cemetery." Xander shook out the shirt and matched the shoulder seams.

Unless I'm meeting Angel, Buffy thought wistfully.

"The music helps." Willow moved to the beat of a Beatles song. "Someone should make sure Devon 'spins the plates' tomorrow."

Xander smiled. "'Platters.' It's 'spin the platters.'"

"Platters or casseroles, Willow's right." Buffy slapped a price sticker on a blue-plaid flannel. "Music makes people feel good, and they buy more stuff."

Xander looked at her askance. "Tell me again why we care if the marching band goes to Sacramento next month."

"Principal Snyder is going with them to chaperone," Buffy said. "Friday through Sunday, Sunnydale will be Snyder free."

"Well, since you put it that way . . ." Xander set the shirt down and paused. "What's this?"

"That? Nothing." Willow winced as Xander pulled Buffy's leather skirt out of the stack.

"Mine." Buffy snatched the garment from Xander's hand and hid it in the shirts again. "I'll never find another one like that for five dollars."

"Women!" Xander scoffed. "Can't resist a bargain."

"I can't," Willow agreed.

Buffy eyed Xander narrowly.

During the next hour, they unpacked a half-dozen boxes containing clothes, curtains, bedding, and other household goods. Buffy pretended not to notice when Xander hid a camouflage vest in a bright orange blanket. She waited until he took an empty box to the discard pile in the corridor, and then she moved the vest to another hiding place. Tomorrow, after he admitted that guys could be suckers for a good deal too, she'd give it back.

When Ms. Calendar announced that everyone had to be out in fifteen minutes, Buffy begged off early. "All this non-lethal activity has been fun, but I promised Mom I wouldn't be late. And you know Giles—he'll get all preachy if I shirk Slayer duty."

"Patrolling home instead of strolling home?" Xander asked.

"Something like." Buffy headed toward the doors before Xander and Willow could offer to tag along. Angel was almost always tracking her when she checked the local cemeteries for new vamps. More often than not he wanted to talk, and talking usually led to kissing—unless she had company.

To all outward appearances, Sunnydale was no different from any small American town on a Thursday night. Sparse traffic cruised well-lit streets and idled unmolested at red lights. A few oblivious joggers ran along park paths, while dog walkers stayed on the sidewalks. Cats yowled in backyards, and TVs blared through open windows. Nothing seemed amiss. No demonic threat registered on Buffy's Slayer radar, but something didn't feel right.

The feeling persisted when Buffy entered the cemetery, but she couldn't pinpoint the source. She couldn't detect the malodorous essence of a demon in the stench of decomposing corpses and moldy dirt. The chirp of insects and the rustle of leaves were the only sounds. Nothing moved except small animals, the nocturnal predators hunting them, and Angel.

Buffy sensed the vampire before he emerged from the shadows. His presence had a distinct signature, a unique combination of the goodness emanating from his tortured soul and the primal power that flowed through his imposing physique. She shivered, feeling warm and chilled as he strode across the manicured ground between tombstones.

Buffy tensed, her breath lodged in her throat, anticipating a kiss when Angel stopped and stared down at her. His words cut the romance out of the moment.

"Something's wrong." Angel turned away, frowning.

"What?" Buffy asked, mortified. *Bad breath? Bad hair?*

"I don't know, it's just . . ." A dark scowl creased Angel's brow. "I've had this creepy-crawly feeling all night."

"Oh, bad vibes!" Buffy sagged with relief and choked

back a laugh. The thought of Angel having the heebie-jeebies was amusing, except for the lethal implications. Anything that unsettled the vampire couldn't possibly be funny.

"Sort of." Angel paced, thinking out loud. "It's hard to describe."

"Like being buried in bugs or smothered in snakes?" Buffy shivered again, this time with revulsion.

"Not exactly." Angel paused, one hand on his hip, the other smoothing back dark hair.

"Oh." Buffy leaned against a large tree, disappointed that Angel wasn't being driven crazy with longing for her. Then again, maybe he was, but the new thing—whatever it turned out to be—was getting in the way. "So you don't have a clue what's going on?"

"No," Angel said, shaking his head. "The demonic street is silent—not a word about anything nasty about to go down."

The concept of demonic gossip made Buffy uneasy. The image of fanged vampires and other foul creatures trading predictions of doom over goblets of blood was deceptively comical—and more insidious because of it.

"But I trust my instincts"—Angel shot her a questioning look—"and yours. Haven't you noticed anything?"

"My early warning system's on alert," Buffy admitted, "but no four-alarm massacres have broken out. Does a socially outcast kid looking for a protection charm his mother donated to the school rummage sale count?"

"I'm sensing something much worse than anything a

superstitious kid could conjure," Angel said. "Still, a threat doesn't have to be big or obvious to be devastating."

"I'll keep that in mind." It was getting late, but Buffy couldn't bring herself to say good-bye. She waited for Angel to make the next move. She had accepted the he-vampire-she-Slayer problem, and they were on equal footing with the demon fighting and passionate kissing, but he was still older by more than a couple of centuries. That was a cultural hurdle she hadn't totally reconciled—yet.

"I'll walk you through the cemetery," Angel offered, holding out his hand. "Then you should probably get home."

"Yeah, I probably should." Buffy smiled and slipped her hand into his. There was nowhere she'd rather be than alone with Angel, even if only for a few minutes walking through a graveyard.

Spike exploded out of his chair when the bottle of vintage French blood hit the wall behind him. He and the ancient text he was trying to translate escaped being splattered, but his train of thought had been thoroughly disrupted.

"Oh, fits and giblets," Drusilla said, pouting. "I missed the mark quite entirely."

Biting his tongue, Spike watched the red rivulets run down the brick factory wall between pipes. He made sure his seething annoyance was under control before he spoke. "So you were trying to hit me."

"Did you hear that, Miss Edith?" Dru murmured into the

porcelain ear of her favorite doll. “I think Spike found his voice and a word or two to go with it.”

Noting the fragile vampire’s pique, Spike stared at the floor. No matter how carefully he chose his words, there was no guarantee he could diffuse her anger or make her see reason. Drusilla was as vicious a vampire as had ever preyed upon the earth. She was also insane. When her twisted mind latched on to an idea, it was practically impossible to dislodge. He wanted nothing more than to cure the wasting disease that had slowly sapped her strength the past few decades. He had devoted his time and energies almost exclusively to the task, but today that mattered not a whit.

“He must pay a penance for ignoring us.” Dru turned toward Spike, the doll dangling from her fist. The glint of madness burned in the darkness of her corrupt gaze. “Perhaps he should lick the remains of Count Le Clerq off the wall. Can’t have all that royal blood feeding the spiders, now can we?”

“It’s not a great loss, Dru. The last time we uncorked a bottle of the count, he tasted musty.”

Drusilla ran the tip of her tongue over teeth as white as her translucent skin. “But he was so handsome, all dressed in blue with a feather in his cap—like the painting, only warmer.”

“Perhaps you’d like something fresher.” Smiling, Spike stepped closer and drew her slim body into his arms.

“A dressmaker would be nice.”

“They’re called designers now, love.” Spike touched his

lips to the dark ringlets that framed her delicate face. "But none of them reside in this forsaken hamlet. I could fetch you a plump, young toddler."

"I'm not hungry." Dru pushed away. "I fancy an outing. Miss Edith needs a new frock, all frilly with lace. A hanging's not the same without white lace to catch the bloody spittle."

"And what's Miss Edith done to deserve hanging?" Spike asked, humoring her.

"Telling tales of beasties swarming and slithering about"—Dru's voice became hushed—"all grim with grit and grime."

"Is something coming?" Spike asked, alerted by her haunted tone. Dru's ramblings were not always nonsensical. Sometimes the riddles were clues to her prescient visions.

"They weren't invited." Cocking her head, Dru looked at him coyly. "I'll need a new dress for the party, with velvet wings for dancing on the ceiling."

Spike had no idea if her references to hangings, beasts, and parties were the disjointed parts of a premonition or simply inconsequential babbling. As a matter of survival, he couldn't risk overlooking any threat. However, the bits and pieces of the puzzle had to be coaxed from Dru's mind.

"You want to go shopping," Spike said. For once he could safely satisfy her demented whim. "I know just the place."

CHAPTER TWO

It's almost dawn." Spike nuzzled Dru's neck, hoping to lure her away from the tables of used wares. They had been in the school for hours, but she wanted to look through the rummage sale items one more time. "We have to go."

"But I need a hat pin, a pearl one—white like chipmunk eyes when the fox bites." Dru added bright green boxer shorts to the other materials and bric-a-brac in her wicker basket. "And more socks."

"You've got a dozen pair there," Spike pointed out impatiently. "All colors and sizes."

"Tiny tunics for voodoo dollies," Dru cooed with a delighted giggle. "But they won't do without pins to stick."

Throwing up his hands, Spike returned to the display cases on the table near the door. As he snapped off the lock and raised the glass cover, he heard a distant door open and close. In her weakened state, Drusilla could barely overpower a teenaged girl. She had only barely escaped Prague, where a brutal mob would have torn her apart and left the pieces to fry in the morning sun.

Scooping up a handful of jewelry, Spike hurried back across the room. "We have to leave, Dru—now."

"But I've not finished looking for baubles," Dru whined.

"Here." Spike dropped the tangle of gold, silver, and rhinestone trinkets into her basket and glanced toward the cafeteria doors. He would like nothing better than to cull a crowd of unsuspecting teenagers for breakfast, but his first responsibility was to Dru.

Dru stared at the glittering jewelry, then recoiled with an alarmed hiss. "Fireflies and bloodstones."

"Come on." Taking Dru's hand, Spike pulled her toward the basement door. The locked dead bolt broke and turned easily in his vampire grip.

They had entered the school through the main doors under the cover of darkness. At sunrise the only safe way out was through the network of electrical tunnels and sewers that ran underneath the town.

Dru balked at the top of the stairs. "Maids and knaves to slaughter in the belly of the beast."

Spike frowned. Her hesitation was rooted in fear, not

obstinacy. They were very close to the Hellmouth, and he assumed the convergence of mystical forces was affecting her addled but highly receptive mind. However, petulant and easily bored, Dru didn't have the patience for hiding in the school until sundown. They had to go underground to escape.

"We'll hurry through," Spike said, drawing her down the stairs. "It'll be all right."

"Lickety-split, then." Dru followed obediently until they entered the cellar corridor. When she saw more cartons of rummage sale donations piled on tables, she dashed ahead, her apprehension forgotten. "It's a bargain basement, all waiting with needles and pins. Knitting needles, pine needles—"

Spike cursed his luck. "We don't have time to dawdle, Dru. They'll be coming to get these boxes."

Dru held up a corkscrew and made a jabbing motion. "Poke it in the eye, blind the mice. But there's more than three, and they won't run—" She dropped the corkscrew when something else caught her eye.

Spike listened to the sounds of people in the halls above. There were more than three, and they were coming closer.

Drusilla picked up a sunburst pendant on a gold chain, turned it over in her hand, and traced the red and green stones with her finger. "It whispers with an aching heart—"

"Who unlocked this door?" a man barked.

Spike recognized Principal Snyder's nasally voice. During the short time he and Drusilla had been in Sunnydale, he had identified and studied everyone who was close to the

Slayer—friends and enemies. The perverse pleasure Snyder derived from giving Buffy Summers a hard time was his only redeeming characteristic and one reason Spike didn't end his miserable life. The thought of feeding on the contemptuous little man made him nauseous.

"It wasn't us," a girl snapped with indignation.

"We just got here," a boy said.

"It's broken!" Snyder snarled, as though the vandalism was a personal affront.

"Who'd want to steal any of this trash?" a second girl asked, incredulous.

As the students started down the stairs, Drusilla shuddered and threw the gaudy necklace into a box. "The longing wiggles and burns—"

It was too late to run without being seen or heard. Cursing the seconds he had lost coddling Dru, Spike pulled her into the shadows behind a pile of boxes under the stairs. A guttural growl rumbled in her throat as Snyder and several teenagers descended into the basement.

"Hide and seek," Spike whispered. The deranged Drusilla had a child's passion for games, and he hoped her desire to win was stronger than the temptation of young prey. "We're hiding."

"They'll never find us," Dru said softly.

"Everyone grab a box," Snyder ordered. "As soon as maintenance fixes that door, it's getting locked and staying locked just like the sign says, so don't leave anything behind."

The guitar player from Dingoes Ate My Baby picked up the box with the sunburst pendant. Dru had been so profoundly disturbed by the necklace that Spike suspected it had some mystical properties. The Hellmouth would significantly enhance even simple folk magick.

"Dullards can't even smell the rats scampering in the walls," Dru whispered with disdain, "and the wee hearts racing all frantic and aflutter with fright. Squealing canapés for the serpent, they are."

Hushing her with a finger to his lips, Spike waited until Snyder and his entourage were back upstairs. When the coast was clear, he led Dru down the concrete passageway toward the basement hatch into the tunnel system. As they turned into an adjacent corridor, the flapping of wings and a high-pitched screech brought him to an abrupt halt.

Dru clamped her hands to her ears. "The song stings, like nettles in my ears!"

The excruciating noise came from a horde of bats unlike any Spike had ever seen. Red, with three-inch fangs and a three-foot wingspan, they flew in haphazard disarray at the end of the corridor. They had no eyes, but they instantly detected the vampires. Alerted by sonar, the bats turned and swept toward them as a cohesive unit.

Spike recalled Drusilla's words as they raced back the way they had come.

". . . with velvet wings for dancing on the ceiling."

The obscure warning was meaningless now that they were

under attack. The bats blocked the route to the tunnel hatch, and there were too many to fight off without endangering Dru. With hundreds of students streaming into the school, taking cover seemed prudent.

Spike ducked into a storeroom, pulled Drusilla inside after him, and turned to close the door. Given Dru's melodramatic musing about beasts and the burning necklace, he couldn't help but wonder if the jewel and the bats were connected.

Drusilla screamed, banishing his reflections.

"It's all right, love. There's nothing in—" The rest of Spike's words hung unspoken in the dark. Drusilla flailed, trying to beat off a crimson bat.

Spike's rage instantly manifested with ridged bone and fangs. Roaring, he clamped his hand over the winged creature's neck and pulled it off Dru. The vicious animal fought with the strength of a thousand beasts its size, erasing any doubt that it was demonic. But Spike felt no kinship with the hellish creature. He crushed its skull against the cinderblock wall, severed the head from the body, and stomped it into a bloody mass of red flesh, acid blood, and splintered bone.

When the killer lust subsided, Spike knelt to examine Dru. "Did it hurt you?"

"Stuck," Dru muttered, "with poison pins."

Spike gently brushed ringlets of dark hair away from her face. The blood of her last meal oozed from two deep puncture wounds in her shoulder.

• • •

Xander unfolded the orange blanket, but the camouflage hunting vest he had hidden inside it last night was gone. "Stolen. The question is, by whom?"

"Someone else with a military fetish?" Willow teased.

"Not a fetish," Xander insisted. He was neither single-mindedly devoted to nor irrationally excited by fabrics that blended in with natural surroundings. "It's an identity thing."

"Yeah, well—okay." Willow didn't press.

That was the latest in hundreds of reasons why Willow Rosenberg had been his best friend forever. She never talked about it, but she understood that a few hours of being a real soldier had made him aware of his own untapped strengths and capabilities.

"There's Devon and that guitar guy." Willow tracked the two boys as they entered the cafeteria with a group of football players and cheerleaders.

"Are you afraid of them?" Xander asked, perplexed when she suddenly stepped behind him. "Are they after you?"

Xander was only mildly acquainted with the members of Dingoes Ate My Baby, but they weren't dangerous. They were musicians. The only threat they presented was ignoring anyone beneath them on the popularity roster, which was just about everyone.

"No, he doesn't even know I'm alive, not that it would make any diff—" Willow faltered. "Just go ask them to keep playing that old music today, will you?"

"You go ask them." Xander couldn't believe that Willow

had a crush on Cordelia's ex, but the signs were obvious. "Devon doesn't bite, and I know for a fact that he's available."

"Devon? You think I want Cordelia's castoff?" A frown hardened Willow's perky, freckled face.

Xander shrugged. "This *is* a rummage sale. Everything's a hand-me-down."

Willow cuffed his arm. "Even *I* have more self-esteem than that. Go ask or . . . or I'll carry the whereabouts of your hunting vest to my grave, which I hope nobody digs for another sixty or seventy years."

"You took it?"

Willow clamped her mouth shut and made a zipper gesture.

"Okay. I'll go ask." Shaking his head, Xander ducked under the table into the next aisle. In the Sunnydale scope of catastrophes, losing a used piece of clothing wasn't even a blip. As omens went, however, it boded well for Buffy's wish. Maybe they would have a weekend where all they had to worry about was not getting the secondhand merchandise they wanted and dying of boredom.

Or getting a month's detention for blocking an aisle, Xander thought as Principal Snyder marched toward him between tables. The man's face was rigid with a look of permanent displeasure, but he charged past Xander without a glance.

"Ms. Calendar!" Snyder waved at the faculty adviser. "It's after nine o'clock. I expect the rummage sale to open on time.

The Mayor will be here at noon sharp for a photo op when the first customers come in."

"We'll be ready," Ms. Calendar assured him. Her tight smile turned into a look of pure loathing when he turned his back. A pagan with a load of smarts but no power, or so she had told Giles, Jenny Calendar could only wish boils or perpetual hiccups on Snyder.

Xander stuck to his usual MO when dealing with the principal. He moved briskly in the opposite direction.

Devon and Oz had stopped to help Cheryl Saunders unload an assortment of potted houseplants, and Xander arrived at the music table ahead of them. Rather than wait like a groupie wanting an autograph, he flipped through the old albums.

"You're in clothes, right?" Oz asked, coming up behind him a minute later.

"Right." Xander held his hands up. "Not naked."

The boy smiled. "No, I meant you and Willow."

When the self-conscious girl caught both boys looking her way, she dropped the roll of price stickers. Xander could almost hear her gasp as she stooped to pick it up.

"She sent me over to ask—"

Oz perked up.

"—if you and Devon would keep playing the golden oldies," Xander finished. "Willow and Buffy think doo-wop and psychedelic rock will make people spend more money."

"That could work." Oz held out the cardboard box. "This

is clothes and some other stuff. Your department, not ours."

"Don't think so." Harmony peered over Oz's shoulder into the box. "I see things that belong in the *expensive* department. I'll take it."

Xander didn't object when Oz handed her the box. He asked a more important question. "Have either one of you seen a camouflage hunting vest?"

"Can't say that I have." Oz turned on the old stereo and reached for a small vinyl record. "But I found a pair of sheepskin seat covers that will look great in my van."

"The van with zebra stripes?" Xander hadn't male-bonded since he had staked Jesse, his best friend turned vampire, but Oz seemed sincere and likeable.

"Yeah, but I'm thinking of painting it blue." Oz pressed a yellow plastic disk into the large hole in the middle of the forty-five, then fit the small hole in the yellow plastic onto the turntable spindle.

"Have you seen the jewelry someone took out of the display case?" Harmony asked.

"Someone stole jewelry? Something specific?" Xander wondered if Michael had come back in the middle of the night to look for his medallion.

"Some chain necklaces, a couple of bracelets, and a pair of rhinestone earrings. Why?" Harmony's eyes narrowed. "What do you know?"

"Not a thing," Xander answered quickly. He wasn't about to sic the insipid, painfully blunt Harmony on the verbally unarmed Michael Czajak. If Michael had stolen his charm back, it was a victory for the little people. "Gotta go."

Xander snapped his fingers and bounced to the rock-and-roll beat of Buddy Holly's "Peggy Sue" on his way back to men's shirts.

Willow was folding and pricing clothes from another box someone had dumped. She didn't ask about the music or his conversation with Oz. She announced, "The glow-green shorts are missing."

"Now *that's* odd." Xander could see why someone might want the hunting vest, but not the can't-miss-me-in-the-dark underwear. *Unless Michael is hiding some bizarre fashion preferences under his bland public image.*

When Michael crept into the cafeteria, trying not to draw attention, Xander dropped him as a suspect. The boy wouldn't have come back if he had found his amulet.

"Nothing happened?" Giles eyed Buffy over the top of his glasses. It was a classic look of adult disbelief designed to rattle teenagers who were hedging the truth.

"Nope." Buffy wasn't rattled, but she wasn't trying to hide anything either. Perched on the edge of the library study table, she met his skeptical stare with a look of unflinching conviction. "No new vamps rising from cemetery cradles, no aspiring Frankensteins or demons that want to be real boys looking for body parts, no monsters itching to put a Slayer notch on . . . whatever they notch—"

Giles cut her off. “Yes, I get the picture. It’s a trifle alarming, actually.”

Buffy frowned. “Right. I can’t sleep unless I’ve had to fend off a few fiends before going to bed.”

“Hmmm?” The Watcher looked up.

“Why is no evil deed for one night a problem?” Buffy asked, puzzled. “Even vampires and demons must need some down time now and then.”

“Not really,” Giles said. “Not unless they’re plotting or saving their strength for a particularly horrendous event.”

“Is there a Watcher rule against humoring a Slayer’s desperate desire to forget about killing or being killed for a couple of days?”

Buffy knew the answer, but the question had to be asked anyway. If she didn’t remind Giles that she was a girl with friends and non-Slayer activities, he would assume she had finally decided to accept the restrictions of being the Chosen One. Sooner or later he’d have to accept that she wouldn’t give up control of her dreams or her destiny.

“Forgetting could be deadly, don’t you think?” Noting her look of consternation, Giles changed tactics. “And what would you rather be doing than keeping evil at bay this weekend?”

“The school rummage sale? We’re raising money to send the marching band to the state competition in Sacramento.”

“Of course.” Giles smiled tightly. “Tooting horns and clanging cymbals while hiking in lockstep is so much more necessary than the preservation of life on the planet.”

Buffy stiffened. "Is something threatening the planet?"

"No, I was just—" Giles pulled up a chair. "I just don't want you to get so involved in other, inconsequential things that you let down your guard."

"Don't worry. I've got this weird Slayer sixth sense that warns me when . . ." Buffy frowned.

"When what?" Giles asked expectantly.

"Last night I had a feeling that something was . . . off," Buffy explained. "Angel felt it too, but . . . nothing happened."

"And now?"

Buffy shrugged. "I can't tell if I'm sensing something weird or if talking about it makes me *think* I am."

"And you're absolutely certain that nothing happened right before this feeling started?"

"Michael Czajak lost a protection charm." Buffy matched the Watcher's worried frown. "Actually, his mom gave it to the rummage sale."

"Do I know him?"

"Probably not," Buffy said, "but he claims this gold medallion protects him from Sunnydale's goblins and ghouls. So . . . do charms work?"

"Some," Giles admitted, "but there's no all-purpose protection spell or talisman. Generally speaking, they have to be conjured for a specific threat, and even then their effectiveness is usually limited."

"So we couldn't have made a thingy to protect me from the Master," Buffy stated flatly.

"No." Giles averted his eyes. He still hadn't forgiven himself for her almost-permanent death at the Master's hands. "If that had been possible, I would have done it."

"I know." Buffy smiled, but now she was on edge. "So what are the chances that Michael's missing amulet has me feeling like mystical centipedes are drag racing in my veins?"

"An amateur spell?" Giles stood up and adjusted his glasses. "I rather doubt it, but we are on the Hellmouth. You might want to keep an eye on this Michael fellow, as a precaution."

"Okay." Buffy slid off the table and glanced back as she headed toward the swinging doors. "Should I tell Ms. Calendar you think the rummage sale is inconsequential, or would you rather owe me one?"

"What? You—" Giles looked stricken. "I'd rather not have cause for harsh words with anyone, thank you."

"I'll keep that in mind." Buffy grinned as she pushed through the doors into the hall. For all his stiff and pompous ways, Giles could be reduced to sputtering incoherence when it came to Jenny Calendar. It was sweet, and despite her teasing, she wouldn't do anything to ruin things for him.

As she headed toward the cafeteria, Buffy wondered if the crate of Joel Shavin paintings had arrived at the gallery yet. Her mom had to take delivery before she could leave to bring the art donations to the school. Buffy wasn't worried about her own reputation in the community, but Ms. Calendar had mentioned the unique pieces on flyers and in a newspaper article about the school sale, hoping to attract customers from Sunnydale's upper crust.

Michael Czajak stayed in the shadows along the wall. The cafeteria had been transformed into a bustling retail enterprise overnight. Students and teachers were still busy unpacking and pricing sale items, rushing to finish before the noon deadline in two hours. Sorting everything into categories would make the sale more convenient for shoppers, but it didn't make his search easier. It kept him rooted in hiding near the objet d'art and jewelry tables where Cordelia Chase was clearly in charge.

"What did you find?" Cordelia asked when Harmony set a box on the end of the table. "You look like you uncovered Blackbeard's treasure or something."

Harmony bubbled with enthusiasm. "I just happened to be looking over Oz's shoulder when he almost gave this box to that zero-charisma Zanzibar—"

"You mean Xander Harris?" Cordelia asked, looking into the box.

"I guess. Does it matter?" Harmony scoffed. "Anyway, I thought we should have that old-timey metal compact and that silver picture frame and that . . ."

Tuning out Harmony's annoying voice, Michael stared at the glass display cases. Gold and silver gleamed under the overhead lights, and he could discern splashes of color—blue and purple, as well as red and green. He had only begun to dabble in magick and didn't know much beyond the fundamentals. However, it seemed likely that his amulet would make itself known to him somehow—if the spell had worked.

Twelve hours had passed since Michael had sent out his mystical call, but there was no sign of his protective charm. Without the amulet, he was vulnerable to every horror that inhabited the dark recesses of the town. Closing his eyes, he recited the incantation again.

Cordis fortis, deiciere,
Adesdum prospecto hodie.

He repeated the spell in English for good measure.

Heart of power, thrown away,
Come back to me today.

CHAPTER THREE

Cordelia tried to ignore the freaky loser hanging out in the corner, but his silent presence was getting on her nerves. She spun around, dark eyes brimming with scorn as she lashed out. "Go hover somewhere else!"

Recoiling from the sharp rebuke, the boy stopped talking to himself and scrambled to get away from her.

Harmony grimaced. "He's so white, like a ghost or something. Could anybody be more repulsive?"

"Zanzibar?" Cordelia shuddered to cover her earlier slip. Xander *had* rescued her from the old science lab fire, and he *was* a great kisser, but that didn't obligate her to defend him. It wasn't her fault he was a buffoon with candy lips.

Are these things great or what?" Opening an engraved metal compact, Harmony removed a fluffy pad. She pretended to powder her nose, then studied her reflection in the small mirror. "Should I get a tan this summer or stick with the pale porcelain doll look?"

"Too much sun causes wrinkles and cancer. Oooh." Cordelia carefully untangled a filigreed silver necklace from a gold sunburst on a heavy chain. "This silver one is mine. The rest can go back to the odds-and-ends table. It's just costume junk."

"I have a crow's claw!" Still gazing at herself in the mirror, Harmony pulled the skin around her eye tight.

"That's crow's *feet*," Cordelia said, clasping the delicate silver chain around her neck.

"But I'm only sixteen!" Harmony squealed.

"And I've been telling you since fifth grade that marathon tanning is bad for your skin. Did you listen? No." Cordelia leaned in for a closer look. Harmony did have creases at the corners of her eyes. "So don't come crying to me."

"But I look twenty!"

Cordelia wasn't in the mood to console the distraught girl. She grabbed the compact out of Harmony's hand and dropped it in the box. "Stop whining. It could be worse. Plastic surgeons can fix premature wrinkles. They can't cure cancer. I'll be right back."

Ordinarily Cordelia wouldn't think of wearing anything someone else had owned. She didn't even buy off the rack at the better boutiques. But it was easy to justify making an exception for the silver necklace. The piece was exquisite, obviously an antique, and a rare find.

That I haven't paid for, Cordelia realized when Principal Snyder suddenly stepped in front of her. *So I can't be busted for buying something before the rummage sale opens—only for stealing!*

"Principal Snyder!" Cordelia flashed him her most ingratiating smile, prepared to use her feminine wiles to wheedle her way out of trouble. He was wearing a gray hat with a wide brim and red band. It was similar to the hats cocky detectives wore in the old black-and-white movies her father liked. "I love your hat! It makes you look so . . . debonair!"

"It does, doesn't it?" Snyder surprised her with a satisfied grin. "I knew you had good taste, Ms. Chase."

"Yes, I do." Cordelia kept smiling.

"I should buy this, shouldn't I?"

"Yes, you should," Cordelia answered with an emphatic nod. Apparently the no-early-purchase rule didn't apply to administration. "It's definitely you."

"Oh, good, because I really like it." Touching the brim, Snyder whistled a jaunty tune as he sashayed away.

"Now *that* was creepy." The tips of Cordelia's fingers tingled as she moved on to the trinket and knickknack table.

"I finally figured it out!" Xander exclaimed.

"What?" Willow asked.

"The shirts must be breeding. The minute we think we've

folded and priced them all, more show up." Xander bent over and opened the flaps on the last unpacked box. He quickly closed them again and left the box on the floor. "Like tribbles, only we can't transport them to a Klingon ship to get rid of them."

"No," Willow deadpanned, "we'll have to sell every single one before they overrun the cafeteria."

"Not possible," Xander said. "The jocks have already pilfered the cool stuff, and the homeless derelicts who might actually *want* yesterday's outfits won't come in to buy them. They'll just wait until we throw them away and dig them out of the Dumpster."

"We're doomed." Willow loved bantering with Xander, especially about old movies and TV shows. It took her back to less complicated, carefree times, when spiders and frogs were the scariest creatures she had to worry about.

"At least we won't have to feed them." Kicking the unpacked box aside, Xander collected and nested the empty boxes.

The original version of "Love Potion No. 9" by the Clovers started playing, and Willow's eyes lit up. "Oh, I love this song!"

"Which reminds me"—Xander tucked the empty cartons under his arm—"we had a deal. I asked Oz to keep playing music, so you have to tell me where you hid my camouflage vest."

"I didn't hide it anywhere," Willow said. "You just assumed I did."

"But you know where it is," Xander stated flatly.

Willow shook her head. "Sorry."

"Can you finish up here?" Xander scanned the room as he spoke. "I've . . . uh . . . got to ditch these boxes."

And look for your vest, Willow thought as he left. Lifting the last box onto the table, she folded back the flaps and pulled out a pink button-down shirt. A strangled scream caught in her throat when a black spider scurried along the collar. She could help dust vamps and defy demons that had downloaded themselves into metal suits, but she had to draw the line at spiders. She dropped the shirt.

A blue forked tongue flicked out, snagged the arachnid, and vanished into the pile of clothes.

Willow had no idea what else was lurking in the box, but anything that killed spiders couldn't be bad—except frogs. However, the only known frog big enough to fit the blue tongue was the Goliath. Thirty inches long and weighing seven pounds, they looked like giant bullfrogs and were native to African rain forests.

The chances were slim to none that the spider killer was a frog, and Willow's scientific curiosity was stronger than her fear. Using her black pricing marker, she flipped over the top shirt.

Round dark eyes set in soft white fur blinked.

"You're not a nasty old frog!" Willow exclaimed, instantly captivated. The size of an average teddy bear, the furry thing had four stubby legs with bright blue paw pads and tufted, pointed ears. The little guy looked like a Japanese anime creature, except that it was alive.

The animal purred.

Absolutely certain the odd but adorable critter wouldn't harm her, Willow placed her hand near its furry face. It snuggled against her palm.

"Hey, cutie." Wrapping the creature in a long blue neck scarf, Willow took it out of the box and held it close. She loved her tropical fish, but her mother had never allowed her to have a pet she could cuddle. This time she wouldn't take no for an answer. She wouldn't even ask. She'd sneak Cutie in and out of her room and carry him to school in a backpack.

"It's okay," Willow cooed. "You're with me now."

Cutie purred.

As Buffy hurried down the hall toward the cafeteria, her Slayer sense suddenly kicked in. Her arm snapped out and her fingers closed around braided leather. She pulled, yanking a short, stocky boy out of the empty classroom on her left. He stumbled into the hall but hung on to the handle end of the bullwhip.

"Jonathan!" Andrew shouted, and ran out behind him. The taller boy had been in Buffy's biology class last year.

She looked Jonathan in the eye. "I thought Principal Snyder was the only one who cracked the whip around here."

"I just got this." Jonathan tugged on the whip, trying to pull it out of Buffy's grasp. She tightened her grip on the main lash. The narrow leather strip, smaller round thong, and cracker that were attached to the end dangled from her closed fist.

"You'll *lose* this if Snyder catches you snapping it in the halls," Buffy warned. "Someone could get hurt."

"Like me," Andrew said, rubbing his arm.

"Sorry." Jonathan swallowed nervously.

"No, you're not. Ever since you found that thing, nothing else matters." Andrew wasn't happy. "We're out here playing Indiana Jones instead of guarding our stash."

"I can't help it," Jonathan said, equally peeved. "Cracking it makes me feel—"

"Taller?" Andrew sneered.

Buffy had better things to do than referee a spat between two pathetic jokers. "Just watch it, okay?"

Jonathan nodded and tugged again.

Buffy let the end of the whip slide through her fingers. Just before the boy pulled the end clear, a small jolt of electricity shot through her hand.

"Ouch." Buffy frowned.

"Uh-oh." Coiling the whip, Jonathan took off down the hall with Andrew in pursuit.

Buffy wished them well in their bumbling efforts to thwart Snyder's regime, but their mortal fate instantly fell off her agenda. After calling the gallery, she pushed through the cafeteria doors and paused to look for Willow and Xander. Ms. Calendar waved her over to the cashier's table.

"I don't want to press, but . . ." Ms. Calendar caught her lower lip in her teeth.

"Mom should be here soon," Buffy said, anticipating the question. "I just called the gallery, and she's not there."

"That's great!" The tension in the teacher's slim body eased. "Someone called about the cloisonné urn I mentioned in the newspaper article. They want something nice for their poodle's ashes."

"They want a super-expensive antique urn for a *dog*?" Buffy's appreciation of art and artifacts began and ended with ancient weapons and occult books. She didn't care what happened to the pot, but her mother would be appalled. "Don't tell Mom they're going to bury it."

"Actually, I think they're going to keep it on their mantel." Smiling, Ms. Calendar turned to help a student find the receipt books.

"Buffy!" Cordelia called from the next table.

Buffy groaned. Despite the fact that she and her friends had saved Cordelia's life more than once, the popular cheerleader never, ever wanted to be seen with the "library losers" unless something dreadfully bad was happening. Buffy wasn't doing bad this weekend.

Cordelia, as usual, wouldn't be ignored. She dashed over, glaring with indignation. "I need help, and that's what you're empowered or whatever to do, right? Help?"

"Is the world coming to an end again?" Buffy asked.

"Not that I noticed." Cordelia grabbed Buffy's arm and

hauled her toward the jewelry display. "Some of these things are very valuable, and I need you to stand guard until Deirdre comes back."

"No can do." Buffy was duty bound to save Cordelia from being hacked up, spindled, or mutilated, but she didn't owe her any favors. "I'm working in shirts with Willow."

"It's just for a minute!" Cordelia insisted.

"But I've got—" As Buffy was about to turn, she noticed a dark speck on Cordelia's front tooth. Fascinated, she hesitated. "—a few minutes to spare."

"Oh, thank you," Cordelia said, relieved. "Deirdre said she'd be right back. I just don't want anyone to walk off with anything while I'm trying to convince Harmony that she isn't turning into an old hag."

"She's sixteen." Buffy couldn't stop staring at the dark spot on Cordelia's otherwise perfect smile.

"She's sun-dried," Cordelia countered, "just like a prune."

"Uh-huh." Buffy's eyes widened slightly when she realized that the dental flaw wasn't a lipstick smear or food wedged between Cordelia's teeth. The gleaming white enamel was marred by decay! Then she noticed that Cordelia's hair was beginning to frizz.

Buffy didn't say a word as Cordelia ran out. Cordelia would scream a few seconds after she looked in the restroom mirror, as soon as the shock wore off.

Frowning, Buffy rubbed her palm where the whip had zapped her. Was it possible for braided leather to build up a static electrical charge? She might not have thought anything of the little jolt except for Cordelia's cosmetic calamity and Harmony's premature wrinkles. Apparently, neither girl had noticed any blemishes before they left home for school or they would have skipped.

"Well, I see you're tending to business properly for a change, Ms. Summers." Principal Snyder gave Buffy a nod of approval, then leaned to look in the glass cases. "Let's see what you've got here."

"This is Cordelia's display, actually," Buffy said. The principal's nonhostile attitude was a bigger shock than the bullwhip zapper.

Snyder turned his head and smiled. "Do you like my hat?"

Is that a trick question? Buffy wondered, wishing Deirdre would hurry back and rescue her.

"It's, uh . . ." Buffy couldn't think and drew a blank.

"Nifty?" Snyder giggled softly.

"Totally," Buffy agreed, feeling numb. The subtle sense of alarm that had nagged her since last night clanged in her head. Trying not to look as frantic as she felt, she glanced around.

Everyone was calm, and everything seemed normal. Most of the kids had finished setting up. With time to spare before the sale opened in ninety minutes, they stood in groups talking or wandered the aisles shopping. Willow sat in a chair by the tables of men's clothing, bobbing her head to the strains of "Proud Mary," the original recording by Creedence Clearwater Revival. Buffy's mom always got nostalgic when she heard songs by John Fogerty's old group. The only oddity seemed to be Xander. He was at the music table playing records instead of helping Willow in men's clothing.

"I'd like to see that pocket watch," Snyder said, tapping on the glass.

Buffy's head snapped back around. "I don't have the keys, but Cordelia will be right back."

"Okay, but I've got dibs." Chuckling again, Snyder tipped his hat and bowed his head slightly. Buffy saw three round red marks on his bald pate before he replaced the hat and sauntered off.

Bites? A rash? Buffy made a note to ask Giles. The marks didn't seem to be bothering Snyder, but they weren't caused by common dandruff, either.

Deirdre looked irritated when she returned and found Buffy standing in for the leader of the popular pack. "Where's Cordelia?"

"Restroom." Buffy studied the girl closely. The cheerleader's blunt-cut brown hair had a healthy shine and no split ends. Her complexion wasn't pitted, pocked, or wrinkled. "Have you been with Cordelia and Harmony all morning?"

"Most of it." Deirdre frowned. "Why?"

"No reason." Buffy shrugged. Getting information from people who thought they were too good to talk to you was a challenge. "Do you really have false teeth?"

"What? No!" Deirdre bared her teeth and pulled on the front ones to prove it.

Buffy peered into the girl's mouth. Not a smidgeon of decay. Deirdre was an insufferable snob, but she wasn't suffering from sudden and inexplicable uglies.

Two imperatives vied for priority in Buffy's mind when Deirdre took over guarding the display cases: Alert Giles that something was definitely wrong, and make sure Willow and Xander were okay. She had no idea if the maladies were mystical or medical, but since they didn't seem to be affecting everyone, she chose friends first.

Sitting with a blue scarf heaped in her lap, Willow looked content and undamaged. Her auburn hair fell straight and limp to her shoulders, but it wasn't dull or frizzy. When she smiled, her teeth gleamed white.

"Hey, Willow. Looks like you finally got all those shirts stacked."

"Yeah, I did." Willow glanced back at the neat piles. "Your skirt's still here."

Buffy had forgotten about the leather skirt.

"But Xander can't find a hunting vest he stashed," Willow added. "He thought I took it, but I didn't."

"I did," Buffy confessed. "But I'm going to give it back—as soon as he admits that guys are just as eager to take advantage of a bargain as girls."

"Good one," Willow said with an impish grin. "I approve."

"Yeah, but it's not all that important right now," Buffy said. "Our no-weirdness weekend may be a total washout. I'm not sure what's happening, but some serious sleuthing is in order. I'll get Xander and we'll meet you in the library."

"Okay." Willow stood up, clutching the bunched-up blue scarf.

"Leave the scarf here, though. Principal Snyder is acting like a complete goof, but why risk getting caught with unpaid merchandise? Tell Giles I'll be right there." Confident Willow would do as she asked, Buffy left without waiting for a response.

The Creedence album was still playing, and Xander swayed to the music as he flipped through the cardboard record covers. He smiled when she rushed up. "Hey, Buffy. Got a request?"

"Isn't this Devon's job?" Buffy asked, giving him a quick once-over. He looked fine.

"Devon is nowhere to be seen," Xander explained. "Oz went to make sure the seat covers he found fit his van. It's in auto shop getting a tune-up or an oil change or something. Anyway, I told him I'd handle the DJ gig until he gets back."

"We have to meet Willow in the library," Buffy said. "Snyder's acting like an adolescent on laughing gas, and Cordelia's teeth are rotting."

"Turning-black-and-falling-out rotting, or a-really-stinky-case-of-halitosis rotting?" Xander looked worried for a moment before he arched a dark eyebrow. "And why is this a problem?"

"Because—" Buffy looked past him. The camouflage vest

she had so carefully hidden in a pile of sheepskin was lying on the CDs. "Where'd you get that?"

"Oz found it in his seat covers. I hid it last night, but someone moved—" Xander's eyes narrowed when Buffy flinched. "You?"

"Yeah, Mr. Girls Can't Resist a Bargain." Buffy winced sheepishly. "Are you mad?"

"Not as mad as I would be if someone else had found it and bought it," Xander said.

"Good. Now let's go see Giles."

"I can't leave until Devon shows up or Oz gets back," Xander said. "Some of these LPs are classics, and you'd be surprised how many people will risk going to jail to steal stuff they can't use."

"LPs?"

"Long-playing records," Xander explained. "Forty-fives were the CD singles of their day."

"Just don't be too long," Buffy cautioned. "We could be dealing with some kind of mutant flu bug or something."

"I am *so* sorry I'm late!" Joyce hurried into the cafeteria carrying a box of donations from her gallery clients. "I had to wait for a delivery, and I think I caught every traffic light between the gallery and the school."

"Don't apologize. The sale doesn't start for an hour. I'm just so glad you took the time to collect all these fabulous treasures." Ms. Calendar took the box. "Is this everything?"

"No, I have two more boxes in the car," Joyce said.

"Great! I'll get Deirdre started unpacking this one, and then I'll help you bring them inside."

"Buffy said she'd"—Joyce's sentence trailed off as the teacher stepped away—"be here to do it."

While Ms. Calendar conferred with a tall cheerleader at the next table, Joyce surveyed the cafeteria. Teenagers waiting for the sale to start stood around tables piled with an impressive array of goods. A song by Blood, Sweat & Tears, one of Joyce's all-time favorite groups, was playing on an old stereo. Xander mimed playing the drums and tapping his foot to the beat. Willow sat in a chair. From a distance it looked like the girl was holding a white stuffed animal. There was something sad about the toys people threw away, a sign that wonder and hope had been lost in the trials of adulthood. She still had a funny stuffed dog with a bee on its nose tucked away in an old trunk, a cherished memento that held the last vestiges of her youth. It was a silly notion, the idea of hanging on to the child she once was. She wished Buffy wasn't so eager to grow up too fast.

More than that, Joyce wished her daughter would learn to keep her word. Buffy was not in the cafeteria, not where she was supposed to be or doing what she said she'd be doing—again. That was disappointing, but not the only thing that worried her. Buffy's grades were barely passing, and her reputation as a troublemaker had followed her from Hemery. Being able to hold her own in a gang brawl was an excellent survival skill, but it wouldn't get her into a decent college. It was becoming quite clear to Joyce that she might have to stop threatening to ground her headstrong offspring and actually do it.

Don't jump to conclusions, Joyce reminded herself. She brought it up with Ms. Calendar as they left for the parking lot. "I thought Buffy was working the sale this morning."

"She is. She just . . . left for a minute."

The teacher sounded suspiciously like a person trying to cover for someone.

Joyce resented not being able to trust Buffy, but Buffy's actions were to blame. As a good parent, she had no choice but to ask, "Was Buffy here last—"

"We already have a buyer for the cloisonné urn," the teacher said, steering the conversation elsewhere. "But *I'm* really anxious to see the Jurojin ivory. The artist carved him standing with a stag, correct?"

"Yes, it's a beautiful piece." Joyce had been surprised and delighted that Mr. Haido had contributed something from his collection of Asian gods. Jurojin, the god of longevity, was one of seven lucky Chinese deities. The deer, another symbol of long life, was often included as his messenger.

"And Mayor Wilkins called to ask if the black jade paperweight comes with any documentation."

"The Mayor wants it?" Joyce asked.

"Only if it's an orb called 'Endless Night,'" Ms. Calendar said.

Jade was symbolic of power, prestige, and immortality. This particular piece had an intriguing history, but Joyce was surprised the Mayor had expressed interest.

"His father lost a bidding war on the orb at an auction in LA back in the fifties," Ms. Calendar explained.

"It's the same piece," Joyce confirmed. "The donor supplied the original sales slip and related paperwork."

"Really?" Ms. Calendar looked impressed. "Why would anyone donate something that valuable to a student rummage sale?"

"Apparently the jade is so black that the donor felt like he was being drawn into infinity when he stared at it," Joyce said. "And the orb has such an intense hypnotic effect that he couldn't stop staring at it. So it's been buried in a desk drawer for five decades. He said he won't miss it."

"Fascinating." Ms. Calendar stood back while Joyce unlocked her car. "The Mayor will be so pleased. He'll be here at noon."

"Mayor Wilkins is coming to the school?" Joyce asked as she hauled a box out of the backseat.

"Just long enough for the *Sunnydale Press* to get a few pictures and quotes," Ms. Calendar said. "I'm sure he'll want to meet the woman who recovered his father's lost treasure."

"That would be nice." Joyce lifted the second box and kicked the door closed. "Don't drop that. Everything is packed in shredded paper, but jade can shatter."

"No pressure there," Ms. Calendar teased.

Joyce relaxed once they were back in the cafeteria and the boxes had been transferred into the faculty adviser's custody. She was no longer responsible for the condition of the precious contents, and she had kept her promise to Buffy.

Who still isn't back from wherever she went, Joyce noted. Perhaps taking her cues from Mr. Giles, Ms. Calendar was cutting Buffy a great deal of slack. Still, it seemed foolish to expect the worst if nobody else was troubled by Buffy's absence.

Joyce had intended to go directly back to the gallery, but Mayor Richard Wilkins III was highly respected in Sunnydale and a patron of the arts. He might appreciate a personal invitation to the opening of Joel Shavin's show. The Mayor's presence would be a boon to the gallery's prestige. She could afford to wait.

An avid bargain hunter, Joyce began a casual walk through the rummage sale. Unusual, collectible, or valuable objects could often be found in thrift shops and garage sales because people didn't know what they had.

As she moved up and down the aisles, Joyce's keen eye flicked over the ordinary and mundane, searching for a junkpile original. Her gaze was drawn to a pair of black lace evening gloves that stood out like a beacon on a stormy night. The gloves were in excellent condition and looked like a pair her grandmother used to wear to the theater. They also fit her hands perfectly.

Sold, Joyce thought, removing the gloves and taking

them with her. As she rummaged through the odds and ends on the trinket tables, she softly sang along to "And When I Die," another old Blood, Sweat & Tears hit that blared from the music table. "'One child born in this world to carry on, to carry on.'"

"Hi, Ms. Summers!" Willow came up beside her. She carried the white stuffed animal wrapped in a blue knit neck scarf. "Did you find anything you just absolutely have to have?"

"Yes, actually." Joyce held up the gloves and scratched an itchy spot on the back of her hand. "I see you've found yourself a must-have item too."

Willow blinked, confused. "I did? What?"

"The white bear or whatever it is." Joyce reached toward the toy.

Holding it closer, Willow lurched backward and bumped into the table. She snapped, eyes flashing. "He's mine."

"Yes, of course he is," Joyce said, taken aback. Willow was a gentle soul and completely without malice toward anyone. Her hostility was unexpected, but not necessarily unwarranted.

"I don't care what Principal Snyder says." Willow spoke in a quiet, intense voice, her expression stony and determined. "Not letting us buy stuff we find before the sale starts is a stupid rule. Who cares where the money comes from, as long as we make enough so the marching band can compete? I'm *not* putting Cutie back, and *that's* final."

"Well, I agree. It's a stupid rule." Joyce smiled. "And I'm not putting my gloves back either."

"Good, because . . . well, finders keepers and first come, first served." Willow had a white-knuckled grip on the bundled plush toy, as though someone might try to snatch it away. "Buffy's at the library."

"What is it with you kids and the library?" Joyce asked, genuinely puzzled. "Does Mr. Giles do your homework?"

"Only if it's about demon stuff. Gotta go." As Willow spun around to leave, the clasp of a gold chain necklace caught on her sweater. The large gold sunburst with red and green rhinestones dangled from her back as she scurried down the aisle.

Joyce called out, but Willow didn't stop. She collided with a dark-haired boy.

"Watch where you're going, Michael!" Willow berated the stunned teenager. "You almost squashed Cutie."

Michael didn't apologize or defend himself. He moved by her and stopped to look through the kitchen wares on the next table.

Willow walked up the aisle at a more leisurely pace and went back to shirts. It was unsettling to see the girl so out of sorts, but Joyce chalked it up to typical teenage angst. Everyone had cranky days.

Paying more attention to the merchandise than where she was walking, Joyce almost ran into another early browser. "Excuse me, I wasn't—"

Joyce whipped the black gloves behind her back when

she recognized Principal Snyder. It was an instinctive reaction, even though his early shopping rule probably didn't apply to contributors. However, she couldn't contain a gasp of astonishment triggered by his startling appearance. He wore his suit jacket, but his blue shirt was draped over the table and his puny, hairless chest was bare.

"Do you like this tie or this one?" Snyder dropped a tie with diagonal blue-gray stripes and held up a muted red tie with tiny golden fleurs-de-lis.

"You took off your shirt." Joyce didn't like the short, scrawny man. He obviously loathed all teenagers and harbored a particularly belligerent dislike for Buffy. Even so, his bizarre behavior piqued her curiosity.

"It clashes with my hat. The band is red." The man tilted his head and a drop of blood trickled down his ear. He held up both ties.

"Do you need a doctor?" Joyce asked, wondering if he had cracked under the stress of running Sunnydale High. She didn't like to think about it, but the school had an alarming rate of student and faculty tragedies.

"No, I need a tie. The Mayor never mixes. He always matches." He held up both choices. "Which one?"

"The red one." Joyce smiled tightly.

If Principal Snyder had suddenly come unhinged, the best thing to do was humor him. The Mayor wouldn't ignore his disturbed state and might even use it as grounds for dismissal. She could only hope, for Buffy's sake.

Joyce hurried back to the cashier's table. During the thirty minutes remaining before the sale officially opened, she could answer any questions the cheerleader had about the pieces she had brought from the gallery.

Besides, Ms. Calendar or one of the girls might have hand lotion she could use. Her skin was much drier than usual, and her hands itched. Large flakes of skin peeled off when she scratched them.

CHAPTER FOUR

On her way to the library, Buffy ducked into the restroom to check on Cordelia. Besides the unfortunate fact that Cordelia knew the Slayer secret and was therefore owed certain inner sanctum considerations, Giles would need as much information as Buffy could get.

Since Harmony would rather die than share with a social outcast, Buffy quietly opened the door and hugged the wall as she slipped inside. Cordelia sat cross-legged on the floor in front of a closed stall. Harmony had locked herself inside.

"This is getting ridiculous, Harmony." Cordelia fidgeted with her silver necklace, a sign that she was antsy and bored. "You can stay locked in there feeling sorry for yourself, or you can come out and look in the mirror. It's not as bad as you think."

"Yes, it is," Harmony sobbed.

Cordelia rolled her eyes, but her tone didn't betray her impatience. "A few teeny-weeny little lines won't kill your chances with Jake. Well, they might. He *is* the Razorbacks' star tight behind or rear or—"

"End." Harmony sniffled. "He's the tight end."

"Whatever. Anyway," Cordelia continued, "they've developed all kinds of new therapies to make old people look young."

"I'm not old!" Harmony wailed. "My life is over."

Buffy couldn't take her eyes off Cordelia, who obviously hadn't looked in the mirror lately. If she had, she wouldn't be calmly chiding Harmony about overreacting to suntan creases.

Cordelia's sleek brown hair was slowly turning to straw. Her pink manicure had sprouted black dots, and the dark decay had spread to all her front teeth. If Harmony's tiny lines were getting worse at the same rate, she'd look like a shar-pei before fifth period started.

Buffy backed out of the restroom as silently as she had gone in and speed-walked to the library. There was a measure of cosmic justice in Cordelia and Harmony's cosmetic disintegration, but she didn't have time to deal with two hysterical girls. If the cause was a magickal spell or curse, Giles was their only hope of reversing the effects.

Even if it's a scientific something—a gene mutation or a failed chem-lab experiment or pollution run amok—Giles is still the go-to guy, Buffy thought.

Her Watcher was shelving books on the upper tier. Very few students used the school library, but he could hardly discourage all non-Slayer access. Sometimes he had to do what librarians do.

Buffy got straight to the point. "You know that weird feeling I had this morning?"

"Something happened?" Giles pushed the book cart aside and hurried down the short flight of stairs.

"In a nutshell." Buffy counted off the odd maladies. "Principal Snyder's gone totally bonkers and may have holes in his head. Harmony's aging, and Cordelia's decomposing."

"Literally, or are those colorful figures of speech?" Giles asked as he slipped back into his tweed jacket.

"Literally," Buffy said.

"I see," Giles sighed wearily. "I was rather hoping you'd get your wish for a slow weekend, and I'd have time to finish cataloging this shipment of books before someone steals another one."

"So I take it the lactose manuscript hasn't shown up on the vampire black market?"

"That's *du Lac* manuscript," Giles corrected. "And no, the trail's gone completely cold."

Buffy was sorry for Giles's loss, but she needed his immediate attention. "The only other weird thing was the shock I got from Jonathan's bullwhip. Although, that might have been a static shock—like you get from a doorknob."

"That happens when friction causes a frantic exchange of electrons, especially between insulating materials," Giles explained. "Leather-soled shoes acquire extra electrons from the carpet and a negative charge builds up in your body. When you touch something with the opposite charge, such as a doorknob, the electrons rush out and you feel a shock. There can be an enormous buildup of voltage."

"One question, Mr. Wizard," Buffy said, annoyed by the lecture. "Could static electricity build up in the end of a bullwhip?"

"Under normal use? Not likely, but not impossible, I suppose." Giles frowned, thinking.

"Okay, but what about the other things?" Buffy asked. "Can a disease go from the first symptom stage to the patient's falling apart in less than an hour?"

"Poisoning could cause a rapid progression," Giles said. "So could a toxic chemical compound or a parasite, perhaps a mutation."

"I thought of that," Buffy said.

"But from what you've told me, the victims don't have the same symptoms." Giles removed his glasses and nibbled on the frame as he paced. "Are you sure the effects were limited to Principal Snyder and the two girls? There wasn't anything strange about anyone else?"

"Not that I noticed, but"—Buffy hesitated—"I wouldn't

have seen the sores on Principal Snyder's head if he hadn't taken off his hat."

Giles looked surprised. "He was wearing a hat?"

"An old-fashioned one he found in the sale stuff. He *really* wanted me to like it." Buffy made a face. "I said it looked great. If Snyder's sudden soft spot for students is permanent, I don't want to lose the good-graces points I just got."

Giles resumed pacing. "Were Cordelia and Harmony wearing anything that was donated to the sale?"

"I didn't actually *see* Harmony," Buffy explained. "Cordelia was wearing an outfit I've seen before—except for her necklace. She's in charge of jewelry for the sale, but I don't know if that's where she got it. I think she's allergic to anything used."

"We must find out," Giles said. "Identifying a common denominator won't tell us if the problem is scientific or magickal, but at least we'll have a sound starting point—especially if all or most of the sale items could have been contaminated by the same agent."

"Almost everything was stored in the basement." Buffy paused. "Mom."

"What about your mother?" Settling his glasses on his nose, Giles started toward the doors.

"She's bringing some donations from the gallery." Buffy rushed out with him, jogging to match his lengthy stride as they hurried down the hall. "If she's not here yet, I need to stop her."

Jonathan and Andrew were arguing in the hall outside

the cafeteria. Buffy was trying to reach her mother's cell phone. Giles stopped to demand that Jonathan hand over the whip.

The usually timid boy refused. He stuffed the whip in his locker, slammed the door closed, and stood in front of it with his arms folded.

"Are either of you feeling anything unusual?" Unwilling to physically force a student to obey, Giles resorted to a less confrontational method: inquiry. "Headaches, nausea—"

"My wrist hurts," Jonathan said.

"That's because you keep snapping that whip at me!" Andrew's temper flared. "And I'm getting really tired of being shocked."

"Repeatedly?" Giles asked.

"Yeah." Andrew glared at Jonathan. "And it hurts worse every time."

Buffy left a message on her mom's voice mail, but she was positive it was too late. Her mother was a stickler for rules. She would have turned off her cell phone in the school. "I think she's already here, Giles. Come on."

Buffy saw her mom the instant she entered the cafeteria. She was helping Deirdre arrange the gallery pieces on the collectible table and, judging from the animated conversation, educating the girl on the histories and values. Hiding her dismay, Buffy smiled and waved.

Spotting her, Buffy's mom started to leave the table. Deirdre, however, still wanted her help and pulled her back.

Joyce shrugged and held up a finger, signaling Buffy that she'd break away as soon as she could.

Take your time, Mom, Buffy thought. In addition to the danger of contracting a creeping crud disease, having her mother around made being a fully functional Slayer harder.

"Hello, Mr. Giles," Ms. Calendar greeted him with a warm smile. "I'm surprised to see you here."

"You are? Why?" Giles asked, perplexed.

"We don't have any books with a copyright date older than 1943," she joked.

"You're not referring to a book published in 1943 by a Hungarian chap called—" Giles caught himself and coughed self-consciously. "Actually, I think it's important to support the student body in its charitable efforts."

"Yes, it is." Ms. Calendar smiled as they looked deep into each other's eyes.

Buffy nudged Giles to get him back on track. "Except certain student bodies are having a really bad day."

"What? Oh, yes." Giles drew Ms. Calendar over to the wall where they wouldn't be overheard.

It was 11:50, ten minutes before the sale opened. Housewives, retirees, and wealthy bargain hunters were probably already lined up at the building entrance Principal Snyder had designated for rummage sale use.

Buffy made a quick survey of the room as she moved aside with Giles and Ms. Calendar. As before, nothing seemed wrong at first glance. Willow was straightening the stacks of shirts. The blue scarf and a furry white thing—her illegal early sale acquisitions—were on the chair. Oz ran back in and hurried over to Xander at the music table. Devon either had blown them off or hadn't returned. Xander was wearing the camouflage vest. Michael Czajak was looking through everything on every table, still searching for his lost protection charm. As she watched, he jerked his hand out of a woman's handbag and put his thumb in his mouth, as though something sharp had stuck him.

Or bit him? Buffy wondered. Karl Torlette, a lanky basketball player, sat with his head in his hands. Traci Benedict was curled up in a donated reclining chair, asleep or unconscious.

Her sweeping Slayer gaze stopped on Principal Snyder. He still wore the hat, but he had taken off his shirt, shoes, and socks. Barefoot and bare-chested, he stood with several colorful and drab, narrow and wide ties hanging from his neck and arms. His movements were spastic, like a robot that had short-circuited and couldn't complete a command. A thin line of blood had dried on the skin in front of his ear.

"How sure are you about this?" Ms. Calendar asked Giles.

"I'm sure," Buffy said, interjecting her opinion into the discussion. "Something's not right."

"I wish we could be more specific," Giles added, "but until we know more, we should isolate the affected areas."

"A quarantine?" Ms. Calendar frowned. "The cafeteria or the whole school?"

"The whole school, I'm afraid," Giles said. "We don't know what it is, where it started, or how far it's spread. Will you contact the school office and have them post teachers at all the exits? No one can be allowed to enter or leave."

Ms. Calendar hesitated. "We can't tell the staff they might be infected with something. They'll panic."

"Excellent point." Giles ran his hand over his head and stared at the floor. "I might be able to conjure a ward to seal the building, to keep everyone inside in and everyone else out"—he looked up—"but it will take time."

"Just tell the teachers a rival school gang is loose in the building," Buffy suggested, "and Principal Snyder doesn't want them to get away before the cops arrive."

Giles nodded. "That might work temporarily."

Buffy glanced at the deranged principal. "And he won't contradict you."

"At least the sale hasn't started." Ms. Calendar spoke as she moved to the intraschool phone on the wall. "And I'd better call the Mayor. Maybe he hasn't left his office yet."

With the initial emergency response implemented, Buffy's thoughts focused on her mother. So far the evidence suggested that the unknown bad thing was probably connected to the sale donations. The gallery items hadn't been inside the school when the first symptoms erupted. Her mom might not be infected—yet. No one could leave the school, but her mother would be safer in the library.

Xander came up as Buffy turned to go get her.

"The vest looks good on you," Buffy said.

"It's a little tight, but I'm afraid to take it off."

"For what reason?" Giles asked.

"If I put it down"—Xander looked at Buffy—"*someone* might hide it as a childish act of revenge."

"Let's just call it even, okay?" Buffy didn't want to be distracted by silly, adolescent games. "We've got other things to worry about."

"Right," Xander agreed. "Like Willow."

"Willow?" Buffy's heart lurched with alarm. "What's wrong with Willow?"

"Her personality's taken a distinctly nasty turn." Xander tugged on the sides of the zippered vest, trying to loosen it. "She's turned into a supershrew, just like that Kate lady in the play."

Giles looked stunned. "You're familiar with *The Taming of the Shrew* by William Shakespeare?"

"We read it in class," Xander said. "I even took notes, for pointers on how to deal with Cordelia—and other shrewish females, like Willow the raging maniac."

"She's raging?" Buffy frowned.

"Truth." Xander mimicked a shrill female voice. "'Get away from my cute thing!'"

Buffy looked at Xander askance. "What thing?"

"Some weird stuffed animal she found." Xander shook his head, bewildered and upset. "She calls it Cutie."

"Oh, dear." Giles squinted, his gaze riveted on Willow. She

was sitting in the chair again, rocking with the blue scarf and fuzzy thing. "I don't believe that's a toy."

"What else could it be?" Xander asked.

"Not a myth, as most scholars have assumed." Giles was suddenly a torrent of information. "It's a *kur*, a lesser creature indigenous to the Hellmouth—a demonic rat, so to speak."

"Hellmouth rats are white, furry, and adorable?" Buffy asked. The concept was difficult to process.

"Apparently, yes," Giles said. "Every ecological system has lower life forms that support the higher ones, and it's been hypothesized that the Hellmouth is no exception."

"And demons eat cute things like treats." The disgusting idea made Buffy cringe. During one of his dire warnings, Angel had let slip that demons craved kittens.

"Will it eat Willow?" Xander asked, aghast.

"No, but"—Giles jumped right into lecture mode, but this time Buffy was all ears—"such a creature would be completely defenseless in any environment without a protector. The kur establishes a psychic link with a stronger being, who becomes obsessively protective of it. It's a remarkable, if somewhat insidious, survival mechanism."

"That explains why Willow almost bit my head off—verbally speaking," Xander said. "But how did a Hellmouth rat get into the Sunnydale High School cafeteria?"

"We've got more than Hellmouth rats," Buffy pointed out. "Whatever's eating Cordelia's teeth and Principal Snyder's head are not cute and cuddly."

"I'm sure," Giles agreed. "If a kur breached the barrier, then we can assume that other varieties of Hellmouth pests did as well."

"And infested the rummage sale items we stored in the basement," Buffy concluded. "So is this the mystical convergence, only-a-matter-of-time, fresh hell breaking loose you warned me about?"

"It's not a manifestation I anticipated, but yes, that would describe it," Giles said.

Ms. Calendar entered just in time to catch the last few comments. "The school's locked down, but did I hear you correctly? We've got a Hellmouth infestation?"

"Evil bugs and other assorted lowlifes," Xander said.

"But we closed the Hellmouth," Ms. Calendar reminded them. "How could anything get out?"

"Closed, yes, but the barrier must have been weakened when the Master was released," Giles said. "Apparently, it leaks—just enough to let the vermin through."

Buffy stole a glance at her mother. She was still with Deirdre by the gallery boxes and showing no signs of disease or distress.

A shrill scream echoed in the hallway.

"Sounds like somebody looked in the mirror," Buffy said.

Cordelia burst through the doors. Her strawlike hair stood straight up, forming a scarecrow halo around her head. Her front teeth were almost entirely black. Wild-eyed and in shock, she stopped in front of Giles and held out her hand.

"They—they just . . . fell off." Several fingernails lay in Cordelia's palm. They had turned to brown mush embedded with bits of pink polish.

Giles turned to Buffy and Ms. Calendar. "I'll go see about casting the spell to seal the building. Let's just hope nothing has escaped the school."

"None of the sale items were taken out, so we're probably good on that," Buffy observed.

"We'll find out soon enough," Giles said.

"Teachers are covering all the doors to make sure no one leaves or comes in," Ms. Calendar reported. "They didn't question the gang story, and they're telling everyone the sale opening will be delayed until the police apprehend the troublemakers. I doubt many people will wait long."

"Disappointment is infinitely preferable to mystical disease," Giles observed drily. "Once the binding spell is active, nothing will be able to exit or enter. In the meantime, it would be wise to move everyone with symptoms into an isolation ward. We may be too late to stop the spread within the school, but every precaution must be taken."

"We'll take care of it," Ms. Calendar said.

"Is middle-age weight gain catching?" Xander pulled on the edge of the camouflage fabric around his waist. "I'm gaining weight just standing here."

Spike stood with his back against the door. He didn't know how long they'd been under siege in the storeroom, but their ordeal was far from over. When he'd cracked the door to look out ten minutes back, a sentry bat had almost forced its way in. The other red beasts were hanging from pipes and rafters, taking a nap while they waited for their cornered prey to emerge. The bats had the advantage.

He also had to make sure Dru didn't get out.

A potential ally of the bats, Drusilla huddled in the corner, staring at him with a vampire's yellow eyes. However, the heavy bone that formed her demonic brow was receding. Scalloped ridges were forming in her ears, which had elongated into large, triangular shapes. Her fangs glistened against the bloodred interior of her mouth, and her nose had flattened.

In a bizarre twist of fate, his beautiful Drusilla was being transformed into one of the beasts that had bitten her.

"I smell fresh blood all packaged nice, like in tender teenagers," Drusilla snarled. "But she's in the cave with them, all shrouded in a dark where I can't see."

Spike assumed she was referring to Buffy. The Slayer's powerful presence befuddled Dru's senses, but he had no doubt the girl was nearby. She was always in the middle of it when mystical mayhem erupted, and something dreadful had gotten all bollixed up.

Vampires turned people into vampires. They did not get turned into bats.

"See that, now." Dru held up her arm and touched the leathery skin flap that connected her elbow and ribs. They were growing on both sides, expanding to form membranes between her wrists and ankles. "Feathers wilt if the sparrow doesn't fly, and now she has naked wings."

Spike's dead heart broke for her. She was stalked by many irrational fears in her mad mind, worrying that her hair might fall out or that she'd fade out of existence. He felt guilty now for being impatient with her crazed concerns, even though he usually suppressed it. She had once fretted that her long nails would turn into talons, but she had never imagined this.

"Your darling Dru wants her dinner, Spike." Dru's words slurred slightly as her mouth and chin began to change into a short snout.

Logic was all too often beyond Dru's ability to comprehend when she was her daft and vicious self. Spike doubted his reasoning about anything would make sense to the animal personality asserting control. He tried nonetheless, more to work things out in his own mind than to convince Dru.

"Well, here's the rub about feeding," Spike said. "First, all your cousins are hanging between us and a way out of here. We can't get upstairs or out the hatch into the tunnels."

A look of total terror widened Dru's eyes. "The wretched li'l munchers have eaten the basket!"

"It's by your foot," Spike said calmly, "under your skirt."

Frantic, Dru clawed at the fabric with fingers that had fused together. When she uncovered the basket, she hooked her hand through the handle and heaved it toward Spike.

The basket smashed against the door a few inches from

Spike's head, and the contents spilled when it hit the floor. He didn't flinch. A sudden move might trigger an attack, and he wanted to save Dru, not kill her to save himself.

Dru's fit of temper passed. Crawling forward, she mumbled as she collected her treasures. "I can hear Miss Edith laughing, making fun of Mummy, all elbows and knees. There'll be no bedtime torture for her tonight, and no songs until someone fetches a mouse."

There won't be any prey today, Spike thought, *unless she wants to foul her fangs on four-legged rodents.* Students and faculty were off the menu until he figured out how to counter the poison in her system. The demonic world had a plethora of bad omens and cautionary tales, but in all his travels he had never heard a word about red bats with vampirelike venom in their bite. It followed that a cure, if one existed, might have to come from the good guys.

The Slayer and the librarian were his only hope for making Dru better. Killing anyone in the school would end his chances of getting their help.

"Is that everyone?" Giles asked as he joined Buffy and Ms. Calendar outside the cafeteria. The double-size classroom across the hall was serving as a triage area and infirmary for the afflicted. Sale volunteers who hadn't exhibited any symptoms were isolated in the next room down.

"Everyone who's got something that can't be missed," Ms. Calendar said.

Not quite everyone, Buffy thought, glancing down the hall. Xander and her mother were pleading with Cordelia to come out of the utility closet. Harmony was still hiding in the restroom. As long as they stayed locked away, neither girl would pass their Hellmouth afflictions on to anyone else. Willow had shrieked, then held her breath until she turned blue when they had asked her to leave Cutie behind. She had stayed in the cafeteria, content to hold Cutie and rock. The white kur seemed to be the only one of its kind that had made it through the barrier. At least, they hadn't discovered any others.

"How bad off are they, do you think?" Giles asked.

"I'm really worried about Principal Snyder," Ms. Calendar said. "Buffy's assessment was accurate. He actually does have holes in his head."

Buffy glanced through the classroom door. Principal Snyder lay on his back across three student desks that had been pushed together. His mental capacity had undergone several downgrades in a couple of hours, from foolish to imbecilic to catatonic. The hat had been removed and put into a kitchen trash can along with everything else they knew was a source of pestilence. However, they didn't know if they had found everything or if the contagions could be controlled.

"Possibly some kind of brain bore," Giles muttered, studying the comatose principal from the doorway.

Ms. Calendar took exception to Giles's pragmatic tone. "All these people are going to die if we don't find a way to fix this."

"Then we'll fix it." Buffy's confident attitude was all bravado. She didn't want to admit that she felt overwhelmed by the task.

Killing one huge scary thing was a lot easier than trying to identify and combat a hundred little demon thingies. A lot of the creepy critters were microscopic and invisible to the naked eye. There could be a thousand or a million different Hellmouth bugs crawling around the school. One magickal bug bomb or an enchanted fly swatter probably couldn't exterminate all of them.

"What do we do now?" Ms. Calendar asked.

"Back to the library for me," Giles said. "Assuming the binding spell was successful, it will keep everything locked in—"

"And everyone else locked out?" Buffy didn't want to add police and other municipal officials to the list of pests she had to deal with.

"The Mayor agreed to honor the quarantine," Ms. Calendar said. "I told him we could be dealing with food poisoning or a highly contagious plague."

"The plague of a zillion wee beasties," Buffy said.

"Which we have to kill or neutralize." Giles turned to leave, then stepped back. "We should probably isolate Willow and the kur. Tell her I need help with some computer research in the library."

"You're not worried she'll smash the screen and then rip your head off?" Buffy asked.

"She seems to function normally as long as her furry friend feels safe," Giles said. "If you don't threaten the kur, I'm sure she'll agree to help. In light of that, it probably wouldn't be a good idea to reveal that her new pet came from the Hellmouth."

"Don't mention that Cutie's a demon rat. Got it." Buffy paused, bracing herself. She wasn't sure how to handle Willow if she became violent.

"I realize there's a good chance of becoming infected yourself," Giles said to Ms. Calendar, "but these children need attention. Would you—"

"Stay with them? Of course," Ms. Calendar said. There was no question that she would do whatever was necessary.

"Me too." Joyce walked up, smiling through her worry and stress. "Since we're quarantined, I might as well make myself useful."

Buffy didn't even consider trying to talk her mom out of helping Ms. Calendar. Joyce Summers never turned her back on people in trouble, and Buffy knew she wouldn't start now. On the plus side, her mom didn't seem to be breaking out with a corrosive microbe infection. *At least, one that I can see,* she reminded herself.

"How are you feeling, Mom?"

"I'm fine." Joyce smiled to reassure Buffy and turned to Giles. "Do they have any idea why so many kids are getting sick?"

"They?" Giles frowned, forgetting for a moment that Joyce Summers wasn't in the Slayer loop.

"The medical authorities in charge." Joyce turned to Ms. Calendar with an irritated expression. "Do you have any hand lotion? I've had dry, chapped hands before, but never like this. The itch is driving me crazy."

Giles and Ms. Calendar both looked at Buffy.

Buffy was focused on the large flakes of paper-thin skin peeling off her mom's hand and drifting to the floor. *Not just unsightly dandruff and an itch,* she thought. Some of the other conditions had seemed harmless at first too. Considering how those were progressing, her mom could shed enough skin to expose the muscle. If that happened, the pain would be excruciating, and death would be a blessed relief.

"I have some cream in my desk," Ms. Calendar told Joyce. "It's an herbal blend, an old family recipe I make myself. I'll send one of the boys to get it."

"Thank you." Joyce glanced at Buffy, frowning with maternal concern. "Do you have any symptoms, Buffy?"

"No." Buffy answered honestly. Her mother, however, didn't seem to realize that she was being skinned alive, like an onion—one layer at a time. "But I don't think a cream is going to—"

"Go help Willow, Buffy," Ms. Calendar interjected. Her gaze was as commanding as her teacher tone. "We'll take care of things here."

"The sooner all the *medical authorities* are on the job," Giles added pointedly, "the sooner the afflictions can be cured. I'll be in the library."

Message received, Buffy thought as Giles hurried away. The best way to help her mom and the stricken students was to get the Scooby medics moving. "I'll, uh, go see Willow."

The deserted cafeteria reminded Buffy of a movie ghost town—everything had been left in place when the people suddenly or mysteriously vanished. The carefully collected, sorted, and priced merchandise waited for shoppers who wouldn't come. The cash box on the table near the door sat unattended and in no danger of being stolen. Nobody wanted money that would burn a hole in a pocket, then eat through flesh and bone. It all seemed so normal, except for the quiet and the bright orange six-legged lizard that crawled out of a mug of cold coffee.

Buffy headed down the center aisle toward Willow, taking care not to touch anything. When she arrived, Willow watched her warily, waiting for her to make the first move.

"Giles needs you in the library," Buffy said lightly.

"Why?" Willow eyed her with undisguised suspicion.

"For the same reason he always needs you," Buffy said. "You're the computer genius. *I* don't have a clue how to track down some weird evil disease on the information highway."

"A disease?" Willow perked up, intrigued. "Like demon pox or monster measles or fiend flu? That kind of disease?"

"That's pretty close, actually. Giles thinks Principal Snyder has brain bores."

"That can't be good." Willow shuddered at the gruesome thought.

"It's not. So come on. Grab your stuff and let's go." As she walked away, Buffy sensed Willow's hesitation, but she didn't look back. Willow's indecision only lasted a moment and she ran to catch up.

"If there are demon germs, are there demon doctors?" Willow clutched the blue scarf close to her chest. Curls of white fur gave away the kur hidden inside.

"Good question. I don't know, but Giles might." Buffy saw the furry rat watching her from the corner of her eye, sizing her up or trying to gauge her intent. Since being discovered might prompt Cutie to engage its defenses—a.k.a. Willow—she pretended not to notice it.

"Why is Xander talking to a door?" Willow asked as they stepped into the hall.

"He's talking to Cordelia," Buffy clarified. "She won't come out. I wouldn't either if I was turning into compost."

"That doesn't sound good either," Willow said as they drew closer. She pulled the edge of the scarf up to hide a tuft of Cutie's white fur. "Giles needs the search-and-research team in the library, Xander. Coming?"

Buffy stood behind Willow, ready to signal Xander to ignore the little beast. However, his thoughts were solely on Cordelia.

"Can't." Xander shrugged an apology. "I don't want to leave Cordelia alone while she disintegrates into a disgusting heap of demon decay."

Willow frowned. "I know Cordelia is mean and insulting

and selfish, but if she's sick, you probably shouldn't gloat."

"I'm not gloating," Xander explained. "Would you kiss a mush mouth?"

"Why do you care about Cordelia's rotting romantic appeal?" Buffy asked. Had he contracted a vigilance virus that compelled him to watch his tormentor suffer and maybe die?

"I don't! It's just that . . ." Xander squirmed uncomfortably. "Cordelia may be rich and conceited and convinced she's better than everyone else, but she doesn't deserve this."

"Yeah, I know," Buffy agreed with a wan smile. Despite his tough talk and the justifiable grudges Xander harbored against Cordelia Chase, he would never wish her harm.

"Are you okay?" Willow asked.

"Nothing a no-doughnut diet won't fix," Xander quipped.

Willow scowled. "Did you have doughnuts today? And you didn't bring me one?"

"We'll be in the library if you need us, Xander." Buffy moved out, waving Willow to follow.

When they walked through the library doors, Giles was beside himself with exasperation. "There you are! It's about time, which we don't have much of, according to my calculations."

Buffy and Willow exchanged a glance as he picked up a yellow pad and adjusted his glasses to read. Giles was so intensely dedicated to his duty as the Slayer's Watcher that he didn't realize he took Buffy and her friends' presence for granted. They got annoyed, got over it, and got to work.

"What calculations?" Buffy asked.

"Based on the observable progression of the various disorders, everyone in the school could be dead by dawn—or permanently scarred." Giles stole a glance at Willow. "Physically or mentally."

"That bad, huh?" Buffy's stomach churned with anxiety. "How do I fight bacteria from hell? We can't get a prescription for an antibiotic from the demon drugstore. I mean, I can probably catch the orange lizard with a cup of coffee, but I can't catch what I can't see."

"Unless you catch an evil illness," Willow said. She sat down and put Cutie and the scarf on her lap. When she pulled the chair closer to the study table, the kur was hidden from view.

Buffy focused on Giles. "I can't take out a fungus with a crossbow or stake a swarm of gnats. So what am I supposed to do?"

"Until I find a remedy, which I am determined to do," Giles said calmly, "it might be a good idea to keep an eye on things at our makeshift infirmary, in the event a creature you *can* see shows itself. I doubt that all the intruders have found victims."

"That works." Buffy accepted the assignment with a definitive sense of relief. However, she intended to take the plan one step further to include a patrol of the school. She was the Slayer. She hunted and killed bad things. It would not go well for any Hellmouth pest that crossed her path.

• • •

"Do you need anything, Willow?" Giles lifted the stack of books he had selected and paused, waiting for a response.

He tried to sound casual, which was difficult when his every move was being tracked by dark, demonic eyes. Part of the kur's face was visible in the gap between Willow and the table.

"I'm about to make a pot of tea," Giles added.

"No, thanks. It'll take a while to check out everything you gave me." Willow flashed an innocent smile, which was familiar yet not to be trusted while she was under Cutie's demonic influence.

"I'll be in my office, then," Giles said, "doing some research in the texts."

"I hope you have more luck than I'm having," Willow said. "I haven't found a single reference to these source words anywhere online."

"Yes, well—persevere." Balancing the books against his chest, Giles entered his office and kicked the door closed. He set the stack down, turned on the kettle, and sank into his desk chair.

He'd be quite surprised if Willow's searches turned up a result. The words he had supplied were meaningless, intended as busy work to keep her in the practically deserted library where the kur would feel secure—he hoped. The animal was only a threat if it felt threatened, and Giles could only guess what it would construe as a danger. He had no doubt that

Willow would kill to protect it, and he didn't have any spells to save her from the mortal world's justice system. Preventing an incident was the best way to protect her. Of all the creatures that had breached the barrier, he suspected the cute beast might prove to be the most dangerous, and perhaps the most difficult to dispose of.

While he waited for the water to boil, Giles shuffled through the books. Finding a means of eliminating the Hellmouth pests and curing the maladies was only one of the problems confounding him. Months had passed since the Master had breached the barrier, and no underworld animal life had broken through—until today. Something had driven them to leave their supernatural environment, but what?

The question nagged, but the health of the students was the priority. With nothing to go on but rational conjecture, Giles had formulated a theory utilizing the principles of scientific method.

Presented with solid evidence, Giles had established that a pyramid of lower to higher life forms existed within the Hellmouth. Every ecological system required balance to be self-sustaining, but no system was perfect. Human use of modern technology over a hundred years had altered the natural balance of the planet. Consequently, unnatural practices had to be instituted to offset the ecological disruptions. Logically, he could conclude that the Hellmouth operated on a similar premise.

Where there were pests, there had to be something to control them.

Buffy was a good example. As had the generations of Slayers before her, she kept vampires and other demonic entities from taking over the world. Without the girls who were chosen and trained to assume that responsibility, humanity would have long been extinct.

Or kept and raised as cattle to satisfy demonic appetites, Giles thought as he poured hot water into his cup.

Preferring the breakfast blends strongly brewed, Giles carried the tea to his desk to let it steep. He smiled as he sat down, pleased with the intensity of Buffy's desire to take action. The infestation *did* present unusual circumstances the Slayer couldn't combat with the weapons in her arsenal, and her frustration was understandable. Sending Buffy off on a vermin search-and-destroy mission amounted to Slayer busywork, an activity to keep her from feeling too restless.

Giles opened a volume that a monk had penned during the Dark Ages. *The Bestiary of Hell* had long been viewed as a fanciful work of macabre fiction. Even so, there were theories that during the centuries between 500 and 1000 A.D., the fabric between the mortal realm and the underworld may have been exceptionally porous. *Could it have leaked, allowing small demonic animals to escape?* Giles wondered as he checked the index. One of the illustrations answered the question.

The kur sitting on Willow's lap was an exact match for a beast staring at him from the page.

The odds that a monk would accurately imagine a kur without having seen one or heard an eyewitness report were astronomical. Given evidence that Hellmouth vermin had breached the barrier thirteen centuries before, Giles could safely deduce that all those invading beasties had been destroyed or sent back. Spurred by hope, he turned the pages quickly, perusing each entry and moving on to the next, looking for the solution.

He found the answer on the last page, where the documenting monk had recorded his firsthand experience.

Higher forces within the Hellmouth had empowered a lower-level demon to control pests. All Hellmouth animal entities were compelled to follow Pragoh when he called. In addition, the poisons, infectious agents, and other noxious effects the creatures spread were neutralized when the carriers fled. With the exception of those who had already died, victims were cured.

Pragoh was in essence a pied piper who might already be in the school tracking down the Hellmouth escapees. The relief Giles felt was quickly curbed by the thought of Buffy. The demon demon-hunter was the only means of saving the school and everyone in it—if Pragoh didn't encounter Buffy first!

CHAPTER FIVE

Buffy was only mildly concerned for Giles's safety. The Watcher was educated in the ways and wiles of evil beings and was always vigilant. He knew the danger Willow and the kur presented and wouldn't provoke them. Her mother, on the other hand, was oblivious to the danger she faced.

At least, she was the last time I saw her, Buffy thought, breaking into a jog. If her mom's skin was peeling faster or coming off in thicker layers, she would be panicked and in terrible pain now. Postponing a patrol of the halls, Buffy went straight to the infirmary room from the library, passing Xander on the way. He was still sitting in the hall by the utility closet, but he was no longer trying to coax Cordelia out. He told Buffy that she had stopped talking.

"Can't or won't talk?" Buffy asked.

"Hard to say. She sounded better when I mentioned that she could wear professional fake nails until her own nails grew back out," Xander explained. "But she started crying when I said that implants look just like real teeth."

"Toothless grin would not be an image Cordelia could handle," Buffy observed.

"Me either." Xander gripped his stomach.

Buffy studied him closely. "Are you sick?"

"Nothing a rigorous exercise routine won't cure," Xander said. "Which I plan to start first thing tomorrow."

Buffy doubted Xander would follow through, but it wouldn't matter if they didn't survive today.

The infirmary was a madhouse of chaos and calm. Some of the students had fallen into comas. Others displayed varying degrees of emotional and physical trauma, depending on their ailments. Girls and boys sobbed, threw fits, or writhed with seizures. A few were in shock and just stared at the floor, walls, or ceiling. Michael Czajak was curled up on the floor with his eyes closed. Two teachers had been admitted, one with uncontrollable coughing. Mrs. Monroe had purple hives growing in huge clumps all over her body.

Buffy's gaze settled on her mother, who was sitting with Karl, the weepy basketball player. The boy's eyes were sunken and his face gaunt. Joyce's hands were tucked out of sight in her folded arms. Buffy crossed the room to confer with Ms. Calendar. The teacher wouldn't try to soften the blow of difficult news.

Ms. Calendar stood over Principal Snyder's makeshift bed. The first extraordinary anomaly that struck Buffy was his peaceful smile. Despite the worms sticking out of the honeycombed holes in his hairless head, the characteristically cranky man looked happy.

"Gross." Buffy choked back the bile that rose in her throat. The irony of her reaction was not lost on her. She could face and fight hideously vile vampires and demons, but the sight of little green worms with razor-sharp mandibles boring through bone into a man's brain made her queasy.

"The stuff of nightmares," Ms. Calendar said.

Principal Snyder giggled.

Buffy noted the slimy pink secretions on the tiny worm teeth. "They must be injecting him with joy juice."

"Must be," Ms. Calendar agreed. "Or having your brain consumed by minimonsters tickles."

"Too bad the happy side effects will probably kill him," Buffy quipped, then turned serious. "You haven't gotten too close to them, have you?"

"Absolutely not," Ms. Calendar said, appalled. "But proximity might not be a problem. I've noticed that no two people have developed identical symptoms."

"That's good, isn't it?" Buffy asked.

"If people aren't passing their infections on to other

people, yes—very good. It would mean that once a Hellmouth parasite or disease finds a host, it's content to stay put. I should probably call Giles."

"I would," Buffy said. "How's my mom doing?"

"Not too badly so far." Ms. Calendar glanced toward Joyce. "I made her give up a pair of lace gloves she found at the sale. She told me she had tried them on."

"And exposed herself to the Hellmouth horror that's stripping away her skin." Buffy sighed.

"That's not your fault," Ms. Calendar said.

Buffy wasn't sure that was true. She couldn't protect everybody from everything all the time, but she had known her mom was coming to the school, and she had promised to help unload the car. If she had been there, maybe her mother would have left immediately and avoided the contamination.

Bobby Farrow walked up. "Here's that stuff you wanted, Ms. Calendar." He handed her a small, wide-mouth jar and the key to the computer classroom. He left quickly.

Ms. Calendar gave Buffy the jar. "This is just an ordinary herbal balm. It won't cure the infection, but it might relieve your mom's itch."

Buffy walked over to her mom, trying not to jostle the teenage patients and wishing she could mute the moans and sobs. Few knew the true nature of the enemy, and somehow that made the misery more heart wrenching.

The school nurse and two other healthy teachers had pitched in to staff the sickroom. Like her mom, they probably assumed that an official disease-control agency had been contacted and that medical help would arrive soon. They didn't know their fate was in the hands of a librarian and two teenage girls.

Buffy paused by Michael, who blocked the aisle. He was still in a fetal position and appeared to be asleep, but he didn't seem to be in pain. She stepped over him.

"Buffy! Sit down." Her mom patted the empty desk chair beside her.

"Here's Ms. Calendar's skin cream." Buffy held out the jar. When her mother didn't reach for it, she set it down. "How are you doing?"

"Better than this poor boy." Joyce's voice was filled with pity for Karl. His closed eyelids were as depressed as his cheeks, covering empty sockets. "He couldn't stop crying, and now he's completely dehydrated."

Buffy averted her gaze and touched the jar. "This might help your itch."

"I hope so. I think it's spreading." Joyce leaned in, speaking softly. "Ms. Calendar took these beautiful black lace gloves I wanted to buy. Your great-grandmother had a pair just like them."

"All the sale stuff is probably contaminated," Buffy explained. That wasn't a lie. She just didn't mention the demonic origins part.

"You seem to be okay." Joyce looked relieved.

"So far," Buffy said. She hadn't touched any of the rummage sale donations since last night. "Look, I've got to go. I just wanted to make—"

"Go?" Joyce looked surprised. "I thought you'd stay here and help. There aren't enough staff volunteers, and all these kids are suffering so much."

"I will be helping, Mom. Just not here." Buffy knew that sounded lame, but telling the truth wasn't an option. "Try the cream."

Joyce picked up the jar, but her fingers were so raw she couldn't twist the lid off.

"Here, I'll do that." Buffy reached out, but her mom pulled the jar back.

"I'll get it," Joyce said. "You go on and do whatever it is you think you have to do."

Buffy stood up, ignoring the hint of accusation in her mother's tone. The strangling sound of acute respiratory distress diverted their attention.

Ms. Calendar raced over to Mrs. Monroe, the teacher stricken with hives. The woman was covered with masses of purple welts and mounds. She heaved, wheezing and struggling for air.

"The hives are blocking her nose," the nurse said.

Ms. Calendar tried to force the teacher's mouth open. "Her mouth is swollen with welts. They're blocking off her airways!"

The nurse pulled a ballpoint pen out of her pocket. "I've never done an emergency tracheotomy before, but—"

Mrs. Monroe gagged and convulsed.

Buffy watched as the nurse tried to drive the pen into the teacher's bulging flesh. She couldn't pierce the skin.

"The hives are choking her from the inside," Ms. Calendar announced with commendable calm. "They're clogging her throat. There's nothing we can do."

"There must be something," the nurse objected.

"You can stand back," Ms. Calendar said. "No one must touch her after . . . she's gone."

"We can't just leave her here!" the nurse protested.

"You can if you don't want to die the same way," Ms. Calendar said bluntly. "The hives weren't a threat while she was alive, but chances are they'll be looking for a new victim after she dies. If so, they'll move to whoever touches her first."

The nurse quickly stepped back.

Buffy's chest constricted as she watched. There wasn't anything she could do to save the woman either, and it tore her apart.

So I'll just have to save the day, she thought as she hurried out. Patrolling would restore her sense of being in control, of doing something useful, of fighting back. She turned toward the cafeteria, setting her sights on the six-legged coffee lizard.

Halfway across the corridor, Andrew almost bowled her over. Thrown off balance, Buffy stumbled but stayed on her feet.

Andrew ducked behind her, using her as a shield. "He's trying to kill me!"

Jonathan barreled down the corridor toward them, cracking the bullwhip and laughing maniacally. As he closed in, he drew the whip back.

"Oh no, you don't!" Xander sprang to his feet and lunged at Jonathan, intending to tackle and take him down.

Surprisingly faster and more nimble, Jonathan jumped clear. He snapped the whip, striking Xander.

Xander collapsed to his knees, his torso and arms shaking violently.

"Hurts like hell, doesn't it?" Andrew yelled.

"That's not simple static buildup," Buffy observed as Jonathan drew back to hit Xander again.

"Static electricity doesn't pack a million volts," Andrew said. "And the shocks get stronger every time Jonathan snaps that whip. He's working his way up to electrocution."

"Xander!" Buffy shouted a warning. "Look out!"

"Yeehaw!" Jonathan let the rawhide fly.

Xander came to his senses and scrambled aside, narrowly escaping the lash.

"Stop it, Jonathan!" Buffy was sure the boy's zealous whip-snappy compulsion was being fueled by another Hellmouth culprit. She didn't want to hurt the kid, but she couldn't let his electric reign of terror continue unchecked. "I mean it!"

"I don't care!" Delirious with power, Jonathan flipped the whip back and snapped it toward her.

Buffy snatched the thong out of the air, breaking the momentum of the lash. However, that didn't stop the electrical jolt that sizzled through her, zapping every nerve and muscle in her body. Unlike Xander, she had the Slayer's healing capacity and quickly recovered from the massive shock.

The eel-like critter twined around the dangling strip of thin leather caught Buffy's attention. She held on to the heavier part of the whip and yanked the handle out of Jonathan's grasp, wrapping a loop of leather around the base of the eel's head and pulling on both ends.

The creature uncoiled from the thong and twisted, trying to get away from Buffy's leather stranglehold. Blue-white electrical bolts and red sparks crackled and spewed out of its round mouth. A series of shocks shot through Buffy's hands and arms, each one diminishing in intensity. When the eel's energy was spent, she gave a final tug and severed the blackened head from the elongated body.

For a moment Buffy and the three boys stared at the dead parts on the floor.

"What's that?" Jonathan asked, bewildered. "Where am I? What's happening?"

As Buffy started to explain, Andrew grabbed the whip out of her hand.

"Take my advice, Jonathan." Andrew grinned with evil intent. "Run!"

Jonathan's big brown eyes got bigger when Andrew snapped the bullwhip. He turned and ran.

"Get him, Andrew!" Rubbing his arms to restore the circulation, Xander watched the boys skid and disappear around a corner. "Are there any more of those living electrical sockets hanging around?"

"Actually, I saw a tiny one come out of the leather and wrap itself around the cracker just before Andrew grabbed the whip. But on the bright side, one down and who knows how many gazillion to go," Buffy said.

"That many?" Xander looked up and down the corridor as he moved back to the utility room door.

"At least," Buffy teased. She wanted Xander to stay put. No place in the school was safe from airborne microbes or other too-tiny-to-see pests. But if something larger came down the deserted corridor, he'd have a chance to escape. "And at my current critter-slaying rate, it'll take a few centuries to kill them all, so wish me good hunting!"

"Centuries?" Xander asked anxiously. "You mean hours, right? Or maybe a couple of days?"

Waving over her shoulder, Buffy ducked into the restroom. Despite her lack of symptoms, she reminded herself that she could be infected with something that took longer to disable its victim. If not, just being in the school put her at risk. Still, she had to proceed as though it was possible to stay vermin-free. Paper towels were handy and might protect her if she had to touch something in the cafeteria.

Before she touched the paper towels, Buffy leaned over to check on Harmony's condition.

The blond girl was lying on the floor in the stall, but Buffy couldn't tell how deep the wrinkles had gotten. A lacy network of pink and green fibers grew out of the creases that covered her face. *But they won't be looking for a new host just yet,* Buffy thought as she stuffed paper towels in the waistband of her skirt. Harmony was still breathing.

Buffy's spirits improved as she entered the cafeteria. Throttling the sparks out of the electric eel made her feel less like a helpless bystander and more like an empowered warrior. That feeling only lasted until she saw a flash of orange zoom past a black orb near Cordelia's jewelry display. She was hunting animals that acted on fight or flight instincts, not cunning evil intellects with major reps in the underworld. She had been demoted to Demonic Lizard Slayer.

For the moment only, Buffy thought as she used a paper towel to grip the handle of Ms. Calendar's coffee mug. She didn't know if cold coffee would work as bait, but it was worth a try.

Buffy moved slowly past the table that held the gallery donations, looking around, under, and behind all the collectibles and antiques. Her gaze swept over the black orb the lizard had darted by then zipped right back. Most black things had tinges of color or weren't even black, but shades of very dark browns. The space occupied by the black orb looked like a bottomless hole in the table. She stared at the piece, reminded of the day her dad had taken her to Lancaster to see the stealth fighter fly. The plane was so black, it had created a similar optical illusion, like a hole in the sky. The fascinating darkness of the orb drew her in.

Something sticky touched her arm, snapping Buffy out of her daze. She inhaled slightly but didn't jerk her hand out from under the little lizard. She had no idea how the beast had climbed up without her noticing.

Only the orange lizard's back two legs touched her skin. Its middle two feet were stuck to the side of the coffee mug, and the front two feet gripped the rim. It lapped cold coffee with a tiny black tongue. Buffy's first impulse was to smash the creature. However, she didn't want to risk being burned by acid blood or poisoned by a toxin that seeped through the skin. Catch and then kill was a more prudent plan.

She glanced at the cloisonné pot someone had wanted for poodle ashes. It had a lid and could contain the lizard until she decided what to do with it. As she reached for the urn, her eyes were drawn back to the black sphere. She remembered how her attention had been absorbed by the darkness, and she forced herself to look away. The orb had to be a Hellmouth hazard too. Its hypnotic effect had certainly proved more dangerous than the lizard with a taste for liquid caffeine.

Since she could bait and catch the lizard again, Buffy wiggled her hand out from under its sticky feet. She expected it to run, but it clamped its back feet to the side of the mug and kept drinking.

Using a fresh paper towel, Buffy picked up the black ball, but she did not look at it. She threw it hard against the wall, and ducked to avoid the fallout. There was no explosion when the piece shattered, and nothing liquid or gaseous was released in the shower of splinters and fragments.

She was, however, astonished that the lizard had not been scared off the coffee mug.

"You won't sleep a wink tonight," Buffy quipped. She wished there was a way to get rid of the little guy without killing it. But in her Slayer soul, she knew that wasn't possible. The lizard didn't seem to pose a threat, but she couldn't assume that it was harmless. "It's the dog-coffin pot for you, I'm afraid."

As Buffy reached for the urn, the lizard suddenly raised its head. A ridge of collapsed black scales along its back stood straight up. Then it leaped off the table and zoomed away at lizard hyperspeed.

Buffy hesitated. The creature couldn't have known she was about to trap it . . . or could it? Had it established a psychic link with her the way the kur had with Willow? If so, the connection wasn't very strong. She had absolutely no desire to chase after it. She had other Hellmouth invaders to track down and eliminate.

"At least I have to try," Buffy muttered as she started a quick tour of the cafeteria. She didn't flush out anything that slithered, scampered, or flew, but she caught sight of an orange flash every now and then. Armed with paper towels, she was careful not to touch anything, and she wasn't exhibiting strange symptoms when she left the sale area and headed down the hall. Every critter that needed a victim had either found one or gone in search of one. There was, she was certain, no chance that pests without hosts would simply die, like 1950s-movie Martians. Sunnydale luck wouldn't allow such an easy solution.

Having come up empty in the cafeteria, the next likely place to look was the basement, where the contamination had started.

Buffy cautiously eased through the access door. Midway down the stairs, she paused when she heard the staccato beat of many padded feet. *Or wings,* Buffy realized. She bent over just in time to see a slew of large red bats fly down the wide corridor and disappear around a corner.

Then she noticed the odd, flickering crack in the basement wall. The area around the crack shimmered as a dwarf-size demon squeezed through.

That's what happens when you have a leaky Hellmouth barrier, Buffy thought as she studied the new intruder.

The demon was roughly forty inches tall with stubby arms and legs. Splotches of green and black, similar to Xander's camouflage vest, mottled its leathery gray skin, and large black scaly plates protected its chest and groin. Two tapering horns curved back from a face that reminded Buffy of a pug. The beady eyes were deep set under a ridged brow above a black flattened nose. Twin canine fangs pointed upward from a jutting lower jaw and extended past its upper lip.

Buffy watched, wondering what it wanted. The red bats, like the kur and the orange lizard, were larger than most of the icky things that had escaped the Hellmouth. Was the ugly guy just another animal, only bigger? Or was it smart? Had it come through the barrier out of curiosity? Or did it have a sinister agenda?

Not knowing the answers to so many questions made Buffy nervous, but at least she was on even terms with the dumpy demon. Slayer skills were useless against infectious microbes and caustic fungi. She could hit the new guy.

The demon's nostrils flared, and a low growl rumbled in its throat.

Buffy felt a familiar tickle on her ankle. She looked down, startled to see the little orange lizard sitting by her shoe. Coincidence, or had it followed her? Or had it yanked her psychic chain and led her into an ambush?!

The lizard squeaked, drawing the newly arrived demon's attention. When it spied Buffy, it flexed claws and talons that looked sharp enough to pierce muscle. The lizard fled upward when the dwarf demon curled its lip back and roared.

"Take it easy, short stuff." Buffy eased down the steps, holding the brute's glittering gaze.

The demon snorted and puffed out its chest.

The instant Buffy's foot touched the floor, the demon charged. She deftly deflected the attack, grabbing a horn and heaving the demon across the cement corridor into a storeroom door. It quickly regained its feet, glared at her, and grunted.

"Not the talky type, huh?" Buffy braced herself when the demon charged again.

It slammed its heavy head into her midsection, driving her backward. Mindful of the slashing claws, Buffy ducked clear, spun, and kicked, catching the demon under the chin. It yelped and attacked in a frenzy of gnashing teeth and punches. A talon raked her leg, drawing blood. She knew if it got an opening, the demon could easily disembowel her.

"Gutting the Slayer is a definite no-no." Fighting for her life now, Buffy unleashed the Slayer fury she needed to survive. She flipped the creature onto its back. Within another second, she had a knee on its chest, one hand on its throat, and her other fist raised.

The demon threw a tantrum—roaring, shaking its head, and kicking its feet. Spittle flew from the creased corners of its leathery mouth, but Buffy didn't loosen her hold. Judging by her adversary's undisciplined attacks and defensive responses, she was pretty sure it wasn't high on the demonic evolutionary scale. She punched it in the nose, which seemed to knock it senseless.

As Buffy raised her arm to strike again, someone grabbed her from behind and pulled her off.

"Bad move, Slayer!"

Spike? Pulling free, Buffy whirled and backed up to keep both demons at a distance until she got her bearings. The dwarf demon was still stunned. She unloaded on the vampire.

"What do you think you're doing?" Buffy demanded.

"The bats ran away from him." Spike kicked the prone demon's foot. "Like maybe they were scared."

Buffy frowned. "So?"

"There was a whole bloody colony hanging about until this wanker popped in." Spike crouched slightly, scanning the ceiling. "Vicious creatures with a nasty bite."

Sensing his dread, Buffy dug in with a cutting remark. "Vampires, bats. What's the dif?"

Before Spike could respond, the short demon scrambled upright and snarled. Its alert eyes shifted back and forth between them before it suddenly broke for the stairs.

"Stop!" A voice called out from the access doorway above.

Buffy spun at the sound of Giles's voice.

The Watcher started down the stairs as the demon ran up, but he averted a head-on collision with a word: "Pragoh!"

The demon stopped and backed down, growling softly.

Buffy stared, noting that Spike seemed as astounded by the mild librarian's brazenness and the demon's cowed reaction as she was.

"Thank the gods I'm not too late. Ms. Calendar said you'd taken off, and I was afraid"—Giles paused, surprised to see Spike—"you'd kill our only salvation before I arrived."

"Spike?" Buffy asked, confused.

"I daresay not." Giles motioned toward the other demon. "I meant Pragoh."

Buffy watched the pug-nosed demon from the corner of her eye. It sniffed, as though it could discern intent by the odors they gave off. It remained tense and wary. Apparently, it still felt threatened.

"Stupid girl would have killed it if I hadn't pulled her off," Spike said.

"Okay, Spike," Buffy fumed. "Let's just finish this now and get it over with."

"Without the element of surprise?" Spike eyed her with disdain. "Where's the sport in that?"

"A truce would be in order, actually," Giles said. "As distasteful as I find it, we'll all have to cooperate to prevent a disaster everyone inside and outside the Hellmouth will regret."

"Seriously?" Buffy wasn't sure she had heard him correctly. "You want me to work *with* Spike and Play-Doh?"

"It's *Pragoh*, and I'm deadly serious."

Buffy wasn't happy about teaming up with the enemy, but she trusted Giles. Despite the almost fatal fiasco with the Master, she owed him. Stuffy and old-school, he didn't always understand or agree with what she did or what she wanted, but he tried to see her side. He knew—beyond doubt—that she wasn't selfish and irresponsible. That didn't negate the sting of her mom's misconceptions, but it helped.

Giles eyed the vampire narrowly. "What are you doing here, Spike?"

"Just checking out the rummage sale."

"We can do without the insolent sarcasm," Giles snapped.

"It's the truth!" Spike bristled at the insinuation he was lying.

"The survival of the entire planet may be at stake," Giles added. "If you know anything relevant—"

"We were shopping!" Spike insisted hotly.

"Is survival of the planet worse than the typical saving-the-world scenario?" Buffy asked. "Because it sounds worse."

"Actually, it could be." Giles turned to Pragoh. "My hypothesis is based on certain assumptions. Please correct me if I'm wrong."

"Yesssss," Pragoh agreed in a gravelly voice.

Spike rolled his eyes. "Just get on with it, will you? Some of us have other things to do."

Buffy bit back a scathing taunt about secondhand style, ending the verbal joust. Giles did not make jokes about the end of everything, and he needed her undivided attention.

"As I explained earlier," Giles began, "the Hellmouth has a pyramidal structure of lower to higher beings. However, the higher-level demons cannot break through the barrier and escape without assistance, such as the Master provided."

"That's why I'm here," Spike said, needling the librarian. "In Sunnydale. Because the big bloke bought it."

"Irrelevant, Spike." Giles waved him off like a pesky child. "These dominant demons empowered a lower-level demon—"

Pragoh snarled.

"My apologies, Pragoh." Giles cleared his throat. "They empowered Pragoh to have dominion over all the lesser entities in the Hellmouth. He is charged with ensuring that they don't infest our world, which would bring an end to all life as we know it."

"Impossible," Spike scoffed.

"It's entirely possible, I assure you," Giles said.

"How?" Buffy asked, perplexed. "Ms. Calendar said that the disease bugs don't infect more than one person at a time. They wait until that person dies before they look for someone else."

"A fortunate, but temporary reprieve, I'm sorry to say." Giles wiped his glasses with his handkerchief. "Without natural enemies in this world to control them, the Hellmouth organisms will undergo explosive growth. The same natural mechanisms affect Earth life. If certain animals didn't feed on insects, bugs would overrun the Earth, wiping out everything else."

"Oh." Buffy nodded. "I think we studied that in biology last year."

"And if Hellmouth flora and fauna are allowed to multiply without restriction," Giles concluded, "they'll require more and more victims exponentially, until all Earth life is extinct."

"Yesssss," Pragoh agreed.

"And Pragoh is here to do what?" Buffy asked. The idea that the smallest entities in either reality could finish off everything was very unsettling.

"He's here to lure the vermin back through the barrier," Giles explained. "Most of those who've been taken ill will be cured after the beasts abandon them."

"Most but not all?" Buffy frowned, her thoughts on her mother and Willow. "What things won't be cured?"

Spike took a sudden interest. "I'd rather like to know the answer to that myself."

"Quite honestly, I haven't the foggiest." Giles stuffed his handkerchief back in his jacket pocket. "We'll, uh, have to wait and see. The important thing is that Pragoh's superiors want to preserve the natural balance in our world—"

"Why?" Buffy asked. "Evil things don't do good things unless they're going to get something out of it."

"Good point, Slayer." Spike scowled. "The big bad beasties must be planning a bash."

"The old ones will kill all things here." Pragoh made a throaty noise that might have been a laugh. "Someday."

Buffy wasn't amused. "Someday when?"

"At an undisclosed time in the future," Giles said. "Give or take a few years or millennia."

"Is that written down?" Buffy asked. The monstrous scope of the Hellmouth bigwigs' ulterior motive was chilling. However, a plan to end all life on Earth wasn't guaranteed to succeed unless some ancient killjoy had left a note.

"Not specifically, that I'm aware of, but it doesn't matter at the moment." Giles looked at Buffy. "What matters is that Pragoh alone has the necessary abilities to round up the escaped vermin and send them back into the Hellmouth. That's the only way the afflictions will be cured."

"Starting with Dru." Spike took a stride toward Pragoh. "C'mon, you."

"Not so fast." Buffy blocked his advance. "I may have to work with Pragoh, but our salvation won't be at risk if I kill you."

"I wouldn't be too quick to test that theory, Slayer," Spike said. "The part about your health and welfare not being at risk."

"Why would I need you?" Buffy smiled, refusing to be baited by his mocking tone.

Spike was matter-of-fact. "You need me to save you from—"

Buffy's cocky attitude crumbled when the storeroom door slammed open.

The grotesque beast standing in the doorway looked like a bat-vampire hybrid experiment gone terribly wrong. Dark hair fell in long, matted tangles around large, pointed ears. A sloping skull had replaced the heavy brow, and a flat, puckered nose capped a short snout. Tatters of a white dress hung from narrow shoulders. The seams had been ripped apart as membranous wings grew outward from the down-covered body, legs, and arms. The velvet edge of the wings stretched from wrist to ankle, and venom dripped from viscous fangs.

"Is that—" Giles stumbled backward when the deformed demon lunged toward him.

"Drusilla!" Spike shouted.

CHAPTER SIX

And Cordelia thinks she's having a bad day! The sight of Drusilla's shocking transformation did not inhibit Buffy's timing. Her reflexes were as quick and ruthless as her catty observation.

Giles jumped back as Buffy raced forward and kicked, landing a foot squarely on the vamp-bat's chest. Dru was thrown off stride, but only for a second. When she launched an immediate counterattack, Buffy ducked, struck out with her leg as she came back up, and repelled Dru's charge.

"Don't kill her!" Spike tried to insert himself between Buffy and Dru, but the beast batted him aside.

"It's her or us, Spike!" Buffy planted her feet, poised for the vamp-bat's next move. "She loses."

Giles flattened himself against the wall and took off his belt. He wrapped the leather end around his hand twice. If swung with enough force, the buckle end was an effective weapon.

But not against the supersize bat out of hell, Buffy thought. As a hybrid, Drusilla was a lot stronger than a vampire and a lot smarter than a bat. She wasn't sure how they were going to defeat her.

"So where's the Beastmaster gotten to, then?" Spike asked, brushing dust off his long coat. His eyes narrowed when he spotted Pragoh under the stairs. "Hey! No hiding. Get out here and cure her!"

Pragoh shook his head. "She bites."

Spike stopped, then sidestepped, swinging his upper body low as he moved. Drusilla's fangs grazed dead flesh without breaking the skin on the back of his neck. His brow furrowed as he took several quick steps over to Buffy. He was visibly shaken.

"Too bad she missed." Buffy smiled, but the brash vampire's fear gave her pause.

"Is it?" Spike's surly tone had a serious edge. "If she'd bitten me, you'd have two monster bat people to fend off."

Drusilla raised her arms, gracefully unfolding her scalloped wings. The fingers on each hand had fused into a single curved claw at the midpoint on the membranes. She stared at Buffy with unblinking golden eyes. A menacing growl sounded deep in her throat.

"Why doesn't Pragoh *do* something?" Buffy hissed at Giles.

"Technically, Drusilla isn't a lesser Hellmouth creature," Giles said. "Pragoh can't control her."

"Then I'll bloody well have to." Spike threw up his hands as he moved by them and continued on past the stairs.

"By running away?" Buffy huffed.

"Teeth!" Giles yelled.

Pivoting, Buffy fired off another kick to stop the vamp-bat's forward surge. Dru snapped clear before the blow connected, then hooked Buffy's ankle and pulled her off her feet. Rolling as she hit the floor, Buffy sprang back up in an unbroken fluid motion of Slayer agility. Enraged, Dru prepared to strike again.

Buffy wondered how Angel would react to Drusilla's hideous transformation. The torment of driving her crazy and killing her family before he changed her into a vampire was almost more than he could bear. At least he was locked out of the school by Giles's quarantine spell. She missed having Angel by her side in a fight, but she was glad he wasn't in danger of being bitten or infected.

"Okay, Slayer. Just so we understand each other—"

Buffy's heart lurched, lagging Spike's sudden return by what could have been a fatal second. She had been so fixed on Dru that she hadn't heard him coming. She cocked her elbow, ready to deliver a swift and painful jab.

"I'll put bat-girl back in her cage *and* keep her there," Spike said.

"Right. You've done such a good job of controlling her so far," Buffy interjected sarcastically.

"In exchange for what, Spike?" Giles asked.

"We don't try to kill each other until hell's zookeeper cures Dru and gets the bats back in their proper belfry."

"*You* won't kill *anyone*," Buffy countered. "Everyone in this school is off-limits."

"All right, for today." Spike paused, then added, "And Dru and I get a free pass out of here when it's done."

Buffy looked at him askance. "Why am I even thinking about trusting you?"

"Make the deal, Buffy," Giles advised, "before Drusilla bites you—or me."

"Okay. Deal." Buffy had to agree. The risk of being turned into a bat-babe was too great not to give Spike the benefit of the doubt. He wouldn't jeopardize his only hope of having Dru restored to her insane, savage self. And in the event he couldn't confine her, Dru would turn them all into bats and the fighting odds would be even again.

Buffy watched closely, intrigued as Spike took immediate command of the situation. He carried himself with the confidence of someone who was accustomed to giving orders and being obeyed. He showed no fear or doubt as he advanced, and his intimidating bearing cowed the animal essence that had supplanted the insipid but cunning Dru.

"Fun's over, love. Time to fold up your wings and take a nap in the nice comfy dark." Spike motioned toward the open storeroom. When Dru snarled and rustled her wings to test his resolve, he whipped out a flashlight and trained the beam on her eyes. "In the storeroom, Dru. Now!"

Buffy tensed as Dru pulled her wing over her eyes. The dramatic move was eerily reminiscent of Bela Lugosi's Dracula in the 1931 movie, but the light had worked. She backed up.

"Where'd he get the flashlight?" Buffy whispered to Giles.

"The boiler room, I think."

He's not a dimwit either, Buffy realized, cataloging Spike's every move. She would just as soon kill both vampires now, but she had to honor her word. Eventually she would turn Spike to dust on the business end of her stake. It wouldn't be easy, but she would kill him.

"Enough with the lollygagging," Spike said as he prodded Drusilla to the door with the light. As soon as she was inside the storeroom, he dropped the flashlight and pushed the door closed. The beast threw herself against the door from the other side, then hit it again. The heavy door bounced as Spike leaned in, trying to hold it closed. "Some help here, people!"

"I'll go," Buffy told Giles. "You get Pragoh, and let's get this circus back on the road."

"That cannot possibly happen quickly enough, as you Americans like to say."

"More or less," Buffy said, moving toward the storeroom

as Giles went to the stairs. When she added her weight to the door, Spike was able to hold it closed long enough to secure it. However, the door didn't lock.

"Won't she just open the door from the inside?" Buffy asked, concerned.

"She would if she still had her wits and her hands, her fingers and toes." Spike shrugged. "But she doesn't."

"As odd as this sounds, I hope we can remedy that." Giles slipped his belt back on as he and the demon approached the door. "We've lost far too much time, Pragoh. Please, do whatever it is you do."

"First thing." With a stiff bow, Pragoh turned to face the stairs. Holding up his plump arms, he closed his eyes and hummed. After a moment, he mumbled a few unintelligible words, then hummed again.

"Can't anyone do what they do without chanting?" Spike flinched each time Dru slammed into the door. "Damn cults and magick makers always with the incessant blathering."

"The cadence enhances the power of a ritual," Giles explained. "Chanting concentrates—"

Spike smashed the door with his fist. Giles stopped talking, and Dru stopped trying to break it down. "I just hope the ritual works."

Ditto that, Buffy thought.

Giles watched Pragoh and checked his watch, his frown deepening as the minutes passed.

"Bats now," Pragoh said when he finished his litany.

"What have you been doing?" Giles asked, still frowning.

The demon didn't acknowledge the question. He waddled partway down the corridor, where the bats had last been seen. Cupping the sides of his face with his hands, he closed his eyes again. This time he was silent.

More minutes passed before Pragoh lowered his arms.

"Is that it then?" Spike asked, placing his hand on the door handle.

"Don't open!" Pragoh waved his arms, his little eyes alight and frantic. "No bats come."

"Meaning?" Spike asked.

"Power *pfft*!" Pragoh made a gesture of helplessness. "I call. No bats. No bats, no get better."

"The ill effects created by the vermin aren't neutralized until the source animals are back inside the Hellmouth," Giles explained.

"No bats, no get better," Buffy repeated. *Not good,* she thought. "Try calling that little orange lizard that drinks coffee—the one with the black scales on its back."

Pragoh stared at her then took a step back. "Did the fire dragon smoke you?"

"Like blow smoke out of its nose?" Buffy shook her head. "No. Why? What happens if you get smoked?"

"Fire start." Pragoh poked the scales over his stomach. "Slow cook and all burn up inside. *Pfft!*"

"Oh, now there's a picture to savor." Spike smiled.

Buffy felt sick.

Giles peered down at her. "Are you absolutely sure this fire creature didn't . . . smoke you?"

"In face?" Pragoh asked, patting his cheeks.

"I'm sure," Buffy said. "I can't believe I felt sorry for it."

"Good thing not try to catch it," Pragoh said, nodding sagely. "All over for you then."

"Yeah." Buffy didn't elaborate. Her merciful decision to catch rather than squash the orange lizard had almost gotten her incinerated from the inside out. However, she didn't have time to dwell on calamities that wouldn't happen. She had to stop the horrible things that were in the process of killing her mother and friends. "So can you call it?"

"Can try." Pragoh assumed the stance with his hands cupped to his face and held it for a minute.

The fire dragon didn't show.

Xander knew he was in trouble when he tried to take off the vest and the zipper wouldn't unzip. He wasn't putting on pounds. The vest was slowly strangling him.

Xander glanced at the utility room door. He didn't want to leave Cordelia alone, but she hadn't even sobbed since he had come back from a quick trip to the restroom. He had tried to comfort her and failed, and continuing his vigil wouldn't accomplish anything either. They were both on a fast track to tombstone park unless Buffy, Giles, and Willow figured out how to save them.

"And if I don't want my supersecret Scooby license

revoked, I should probably help." Xander put his ear to the door, but there was only silence on the other side. He had to do something before Cordelia completely decomposed.

The tight vest prevented Xander from bending at the waist. Getting to his knees, he used the doorknob to pull himself upright. His breathing was only slightly restricted, but it wouldn't be long before the python effect crushed his ribs and collapsed his lungs.

Xander looked toward the basement access door, where Buffy had gone a while ago. She could demolish most demons without breaking a sweat, but her butt-kicking prowess wouldn't solve this problem. Slayer action against the vest would just get his bones broken more quickly. He needed brains, and both of them were in the library.

Xander refrained from running, but he almost passed out when he pushed through the library doors. He hadn't realized how greatly walking fast would affect his respiration rate. Unable to fully expand his chest, he leaned on the book counter and took rapid, shallow breaths.

"Xander!" Willow pushed her chair back and stood up. She was still clutching the kur in the blue scarf. "Are you all right? What happened?"

Xander held up a hand to convey that he was all right. Then he waved, hoping she'd understand he wanted her to stay back. The last thing he needed was to inadvertently upset the kur. If Willow attacked, he wouldn't be able to defend himself.

"Is something chasing you?" Willow tightened her grip on the blue bundle, but she didn't move toward him. "Something bad? It better not try to hurt Cutie, because I'll have to leave or—" Her gaze snapped to the cage where Giles stored staffs, crossbows, swords, and other medieval arms. "I just might have to take drastic action."

Xander used precious air to force out two words. "Nothing . . . coming."

"Good, because Giles would freak if I wrecked the library." Willow smiled. Then, with her protective passion for Cutie diffused, her apprehension shifted back to him. "You really are out of shape, huh? Guess you were right about the doughnuts."

"It's the vest." Breathing more easily, Xander tugged on the lower edge of the vest. "It's getting tighter, and it won't come off. Got any scissors?"

Willow's face clouded with a bewildered frown. "What for?"

"Maybe I can cut it off."

Willow sneered. "Don't you dare try to cut Cutie!"

"The vest," Xander clarified. "I can't unzip it, but maybe I can cut it. It's worth a try, right?"

"Oh!" Willow brightened as quickly as she had turned belligerent. "There's a pair behind the counter."

"Thanks." Moving to the other side of the counter, Xander found the scissors on the shelf. He carefully placed the blades over the bottom edge of the vest. "Where's Giles?"

"He went to find Buffy." Willow fussed with the scarf, then nuzzled her furry white psycho pet.

"Why?" Xander tried to cut, but the fabric hardened where the blades touched. It was like trying to slice through an armor plate. He put the scissors back on the shelf without showing them to Willow. One glint of steel might send her into a defensive frenzy.

"To stop her from killing the only demon in the universe that can help us," Willow said.

"Seriously?" Xander frowned. "What demon is that? Because I didn't see Giles go to the basement, and Buffy's in the basement."

"It's not a big deal. I mean, Cutie's the only thing that's worth saving, and he's got me!"

"I know that makes perfect sense to you right now, Willow, but . . ." Xander hesitated to explain. Anything he said could be misconstrued as a threat, especially if the kur was sensitive to emotional states. Thanks to being choked to near death by a piece of quilted clothing, his anxiety level was extraordinarily high.

"Principal Snyder has worms," Willow said. "What have you got? No, wait. That's not right. It's more like, what's got you?"

"To be honest, Willow, the fact that some creepy crawly from the Hellmouth set up shop in this vest and has me in a vise grip is all I need to know." Xander wasn't kidding. Details about the unidentified plant or animal wouldn't change his circumstances except to give him a worse case of critter jitters. "I've got to find Buffy before she kills something."

"I'll go with," Willow said.

"That's okay." Xander tried to discourage her as he eased toward the doors. "Cutie's probably a lot safer in the library."

"I'll take care of him." Oblivious to the danger she posed, Willow followed Xander out the doors. "I finished the research Giles gave me, but it was a big bust. There's nothing online about a jat-sliver or a flitcha-my."

"Imagine that." Xander couldn't outwalk her and breathe simultaneously, so the next safest course was to say as little as possible. Willow's enthusiastic output filled the verbal gap.

"Giles is acting really weird, like he thinks I'll go disgruntled employee without warning him first. I mean, I know he's way too cautious sometimes, but he's not usually paranoid! Unless—what if he caught something in the cafeteria this morning? A gonna-get-me bug or something. That could explain it, right?"

"Could be," Xander replied curtly, eyes straight ahead as they turned into the cafeteria corridor. Willow's rambling was usually entertaining. Now he was relieved because it seemed to be calming the kur. As long as she kept talking, he had a good chance of making it to the basement alive.

". . . and I don't care what my mom says, I'm keeping him. No discussion, no argument—that's what she's always telling me! Cutie stays or we both go. I've made up my mind." Willow slowed to peer into the classroom Ms. Calendar had set up as an infirmary. "Wait a minute."

"I can't wait, Willow. We have to find Buffy just in case Giles hasn't."

"But everyone looks so sick." Willow stared through the window in the closed door. "Even Buffy's mom is lying down. Maybe we should see if they need—"

"They need Giles, who apparently has some idea about what's going on." Xander wished he could ditch Willow, but Ms. Calendar was too busy to worry about a beast with a hair-trigger defense system. If provoked, Willow could do serious damage in the crowded classroom. "So let's find him."

Willow murmured to the kur as she trailed Xander to the basement access door and down the stairs.

"I hear something," Giles's voice said.

"The fire thing only weighs half a pound. Its footsteps don't clump." Buffy looked over as Xander and Willow came down the last few steps. "Oh no. Did Cordelia—"

"Die? Unknown." Xander put out an arm to hold Willow back when he saw that Buffy and Giles weren't alone. "There's a vampire and a demon down here—with you."

"A necessary truce, Xander." Giles centered his belt buckle and shoved a hand in his trouser pocket. "Pragoh here is the equivalent of the Hellmouth dogcatcher."

"Cutie doesn't like him," Willow said.

Xander glanced back. Willow glared at the short gray demon. If it made the slightest move toward the kur, she would willingly gouge out its eyes. Normally he'd be one hundred percent behind that plan, but a catcher caught things. He assumed the cease-fire had been declared because Pragoh caught Hellmouth things. That, however, didn't explain Spike.

"What's Spike doing here?" Xander asked.

"Just waiting for a juicy Xander steak to show up," Spike quipped.

"He's keeping Drusilla, the big bad bat lady, in the storeroom," Buffy said. "What are you doing here?"

"His vest is squeezing the life out of him," Willow explained. "He thought you could save him, Buffy, but I guess you can't."

Xander stiffened. "What does that mean?"

"Cutie was a little nervous for a minute," Willow explained, "but he's not afraid anymore."

"Something is interfering with Pragoh's ability to call the underworld pests back to the Hellmouth," Giles said. "The only positive aspect of that situation is that the kur doesn't feel endangered."

"There must be something we can—" Xander gasped as the vest tightened suddenly. It felt like a bear trap had snapped closed around his waist. His airways weren't completely blocked, but his middle hurt like hell. "Too tight—" He could barely talk.

"There's another plus," Spike said. "The obnoxious one's juvenile prattle has been shut down."

"Did I forget to mention that verbal abuse violates our deal?" Buffy asked.

Spike raised Buffy's seething look of contempt with a derisive laugh. "Just try to enforce that."

Xander desperately wanted to add a disparaging word or two, but he didn't know what had prompted the vest to clamp down. His bones could only withstand so much pressure before they cracked. A couple more Hellmouth hugs like the last one and he'd be a candidate for technology that could rebuild him.

"So what's blocking the mojo, Pragoh?" Buffy asked.

"You're wasting your breath, Slayer," Spike said. "He's empowered to use the power, not to think about why it does or doesn't work."

Xander gripped the end of the banister on the stairs to keep from falling over. His knees threatened to buckle, and he knew if he went down, he might not be able to get back up—even with help.

Pragoh snorted with indignation. "One power work."

"And which power might that be?" Giles looked profoundly disturbed.

"Put spell all around whole place." Pragoh seemed to smile as he opened his short arms.

"Around the school?" Giles scoffed. "At the risk of wounding your demonic pride, that did not help. I already have a binding spell in place and functioning."

"A spell you could break." Pragoh met Giles's gaze with a jutting jaw set in stubborn defiance. "No break Pragoh's spell."

"Is that good or bad?" Xander asked.

"Two things good." The demon counted on his fingers. "All runaways and bad magick still here."

"Bad magick?" Buffy asked, puzzled.

"I believe he means that, in addition to all the Hellmouth

escapees, whatever's hindering his magick is still in the building," Giles said, "where we might be able to find it. Then the effects on Pragoh can be neutralized."

Pragoh nodded.

"What's the bad?" Since his initial introduction into Buffy's bizarre world, Xander had learned that there was almost always a downside to offset the good.

"We can't break Pragoh's spell," Giles said. "His masters want this world preserved. If he can't collect the Hellmouth pests and send them back, he's made sure they'll be confined. They'll die here—along with everyone else in the school."

Jonathan hid behind the science lab station, listening to Andrew's footsteps recede down the hall. Revenge wasn't the only reason his friend had attacked him. The electric eel on the bullwhip had filled him with an incredible sense of power. He hadn't been able to resist the overwhelming urge to crack the whip—over and over, preferably at something alive. Buffy had killed the eel, breaking the psychic bond, but another one must have taken its place. Now Andrew was in the whip's thrall.

That wasn't all, Jonathan realized. If Andrew hadn't been exaggerating to impress Buffy Summers, the creature built up a stronger and stronger electrical charge with each strike.

I almost killed my best friend! Jonathan was appalled, but not just because he had almost electrocuted Andrew. They were both misfits, had been their whole lives, but they had each other. If Andrew moved away or got mad and stopped hanging out with him or died, he wouldn't have anybody. That was the fate he dreaded most. He'd rather die than be alone.

But he didn't want to die today.

Jonathan crept to the classroom door and paused to plot his next move. It was a no-brainer. Since Andrew had run back toward the cafeteria, he ran as fast as he could in the opposite direction.

Something weird was always happening in Sunnydale. Jonathan didn't know exactly what was going on today, but the cops had arrived with sirens blaring to surround the school. Escape from the building wasn't possible, but he just needed a secure hiding place to wait out the crisis—somewhere he had never been, where Andrew would never think to look. A sign on the corridor wall directed him to the perfect spot.

Jonathan raced around the corner toward the auto shop. Andrew probably didn't even know Sunnydale High had a garage! Even if he did, nothing less than an emergency droid repair could lure him inside the student mechanics' grimy habitat.

Jonathan's elation evaporated twenty feet from the auto shop double doors. He skidded to a halt.

"Hey!" a redheaded boy called out. He was almost entirely engulfed in a mass of pulsating gunk that filled the doorway and looked like bread dough.

Jonathan recognized Oz, the lead guitar player for Dingoes

Ate My Baby. Ordinarily he wouldn't dream of talking to a popular musician from the Bronze, but Oz's plight evened out the social differential.

"What?" Jonathan took a tentative step closer.

"Pull me out." Oz extended his arm. He seemed remarkably calm for a kid who was being consumed by a real-life blob.

In his daydreams, Jonathan envisioned himself as the ultimate leading man who knew everything, had everything, and could do everything. That Jonathan would rush to the rescue without a second thought, deflate the victim's doughy prison with a pencil, and yank Oz free.

The real Jonathan inched closer, but didn't commit. "What is this?"

"My van seat covers," Oz said. "They just started growing and won't stop. I tried to run, but my foot got stuck."

"Does it hurt?" Jonathan winced.

"Not so far, but I have a really bad feeling that this is some kind of giant fungus that's slowly digesting me, like a Venus flytrap without leaves." Oz pushed against the dough. "Grab my hand."

"Okay." Taking a deep breath, Jonathan reached out. Just as he touched Oz's callused fingertips, the mass bulged outward. He jumped back as the dough enveloped Oz's arms and oozed farther into the hallway. "I'll go get help!"

"Wait!" Oz yelled.

Jonathan didn't look back or pause until he reached the

corridor outside the cafeteria. Ms. Calendar was in the classroom across the hall. He threw open the door and yelled, "The blob is coming! Run for your lives!"

"Andrew is here," a familiar voice said behind him. "Gotcha!"

"Everybody dies is *not* an acceptable ever after." Buffy fumed. Part of her success as the Slayer was the unshakable belief that every problem had a positive solution. The projected outcome of the present situation—that the trapped Hellmouth mini-monsters would die out *after* they had infected and killed all the available hosts in the school—wasn't good enough. "There's got to be another way to save the world."

"I certainly hope so," Xander said.

"Rupert? Are you down there?" Ms. Calendar hurried down the stairs. Rather than barge past Willow, she stopped before she reached the bottom. She looked frazzled and sounded frantic.

Giles blanched, assuming the worst. "Are you infected?"

"I don't think so, but three people have died. And Jonathan Levenson just told me that a blob creature ate a guitar player."

"Fascinating. Which one? That band Wretched Refuse has a raw, savage sound that hits right here." Spike placed his fist against his stomach. "I'd miss them."

"Is this blob entity in the vicinity of the infirmary?" Giles asked.

"I haven't seen it," Ms. Calendar said, "and Andrew

chased Jonathan away before he finished his report. Are you any closer to fixing this? Dozens more are critically ill."

"How's my mom?" Buffy was afraid to ask, but she had to know. "The hard facts."

"The dry peeling skin only affected her hands," Ms. Calendar said. "But she's broken out in green blotches on her arms and face. The, uh, green skin cracks and bleeds if it's touched. She's lying down and trying not to move."

"I have to go to her." Buffy took a step toward the stairs.

"Your impulse is commendable, Buffy, but it won't cure her." Giles spoke in an even, unemotional tone. "In fact, as much as I'm sure your mother would appreciate your presence, it would be a deathbed watch."

Buffy whirled on the librarian, eyes flashing. "Then let's stop talking and do what we have to do to save her!"

"And everyone else, too," Xander said hoarsely.

"Agreed," Giles said. "First we must identify and remove the magick that's preventing Pragoh from using his powers."

The kur's head suddenly emerged from the blue scarf. It hissed and spit with the ferocity of a cornered wildcat until Willow hushed it.

"Rebooting Pragoh's power isn't a good idea." Holding the kur close, Willow glowered at Buffy. "He wants to hurt Cutie. You can't let him. *I* won't let him!"

Willow was on the verge of a violent outburst, and Buffy hastened to calm her. "Nobody's going to hurt Cutie, Will."

"Promise." Willow's eyes narrowed.

Giles shielded his mouth with his hand and whispered, "The psychic link won't be severed until the kur is back in the Hellmouth."

Buffy nodded slightly to let him know she understood. Until the kur was gone, Willow wasn't in control of her own emotions. Buffy would promise to marry Spike if it would keep Willow from going off the deep end and hurting herself or someone else. "I promise."

"People are dying, Rupert," Ms. Calendar said anxiously.

"We haven't forgotten," Giles assured her.

"At least their problems are over." Spike punched the door when Dru slammed into it again. "Dru could be a ghastly bat forever, being immortal and all."

Buffy held back a quip about justified fate and focused on the problem. "So how do we find the bad magick? We don't even know where to start."

"Actually, I have a theory." Giles slipped into intense mulling-it-over mode. "It's possible that the magick hindering Pragoh's power attracted the vermin in the first place. Something induced the creatures to leave the Hellmouth, and nothing else adequately explains why an infestation hasn't happened before in the months since the Master weakened the barrier."

"Amy Madison," Buffy said. The young witch was the only student Buffy knew with the power to counter a demon's magick.

"She's absent," Willow said. "With the flu, the real flu. Fever, throwing up, feeling yuck."

Buffy glanced at Ms. Calendar. "Have you—"

Ms. Calendar quickly set the record straight on her magickal abilities. "I can cure hiccups and leg cramps. I can't disarm a demon."

"Well, someone did something," Giles said, exasperated.

"It wasn't me!" Willow exclaimed, flustered. "I've just been reading a few books about spells and potions and . . . and stuff. Strictly dabbling. I mean, not *real* magick that could actually *do* anything—"

Buffy wasn't surprised that the ultrasmart techno-whiz was investigating the magickal arts. Knowledge was power. Willow's mind was one of the Slayer's greatest assets.

Giles didn't dismiss Willow's dabbling as unimportant either. "An amateur spell might be responsible. The most simplistic incantation or ritual could be increased by magnitudes of power this close to the Hellmouth."

"Really? Whoa!" Willow blinked. "But I didn't do any magick. Honest."

"Oh! Oh!" Xander hit the banister with the heel of his hand. "Michael."

"Michael Czajak?" Buffy asked.

"He was muttering . . . while he looked for . . . his charm." Xander explained in halting phrases between labored breaths. "Didn't hear what—"

"If Michael believes the gold medallion has the magickal power to protect him," Giles concluded, "he might cast a spell to find it."

"Makes sense to me," Buffy said.

"Assuming that's what occurred," Giles went on, "Michael's spell would have to be satisfied in order for the magickal interference to end."

"Meaning the spell will be broken when Michael gets his charm back?" Buffy asked.

Giles nodded. "Theoretically, yes."

Pragoh agreed. "No more bad magick."

"Except that we don't know what happened to the medallion," Buffy pointed out.

"Is it a gold sun studded with red and green stones?" Spike asked.

"Yeah. Do you have it?" Buffy tensed. She didn't have time to spar with the vampire.

"No, but Drusilla did for a few minutes this morning, before the bats attacked." Spike hesitated, then added, "She said the bit burned, like an 'aching heart.'"

Buffy had no idea if Drusilla's gibberish meant anything, but at least Spike also thought the circumstances were too dire for games.

"A lost heart, perhaps?" Giles mused.

Spike shrugged. "'The longing wiggles.' She said that, too."

"An odd choice of metaphors," Giles said.

"Where amulet *now*?" Pragoh asked pointedly.

Buffy shared his impatience with the literary riddles, but it was disconcerting to be thinking like and working with a certified Hellmouth demon. *Having the same goal doesn't mean we're playing by the same rules,* she reminded herself.

"Drusilla dropped the medallion in a box." Spike motioned toward the stairs. "The short guitar player from that Dingo boy band took it upstairs."

"Oz?" Xander looked up. "Harmony took it. . . ."

Buffy sympathized with the difficulty Xander had speaking and asked yes or no questions. "Harmony took it where? To the high-dollar table?"

Xander nodded.

Buffy didn't remember seeing it, but she hadn't looked at the items in the display cases.

"Uh—I found Michael's amulet stuck to my sweater." Willow shrank back slightly. "But I gave it away."

CHAPTER SEVEN

As Willow trudged up the stairs behind Giles and Ms. Calendar, she cast a wary glance back. Buffy and the kur-hunting demon were too busy helping Xander to harm Cutie—for now. Spike had stayed in the basement to make sure bat-Dru didn't break out of the storeroom. It was weird, but the vampire didn't seem so scary—maybe because Willow and Spike both had to protect the one thing they loved most in the world.

Of course, Drusilla had fangs and could fight back if she had to. Cutie was soft and cuddly and totally vulnerable without her.

But there wasn't an immediate threat, and Willow relaxed

as she hugged the kur. The warm fuzzies wasn't just a sappy saying. It was exactly how she felt when Cutie felt safe and purred, like toasty mush.

"And you have no idea what became of the necklace, Willow?" Giles asked.

"I told Brad it belonged to Michael," Willow answered, annoyed. She was so wrapped up in Cutie, she hadn't followed every nuance of the discussion in the basement. The idea of finding Michael's medallion was unsettling, but since the kur wasn't in imminent danger, she put it out of her mind.

"Did Brad say he'd give it back to him?" Ms. Calendar stepped out of the stairwell and moved aside.

"He said he wanted to give it to his girlfriend." Willow hurried past the computer teacher. Xander stumbled into the corridor after her with Buffy and Pragoh supporting him on either side.

"Brad Corelli has a girlfriend?" Buffy released Xander's arm but held her hand up for a moment in case he started to fall.

"He's been dating Cheryl Saunders for a month." Nudged by a twinge of kur anxiety, Willow moved across the hall.

"House plants," Xander said breathlessly. "Devon and Oz helped her—" He leaned against the wall, gasping for air.

"Where is Brad?" Buffy asked. "We need to know if he gave the necklace to Cheryl or Michael."

"I'm not sure Brad will be able to tell you," Ms. Calendar said. "He's literally taken root at a desk. I haven't seen Cheryl."

Buffy pulled a wad of paper towels out of her waistband.

"I can search the cafeteria for the amulet, on the off chance it's still there."

"Some of these kids don't have much time." Ms. Calendar's voice was tight with urgency.

Willow began to inch away. She felt bad that so many people were sick, but they weren't her problem. Cutie was feeling nervous again, and she had to keep him away from the ugly gray demon.

"Given the number of people who have been in contact with Michael's amulet, it would appear the charm is working its way back to him. Eventually it will succeed." Giles looked at Ms. Calendar. "Is Michael in the infirmary?"

Ms. Calendar nodded. "Drifting in and out of consciousness and wasting away to skin and bones."

Giles turned to Buffy. "Sweep the cafeteria for the necklace, but do it quickly. If we lose its trail, perhaps we can backtrack it from the boy."

Willow felt a surge of fright when a small orange-and-black lizard darted out the basement door and skittered between the demon's legs.

Pragoh jumped suddenly and started stomping his wide foot. The lizard leaped to avoid being flattened.

Cutie screamed in Willow's head, transmitting the same terror she had felt in the basement. The kur wasn't afraid of Pragoh. He was terrified of the fire dragon.

"Stop!" Buffy yelled, and bopped Pragoh on the head. She pulled the startled demon back before he injured the fire dragon.

"Are you trying to get us all turned into Easy-Bake ovens?"

"Not cook me," Pragoh said.

"Of course." Giles commented on the demon's casual assertion as a matter of interest. "Pragoh would have to be immune to the creatures to be effective, wouldn't he?"

"Don't like fire dragon," Pragoh explained.

"Don't care!" Infuriated, Buffy pushed Pragoh back against the wall.

The fire lizard had been nearby the whole time they had been in the basement, and it hadn't smoked anyone. It hadn't even tried to smoke her when she had reached for the pot to trap it. The lizard had run away instead. And it hadn't used its deadly defensive mechanism when Pragoh had just tried to squash it. She felt confident the fire dragon wouldn't attack unless smoking was the only way to avoid being caught or killed. At the moment it was sitting up on its haunches a few feet away, watching.

"Everyone would probably be safer in the infirmary, Giles." Buffy glanced at Xander. Every breath he took seemed harder to draw than the last. "Where's Willow?"

"Run away." Pragoh pointed down the corridor. "Kur don't like fire dragon."

"Don't blame him." Ms. Calendar opened the classroom door, and Giles waved her inside.

"I know how to handle the lizard, Giles," Buffy said, "but you'd better take Pragoh with you. I don't want to get smoked by mistake."

"Understood. A hand here, please, Pragoh." Giles kept a wary eye on the lizard as he and the demon helped Xander hobble into the classroom.

After the door closed behind them, Buffy headed down the corridor. The lizard seemed to be tracking her movements, and she hoped it would follow her. Ms. Calendar's mug was still half full, which was more than enough cold coffee to keep the little guy occupied until Pragoh called it back into the Hellmouth.

Provided we get his magick working, Buffy thought as she strode through the cafeteria doors. The floor was still covered with black splinters and shards. With so many bizarre beings on the loose, she wouldn't have been surprised if the black ball had reconstituted itself like liquid metal, *Terminator 2*–style. She was relieved to discover it had not.

The coffee mug was where she had left it, on the table with the other art pieces her mom had brought in. Buffy tensed when the little lizard leaped onto the table, but it ignored her and clamped on to the mug. As she stepped back, she noticed the slogan the lizard's body had covered earlier: PARTY PAGAN.

"May we all live to party another day," Buffy said as she turned. The potted plants were on an end table one aisle over from CDs and old records.

Buffy's alert gaze flicked over everything as she walked. An animal that looked like a purple armadillo-porcupine combo with boar's teeth and three horns burrowed in the orange blanket where Xander had first hidden his vest. She realized that if she had left it there, he might not be facing a slow death by crushing, but she shook off the pang of guilt. For all she knew, the purple creature had poison quills that killed instantly.

The leather skirt she had stashed in defiance of Snyder's rules was still tucked in the stack of shirts, but she didn't want it anymore. Even after all the Hellmouth horrors were gone, she wouldn't be able to wear it without imagining that something vile was swimming through her veins, chomping her white blood cells, or turning her hair into cactus spines and seaweed.

A puddle of gray slime was devouring the brim of a Razorbacks baseball cap someone had left with the artificial flowers, baskets, decorative planters, and garden tools. The rows of potted ivies, philodendron, and ferns on the end of the table looked undisturbed, but that didn't mean the leaves weren't crawling with flesh-eating mites or pod-people spores.

Finally, convinced that nothing but hell beasts were wandering the rummage sale aisles, Buffy headed toward the exit. The unexpected snoring sound rising from behind a stack of boxes brought her to a sudden halt. At first, unable to tell if a person or a critter was making the noise, she approached with extreme caution. Even when she saw the toe of a sport shoe, she didn't let down her guard.

"Cheryl?" Rising on her toes, Buffy craned to look over the boxes.

"Ummmmm." The girl was lying on her side with her

hands pillowing her head. A brown, gold-flecked flat worm with a million tiny legs was wrapped around her neck. She appeared to be asleep.

"Cheryl?" Buffy called softly. "Can you hear me?"

"Uh-huh." Cheryl rubbed her nose with her finger, but she didn't open her eyes.

"Did Brad give you a necklace?" Buffy crossed two sets of fingers. "A gold sunburst?"

"Uh-huh."

Buffy didn't see the medallion, but the girl might have put it somewhere before the millipede hit her with the Rip Van Winkle whammy. "Can I borrow it?"

"Don't have it." Cheryl frowned.

"Where is it?"

"Brad has it."

Buffy couldn't be sure the girl had understood the question and took a stab at a follow-up. "You gave it back to Brad?"

"Uh-huh." Cheryl turned her head and began snoring again.

Buffy stepped back from the boxes to think. Brad was rooted to a desk in the infirmary, but Willow had told him the necklace belonged to Michael. Since Cheryl didn't want it, he might have decided to do the right thing and return it. If not, the infirmary was still the best place to look. *Everyone* from the rummage sale who showed symptoms had been isolated in the classroom, including Michael. Given the medallion's steady progress back to him, the protection charm had to be there too.

Buffy was hesitant to leave Cheryl, but the girl was sleeping peacefully and wasn't in pain. Even if the millipede was draining her life force or turning her into a moron, moving her wouldn't arrest the process. The disturbance might make her condition worse. Buffy decided to let her sleep and went back to the infirmary alone.

Despite the nonaggressive, academic facade Giles maintained, he was neither squeamish nor weak. He could not hold his own against the Slayer, but his combat skills were much more advanced than anyone knew. His wealth of knowledge was invaluable, but it was not all he had to offer. He believed that one day the sudden and unexpected implementation of his physical abilities during battle would be crucial to victory.

Nothing, however, had prepared him to deal with children and friends who were dying of horrid and excruciating demonic infections.

"Are the ambulances coming, Mr. Giles?" Joyce asked, her voice weak and hoarse.

"Yes," Giles lied. "They'll be here soon."

"So thirsty—"

"Ms. Calendar has some water up front. I'll get some for you. Just lie still." Giles smiled, but the sight of Joyce's cracked lips and oozing green sores was deeply disturbing.

Although he was quite enamored of Jenny Calendar, he had always found Joyce Summers attractive. It was a purely aesthetic observation he kept private, not only to avoid being teased but out of respect for Buffy's mother. He liked her, and it pained him to see the woman's loveliness violated by a species of hellish algae. More distressing was the undeniable fact that Buffy would be devastated if her mother died, perhaps to the point of dysfunction.

Giles tried not to think about the consequences of failure as he moved toward the front of the classroom to get a moist towel and some water for Joyce. Jenny had set up a headquarters of a sort at the teacher's desk. From there, she rationed first aid and other supplies and delegated tasks to the volunteer teachers who had not been frightened off by the three deaths. No one else had died, but all the afflictions were worsening at an alarming rate.

Giles paused to peer down at Michael Czajak. Curled into a fetal ball on the floor, the boy was oblivious to the plagues and pestilence his seeker spell had unleashed. He did not know for certain that Michael was responsible, but it seemed likely. The protective amulet's relentless journey from person to person back to the boy was hard evidence to ignore. And, Giles had to admit, he wanted to believe it. If Michael's spell wasn't the catalyst, there probably wasn't time to locate the source before everyone inside Sunnydale High perished.

After quickly tending to Joyce, Giles had no luck trying to backtrack the amulet from Michael. The few students he questioned had not seen the amulet or couldn't answer.

Cutting a diagonal across the room, Giles could not help

but gawk at Principal Snyder as he went by. The malicious man's contented smile was a maddening side effect of the brain bores drilling through his scalp. It seemed terribly unjust that the worms pumped a numbing substance into Snyder to counter pain while Joyce and the students suffered.

Jenny was not at the desk, and Giles took a moment to check on Xander in the corner behind it. The boy was pale and shaky, but still on his feet. Xander had tried stretching out on the floor, but the vest had reacted to the external pressure by squeezing harder. The vise effect was alleviated somewhat when Xander was vertical. Giles suspected the vest was infested with hive-mentality creatures that worked in concert—toward what end was unknown and irrelevant, given that Xander was being strangled in the process.

"How are you doing, Xander?" Giles remembered too late that speaking required more air and effort than Xander could safely expend. "I'm sorry. I'm sure Buffy will be back any moment with the amulet."

Fighting to keep air in his lungs, Xander didn't react.

"There she." Pragoh looked toward the door when Buffy entered. The demon stood beside Xander, concealed in a yellow rain poncho Jenny had found in the teacher's desk. The hood slipped off his horned head when he turned.

Giles pulled Pragoh's hood back up. Several people in the room remained conscious. No one needed to see a being that couldn't be explained away as a mutant pathogen.

"Let's hope she's had some success." Even as Giles said

the words, his hopes were dashed. As Buffy came toward them, he could see that she wasn't holding a gold necklace.

"Where fire dragon?" Pragoh scrunched up his pug nose and sniffed.

"Safe from you, bingeing on caffeine," Buffy said.

"You didn't find Michael's charm," Giles stated flatly.

"No, but it's got to be in here somewhere." Buffy quickly scanned the room. "Cheryl gave it back to Brad."

Giles cast a glance at the boy who was being transformed into a tree. The small roots sprouting from Brad's lower torso and legs had intertwined into a network of larger roots that had grown into the floor. Small limbs were shooting out from his shoulders and arms.

"How is she?" Buffy's eyes locked on her mother.

"As comfortable as she can be," Giles replied. "Finding that medallion is critical, for her and everyone else."

"I know." Buffy shifted her gaze to Brad. "Have you talked to him?"

"No." Giles shook his head. "He's too catatonic to talk or notice that he's turning into a tree. A mercy for him, I suppose."

"But it won't help us." Buffy sighed, then moved on. "Maybe Donnie Appleton can."

"Who?" Giles frowned as Buffy breezed by him. He jotted a quick note to Jenny, asking her to take more water to Joyce, then followed Buffy.

The boy sitting next to Brad had blue fuzz growing on his arms, but he was awake.

"Can you talk, Donnie?" Buffy asked.

"Yeah, why?" The boy's speech was slurred.

Buffy was blunt. "Did Brad have a gold necklace when he came in here?"

"Think so." The boy squinted, as if trying to keep Buffy in focus. "He was mad because Cheryl broke up with him."

"What became of the necklace?" Giles pressed.

"He threw it away. No . . ." Donnie's brow furrowed and he scratched his head, trying to remember. "He was going to toss it, but he didn't. He gave it to"—Donnie waved his arm, then snapped off a point—"Juan."

Giles's spirits sank lower as he walked behind Buffy between desks. None of the boys in the aisle appeared cognizant, but his stomach didn't rebel until she stopped in front of a boy with dark curly hair. Black gel oozed out of Juan's nose, mouth, and ears.

"Juan, where's the necklace Brad gave you?"

"He can't answer, Buffy," Giles said, feeling nauseous. "He's dead."

"He can't be dead. We have to find that amulet!" Buffy's temper simmered below the surface, nearing an explosive tipping point. "I'm not going to let my mother die."

"Don't touch him!" Giles barked, and jerked Buffy back. The black sludge would be looking for a new host, but it would not be the Slayer.

"Thanks, but I wasn't going to touch him." Buffy's intemperate tone softened as she explained. "I was looking for the medallion, but I don't see it. It's not in his hand, and there're no bulges in his pockets—"

"Boy fall!" Pragoh yelled excitedly.

Giles snapped his head toward the corner. The short demon was desperately trying to keep Xander upright. Jenny had been on her way to Joyce, but she abruptly turned back to assist Pragoh. They couldn't hold Xander up, so they broke his fall. Giles's throat went dry when the teacher put her ear to Xander's chest. She looked up suddenly, caught his eye, and shook her head.

Xander wasn't breathing.

Jenny started mouth-to-mouth resuscitation, but she could only buy him a minute or two at best.

Buffy remained intent on the one thing that could save him. "That necklace has to be here—*right* here, close by."

Giles agreed. When the amulet moved from Brad to Juan, it had drawn closer to Michael. He had no doubt it was nearby, but twenty teenagers surrounded the boy lying on the floor. They would find his protection charm, but would they find it in time to save Xander?

"Lucy Lopez found a necklace." A girl in the next aisle sat with her arms wrapped around her knees. "She picked it up when Juan dropped it."

"Lucy Lopez?" Giles wasn't familiar with the name.

"Over there." When the girl raised her arm, something undulated under her skin.

"I know her." Buffy rushed over to a girl with long dark

hair. A crusty substance had grown over her eyes. She sat perfectly still with one hand resting in her lap, clutching the medallion. Buffy pried her fingers open. "Sorry, Lucy, but I need this."

"Amazing," Giles mumbled as Buffy vaulted over a desk into the next aisle, where Michael lay crumpled on the floor. Lucy was sitting less than five feet away from him. His spell had worked with crude but impressive precision.

"Here's your protection charm, Michael." Buffy pressed the amulet into his hand and stood back. She glanced at Giles expectantly. "Now what?"

Giles exhaled. With the return of Michael's medallion, there was nothing left but to determine whether they had succeeded.

"Let's hope Michael's spell is broken and Pragoh's power works." Giles called out to the demon as he started for the door. "Pragoh!"

Buffy hesitated. "My mother—"

"Yes, you must go to her. I'll see to the . . . exodus." Giles hurried up the aisle. He and the demon reached the door at the same time.

"Bad magick gone?" Pragoh asked. The demon's squashed, pug-nosed face looked comical framed in the yellow slicker.

The next few minutes were no laughing matter, but Giles was oddly touched by the earnestness in the demon's tiny eyes. A less complicated being than his masters, Pragoh was a pawn, blindly doing the job he was assigned without concern for the consequences—except as it affected him. He wouldn't survive failure either.

"Let's find out, shall we?" Giles opened the door and said a silent prayer as Pragoh stepped into the corridor.

"Try now." Pragoh slipped out of the poncho, took a deep breath, and snorted loudly. Then, cupping his hands to the sides of his face, he closed his eyes and concentrated.

Giles didn't know what to expect. He glanced back into the classroom, targeting the corner first. Jenny was still kneeling over Xander, trying to revive him with her own life's breath. He didn't detect any changes in the victims until his gaze found Michael.

The boy opened his eyes slowly and inhaled sharply, obviously surprised to see the sunburst medallion in his hand.

Giles extrapolated the boy's future endeavors based on experience. Michael would assume, correctly, that his spell had worked. As he had learned at university, no one who discovered they had magickal power ever left well enough alone. Having no concept of the Hellmouth or the role it had played in his success, Michael would continue to explore his abilities.

And if the fates are kind, his parents will move him to Kansas, Giles thought, jumping back to avoid the stampede of Hellmouth life forms that slithered, flew, oozed, and scampered out the classroom door.

Engulfed in a swirling darkness that sparkled with specks of light, Xander felt himself being carried away. He didn't have the energy to fight the current, but it almost didn't matter. The pain he had felt just a moment before, like someone had parked a truck on his chest, was fading. He wanted to grab the pain, to cling to it before it was gone and the last tie to his life was irrevocably severed. Yet the lure of the darkness, of the painless nothingness, was so tempting—

Being snapped back to consciousness with his lungs bursting and his ribs bound in a vise grip was brutal by comparison.

Xander gasped, and it hurt. However, he was alive, which made the trade-off worth it.

"Xander, you're back." Ms. Calendar knelt beside him. "I thought we had lost you."

Xander struggled to breathe. The vague feeling of slipping into a dark void faded away as he took in more and more air. The grip of the vest loosened slightly, and he tugged on the fabric. "Off."

"No, wait." Ms. Calendar lifted his hand off the vest and held it.

"But—" Xander squirmed, revolted by the idea of spending one more second wrapped in the vest. Still, the teacher was far wiser than he about many things that probably included infestations of Hellmouth germs. Every muscle in his body tensed, but he gritted his teeth and waited.

"There they go." Ms. Calendar smiled.

Xander watched, fascinated as a transparent sheet of interconnected, paper-thin amoeba-like animals rose off the surface of the camouflage material. The colony flowed off the vest like a sheet of cellophane off a cardboard roll, and continued across the floor toward the door.

"That's it?" Xander was still hoarse, but his chest was no longer being crushed. He patted the vest. The quilted fabric was soft and resilient. "They're gone?"

"Yes, they are." Ms. Calendar stood up. "Will you be okay? I've got to check on the other students."

"I'll be fine." Nodding, Xander pulled himself into a sitting position. He was anxious about Willow and Cordelia, but he needed a minute to make sure he was all systems go.

The vest unzipped easily, but as Xander started to shrug out of it, he paused. Now that the python element had vacated, the vest was just a vest that appealed to his inner military man—and that had almost killed him. He took the vest off and lobbed it into the wastepaper basket by the desk.

Not everyone had been as lucky, Xander realized as he looked around the room. Dark streams and colorful clouds of minuscule creatures abandoned victims and drifted toward the door, along with larger bugs and beasts. Most of the stricken people in the room showed immediate signs of recovery, including Joyce Summers. She was sitting up and talking to Buffy, but she seemed more concerned about Karl's condition than her own.

The roots and branches Brad had grown were absorbed back into his body. A seed pod popped out of the boy's shoe and attached itself to a hairy, mouse-size, multilegged beetle.

Hitching a ride and Hellmouth bound, Xander thought as the bug skittered away and Brad keeled over dead.

Cordelia's affliction could also be a killer, he realized. Getting to his feet too fast, Xander gripped the back of the teacher's chair until the dizziness passed. The sickening sensation in the pit of his stomach wouldn't go away until he knew Cordelia's fate. He was worried about Willow, too, but the kur needed her too much to harm her.

Despite his bruised ribs and wobbly knees, Xander felt almost normal when he entered the corridor. Giles stood by the wall, watching Pragoh gather his wandering charges.

"The nightmare menagerie," Xander said with a grimace.

"Xander! You're all right!" The librarian's eyes lit up, and he grabbed Xander's shoulders. The moment of excessive exuberance passed quickly. Pressing his lips together, Giles let go and sheepishly backed off. "Did you notice Buffy or her mother?"

"Both fine, as far as I can tell," Xander said. "I, uh, need to check on Cordelia, though. She's just down the hall, in the utility closet. If she's—"

"I'll be right here if you need me. If she's—" Giles cleared his throat. "I hope she's not—"

"Me too." Xander didn't mention the enemies-with-benefits angle. "Thinking up comebacks to Cordelia's insults keeps me sharp."

"Do tell." Giles raised an eyebrow.

Xander hurried to the closet, but he stood outside the

closed door for a minute before he worked up the courage to knock. "Cordelia?"

"Go away!" Cordelia's voice was weepy but strong.

"It's alive!" Xander was so happy, the unkind quip just slipped out. "I mean—"

Cordelia screamed, emitting several short, sharp, ear-splitting blasts before she reverted to uncontrollable sobbing.

A pattering sound drew Xander's gaze to the bottom of the door. He shivered as a hundred ultratiny spiders scurried out of the closet and down the corridor.

"You can come out now, Cordelia," Xander said.

"No one is going to see me in this condition," Cordelia said. "Especially you."

"But the spiders are gone," Xander explained. "All your symptoms will go away."

"Do you have any idea how much damage mutant bugs can do to a manicure?"

"Apparently not," Xander muttered. The withering tone and skewed priorities proved Cordelia had been unchanged by the ordeal. However, he really wasn't up for being put down with sarcasm and welcomed the diversion when a shriek sounded from the restrooms.

"What are you doing in here?" Harmony's shrill voice was full of outraged contempt. "This is the *ladies'* room, doofus!"

The door flew open and Jonathan ran out. He wasn't red-faced with embarrassment or armed with a whip. He was white as a sheet and terrified. "Have you seen Andrew?"

"Not since he took your bullwhip, making the halls safe for innocent bystanders," Xander fumed, remembering the shock that had driven him to his knees. Apparently, Jonathan had been hiding from Andrew in the ladies' restroom.

"Catch it!" Andrew shouted as he raced around the corner—chasing the bullwhip.

Xander and Jonathan both stared as the bullwhip zoomed along the smooth floor. The leather thong had not suddenly come alive, Xander realized as it snapped and slid by. The snake curled around the cracker was pulling it. He stepped out in front of Andrew, stopping the boy's pursuit.

"Let it go, Andrew."

"But it doesn't have enough power," Andrew whined. He tried to pull free, but Xander was bigger than the nerd and held on.

Xander looked at Jonathan. "Is he talking about that snake?"

"Yeah." Jonathan sighed. "It kind of takes control of your mind and makes you hit people so it can build up an electrical charge. Andrew's still bonded to this one 'cause it isn't dead."

Xander recalled that Jonathan had snapped out of his murderous trance when Buffy cut the head off the first eel. He glanced at Pragoh. The demon picked up the bullwhip and shook a few wiggly things out of it.

Andrew kicked Xander in the shin and bolted when he let go to grab his leg. Wincing, Xander didn't try to stop him. If Andrew wanted to aid and abet a demonic eel, there wasn't a thing he could do about it. Unfortunately, it looked like Andrew's psychic link might get him killed.

"What's he doing?" Jonathan asked.

Andrew charged Pragoh and tried to scoop up the handle end of the whip.

The little gray demon was still holding the cracker end. Immune to the shocks, Pragoh ripped the large, charged eel off the cracker and tore it in two.

Abruptly freed from the eel's mental grip, Andrew came to his senses surrounded by swarms of hideous Hellmouth vermin. He ran back past Jonathan and Xander and kept running.

Jonathan waited until Andrew was out of sight around the corner. "So are all these whatever-they-are leaving with the short kid in the monster costume?"

"Yeah." Xander nodded, hiding a smile. Jonathan rarely ran into someone older than twelve who was shorter than him.

"And there's nothing left at the rummage sale except rummage?"

"Probably not," Xander said. Judging by the creatures amassing around Pragoh, it certainly looked like all the Hellmouth beasts had answered his call.

"And it's past noon, so the sale's officially open, right?" Jonathan gave Xander a sidelong glance. "So I can officially put my money on the cash table to pay for some action figures."

"And cheat Andrew out of them?" Xander nodded again. "Yeah, you could do that. He'll get even someday, though."

"I'm not going to *keep* them all to myself. I just want him to sweat it a little." Jonathan paused outside the cafeteria door to make sure the way was clear, but he walked in with a definitive spring in his step. He didn't get the upper hand very often.

Winded from the tussle, Xander leaned against the wall. When Harmony squealed again, he watched the restroom door. A cloud of pink and green mist trailing clusters of pink and green strings emerged. As the cloud drifted toward Pragoh, the strings dropped along the corridor floor, the residue of Harmony's infection.

When Giles and Ms. Calendar approached, Xander was ready for company that didn't freak in the face of horrifying evil. "What's happening?"

Giles did not react as though he had been asked a foolish question. He answered, "Buffy will need to get down there and keep track of Pragoh and his beastly entourage until Ms. Calendar and I return with a spell to seal the Hellmouth."

"You have one of those just lying around in case of a Hellmouth emergency?" Xander asked.

"After that dreadful business with the Master, I made a point of looking one up," Giles said. "There's a binding spell in the *Hebron Almanac* that should do the trick."

"Have you seen Willow?" Ms. Calendar asked.

Xander shook his head. "Not since we came up from the basement. Why? She's not in danger, is she?"

"We're not sure, actually," Giles said. "I've assumed the link to the kur will end once it's back in the Hellmouth where it belongs."

"Unless we can't separate them," Ms. Calendar added. "The beast's influence is so strong, Willow might very well waltz right into the Hellmouth with it."

Giles's voice shook slightly, as it did whenever he was upset because Buffy had taken a particularly dangerous risk. "Where she will die quite painfully of something atrocious within moments."

CHAPTER EIGHT

"Are you sure about that?" Willow stared into Cutie's big brown eyes. The library was the safest place in the whole school, quiet and mostly deserted. Nobody used it except Giles and the Scoobies, and they were all off helping the demon. Still, Cutie was pushing her to leave.

The kur twitched his button nose and purred, snuggling against her chest.

"Okay, if that's what you want." Willow adjusted the scarf around the precious creature as she walked toward the doors. She heard Xander talking as he approached from the other side.

"We have to kill the kur," Xander said. "It worked for Andrew and Jonathan. This electric eel thing—"

Willow was frozen in shocked outrage when the doors opened. Xander, Ms. Calendar, and Giles smiled when they saw her, acting like nothing was wrong. Like they hadn't been plotting to murder the one thing in the universe that made her really happy.

"Uh—" Xander's mouth moved but nothing came out.

"How could you?" Willow glowered at Xander. Cutie trembled in her arms, sensing the danger.

"Willow, I'm so glad you're all right." Ms. Calendar tried to embrace her.

"Don't touch me." Willow shrugged out of reach. "I trusted you! All of you! I thought you were my friends, but you're not. You want to kill Cutie!"

"No, we don't, Willow," Giles said. "You didn't hear every—"

"I heard him!" Eyes flashing, Willow pointed at Xander. She was so angry, her chest heaved and she had to speak through clenched teeth to stay in control. "He said 'kill the kur.'"

"Kur? You thought I said 'kill the kur'? No, I said 'her.' Kill *her*. The, uh, Cordelia!" Xander smashed his fist into his hand. "She makes me so mad sometimes, I just want to . . . kill her. But I wouldn't."

"And you expect me to believe that?" Willow didn't hide her disdain.

"Well, yeah." Xander shoved his hands into his pockets and smiled his lopsided smile. "You know me. Speak first, think too late, and then regret."

Xander fumbled for words that could make it right, but

nothing could fix it this time. She didn't need friends who wanted her pet to die. She didn't need friends who betrayed her. She didn't need anyone now that she had Cutie.

Willow calmed down when she realized that it didn't matter what Xander *thought* should happen to the kur. He'd have to kill her first to get to Cutie, and he wouldn't do that, not in a million years.

"Were you going somewhere, Willow?" Giles asked.

"Cutie wants to take a walk, so we're leaving." Nudged by the kur's intense desire to move, Willow marched out the door. She heard her ex-friends talking behind her back again.

"Is she—" Xander stuttered. "Should I—"

"Just tell Buffy." Giles coughed. "And that Ms. Calendar and I will be there shortly with the spell and accoutrement."

"Huh?" Xander sounded puzzled.

"Spell stuff," Ms. Calendar explained. "Candles, incense, charcoal—"

Willow smiled as she ambled down the corridor. Cutie was serene and all was well. She wasn't even upset when Xander caught up with her, still pretending that everything was fine between them. The kur wanted her to take him home.

Buffy stood against the wall on the perimeter of the Hellmouth varmint herd. Unwilling to leave her mother's side until the green sores began clearing up, she had fallen out of the disaster loop. With the exception of Pragoh, she didn't know where everyone was or what they were doing. She had to trust that

Giles would find a way to fill in the gaps. The demon didn't know anything.

"Where's the fire dragon?" Buffy asked, worried.

It bothered her that she cared about the lizard's welfare. She didn't feel an overwhelming desire to protect it like Willow did the kur, nor was she compelled to commit violent acts as Jonathan had been with the eel. She just liked the little guy. It was adorable in an orange-and-black, has-a-coffee-habit, and can-turn-people-into-human-torches kind of way. She also wanted to make sure it went home to the Hellmouth before Giles sealed the leaks.

"Dragon *never* hurry." Pragoh threw up his hands.

"He's dawdling?" Buffy asked, amused. She had a pretty good idea why the lizard wasn't in a rush to leave. "Maybe I can get it."

"Should have stomped it. Easier." Pragoh continued to complain as he waddled down the hall toward the basement access door. "Everybody else ready to go!"

Following the demonic pied piper's lead, the huge assortment of Hellmouth critters started to move. The purple armadillo-porcupine animal trundled by, flanked by a winged caterpillar and the puddle of gray slime. The faint outlines of the letters *Z*, *O*, *R*, *B*, and *A* from the Razorbacks baseball cap were visible in the slime.

Buffy moved in the opposite direction, staying close to the wall until she was past the migration. Then she ran for the teacher's lounge. The pot sitting on the coffeemaker burner was empty, but several teachers hadn't taken the time to clean their mugs when the emergency had been declared.

After collecting a full mug of cold coffee to use as bait, Buffy walked back to the cafeteria so she wouldn't spill it. She felt terrible about the eight people who had died. She would never know how many students and residents of Sunnydale were still alive because of her efforts, but she bore the burden of every death by demonic evil that occurred in the town. Still, the casualties could have been a lot worse today, and she couldn't help but feel a little jubilant. The evil zoo was en route back to the Hellmouth, her mother would recover with no permanent scars, and Xander had survived.

When she stepped through the cafeteria doors, Buffy realized her premature happy thoughts might have jinxed the mostly happy ending. Not everyone was out of danger yet. Jonathan had several action figure blister packs tucked under his arm, and he was poking through the gallery donations—less than twelve inches from the fire dragon.

The lizard had four feet perched on the rim of Ms. Calendar's mug. Its head, long neck, and upper body were inside the mug so it could get that ever-so-good last drop.

Jonathan and the lizard both seemed oblivious to or unconcerned about the other's presence. She had to get the lizard's attention without startling Jonathan. Since he was in the cafeteria helping himself to collectible goodies, his nerves were probably hair trigger. If he jumped, ran, or shrieked in surprise, he might inadvertently scare the creature into a false-alarm smoking.

She was fairly certain that Jonathan never rocked the boat, avoided trouble at all costs, and unquestioningly obeyed authority. Trusting her instincts, Buffy issued an order. "Don't move, Jonathan. Your life depends on it."

Jonathan didn't move.

"Now, back away from the table—slowly," Buffy instructed. Holding her breath, she shifted her gaze between Jonathan and the fire dragon. The lizard had all six feet clamped on the rim of the cup, and it was watching Jonathan. "Turn around, Jonathan. Slowly. No sudden moves."

Jonathan turned his back to Buffy and the animal. "I was going to pay for—"

"Quiet." Buffy held out the cup when the dragon snapped its head around to stare at her. She didn't care if it was her voice or the coffee that snared its rapt attention. Jonathan was forgotten as it leaped off the table and scampered toward her.

Buffy didn't have time to give Jonathan an all-clear. Coffee sloshed and spilled as she hurried to the door. She smiled when the lizard stopped to lick the drops off the floor with its black tongue. It would follow a spilled coffee trail all the way to the basement.

"Still a little shaky, huh?" Xander stopped to watch as Buffy flipped the stopper to prop the door open.

"Just baiting a Hellmouth delinquent," Buffy said, pouring more coffee on the floor. She noticed that Willow was still carrying the kur bundled in the blue scarf. "And looks like it's not the only one."

Xander shifted his weight, suddenly nervous. "Willow and I were just taking Cutie for a walk."

Willow laughed. "When he wants to go somewhere, I just don't have the heart to say no."

Or the mind, Buffy thought as Willow murmured sweetly to the vile little beast.

"I think it's safe to say that Willow would follow Cutie *anywhere,*" Xander said, holding Buffy with a fervent stare.

It wasn't hard to interpret Xander's words, emphasis, and look, and the message made Buffy's stomach hurt. Giles had been quite clear that Cutie's mental hold on Willow wouldn't end until it was back in the Hellmouth. Apparently, Giles also thought Willow might hand deliver the kur.

Buffy's first solution was to snatch the creature out of Willow's arms and kill it, but she realized that taking such drastic action would backfire. The psychic connection would be severed, but Willow's affection for the creature could be genuine. Her mom wouldn't let her have a pet she could cuddle, and Willow might never forgive her best friend for wringing Cutie's neck.

"Can we please get moving?" Willow asked.

Bad, bad idea, Buffy thought. They had to keep Willow as far away from the basement as possible for as long as possible to minimize the chances of losing her. Unlike the fire dragon, the kur obviously couldn't resist Pragoh's call. And Willow couldn't resist the kur's psychic imperative to return to the Hellmouth.

"Shouldn't we wait for Giles?" Buffy didn't honestly

believe reason would work with Willow, but posing the question bought a few more seconds. She caught Xander's eye and nodded vigorously, hoping he'd catch a clue.

Xander was quick on the uptake. "We should wait. Absolutely. Giles and Ms. Calendar might need help carrying . . . stuff."

Willow was only half listening. The kur was the center of her shrinking world. "You guys can wait. We're leaving."

Buffy cast another frantic glance at Xander. He shook his head, at a loss. If they tried to physically restrain Willow, the kur would have a fit. Willow would react violently, pulling out all the stops to do the beast's bidding. She could get hurt, but that was a chance Buffy had to take.

Better than taking a long walk into hell, Buffy thought, bracing to stop Willow.

Instead of moving forward, Willow gasped and stumbled back from the door.

Puzzled, Buffy glanced into the cafeteria just as Jonathan risked looking over his shoulder. When he spotted her watching him, he jerked his head back around and resumed his motionless stance.

The fire dragon scurried out the door to the second coffee spill.

"Oh, look who's here." Xander prudently eased back. "Hellfire on six little legs."

"Get it away, Buffy!" Willow pleaded.

Xander cocked an eyebrow. "Apparently, Cutie isn't wild about going out in a blaze of glory either."

"Not funny, Xander," Willow said. "That thing makes combustible fevers *inside* other things. One minute you're napping by a lava flow in a cave, and the next you're a campfire."

The fire dragon's incendiary nature gave Buffy new angles to consider. If the lizard turned the kur into a fireball, Willow wouldn't blame her—except that the dragon couldn't smoke Cutie without smoking Willow, too. But Buffy could use the kur's fear to delay Willow's arrival in the basement.

"Okay, Will." Buffy held up a hand and explained, for Xander's benefit more than Willow's. "I can keep the dragon calm if we move *slowly*. Just stay back and you'll be fine."

"Right," Xander said. "If you went first, it could sneak up on you and *wham!* You're charbroiled before you know what hit you."

"Okay," Willow whispered.

Buffy moved a few feet closer to the basement access door and spilled more coffee. When the lizard finished the second spill, it moved on to the third. Willow and Xander stayed six feet back.

"Where's my shirt?" Principal Snyder bellowed through the open classroom infirmary door. "And why am I wearing all these ugly ties? Is this somebody's idea of a joke? I'm not laughing."

"Nobody's laughing," Buffy's mom said sharply. "Now sit down and calm down, or those big holes in your head won't heal properly."

"Where's my hat?" Snyder asked. "Somebody took my hat."

"Oh, joy. Sounds like Principal Snyder's back to his old self." Xander sighed.

"Which is oddly comforting," Buffy muttered. The principal made her life difficult and unpleasant, but he had never tried to kill her.

Giles and Ms. Calendar still hadn't arrived when Buffy reached the top of the stairs. Cutie's fear wouldn't override Pragoh's call indefinitely, and Willow was getting impatient with the snail's pace. Buffy wouldn't be able to delay much longer.

Maybe no more than a few seconds, she thought when the fire dragon jumped over the last coffee puddle and bounded through the door.

"Guess he reached his two-cup limit," Xander joked.

Once the threat was out of sight, it was also out of the kur's mind. Willow's cautious demeanor vanished in an outburst of hostile irritation as she tried to barge past Buffy. "Out of my way."

"Not so fast." Buffy put a hand on Willow's chest. "You wouldn't want to run headlong into something else that could hurt Cutie, would you?"

"No, but Cutie's not upset, so there's nothing to worry about." The kur hissed at Buffy as Willow pushed by her. "Except you!"

"Willow! Wait!" Buffy rushed down the stairs with Xander close behind. She reached out to grab Willow's shirt, determined to stop a misguided charge through the Hellmouth barrier. But Willow didn't fight when Buffy pulled her to a stop on the bottom stair.

The basement teemed with Hellmouth creatures. The small openings into the underworld only allowed a limited number of beasts through at one time. The rest had to wait their turn to leave, including the kur. The presence of the fire dragon directly ahead on the floor was another plus. It negated any impulse Cutie had to push to the front of the line.

"Slayer!" Spike had his back to the storeroom door, but he was losing the battle against Dru's incessant battering. "Will you please tell your short, stubborn friend to do something?"

"Is there a problem?" Giles paused behind Xander. He had a bag slung over his shoulder and his arms were laden with a book and candles. Ms. Calendar stopped on the stair above him with more magickal paraphernalia.

"He won't call the bats!" The door banged, and Spike leaned into it with his shoulder. "And she's getting stronger!"

Rolling her eyes, Buffy raised her voice to be heard over the thrum of wings and feet. "Pragoh! Why haven't you called the bats?"

The demon's upper lip curled back in a snarl. "Don't have to do what puny vampire say."

"Puny?" Spike's ability to cope was strained to the limit, and the insult pushed him too far. He vamped out and whirled to menace the demonic beast master.

"That cannot be good for our side," Xander said.

"Excuse us. We have a spell to cast." Giles squeezed past Xander, Buffy, and Willow. Taking care not to step on the fire lizard, he moved under the stairs and dropped the spell supplies.

"Couldn't we have used a simpler version of the binding spell?" Ms. Calendar asked as she joined him.

"To ensure success, no." Giles pulled a round, metal censer out of his bag and tested the chain.

Buffy concentrated on the clash of demonic male egos. She did not want to referee a fight between Spike and Pragoh. She wanted to stop it, and barged forward as Spike charged, but she wasn't quick enough to intercept. Arms folded and snorting defiance, Pragoh stood his ground. Just before Spike barreled into him, the storeroom door flew open.

Spike's face returned to human form in the split second it took him to stop and look back.

A hush fell over everything as Dru's grotesquely majestic presence emerged from the doorway. Draped in torn streamers of a white gown with long, dark hair and black velvet wings, the tall, exotic she-bat exuded primal power. A low guttural growl sounded in her throat as her golden gaze bore into Spike. There was no affection in her eyes, no trace of weakness in her bearing as she brandished winged claws. She wanted blood, beginning with the vampire.

"Gone a bit stir-crazed in there, love?" Spike's flippant tone was laced with fearless arrogance, but the tension in his jaw showed that he recognized the danger. "Our little friend here was just getting ready to make it all better. Weren't you, Pragoh?"

"Still mad," Pragoh huffed.

"Say please, Spike," Buffy urged.

The enormous energies Dru generated kept Buffy in a state of total Slayer readiness. Primed to repel an attack, she swept the room with her senses. Clouds of microbes, colonies of mites, and larger solitary beasts continued to flow through the leaks in the Hellmouth barrier. Under the stairs, Giles and Ms. Calendar furiously prepared to cast the binding spell. Xander stood above Willow, ready to grab her.

"'Say please'?" Spike tilted his head back and laughed. "Not bloody likely."

Unfurling her huge wings, Dru flew toward Spike. Light glinted off her fangs, and her high-pitched screech sent chalkboard chills up Buffy's spine. Spike tried to duck out, but Dru's wingspan was too expansive to escape. She folded him in the membranes and threw back her head, mouth open to bite.

The attack was a catalyst igniting all the other potential calamities in the room. Everything exploded at once.

Willow jumped off the stairs. Xander grabbed the back of her shirt and dragged her down into a mass of yellow jelly orbs on the floor. Cutie spit and snarled as the fire dragon sprang clear. Lying on her side, Willow clutched the frenzied kur, kicked, and screamed. With one terrified eye on the lizard, Xander slipped his arms around Willow's waist, buried his face in her back, and hung on.

Giles crept out from under the stairs with a lump of charcoal in his hand. Shooing straggler Hellmouth creatures out of his way, he darted to the basement wall several feet to the right of the main breach. Smaller punctures were only evident because of the mists and streams of ultrasmall beasts moving through them. Giles began to draw a large semicircle on the cement floor with the charcoal. Ms. Calendar drew smaller circular patterns within the outline and positioned unlit candles.

Vamping out again, Spike drove his fangs into the main rib on Dru's left wing. Enraged by the pain, Dru flew into a Cutie-style fit that imperiled every creature still in the basement. She was a riot of slashing teeth and talons, striking out in all directions. Spike threw himself at her, shoving her backward and bringing her down with the momentum. He tried to catch and pin her winged arms, but she eluded his grasp and clawed his cheek.

Willow had stopped fighting Xander, but Buffy didn't know how long Spike could keep Dru down. She was certain that if he lost the battle, someone else would die. "Pragoh! Call the bats now!"

The gray demon jutted his chin to refuse, then fixed Buffy with his beady haze. "What for Pragoh?"

"A bribe?" Buffy asked, incensed. "You want a bribe to do your job?"

"Ow!" Spike wiped a smear of blood off his neck, then smacked bat-Dru with his fist. "Agree now, negotiate later!"

Furious, Buffy advanced on Pragoh. "Call the bats." Her voice was tight, leaving no doubt that she meant it or else.

Pragoh flinched. "You owe."

"Call them." Buffy stared the demon down until he cupped his face and closed his eyes. Then, despite her hatred of the punk vampire, she stood on the edges of Drusilla's wings to help Spike hold her down for the count.

Buffy heard the thunder of wings before the flock of brilliant red bats swooped in. Huge, with saber fangs, they dove through the Hellmouth breach like hot knives through ice cream. When the last bat was gone, Drusilla gave up her struggle.

Spike rolled off Drusilla's still body and stood up. "How long before she's right again?"

Buffy jumped back when the leathery wings suddenly began to recede. "Not long."

Within the space of a few seconds, the furry bat face smoothed into the perfect contours and porcelain complexion of Drusilla's human countenance. Wing membranes seemed to evaporate as talons and claws softened into bare feet and delicate hands. Drusilla's transformation occurred with astounding speed compared to the recovery rate of the human victims.

Must be a vampire thing, Buffy thought as Spike drew the tatters of Dru's dress closed. He slipped out of his long coat and settled it over her shoulders when she sat up.

"I don't like this party, Spike." Dru's head drooped against his chest. "The li'l red pawns tricked the queen and now they've gone and taken all the tea and crumpets."

"But you won the game." Smiling tightly, Spike caressed her cheek with the back of his hand.

"Get a crypt!" Disgusted with the vampire fawning, Buffy

turned to assess the other ongoing dramas. Spike's tenderness toward his vampire mate made her uneasy. She didn't want to watch him lift Drusilla into his arms and whisk her away. They were monsters, not a gallant knight and a damsel in distress. She glanced back anyway, but they were gone, and she put the loathsome couple out of her mind.

"One more candle there should do it," Giles said. He and Ms. Calendar put the finishing touches on the charcoal diagram they had drawn on the floor. Situated directly under the library, the large semicircle encompassed all the shimmering distortions visible against the cinderblock wall. All the breaches, Buffy realized, had occurred on the outer edge of the Hellmouth.

Giles and Ms. Calendar tensed when the fire dragon scampered toward the wall, but it had no interest in them. It stopped to look back at Buffy just for a second before it leaped through the barrier.

Bye, little guy. Buffy allowed herself a brief pout. She was glad the dangerous creature was gone, but it hadn't hurt anyone. It had actually helped her save Willow.

Although, we're not home free on that one yet, Buffy thought, checking on her friends.

"Feeling better, Willow?" Xander asked. They were both sitting up, but he still had a grip on her skirt in case she made another break for it.

"A little." Sighing, Willow rested her chin on the top of Cutie's furry head.

"Except for lighting the candles and the incense, I believe

we're ready." Giles brushed black dust off his hands. "Have all the creatures gone through?"

The moment Buffy was dreading was near, but there was no avoiding the inevitable. "Everything but the kur."

"But he wants to stay with me," Willow said.

Xander, Giles, and Ms. Calendar watched Willow, intent and worried but not knowing what to do. Nothing could make the necessary parting easier.

"Cutie has to go back where he belongs," Buffy said, her voice gentle but firm.

"We belong together." Willow tightened her grip on the creature. "Here or there."

"Good. Kur girl go there." The gray demon waved toward the Hellmouth breach. "Pragoh need prize."

Xander frowned. "Did I miss the part where we all woke up in a box of Cracker Jack?"

Aghast at the implication, Buffy stepped between the demon and Willow. "What are you talking about?"

"You owe bribe!" Pragoh poked her with a stubby finger. "Big demons blame Pragoh for all this escape. Want something make them not be mad."

Buffy grabbed Pragoh's finger and leaned into his face. "Evil weakened the barrier and opened the Hellmouth edition of Pandora's box, and it's your job to round up the strays and take them back. *We* don't owe *you* anything."

"Especially not Willow!" Ms. Calendar struck a long fireplace match and began lighting the candles.

Giles opened the metal censer and snapped an aromatic cone of incense into the holder.

"She want go!" Pragoh snapped, exasperated.

"No, the *kur* wants her to go," Buffy countered. "She stays."

"Only if Cutie stays too," Willow said.

Buffy ignored Willow. Her plan required precision timing, but it wouldn't work if Willow or the kur suspected anything. Until it was time to act, it was safer to let Willow believe she could keep her pet.

Huffing with indignation, Pragoh pulled his finger out of Buffy's grasp. Then he poked her again. "You give girl or Pragoh not take back spell."

"Spell? What spell?" Buffy looked at Giles.

"The spell he used to bind the school," the Watcher explained, stunned. "We do not have the power to reverse it. No one will be able to enter or leave the building unless Pragoh lifts his containment spell."

"So we'll all die of starvation instead of monster measles," Xander said.

"Nobody else is going to die." Buffy fixed Pragoh with a no-nonsense Slayer stare. "He can take me instead of Willow."

"Then you'll die!" Ms. Calendar protested.

Giles placed a hand on the teacher's arm to silence her. His expression of puzzled concern and curiosity suggested that he wasn't sure what Buffy was doing, but he wanted to hear her out.

The demon was just as intrigued, and Buffy had his complete attention.

"I bet capturing the Slayer would please your big demon bosses," Buffy explained. "Who knows? They might even give you a promotion."

Pragoh's nose twitched in agitation, as though he suspected a trap but couldn't discern what it was. "Why Slayer go?"

"It's my job," Buffy said.

"Since when is 'sacrificial lamb' in the Slayer job description?" Xander asked. He still had a grip on Willow's skirt.

Buffy addressed Pragoh. "I put my life on the line to protect innocents every day. Willow is an innocent." Sensing that the demon wasn't convinced, she added, "I'm expendable."

Pragoh frowned.

"Look, here's how the Chosen One thing goes down," Buffy went on. "The instant Giles and Ms. Calendar seal the barrier, I'll be as good as dead and another Slayer will be called. Just like that. No mess, no—whatever." She wasn't sure being trapped in the Hellmouth qualified as being dead, but her reasoning convinced Pragoh.

The demon pointed toward the wall. "Slayer go now."

CHAPTER NINE

"She isn't going anywhere," Giles said.

Buffy flashed him an annoyed look. If Giles didn't understand her motives or what she was thinking or planning, he should trust her enough not to interfere. He did.

"Not just yet," Giles continued. "The bargain—an extremely bad one, in my opinion—is this: You remove the containment spell around the school, and then Buffy will do . . . whatever she's decided to do."

Buffy let the Watcher talk. His carefully chosen words implied that he knew suicide was not her intention. His calm, reasoned approach also lent credence to her proposal.

The short demon snorted, but he didn't argue. He moved

into the center of the corridor and faced the stairs, just as he had when he cast his binding spell. With his plump arms raised, he closed his eyes. After humming for several seconds, he mumbled an incantation, then hummed again.

Buffy watched Willow, looking for signs of unrest, but for now, she wasn't a flight risk. The kur was insensitive to Pragoh's humming chant and at ease.

Pragoh abruptly stopped humming and turned. "All done. Now Slayer go."

"I think not!" Giles stiffened. "Buffy stays right here until we *know*—for a fact—that the spell has indeed been removed."

Losing patience, Pragoh stamped his foot. "Pragoh mad."

"Tough." Buffy glanced at Xander. She needed him to execute her plan, but that would wait. "Go check the doors upstairs, Xander. If you can get outside, we're in the clear."

"Uh—" Xander looked at Willow, afraid to let go.

"It's okay. Nobody's going anywhere until you get back," Buffy assured him.

"Okay. See that you don't." Halfway up the stairs, Xander paused to look back. "I mean it."

"I know." Buffy smiled.

After lighting the last candle, Ms. Calendar walked behind Buffy and whispered, "I hope you know what you're doing."

Ditto that, Buffy thought as the teacher returned to the space under the stairs. Ms. Calendar picked up the old book and went to stand beside Giles. When the time came, they had everything in place to seal the Hellmouth.

On edge with anticipation, Buffy watched the stairs for Xander and reviewed all the steps of her plan. Her thoughts were so focused, she almost didn't sense Angel moving toward them through the basement corridors. Every nerve in her body sizzled as she turned to greet him.

"Angel!" Giles exclaimed, surprised when the vampire suddenly appeared by the storeroom.

Angel didn't respond to the Watcher. His dark eyes captured Buffy's gaze and held her with the intensity of his caring. When he stood over her, the cosmos took a breathless pause. Buffy clung to the intimate moment. Things didn't always work out as planned, and it might be their last.

"When did you get here?" Giles asked. "Into the school, I mean."

Angel dragged his attention away from Buffy. "I've been hanging out in the tunnel for the past hour. I couldn't shake the feeling that something was off."

"You could say that," Buffy agreed. "The Hellmouth sprang a few leaks and a horde of low-life demons flew the coop."

"That explains why the building was sealed," Angel said.

"Yes, to prevent the contamination from spreading." Giles looked up sharply. "How did you get in again?"

Buffy was way ahead of the librarian on that one. The fact that Angel was *inside* the building meant that Pragoh's containment spell was no longer in effect. Without being obvious, she took stock of all the players. Fate had replaced Xander with Angel, a switch that could prove critical. The vampire was stronger, with a higher tolerance for pain.

"I walked in after Spike and Drusilla ran out," Angel said. "Drusilla looked a little frazzled."

"Turning into a giant bat takes a lot out of a person," Ms. Calendar said.

With the pests gone and the containment spell broken, there was no reason to delay. Buffy plotted her moves while Giles, Ms. Calendar, and Angel talked, taking it for granted that they would know what to do and when to do it. Her life and Willow's depended on it. Once she set events in motion, they would all be committed.

"Drusilla turned into a bat?" Angel raised an eyebrow. "I can see how that would make for a bad day."

And it's going to get worse for some of us.

Without a whisper of warning, Buffy charged Pragoh and pushed him toward the wall. Grabbing his horns, she lifted him off his feet and kicked him through the distortion into the Hellmouth.

"Open the book!" Giles called to Ms. Calendar.

A gazillion and one down, and one to go, Buffy thought as she grabbed Willow by the arm. She pulled the startled girl toward her, then pushed, driving Willow into Angel. The vampire instinctively threw his arms around her.

"Hold on to her, Angel," Buffy yelled, "and do *not* let her go!"

"What are you doing?" Willow's frightened confusion

was a fleeting concession to her humanity. When the kur's fear kicked in, her face contorted with rage. "Let me go!"

Buffy glanced at Giles.

He nodded, understanding with no words spoken.

Buffy sprang forward and wrenched the kur from Willow's grasp.

"No!" Willow stretched out her arms as Buffy spun and ran for the barrier. "Give him back! Buffy!"

Angel tightened his hold around Willow's waist and chest. She fought with the ferocity of a mother tiger defending her cubs, twisting to wrench free, kicking and scratching.

Buffy yanked the blue scarf off the spitting beast and held it at arm's length as she ran. It had two rows of short, sharp teeth and a pitiful ear-splitting howl. It snapped its jaws, clawed her arms, and flailed furry feet.

Swinging the smoking censer, Giles studied the spell in the book Ms. Calendar held open.

Unable to free herself from Angel's grip, Willow changed tactics. "Buffy, please don't. He's so cute and helpless. Please—"

Buffy blotted out Willow's plea and kept her eye on the wall. When she reached it, she rammed the kur through the shimmering crack.

"No!" Willow's tortured scream reverberated through the basement.

Buffy stood facing the Hellmouth, tense and breathless from the emotional exertion. The sound of Willow's suffering was almost more than she could bear, and the cadence of the Watcher's chant was a numbing balm.

"Terra, vente, ignis et pluvial," Giles recited, swinging the censer in an expanding arc.

"Easy, Willow," Angel said, his voice low and soothing. "It's going to be all right."

Willow wailed and pounded on the vampire with her fist. A prisoner of the psychic link until the Hellmouth closed, she was inconsolable.

". . . numina vos obsecro."

Hurry, Giles, Buffy begged, wishing she didn't have to listen. Then she saw the gray arm.

Pragoh was trying to come back!

Pragoh want a prize? Buffy fumed as she positioned herself in front of the distortion. She had no qualms about breaking a deal with the little devil—none at all. He had made *his* bad bargain when he'd asked for a bribe. The instant the gray demon's snout appeared, she let fly with a kick and punched him back in.

". . . nos a recente malo resoluto."

"The spell's broken, school's open!" Xander's excitement stalled at the base of the stairs. "When did Mr. Tall, Moody, and Annoying get here?"

Buffy watched in disbelief as Pragoh tried to scramble through the leak again. He thrust an arm and leg out with his head. Buffy put her hands on his horns and pushed, but he resisted.

"Uh, Buffy," Xander said. "Giles's eyes are bulging. You don't think one of those critters—"

Buffy knew exactly what to think. Giles couldn't interrupt the incantation to warn her—

"Omnia vasa veritatis!"

—that the Hellmouth was going to close!

Now! Buffy let go of the demon's horns and jumped back as the barrier sealed. She had narrowly missed having her hand severed. Pragoh's snout, arm, and leg fell on the floor, gushing green blood.

Willow sagged against Angel and wept. The psychic connection to Cutie and her heart were broken. The vampire held her close, saying nothing. Only time could turn her raw wound into a tolerable scar.

"We did it!" Raising victorious fists, Ms. Calendar grinned and hugged Giles.

"It would appear so." Giles nodded at Buffy, his eyes brimming with relief.

Buffy smiled back, but the good feeling for a job well done was tainted. Everything had worked out exactly as planned, leaving only one loose end. Willow didn't hold grudges as a rule, and on an intellectual level, she knew that Buffy had had no choice. Still, her sorrow over Cutie's loss was so deep that it might be the exception to Willow's generous ability to forgive.

That's another injury time will heal or not, Buffy thought with a glance at Angel. Unlike men who treated distraught women like embers that were too hot to handle, he held Willow close and murmured reassurances, giving her all the time she needed to cry it out.

Xander peered down at Pragoh's remains. Flesh and gore smoked, burning away into a pile of ash. "The Hellmouth's demon dogcatcher is dead."

"It was his own fault for trying to pull a fast one," Buffy said. "Extortion is a crime."

"So if the seals fail—" Xander turned to fire off a few words of apology. "No offense, Giles, but if they do, who's going to come and take the mini-invaders away?"

"I'm pretty sure the Hellmouth has a long line of varmint hunters," Buffy said. "Pragoh wasn't the least bit skeptical about how a dead Slayer is automatically replaced with a new one. I bet another demonic pied piper is being chosen as we speak."

"Brilliant deduction, Buffy!" Giles looked proud, but Buffy wasn't sure she should take his surprise as a compliment.

"We should probably collect all this accoutrement and get it out of here before Principal Snyder decides to inspect for rabid termites." Handing the book to Giles, Ms. Calendar began extinguishing the candles. "He has to explain this away somehow."

"I don't suppose he retained a trace of lackadaisical good nature?" When Giles caught everyone's incredulous stares, he sighed. "No, I suppose not."

"Maybe I should take Willow upstairs," Xander said. "Away from the scene of the crime."

"Good idea," Buffy agreed.

"And I must get back to the library to record the details of this incident while they're still fresh in my mind." Giles shouldered his bag. "Your input would be helpful, Buffy."

"You've got it," Buffy said. "Later."

She stood back until everyone but Angel was gone. Even though she and the vampire were in love, they couldn't get by feeling awkward—until the kissing started. She stumbled into the dialogue first this time. "You missed all the fun."

"Playing Batman with Drusilla in the Batcave?" Angel grinned. "Not my idea of a good time."

"I've had better mornings too." Buffy desperately wanted to feel his embrace and the softness of his lips on hers. With him standing so near, the temptation was overwhelming, but not enough to countermand the other things she had to do. "I, uh, have to go see how my mom's doing."

"Joyce was here? With the bats?"

"No bats," Buffy said. "Just a terrible case of gross green junk eroding her face, but she's getting over it."

Angel nodded. He understood. "Yeah, you should go."

"I know." Buffy sighed. Her mom was already upset with her for deserting sick friends. As much as she wanted to stay with Angel, she couldn't neglect her responsibilities. "Will I see you tonight?"

Angel's smile brightened her heart. "Midnight at Myra's?"

"I'll be there." When the vampire was out of sight, Buffy shivered in the cold he left behind.

• • •

On her way back to the cafeteria, Buffy paused outside the classroom that had served as an infirmary. Police officers and paramedics were filling out forms and checking the corpses. A doctor and the detective in charge were discussing a press release with Principal Snyder, who had retrieved his clothes. They had decided to call the outbreak a noncontagious variation of Legionnaires' disease. Buffy had no doubt the lie would work. The people in Sunnydale would believe anything to avoid dealing with the truth.

A little sickness won't even keep them away from the rummage sale, Buffy thought.

Before she returned to the cafeteria, Buffy ducked into the restroom and caught Cordelia and Harmony taking stock of the damage to their appearances in the mirror. She was surprised the two girls hadn't vacated the school as soon as the quarantine was lifted. When they saw her, they reacted like they wished they had.

"What are you doing here?" Cordelia demanded.

"We're in the middle of serious cosmetic repairs, if you don't mind." Rolling her eyes, Harmony turned back to squint at her reflection.

Buffy was very much aware that the cool crowd claimed territorial rights to all the restrooms on campus. If anyone in the not-so-cool majority entered when Cordelia and company were present, they risked being chased away or publicly humiliated. *A little harmless payback is in order,* Buffy thought, taking her cue from the conversation she had had with Deirdre earlier.

"Oh, I'm so glad you're all right, Cordelia." Buffy faked being immensely relieved. "When I heard you had lost all your teeth, I figured you'd be—"

"Who said I lost my teeth?" Cordelia gasped. "Xander! That no-good—"

"No, it wasn't Xander." Buffy tapped her cheek, pretending to think. "I don't remember, but everybody's talking about it."

Harmony glanced at Cordelia with a slight smile, savoring the idea of having devastating ammunition to use against her best friend.

"I did *not* lose my teeth!" Slamming her hairbrush on the sink counter, Cordelia opened her mouth and tugged on glistening white enamel. "See? They're real."

"Oh, yeah." Buffy winced with dismay. "I am *so* sorry."

"They do look kind of fake," Harmony said.

"And you still have crow's feet around your eyes!" Cordelia shot back.

Deciding she could wait to freshen up, Buffy left the chilly restroom and walked into simmering pandemonium. The cafeteria was almost as chaotic in the aftermath of the Hellmouth epidemic as it had been during setup for the rummage sale. She paused inside the doorway to eavesdrop on the Dingoes' lead guitarist and lead singer.

"Legionnaires' disease?" Oz asked Devon.

"That's what the cop said."

"One diagnosis fits all? I don't know." Oz shook his head.

"My memory's a little hazy, but I think I was almost smothered by sheepskin seat covers."

"What did you do?" Devon laughed shortly. "Pass out underneath them?"

"Can't say." Oz shrugged. "Maybe I inhaled something that was on the wool and had an asthma attack."

"Could happen, I guess," Devon conceded. "I leaned over to look at a pair of old Chevy hubcaps and woke up in the corner of a classroom."

"Are you okay?" Oz asked.

Devon patted his chest and arms. "Yep."

"Me too. Let's go spin some tunes."

As the two boys walked off, Buffy scanned the room for her mother and friends. She hoped all the survivors had recovered from their various ailments with amnesia. Muddled minds told no tales they couldn't explain.

Andrew walked up and down the aisles, carrying the coiled bullwhip. He looked lost, and he was obviously looking for something. *Jonathan?* Buffy wondered. The short, quiet kid had been standing at rigid attention the last time she had seen him, but he wasn't in the room now.

Willow sat on the chair by the shirts with her head propped on her hand, looking totally dejected. Xander wasn't there, and Buffy put off going over. She couldn't blame Willow if she spurned a sympathetic overture, but she didn't want to go through it alone.

Better to face the music with her mom, who was helping

Ms. Calendar sweep up the shattered black orb.

As Buffy took a step, Principal Snyder stormed in, dragging Jonathan by the ear. The boy still had the action figure blister packs, and Snyder was wearing the hat.

"Stealing will not be tolerated, Mr. Levenson." Principal Snyder stopped by the checkout table and held out his hand. "I'll take those. Then I'll decide whether you'll spend the next month in detention or at juvenile hall."

Alerted to Jonathan's whereabouts by the commotion, Andrew cautiously crept closer. He stopped a few feet from Buffy.

"I was going to pay for them," Jonathan said meekly. "After I got back from the—you know."

"Sure you were." Principal Snyder folded his arms.

Buffy was pretty sure Principal Snyder had been too distracted to pay for the hat. Not that she could point that out without paying a price. Still, as a champion of the underdog with a duty to thwart injustice, she had to do something to help Jonathan.

"Actually," Buffy said, moving closer, "he told me a little while ago that he was waiting to buy them."

"One juvenile delinquent vouching for another juvenile delinquent." The principal sneered. "Why should I take your word for it, Ms. Summers? Everyone knows you criminal types stick together."

"Ask him!" Jonathan pointed when Xander walked in. "Xander knows I was going to pay!"

Xander stopped dead, whipping his hand behind his back to hide a can of soda. "Me?"

The detective stuck his head in the door. "Snyder! We need you to sign these reports."

"Make sure you get a receipt." Principal Snyder glared at Jonathan, then shouted at Ms. Calendar. "The rummage sale opens to the public in an hour! The police are blaring an announcement from their patrol cars all over town. You *will* be ready." He mumbled as he headed out the door. "Next year's fund-raiser for the marching band will be something simple, like selling candy."

Xander continued on across the room toward Willow.

No sooner had Jonathan slipped the Snyder noose than Andrew confronted him about his action figure heist. "Some best friend you turned out to be, Jonathan. You know how much I want that 1978 mint condition Walrus Man."

Buffy joined her mom and Ms. Calendar behind the artifact table just as they swept the last bits of black glass into a dustpan.

"Buffy!" Her mother smiled as she stood up. "I was hoping to see you before I went back to the gallery. It seems I owe you an apology."

"Oh." Buffy waited to find out why.

"Ms. Calendar explained that you were helping other students who were in danger." Joyce smiled sheepishly. "I should have known you wouldn't turn your back on your friends."

"That's okay, Mom," Buffy said with a grateful glance at

the teacher. There was truth in what Ms. Calendar had told her. She *had* saved Willow and herself from certain death in the Hellmouth.

Ms. Calendar held out a wastepaper basket, and Joyce dumped the broken glass. "Such a shame," the teacher said.

"Yeah." Buffy wrinkled her nose. "I guess that black thing wasn't . . . alive."

Ms. Calendar looked at her askance, apparently realizing Buffy knew more about how the orb had been shattered than she wanted to say. She didn't say anything either.

"Hardly!" Joyce exclaimed. "It was a rare piece of black jade called 'Endless Night.' The last owner claimed that it hypnotized him."

"Really?" Buffy didn't volunteer her corroborating second opinion.

"It really is too bad a vandal got in here and smashed it," Joyce said. "The Mayor would have paid quite handsomely for it, I'm sure."

"The Mayor wanted to buy it?" Buffy asked.

Ms. Calendar took the dustpan from Joyce and set it aside with the wastepaper basket and broom. "I'm sure Mayor Wilkins will understand that this wasn't your fault, Ms. Summers. You can still invite him to the Joel Shavin showing at the gallery."

"Oh, no." Joyce shook her head and pulled her car keys out of her pocket. "He doesn't know this was *the* 'Endless Night' his father lost at auction all those years ago, so please don't tell him. I'll just invite him to another gallery event—someday. Next year, maybe."

"All right, if that's what you want." Ms. Calendar smiled, then left to make sure everything was set for the delayed start of the rummage sale.

Buffy felt bad about messing up her mom's opportunity to impress the Mayor, but the black jade was dangerous. Things would have turned out much worse if Mayor Wilkins had bought it and gone bonkers after prolonged exposure. Once again, her seemingly irresponsible actions had responsible consequences. And as usual, she couldn't tell her mom. She couldn't explain that she had been in the cafeteria tracking down virulent demonic vermin and had mistaken the black jade for a heinous Hellmouth beast.

"Is Willow going to be all right?" Joyce looked across the room and frowned with concern. "She looks so depressed."

"She's had a tough day, but I'll go check." Buffy cocked her head to study her mom. "Are you sure you're okay?"

"I'm fine, but . . ." Joyce hesitated. "You might ask Ms. Calendar to find those black lace gloves and put them aside for me."

"Consider them yours," Buffy said.

"Don't be late for dinner." Joyce waved and walked out.

Relieved that her mom was finally leaving the building, Buffy took a deep breath and headed toward men's shirts. She wasn't sure how to approach Willow, and she didn't know if Xander was mad at her too. His lack of wordage at the door was troubling. Snyder might have shocked him speechless, but it was hard to tell.

The rocking rhythm of an old Queen song started playing as Buffy walked up to Xander and Willow.

"Hey!" Grinning, Xander lowered his voice. "It's the Slayer theme song: 'Another One Bites the Dust.'" He sang along to the title phrase. "Makes you wonder how much other people really know."

Xander was joking, but he had a point. Giles would know if a Slayer in the late seventies had lived in Britain, but she didn't want to. The Chosen One of twenty years ago was dead, like all the Slayers before her.

"I always liked that song," Willow said, "before the dusting thing got real. Now it just makes me . . . sad."

"He *was* cute," Xander said, assuming she was really talking about the kur. "*Is*, I mean. Cutie's not dead. He's just in another place, but if you remember how he controlled your mind and twisted your thoughts, maybe you won't miss him quite—"

Buffy cut him off. "I am so sorry, Willow, but I couldn't let you die."

"I know." Willow sighed. "I just don't want to talk about it." She looked at Xander. "Ever again."

"Never it is." Xander tapped his foot to the beat of the Queen song for a moment. "I think Oz likes you."

"The guitar guy?" Willow scoffed. "Oh, yeah. Right. I can just see me holding down the band table at the Bronze."

"Stranger things have happened," Xander said.

Willow smiled. "Well, yeah. But there's strange, and then there's impossible."

"Incoming," Xander announced when the first wave of student shoppers burst through the doors.

All the tension eased out of Buffy as she listened to her friends banter back and forth. Her mother was back in mom mode, and Giles was dutifully keeping Watcher notes. Good had triumphed over evil one more time, and normal reigned supreme.

Best of all, she had a midnight rendezvous to keep at Myra Stanley's tombstone, inscribed in 1953 by her beloved husband of sixty years: MY ANGEL FOREVER.

Afterimage

To Keith DeCandido

Special thanks to
my editor, Patrick Price;
Emily Westlake;
and my agent, Jennifer Jackson

PROLOGUE

They'd thrown the place together in the 1950s, back when land and gas were cheap and no one had ever heard of a compact car. Scores of acres large, the Sunnydale Drive-In sat square in the center of a tract of land just outside the city limits, a reasonable distance from even the farthest houses. The relative isolation meant that the owners could go about their business without troubling the neighbors. Engine noises and fumes alike would be borne away on the night wind, and the light and glare of the movies' operation would inconvenience no one.

It had gone up fast and cheap, but in an era when things fast and cheap were still built to last. The main buildings had solid cinder-block walls reinforced with steel beams, and the plumbing and power lines were buried deep in armored conduits that still held up after decades of disuse. Even the huge screen, curved like a shield and facing the parking area, remained structurally sound. The screen's surface was a lost cause, of course, ruined by long years of exposure and no repair, but its supporting framework was perfectly serviceable.

The place's persistence was somewhat amazing, actually. There weren't many enterprises that could stand abandoned and unattended for so long and survive so well.

"They did good work," the contractor said. He was a big man, with beefy muscle that was slowly turning to fat and calloused hands that came with a career of physical labor. He parked his big pickup on the hill that overlooked the screen, got out, and unrolled the drive-in's original blueprints on his truck's hood. "Look," he said, indicating sections of the diagram. "Projection shack, concession stand, box office—they're all sound. Screen needs a new facing and the sound system will be updated, of course." He paused to glance at the bank loan officer who'd accompanied him on the ride out from Sunnydale. "You've got someone working the FCC thing, right?"

The loan officer nodded and dabbed sweat from his forehead. He wasn't in his element. It was a sunny afternoon and the fair skin of his bald scalp had already begun to redden. More perspiration darkened the shoulders and armpits of his suit. "The license should be ready by the time you finish installation," he said. The resurrected drive-in would use broadcast sound rather than car-side speakers, and the Federal Communications Commission had to approve the equipment. "Assuming you can meet the deadline," he continued.

"Sure, no problem," responded the contractor. He spoke as if uttering a completely self-evident truth. "Run cables, patch pipes, landscape. Re-screen and install new signage. Marquee is a standard issue. Nothing big, really. My boys will have this place up and running in four weeks. Three if we run extra shifts."

"Four will be fine," the banker replied. He opened his briefcase atop the blueprint and began pulling out document folders. "Here," the banker said, handing them to the contractor one at a time. "You'll need these. Letter of credit, insurance forms, detailed specification sheets." Before handing over the last folder, he indicated the papers inside. "Contract. Sign and date."

It was quiet at the old drive-in. Even in the open vastness, the scratch of ballpoint pen was easily heard. As he signed his name, the contractor commented, "I hope you don't mind my saying this, but you don't seem very happy for a guy who's just been told that the job's a piece of cake."

"I'm sorry," the banker said. "I'm sure you'll do good work. I'm just not certain that reopening this place is a good idea. It has a history."

CHAPTER ONE

"No," Buffy Summers said. She shook her head for emphasis, her blond hair rippling like water under the fluorescent lights. "I'm dead serious. He looked exactly like a penguin."

"Well, that doesn't sound very frightening," Willow Rosenberg replied. She looked skeptical. "I mean, penguins are friendly, formal fellows. They make children laugh! How much of a problem could a penguin be?"

They were at the big table in the Sunnydale High library. The school day had ended, but sometimes a Slayer's day, like her work, was never done. Buffy, Willow, and Cordelia Chase were seated, but Giles stood, thumbing through one of his countless books and apparently not paying much attention to Buffy's report of the previous night's activities. Neither was Cordelia, who doodled idly on a composition book cover. But Willow was hanging on Buffy's every word about an encounter near the city zoo.

"Well, this *particular* penguin was eight feet tall, with fangs and claws," Buffy said. "Still formal—"

"—but not so friendly," Willow said, finishing her sentence.

Buffy nodded. Fangs and claws were nearly everyday factors in her life as the Slayer. But a giant-size penguin? Now, that was something new. "Giles, ever hear about anything like that before? That's one for the books, right?"

For a man whose title was Watcher, Giles spent a lot of time listening. Without comment, he reversed the book he held, so that the three girls could see its opened pages.

One page was covered with tightly spaced lines of text in an ugly font. Opposite was an elaborate illustration of a gigantic penguin with fangs and claws. Beside it, evidently to indicate scale, was a human silhouette. The penguin-thing towered over the man.

"Oh," Buffy said meekly as Giles resumed his reading.

"So, um, what did you do?" Willow asked. "You got him, right?"

Buffy nodded again. Pretty and well built, with large, expressive eyes that gleamed when she spoke, she often used gestures and motions to underscore her words.

"Well, the stake wouldn't do much good," Buffy said. "Those things have a thick layer of blubber or something—"

"Birds don't have blubber," Cordelia said smugly. They were her first words since joining the conclave, and it made sense that they'd be a correction.

Buffy and Willow blinked in unison. Cordelia wasn't particularly scholarly, and thus the tidbit of knowledge she offered so casually came as a bit of a surprise. Seeing their expressions, Cordelia explained. "Sixth-grade book report." She tapped her temple with one elegant finger, clearly pleased to have pointed out Buffy's error. "Good memory. I'm not stupid, you know."

"Oh," Buffy said. Resolutely, she soldiered on. "He was coming at me pretty fast. When I had the chance, I reached inside his chest and kept reaching." She demonstrated with a pantomime, her arm extended and open fingers wiggling.

Willow's eyes bulged. Buffy made a note to herself to cut back on the graphic detail. As with the fangs and claws thing, she'd become so accustomed to the nuts and bolts of her work that she sometimes forgot how squeamish civilians could be. And although Willow wasn't quite a civilian, she wasn't the Slayer, either. As for Cordelia . . .

To be perfectly honest, Buffy wasn't entirely sure what role Cordelia Chase had in her life these days. They'd disliked each other since Buffy's first day at Sunnydale High, but recent events had cast the Slayer and the shallow beauty queen as reluctant allies.

But she could worry about that later, Buffy decided.

"I kept reaching," she continued, limiting her account to words, not reenactment, "until I found something hard, and then I squeezed it. The thing made a burp—"

"Real penguins make a sound like a crow's caw," Cordelia said.

"—and then he kind of melted," Buffy said. She favored Cordelia with a sharp look. "I don't suppose regular penguins do that, either?"

"What became of the remains?" Giles asked.

Buffy shrugged. "There are storm drains all over that courtyard," she said. "Last I saw, Frosty was dripping into one. It rained this morning too. I don't think anything was left behind."

Giles nodded, closing his book. Buffy wasn't sure whether he was relieved because of strategic concerns or simply because he was a tidy man.

"Wait until Xander hears about this," Willow said excitedly.

"Where is Xander, anyway?" Cordelia asked. She set down her pen. "That boy's been making himself pretty scarce lately after school."

Willow looked mildly confused. "When did you start keeping tabs on Xander?"

Before Cordelia could respond, the library doors opened and the subject of Willow's question sauntered in. Xander Harris was tall and dark-haired, and usually looked mildly bemused by the world around him. He had good features and better eyes. He grinned as he entered, book bag under one arm and a thick sheaf of papers under the other.

"Hey there, groovy guys and groovy gals," he said, dropping into an empty chair on Cordelia's side of the table. He continued, "Oh, and Giles, too."

"Speak of the devil," Cordelia said.

"You know, Cordy, that's the kind of thing you probably shouldn't say," Xander said. "I mean, since we live on top of the Hellmouth and all." He dropped his book bag to the floor and placed his sheaf of papers facedown on the table in front of him. It was a two-inch stack of orange sheets, clamped together with a heavy binder clip.

"Where have *you* been?" Buffy asked.

Xander made a wry expression. "Had to pick up an extra-credit assignment," he said. "I really blew that history quiz Monday."

"Not just now," Buffy said. "You've been making yourself scarce lately." Not only had Xander nearly missed the current gathering of friends and associates—the Scoobies—he'd completely missed several promised study sessions during the preceding two weeks. And if Xander didn't study, he didn't do well on quizzes. It was one of the secret laws of the universe.

"After-school job," Xander said. He seemed inordinately pleased with himself. "Two or three hours a day and I have enough for comic books, video games, and big bowls of Skittles."

Xander could talk for a long time about junk food and other ephemera. Before he could go any further down that conversational path, Buffy asked, "Where are you working, Xander?"

Xander proudly unclipped the stack of papers he'd brought and passed the orange sheets around. His voice took on the cadence of a carnival barker as he said, "Check it out, check it out, something you will enjoy."

It was a handbill. Halftone images made up the background, clearly of actors and actresses in character, a few of whom Buffy recognized. Overlaid on the collage were increasingly larger lines of type, announcing:

Grand Opening! Grand Opening!!
Grand Opening!!!
The Return of a Great Tradition!
Go to the Drive-In and Have Yourselves a Treat!
Dusk to Dawn Thrillerama Festival of Fun!
Free Corn Dogs and Cola for Late-Stayers!

Next came a list of movies. Giles and the girls read the titles, then stared at Xander with expressions that ranged from confusion to disdain, with many stops in between.

"Great, huh?" Xander asked, obviously delighted and expecting them to be too. "*Double Drunken Dragon Kung Fu Fight* is the one for me!"

"*Mysteries of Chainsaw Mansion*?" Buffy asked skeptically.

"It's a horror movie," Xander said helpfully.

"Not for me, thanks," Buffy said. "I've got enough problems."

"What is this?" Cordelia asked. "*The Lonely Cheerleader*? That's ridiculous! Cheerleaders are *never* lonely!"

"You should know," Xander said, slightly crestfallen. He reached to reclaim the handbill, but she pulled it away.

"Oh, I don't know," Willow said. She pushed back a stray lock of coppery hair. "Some of these look pretty interesting. What's *Caged Blondes* about?"

"It's a women-in-prison movie," Xander said. Much of his habitual good cheer had ebbed, but not all of it. "Good woman, accused of a crime she didn't commit, has to fight her way to freedom. They used to be a staple of drive-ins."

"Which brings us, inexorably, to the next question," Giles said. He sounded patient. He was very good at making patience sound like exasperation, though. "What on earth is a drive-in?"

"Hey, yeah, that's right, G. You're from Jolly Old England," Xander said as if he'd just remembered.

"Yes, Xander, I am," Giles said, sounding even more patient, which meant that he wasn't.

"I guess they don't have drive-ins there," Xander said. Primarily for the Watcher's benefit, he offered up a quick history of drive-ins and drive-in movies. The theaters sprang up early in the twentieth century, as a relatively low-tech, low-investment means of exhibition. They hit their stride in the 1950s with the emergence of teenagers as a specific marketing niche. Their popularity started to fade out late in the 1970s, and though some drive-ins lingered, they were few and far between.

"Home video and rising gas prices conspired to make the business impractical," Xander concluded.

"You've been reading again," Buffy said. She pursed her lips in a mock kiss. "I'm so proud of you!"

Xander looked at her blankly.

"I can tell when you're quoting a reference work," she said. "Your face screws up and I can hear the gears spin in your head." She made a mechanical sound.

"Reading is all well and good," Giles said, handing the sheet back as if he were concerned it might bite him, "but what does this have to do with any of us?"

"The old Sunnydale Drive-In is reopening," Xander said. He took the sheet and returned it to his stack, then reluctantly accepted Buffy's and Cordelia's. Willow kept hers. "I've been working at the construction site," he said, then corrected himself. "The reconstruction site, I guess. You know, doing coffee and meal runs, sweeping up, that sort of thing." He indicated his stack of handbills. "I'm supposed to distribute these."

"So you're a flunky," Cordelia said tartly. Sometimes it seemed to Buffy that Cordelia said *everything* tartly.

"I prefer to think of myself as a 'diversified assistant,'" Xander responded.

"A gopher," Buffy said. "You *gophe* for things."

"If you must put it like that," Xander said.

"I think it's a nice way to put it," Willow said. "Gophers are adorable."

Remarkably, Xander blushed. There were times when Willow could make him do that, if she said just the right thing at the right moment. "Anyway, Boss-man says he's had success in other cities, with festivals and retrospectives. Pick up the facilities for a song, slap some new paint on the place, and voilà!"

He beamed. No one beamed back at him. If none of the other four looked confused anymore, none of them looked particularly interested, either, with the possible exception of Willow. Oblivious, Xander rambled on. "Even better," he said, "I've got passes. Grand opening is this Friday, and you're all invited. On me!"

"This is at night, right?" Buffy asked.

"Yeah, of course," Xander said. He looked wounded by the question, or mildly offended, or some mixture of the two. "Can't watch movies outside in broad daylight."

"I have a date," she said.

"Oh?" Cordelia asked coolly.

"Angel?" Xander asked.

"Mr. Pointy," Buffy said. She cocked her head and leaned in Xander's direction. "Hello?" she asked. "Patrol, remember? 'Dusk to dawn' kind of gets in the way, even if it looks like something I'd enjoy." She paused. "Which I don't think it does, really. *Caged Blondes*?"

"Oh. Right."

"Sorry," Buffy said, managing to sound regretful—not filled with sorrow, but sorry to have disappointed him.

"How about you, Cordelia?" Xander asked.

"I'll be busy too," she said.

"Date?" he asked, sounding a little bit worried.

"Now, Xander, where do I usually go on Fridays? Hmmmm?" Cordelia asked. When he continued to look at her blankly, she explained. "The Bronze. It's girls' night out."

"Well, maybe Harmony and Aura—"

"Oh, yeah," Cordelia said with mild sarcasm, interrupting as he named her friends. "They'd be up for a night out with you. And movies like *these*. Uh-huh. Sure."

Willow raised her hand with just a bit of timidity. She wiggled her fingers for attention, but no one seemed to notice. Xander and Cordelia, especially, were too busy trading half glares.

Giles cleared his throat. When no one noticed that, either, he cleared it again, loudly. "Ahem," he said, secure in his audience at last. "As fascinating as all of this is, I think it's time to turn our attention to more substantive matters than American entertainments. When you made your belated entrance, Xander, Buffy was regaling us with her exploits on patrol last night. Perhaps she'd like to resume?"

Buffy liked. "There's not much more, really," she said. "After the penguin melted . . ."

• • •

He looked like a slender Santa Claus as he window-shopped his way along Sunnydale's Main Street. The man had white hair, thick and wavy, and a matching white beard that was bushy and big, but still neatly styled. He had an air of self-importance, but without any hostility or arrogance; he nodded politely at passersby and consistently yielded the right of way to women and children. He wore a nicely tailored suit and an open-necked dress shirt that looked like silk, and Amanda Hoch was certain that his Italian loafers cost more than she could earn in a year.

Amanda was in full regalia herself. She was wearing her favorite black outfit and silver accessories, with a fresh purple rinse in her hair and her skin painstakingly paled with cosmetics. She stood in the entranceway alcove of the Magic Box, where she worked, sucking down the last of a clove cigarette. It was only Amanda's fifth week in Sunnydale (her second week on the job), and she was still getting the lay of the land. She watched approaching strangers the same way she did most things in this town: with wary suspicion.

Even seen from a distance, the man appeared entirely too genial and pleasant. She didn't like people who smiled easily, or who seemed so at home in the bright sunlight. She had a cultivated fondness for dark things and shadows, which was why she'd applied for the part-time job at the Magic Box. So far, however, the gig was a disappointment, like so much of her life. She spent most of her eight poorly compensated hours a day selling tacky items to New Age wannabes and

Wiccan poseurs, who were surprisingly plentiful in the local population. At least the white-haired guy didn't look like he was another one of *those*.

He *was* headed for the Magic Box, though. Just in time, Amanda dropped the cigarette butt and ground it beneath one booted foot. She opened the door and stepped aside so that the potential customer could enter.

"Thank you, miss," the stranger said, taking the door and waving her in. His voice was warm and gentle, in an accent as Italian as his loafers. "I'd like to look around a bit."

"Make yourself at home," Amanda said as she returned to her station at the cash register. In seconds she was engrossed in her magazine again, though not so engrossed that she didn't glance occasionally in the man's direction. The Magic Box had some pricey wares, after all. Little things that fit easily into pockets. The well-heeled bearded man didn't look like a shoplifter, but you never could tell.

The place was new to him. Amanda could tell that, even with her brief tenure. The stranger browsed the Magic Box's merchandise like an explorer, giving each shelf and display a cursory glance before moving on to the next. He touched little but leaned close to read book spines and jar labels. He was working his way along the bins of herbs when he finally broke the silence.

"A surprisingly well-stocked establishment," he said. "It seems out of place in a town like this."

"Sunnydale is full of surprises," Amanda said sourly, still

trying to read. Despite herself, she continued, "You would not *believe* some of the things I've heard about since I got here. I sure don't."

"Ah," the man said, "you're a newcomer?"

Amanda nodded. Despite her initial distaste for his general manner, she found herself warming to him. "A little more than a month," she said. "My grandmother needed some live-in help with my grandfather."

"I thought so," the man said, smiling again. "I didn't think you were from around here."

"The look, you mean?" Amanda asked. She waggled black-nailed fingers and flashed a smile, black-lipped and brief.

There were other Goths in Sunnydale, but not so many that Amanda didn't cause comment. That was one reason she refused to give up the look, despite her grandmother's pleas. Her appearance was a statement, a demonstration of individuality and rebellion. Amanda liked standing out in a white-bread world.

"It was the dialect, actually," the man said. He stood next to the shop's main cabinet now, where high-ticket items hid behind locked glass. "New Jersey," he continued. "Paramus, I think."

Amanda was impressed. "Wow. How did you know that?"

"Dialect. Regional variations in a language, specifically word choices and pronunciations," the man said. He gestured at the locked case. "I wonder if I might see the crystals?"

Usually Amanda disliked fooling with the display case. Not this time, though—not for this customer. She dug out the keys, knelt, and worked the lock. "I thought I had an accent," Amanda said.

The crystals he'd indicated were square cut and five in number. They rested on a black velvet presentation board. Amanda took the board from the case and set it on the display case's top so that he could inspect them.

He looked, but didn't touch. They glinted slightly as he eyed them. "No," he said. "Accents are when two languages impact on one another. You speak with a distinctive dialect, my dear; *I* have an accent."

It was precisely the sort of mini-lecture that Amanda had always found irritating in the extreme, but somehow the white-haired man made the information sound interesting, even useful. Wanting to repay the favor, she read from the card that accompanied the crystals.

"Latverian Spirit Stones," she read aloud. "Premier quality, certified. They respond to human psycho-etheric potentials." She'd never had to show the gems closely before, and she stumbled over some of the words. The instructions on how to use the things were clear enough, though.

Amanda took one stone in her hand. It was as slick as water against her skin. In the crystal's depths, the slight glint of a moment before became something brighter, a spark that danced and shone brightly. The stone's surface remained perfectly cool.

"Wow," Amanda said. She'd never thought any of the stuff in the Magic Box would actually work. She looked up. "Wanna try it?" she asked.

The man smiled and drew back slightly from the offered stones. "I don't think so," he said. "I'm satisfied that they're genuine. I'll take the set."

"All of them?" Amanda asked as she set down the stone. She blinked. The crystals were very expensive, among the dearest items in the shop.

"All five," the man agreed. He smiled and his pale blue eyes twinkled, reminding her of the crystal's surprising gleam. "Unless there are more?"

There weren't. Amanda packaged the five stones carefully. Each went into its own locked case, and then the five cases went into a larger box, to be secured with packing tape and then deposited neatly into a handled bag bearing the store logo. She rang up the sale and accepted a credit card the color of platinum. Amanda dawdled slightly at each step, far from eager to conclude the transaction.

"Here you go," she said with her very best smile as she passed the charge slip to him for his signature. "Will you be in Sunnydale long, Mr. Belasimo?"

"Balsamo," he corrected her, but so gently that it didn't sound like a correction at all. "Bal-sa-mo. And no, my dear, not for very long. Once my business concludes, I shall depart."

"Oh," Amanda said, trying to hide her disappointment. "Well, I hope to see you again."

"Perhaps you shall," Balsamo said. Then, unexpectedly, he took her right hand and kissed her fingers.

It was a flourish that Amanda had seen before in movies but never in real life. She had no idea of any proper way to respond, so all she could do was smile silently and blush a bit as he turned and exited with his purchase.

More than an hour passed before she could fully return her attention to the magazine. Something about the transaction affected her, and the effect lingered. It wasn't the man's easy knowledge, or his elegance and grace, or even the fact that he'd spent more in ten minutes than the Magic Box took in during most weeks. It was something else, something subtler.

He'd treated her like a lady, Amanda finally realized. He'd made her feel like she was someone special, and not just a Goth shopgirl from New Jersey.

Balsamo forgot about the guttersnipe behind the counter before taking ten steps outside. No, not forgot; rather, he took and filed her image safely away from his consciousness. His knowledge of the purple-haired girl's existence remained available, should he ever need to call upon it, but the distaste he felt no longer distracted him. He had taught himself the mental trick in his youth, and it had proved essential over the many years that followed.

The peasants he shared the walkway with received much the same attention. He nodded politely at other men, stepped aside for the ladies, and made himself smile at the children, and then drove them all from his thoughts. They didn't matter. All that mattered was the paper sack he gripped in his left hand.

He'd been very fortunate, he realized. He never would have imagined that a place like Sunnydale would hold a genuine spirit stone, let alone five of them. Balsamo would have liked to know how the five glistening bits of crystal had made their way to the New World, and to this insipid little township. Perhaps later, after his primary business was done, he'd return to the Magic Box to research the matter.

He imagined that he could make the purple-haired wench tell him anything he wanted to know. Likely, he'd enjoy the process too.

Balsamo's stride was long and brisk. It took him only minutes to traverse the six blocks between the shop and his hotel. He smiled at the doorman as he entered, smiled again at the concierge, and then checked at the front desk for messages. There were none, so he proceeded to his room, pausing only to purchase a Styrofoam container of coffee from the lobby shop. He disliked the local blend but disliked brewing his own even more.

A small suitcase waited for him in his penthouse suite. He inspected its seals carefully before opening it. It was the only piece of luggage that had not been unpacked, and it pleased him to see that none of the hotel staff had been foolish enough to tamper with it. The case was small, but its interior was efficiently designed and held a score of interesting instruments.

After considering his options for a moment, he decided that the simplest method would be best.

It usually was, of course.

He chose a small mortar and pestle, each hewn from ivory that was once a dragon's tooth. Both implements were marked with mystic symbols and discolored from heavy use. They'd been in Balsamo's possession for a very long time.

He unwrapped the purchased stones. One by one they lit up like small suns when he touched them for the first time. They flared brightly enough to singe the skin of his fingertips and make his eyes water, but Balsamo scarcely noticed. He dropped them into the dragon-tooth mortar, applying the pestle as he muttered ancient words of power, and then went to work.

The Latverian pebbles broke with satisfying ease. Each flashed one last time as it shattered, then fell dark. Balsamo broke them into fragments, ground them into powder, and then ground them even more. When he was convinced that they no longer posed any hazard to him, he set his tools aside. The released energy added new scars to the pestle, but he didn't care about that.

His suite had a dining area and a small kitchen equipped with reasonable-quality china coffee mugs. He selected one, filled it with the coffee he'd bought downstairs, and added cream and sugar. Settling into an armchair, he sipped and considered the events of the day.

Casual conversations with the local bumpkins had included

mentions of unexplainable events—screams, disappearances, lights in the sky. The newspaper files in the local library told of numerous mysterious deaths. He'd found five Latverian spirit stones in what was, by his standards, a mere knickknack shop.

Clearly, there was more to Sunnydale than met the eye.

CHAPTER TWO

Dinner at the Summers house that night was comfort food, as it often was. Joyce Summers's marriage had ended badly, and although many aspects of traditional family life had fallen by the wayside in the years since, Joyce refused to let go of them all. After coming to Sunnydale in search of a fresh start, she always tried to make the evening meal a sort of capstone for the day. She wanted it to be a time when she and Buffy could sit and talk and, hopefully, reinforce their bonds. That meant sitting together at the big dining room table, eating solid and substantial food, using real plates and real utensils. Paper cartons, Styrofoam cups, and plastic sporks seldom visited the Summers residence, if Joyce had anything to say about it.

Unless she was very, very busy.

She allowed the first minute or two of the meal to pass in near silence. She liked watching Buffy eat. There was something reassuringly basic about it. And Buffy could eat an astonishing amount. Joyce knew that teenagers had healthy appetites, but her daughter seemed to have a bottomless hunger. Given that the younger Summers didn't seem to have much interest in sports, it was a wonder that the girl was able to keep herself so trim.

Finally, Joyce allowed herself to ask the question. "So," she said, "how was school today, dear?"

"Gloomph!" Buffy said. She chewed rapidly and swallowed. "Good," she repeated, before shoveling more chicken casserole into her mouth.

"Did you learn anything?" Joyce asked.

Buffy shrugged. Joyce supposed that a shrug was about as much of an answer as she would have given her own mother, back in the day.

"Did anything interesting happen?" Joyce asked. She tried not to sound needy.

Buffy took a crusty roll and broke it, then spread butter on the fleecy whiteness inside. As she worked, she spoke. "Kind of," she said. "Someone detonated a frog in bio. Willow thinks she's figured out a new file transfer protocol, but I can't tell what she's talking about. Xander got a job."

"Detonated a frog?" Joyce asked. She set her forkful of food down for a moment.

Buffy shrugged again. "Dunno," she said. "Wasn't my lab section it happened in."

"Oh." For some reason Joyce felt relieved. She wouldn't want her little girl to see something so gruesome. "Oh, well, that's better. What about Xander?"

"What about him?" Buffy asked. She ate half her buttered roll with a single, engulfing bite and set the remainder on her plate.

"You said he got a job," Joyce said. Xander was one of Buffy's friends, but beyond that, she wasn't sure what role the Harris boy played in her daughter's life. From what little she'd seen of them together, there didn't seem to be any kind of romance in progress, though she had a hunch Xander wished differently. "What kind of job?"

"He's a flunky. No, a gopher. We agreed he's a gopher," Buffy said. "That's not as good as a flunky but better than a minion." She was still focused almost entirely on her meal. Asparagus spears disappeared into her mouth with amazing rapidity.

"Don't bolt your food, dear," Joyce said patiently. She generally looked forward to each evening meal with her daughter, but sometimes she wondered why.

"They're reopening the Sunnydale Drive-In," Buffy said by way of explanation.

"Oh. That's right," Joyce said. "I heard about that. I wonder if that's such a good idea."

Now she had Buffy's attention. The blond teenager paused and looked at her mom. "Oh yeah?" she said.

Joyce nodded. "They were talking about it at the gallery today," she said. "One of our bank's loan officers has the property's account. He's working with the people reopening the place." She sipped her iced tea. "Barney's lived here a long time. He says that place has a history of trouble."

"Barney?" Buffy asked. She snickered, with the easy cruelty of youth. "You actually know someone named *Barney*? Is he a caveman or a purple dinosaur?"

"Barney is very nice," Joyce said in mild reproof. More than once in recent years it had occurred to Joyce that the day might come when the name Buffy would be considered quaint or goofy. "He has the gallery's account too. I like him."

A worried expression flickered across Buffy's features. No, not worried, wary. The look of mild apprehension came and went so fast that a casual observer might have missed it. Not Joyce, however. Joyce had seen that look before. Buffy could be remarkably mature about some things, but she tended to view her mother's occasional forays into the dating scene with some trepidation.

That was understandable, considering how some of those forays had played out.

"Not like that," Joyce said half-honestly.

"Oh," Buffy said. "Okay." She helped herself to more casserole and set about making it disappear. "Tell me about the drive-in," she said between mouthfuls.

"Barney says they shut it down about twenty years ago," Joyce said. She ate some of her own meal. The asparagus spears were fresh and tender, bought at a farmers' market and poached in chicken broth. They tasted good. "Home video and the rise in gas prices—"

"—conspired to make the business impractical," Buffy interrupted.

Joyce looked at her, one eyebrow raised in silent interrogation.

"Xander," Buffy explained.

Joyce sighed. She wasn't surprised. Xander was a veritable wellspring of pop-culture trivia. Sometimes she wondered how anyone could know so much useless information.

"They're not gone completely," Joyce said. "And sometimes they come back."

"Sounds pretty retro to me," Buffy said. "And not in a good way. What's the appeal?"

Joyce thought back to her teenage years. She thought about one of her earliest dates, with a boy whose name she'd long forgotten. They'd sat in the front seat of her parents' car, eating bad concession-stand food and watching bad movies. The night air had been clean and cool, and the world had still seemed bright and exciting.

"It was fun," was all that Joyce could think to say. It seemed very distant.

"Sounds like someone paid a visit to Lovers' Lane," Buffy said, slightly mocking. Her wariness about Joyce's social life didn't preclude some teasing.

"It wasn't like that," Joyce said sharply. It was, actually, but she wasn't about to provide her daughter with the details.

"What about the bugs?" Buffy asked. An odd pragmatism was part of her character.

"Bugs?"

"Bugs," Buffy said, nodding. "Pesky things. They drink blood. Lovers' Lane plus bright movie screen must have been mosquito heaven. Didn't you get eaten alive?"

Joyce hadn't thought about the bugs. Rather than answer, she sipped her iced tea again. It was from a powder, but the fresh lemon she'd added made it better.

Evidently realizing that she wasn't going to get the answer she wanted, Buffy asked another question. "What about the trouble, then?"

"Trouble?"

Buffy quoted her mother's own words back to her. "'Barney says that place has a history of trouble.'"

Joyce shrugged. "I don't know what he meant, Buffy," she said a bit sadly. "He didn't say and I didn't ask. I'd heard the same kind of thing so many times before. It seems that every street and every institution in this town has a history of trouble." She paused. "I like Sunnydale, honey, but sometimes I wonder."

"You're not going to move us again, are you?" Buffy asked. She looked anxious. "Don't even think about it!"

"No, of course not," Joyce said reassuringly. "You're happy here, aren't you?"

"I'm fine, Mom," Buffy said. She took a third helping of the entrée. Joyce wondered again where the girl put it all. "My grades are okay, and I haven't fallen in with the wrong set." She grinned, and the expression lit up her face. Her words sounded only slightly forced as she continued. "These days I even hang with Cordelia Chase, the most popular gal in town. I'm with the in crowd, baby!"

"I suppose," Joyce said. Like most mothers, she had done a little research on her daughter's friends, both by meeting them and by asking around. Xander, for example, seemed nice enough, a bit clownish; from what she'd heard of his parents, he could use a good friend, and he had one in Buffy. Joyce wasn't sure that anyone could consider Buffy's immediate circle the "in crowd," but they all seemed to be good kids.

The meal stretched on in relative silence after that, interrupted only by sporadic exchanges about the food, and similar niceties. It was only over dessert (gelatin for Joyce, chocolate cake for Buffy) that the subject of school arose again.

"I need to go out for a bit," Buffy said. The announcement was no surprise. Buffy went out most nights.

"I'd hoped you would stay in tonight, dear," Joyce said. "I hardly ever see you anymore."

Buffy pressed on. "Willow wants some help with the computer thingy," she said. "And then I thought we might go to the Bronze afterward."

"It's a school night," Joyce said. The protest was mild and

probably futile, but it had become nearly ritual. Joyce wasn't sure she liked the Bronze, or approved of the sheer amount of time Buffy spent there.

"Aw, c'mon, Mom," Buffy said in a lightly mocking tone. She started to clear the table. "All the *cool* kids will be there!"

Joyce sighed. She felt fresh sympathy for her own mother, and what she must have gone through long years before. Who could really know what kind of lives their children led?

The night was alive. Something was going to happen, Buffy knew, even if she wasn't precisely sure how she knew. The half-moon hung low in a cloudless sky, and the air was clear and cool for an early autumn night.

Buffy sometimes joked to her friends about her "Slayer-sense." It was the kind of pop-culture allusion that prompted Xander to nod knowingly and Giles to roll his eyes in mild disgust, but sometimes the joke wasn't a joke at all. Sometimes she actually seemed to feel a charge in the air, an electric crackle that made her scalp itch like a bad perm, promising imminent menace. She felt it now as she paced the familiar course of her patrol. When the occasional passerby approached, she took pains to conceal her miniature crossbow in the oversize handbag that did double duty as a weapons cache, but her favorite stake never left her hand.

Her rounds included many of Sunnydale's known psychic hot spots: the empty warehouse that often sheltered a nest of vampires, the deconsecrated church that was headquarters for a coven of devil worshippers, and the seedy strip of taverns rumored to cater to the paranormal crowd. The list went on and on, and Buffy inspected each locus without incident.

She was in the cemetery when something finally happened. Between crypt and neighboring tree, something moved toward her with smooth, liquid grace. She saw it from the corner of one eye and instinctively spun, raising her crossbow.

"Oh," Buffy said. "It's you."

"Hey," Angel said. His voice was soft, and he lifted his hands in mock surrender. He was dressed in his habitual black, slacks and shirt and leather jacket, and his handsome features were fair under the half-moon's pale light.

"Hey, yourself," Buffy said, looking at him, still wary. She felt as if little elves with sandpaper shoes were dancing on her nerves. Something was still wrong.

"What's up, Buffy?" the vampire asked. He sounded concerned. His hands remained raised.

"Not lots," Buffy said. "Helped Willow with some homework, or tried to. Told Mom I was going to the Bronze, but I decided that this would be *lots* more fun than hanging with my peers and scoping out the music scene." She gave him a wry half smile. Being the Slayer meant lying to her mother fairly often, and she didn't entirely enjoy that part of the job.

"Um," Angel said hesitantly. "Okay."

"How about you?" she asked lightly. "What's up?"

"Well, your crossbow is, for one thing," Angel said. The weapon's bolt was trained precisely at his stilled heart.

"Oh!" Buffy said, chagrined. She lowered the weapon with hasty embarrassment. "Reflex action and all that," she continued. "You know, patrol, tombstones, mysterious stranger—"

Immediately she wished she could take back the words. Whatever Angel was, he was no stranger. They'd been through too much together for her to ever call him that.

He *was* mysterious, though. There were endless mysteries in his eyes.

"Yeah," Angel said. "But reflex usually doesn't go on this long. Look at you. You're still on edge."

He was right. Though she'd lowered the crossbow to her side, her trigger finger remained curled around the weapon's release, as if of its own accord. Buffy's muscles were prepared for instant action. It was classic fight-or-flight stuff, not the kind of response she typically felt in Angel's presence.

"Something's in the air," she said. "Something's going to happen, I think. Don't know what."

"You think?" Angel smiled. He was hundreds of years old, she knew, but the expression made his eternally youthful features seem positively boyish.

"Yeah."

"Buffy, you're the Slayer. You live on top of the Hellmouth. Something's *always* happening," Angel said.

"Good point," she said. She forced herself to relax, at least incrementally. She even smiled. "Walk with me for a while, then."

Somewhere in the distance a dog howled. At least, Buffy thought it was a dog. She *hoped* it was just a dog. Buffy's nights on patrol were exercises in contradiction. Night after night she went out looking for trouble, hoping she wouldn't find it.

There were times, though, when life seemed normal. This was one, and she didn't want it to change. Walking through a cool autumn night with a good-looking guy, her footfalls matching rhythm with his, talking about their days and lives—what could be more normal than that?

She was a child of ancient prophecy, likely to live a short life with a brutal end. The most interesting guy in her life was a creature of the night, a vampire with a heart that could love but did not beat, prisoner of a curse.

Oh yeah, there was that. But did any of it really matter?

Right now, alone with Angel in the moonlight, Buffy didn't think so. Her eyes continued to search the shadows, but bit by bit the worst of the tension oozed away as she told Angel about her day. He made her feel secure and safe simply with his presence.

"Detonated a frog?" he asked. She knew that he'd seen much worse—they both had—but he was polite enough to make an expression of amused distaste. "Well, boys will be boys."

Buffy nodded. "Except I don't think it was a boy who did it," she said.

"What else happened?" he asked as they approached one of the cemetery's aboveground crypts. Some family had failed to keep pace with the groundskeeping fees, and the tomb had fallen into a state of mild disrepair. The brass hardware was weathered and dull, and clinging ivy half-covered one wall.

"Else?" Buffy asked. "Must there always be an else?"

"There's always something else," he said lightly.

"Oh, Xander got a job," she said brightly. "He's a gopher at the drive-in."

"The drive-in?" Angel asked.

The last thing she wanted to do right now was talk to him about another guy. She wondered if he felt the same. This close, she could tell that he wasn't breathing. Vampires didn't have to, except for speech.

And it didn't matter that his heart wasn't beating either. Hers was working hard enough for both of them.

"It's a long story," Buffy said. She paused midstep and turned to look at him. There was an old oak next to the tomb, and the moonlight shining down through the tree's branches did interesting things to Angel's face. She leaned closer and gazed into his eyes.

"Feeling better now?" Angel asked.

Buffy nodded. "Much," she said. She made a dismissive gesture. "Meemies all gone."

"Maybe you just need to switch to decaf," he said.

"Maybe," she said. "Or perhaps I need something else."

Angel's skin felt cool when she placed her hands on his cheeks, but it warmed quickly. She pulled his face closer to hers, her lips parting. It was a perfect moment, and she didn't want anything to spoil it.

Then, with a snarl, something rudely did.

Inside the Bronze the night was alive. The air was scented with fog and sweat, and throbbed with the beat of the band. The ensemble *du noir* was a plucky band of traditionalists, performing under the cryptic acronym TDQYDJP. A helpful placard explained that the abbreviation stood for "The Don't Quit Your Day Job Players." The group played mostly cover tunes—plain vanilla rock—but they played loud enough and well enough to satisfy the scores of teens crowded onto the club's worn dance floor. Kids were dancing and bouncing and gyrating with force sufficient enough to send tremors through the place's infrastructure, but Cordelia was not one of them. She was in the Bronze tonight not to dance, but to hold court.

She had secured a good table on the main level, situated to provide a good vantage point but far enough away from the stage that she could hear herself speak. She'd permitted the other members of her personal troika, Harmony and Aura, to join her. They sat on either side of her like mismatched bookends, hanging on her every word. Together, the three passed judgment on the band, their drinks, the other Bronze patrons, and anything else that piqued their interest.

Sitting in judgment had long been one of Cordelia's preferred pastimes. Someone had to do it, after all, and she couldn't imagine anyone better qualified. She had the upbringing and refinement to assess the poor fools that swarmed through her life, and it would have been a shame not to share her insights. Harmony and Aura had similarly good taste (though not as highly developed, of course), and they made good companions on her judicial bench. For years the three of them had moved through life together, in study halls and in classrooms, in restaurants and on the playing field, telling the world the way it was supposed to be. In recent months, since her growing involvement with Buffy and the others, the pastime's charm had started fading, but it was far from gone.

"Look, Cordy," Harmony said. She was a pretty blonde, much blonder than Buffy, and she tended to echo Cordelia's every observation. It was seldom that she made one of her own. "Look at the guy with three chins. Purple-hair there is going to shoot him down!"

Cordy followed Harmony's gaze. The Bronze didn't allow stage-diving, but the more hard-core members of the audience still tended to congregate near the stage's lip. There, only a few feet from the TDQYDJP's booming woofer, a portly gent who had unwisely shaved his head was saying something to a Goth chick with purple hair.

Cordelia didn't much like Goth chicks. She could see the value of making a statement, but surely there were better ones to make. And that amount of makeup had to be murder on the skin. Plus, her outings with Buffy and the Scoobies had made her wary of dark-clad creatures with the wrong color hair.

"How long do you give him?" Aura asked. She had dark

bronze skin and black hair, and she generally showed a bit more initiative than Harmony. She was at least as blasé, however. Even before Cordelia, Aura had stumbled briefly into the occult war that had chosen Sunnydale as its battlefield, when she discovered the body of one of that war's victims.

"Seven seconds," Cordelia said, without pausing to consider. She'd been playing this game for a long time.

". . . six, five, four, three, two . . . ," Harmony and Aura chanted in perfect unison.

Precisely on "zero" the purple-haired girl's hand came up in a short, fast arc. When her hand stopped, the drink she held splashed in the bald guy's face. A security goon, drawn by the disturbance, approached to escort them both away from the stage.

"There's trouble in paradise," Cordelia said as Harmony and Aura laughed. They sounded like magpies in stereo.

The three of them carried on like that for an hour or so, but Cordelia was bored by the twenty-minute mark. She turned down three invitations to dance and accepted one, but when the guy wanted to do more than that, she ditched him and returned to the table. During the break between sets, the band's percussionist approached and invited all of them backstage. Harmony and Aura agreed eagerly, only to backtrack when they heard Cordelia decline. The band was a good act and they made good music, but Mrs. Chase's little girl wasn't going anywhere with rockers who hadn't at *least* made the Billboard Top 100.

"Hel-lo," Aura said as Cordelia bade the TDQYDJP

emissary good-bye. "There's a fresh face in town."

Threading his way through the milling crowd on the dance floor was someone Cordelia had never seen before. Tall and Mediterranean dark, he was handsome in an insolently casual way, with heavy-lidded dark eyes and black hair styled in an elaborate pompadour. He wore old-style biker's leathers, festooned with buckles and straps, and he moved with the grace of a jungle cat.

As Cordelia watched, it hit her that the stranger was hot. No, he was *Hot*, and he knew it.

"Yum," Aura said softly.

"Yum, indeed," Cordelia agreed. There was no denying it. Oddly, though, she found herself only slightly intrigued by the newcomer. One reason was what she coined "the Xander situation"; the other was something else.

Cordelia recalled when another leather-clad stranger, tall and dark and handsome, had drifted into the Bronze late one rockin' night. She had all but thrown herself at him, only to draw back in chagrin when he'd brushed her aside. That stranger proved to be a vampire, specifically Buffy's associate, Angel, and the experience had reaffirmed one of Cordelia's long-held beliefs: better to let the guys do the chasing. She turned to Aura, intending to grant the other girl the benefit of her experienced wisdom. But she was just in time for a rear view as Aura disappeared into the crowd.

Cordelia sniffed. Some people didn't understand basic courtesy.

• • •

The beast leaped down onto Buffy and Angel from the crypt's slanted roof, driving them both to the ground with the force of his fall. The creature snarled as he struck, lashing out with cruel claws. Slayer and vampire alike rolled desperately, barely avoiding the raking swipes. Buffy's weapons bag went flying.

Angel was right, she realized, drawing a stake from her jeans pocket. Something else *always* happened.

She scrambled back to her feet, but Angel acted faster. Even as the beast turned to lunge at him, the vampire struck, stabbing the creature with a savage, spearlike strike. He drove the fist of his right hand into his assailant's solar plexus, making the beast double over in pain. The exchange took only a split second, but it gave Buffy a chance to assess the situation.

Their adversary seemed to be some kind of a werewolf, but like none that she'd seen in any of Giles's books. He had a human frame and build but moved in a low, bestial slouch that made his full size difficult to gauge accurately. He had a man's hands, but they were overgrown with thick fur and had hooked, talonlike claws. Human eyes that were clouded with rage stared out from his face, and his features, like his hands, were layered in fur. White froth, liquid and foamy, drooled from a mouth of ragged teeth.

Absurdly, the creature wore denim trousers and a varsity jacket—not in Sunnydale High's red and gold but in colors that Buffy didn't recognize.

"And I thought the penguin was weird," Buffy said softly.

Her words drew the wolf-man's attention. With a low growl he crouched, then sprang. His outstretched hands raced for Buffy's throat.

"Buffy!" Angel said.

She didn't need the warning. She'd already braced herself, her favorite stake poised. When the wolf-man slammed into her, she brought the weapon up, fast and hard. The impact of the beast's lunge was enough to topple her, but not to ruin her aim. The pointed piece of wood stabbed deep into the wolf-man's chest.

Buffy had encountered many varieties of monster since commencing her career as the Slayer. Whether vampire, demon, or zombie, they each had their modes of attack, their specific strengths and weaknesses. One thing, though, was reasonably constant. Heart strikes almost always killed.

This one hadn't.

The quasi-werewolf was on top of her now, pinning her with his weight. His claws found her throat and began to squeeze. From the wolf-man's snarling lips she could feel hot breath against her skin. Buffy's hands found the creature's wrists and she squeezed too. The monster grunted in pain, but his grip didn't falter, not even when she increased the pressure and felt bones grind together.

She felt something else, too, and some corner of her mind duly took note of it. Even as she applied crushing force, she could feel the creature's pulse in her hands, strong and vital.

The thing had a heart, then. Why hadn't the stake done its job? That was a question for later, something to ask Giles. Perhaps he'd favor her with one of his rare direct answers.

The wolf-man's attack had driven the air from her lungs, and she was having difficulty filling them again. Her own pulse pounded in her ears and spots swam before her eyes. The dark night seemed to grow darker. He was trying to kill her and was doing a reasonably good job.

She gritted her teeth and redoubled her efforts to free herself. The angle made the work awkward, but she struggled to pull the wolf-man's arms apart. The monster's clawed hands shifted, just a bit, and Buffy sucked cool night air greedily. Her vision began to clear.

As the world came back into focus, she saw another pair of hands. Angel's. He reached around from behind and grasped the wolf-man's chin with his left hand, then clamped his right fist atop the brute's head. The vampire forcefully yanked back and up, which made a sound like pottery breaking. Buffy's grasp broke as the beast released his grip on her neck. Angel tore the creature away from her.

"Thanks," she said. She managed a smile. He'd shifted into full vampire mode, the handsome contours of his face morphed into something harsher, but he was still a welcome sight.

"It was my turn," he said. The words came in a rush as he pivoted. Moving with inhuman speed, he slammed the wolf-man against the nearby crypt's marble wall. Before the creature could react, he repeated the action a second and third time. When Angel let go at last, the beast's eyes had closed. For a moment he remained standing, slumped against the wall, and then he slid into an unconscious heap. It was like watching a cartoon.

Buffy pulled herself together and stood, waving aside Angel's offer of help. She gathered up the weapons bag and took hasty inventory. The compact and collapsible crossbow, the bolts, the knives, and the other implements were all there. Only the single stake was missing.

"That's odd," she said.

"Hmm?" Angel asked.

She pointed at their attacker. Even in the shadows her stake was conspicuous. It was buried deep into their assailant's chest, but that chest still rose and fell steadily. Even with a stake in his heart, he was still breathing.

"Shouldn't he be, like, dead?" Buffy asked. "I mean, very dead?"

"I don't know," Angel said. Usually cool and unflappable, he too seemed puzzled now. Warily, he knelt and examined the damaged monster. He sniffed, and shook his head. "He's bleeding," Angel said.

Buffy wondered if the wolf-man's blood tempted Angel, then forced the question from her mind. It seemed rude, somehow.

"Lots of blood," Angel said, musing. He opened the varsity letter jacket. Beneath it was an equally absurd football jersey. It glistened wetly beneath the moon's rays. "Between this and the neck, he should really be dead."

"It's a wooden stake, not silver," Buffy said. Some intuition, vague and half-formed, prompted her to reach again into her weapons bag. "Doesn't it take silver, for werewolves?"

"But this isn't a werewolf," Angel said. He looked up at her again. "I mean, I've met werewolves. They're not hind-leggers. Strictly all fours." He pointed at the night sky. "Besides, it's not a full moon."

"So," the Slayer said, "it's not a werewolf but, rather, an incredible simulation of one."

The conversation had taken on an absurd, otherworldly feel, Buffy realized. She was standing in the moonlight, talking to her more-or-less boyfriend, comparing notes on the operational specifics of werewolves. What had her life come to?

"Whatever he is, he's down for the count," Angel said. He shrugged. "What now?"

"Don't know," Buffy said. With most such encounters, disposing of the evidence wasn't a problem. Vampires collapsed conveniently into dust. Elementals found their, well, element and disappeared. Robots had a welcome tendency to explode and reduce themselves to components that defied easy identification. But a wolf-man, unconscious—

"I don't know how long he can last like this," Angel said, echoing her thoughts.

"Put him out of his misery?" Buffy asked tentatively. She didn't like the idea. It was one thing to slay in battle, but executing an unconscious foe was something else entirely.

"Misery. That's another point," Angel said. Satisfied that their foe was, indeed, out like a light, he turned to face her. "Werewolves are usually victims themselves. They're cursed." The vampire paused, clearly troubled.

Buffy knew why. He had a curse of his own. "Maybe, if we can restrain him, Giles can give us an answer."

"How do we do that?" Angel asked. There were times when he was annoyingly pragmatic. "Do you have anything?"

"Not really," Buffy said. She thought for a moment. She wasn't in the habit of bringing handcuffs on her patrols. "Maybe we can box him up?"

"Where?"

Angel was still kneeling, facing her. She looked past him, at the crypt. "There," she said. "We could come back—"

She noticed the movement just in time. Behind Angel the wolf-man's eyelids fluttered, then opened a split second later. The brute rose to his feet, moving at a startling speed that belied his injuries. Clawed hands neared Angel's throat.

Buffy no longer worried about executing an unconscious foe. The realization came almost as a relief, but then the thought faded and trained reflex took over. Inside the weapons bag, her fingers found the hilt of a *boka,* a bent knife with two razor-sharp curved edges. It was shorter than a machete but better balanced and just as deadly. Buffy hurled the blade without pausing to look, think, or take aim.

The *boka* spun through the moonlit air, passing over

Angel's shoulder. Genuine sparks, harsh and electric, flew as the weapon sliced though the wolf-man's neck and dug into the stone beyond.

Heart strikes usually worked. Thus far, at least, outright beheadings *always* did.

"There," she said. "Next time's your turn again."

"I'm not keeping count," the vampire replied, turning to look behind him.

The wolf-man collapsed once more. This time, however, the creature's form slumped forward, caving in on itself. The contours of his remains softened and faded. As they watched, his substance seemed to evaporate, boiling away, first into mist and then into nothingness. In moments, flesh, blood, and clothing alike had all vanished completely. Only Buffy's stake and blade remained.

"Blood's gone," Angel said. He sniffed again. The vampire had a terrifically keen sense of smell, a handy ability, but it wasn't one of his most endearing qualities.

"I can see that," Buffy said. "He cleaned up after himself. And I thought vampires were tidy." Seeing the pained expression on Angel's face, she shrugged. "Sorry," she said meekly. "Nothing personal."

"No, it's not like that," he replied. "It's the blood. The blood scent should last for hours at the very least, but it's gone already." He retrieved her weapons and handed them to her. The blade was chipped where it had struck stone, but both instruments were spotlessly clean. "What was on these and in the air is gone," Angel continued. "There's no residue at all. It's like he was never here."

"The bruises on my neck say different," Buffy said, but without any particular concern. Slayers healed fast. "He wasn't a werewolf, then?"

"I don't know what he was," Angel replied.

"Definitely one for the books, then," Buffy said. "Giles's books, that is."

Angel nodded in agreement. He knelt to study the soil where the wolf-man had fallen. The surrounding grass was bent and disturbed but perfectly dry. Angel seemed fascinated by the phenomenon of blood that could disappear without a trace. Buffy put it down to professional interest.

She put the *boka* back in her bag where it belonged, but kept a secure grip on the stake. The night was still young, after all.

The band was just about to start its second set when Aura made her escape. Cordelia was a sweetheart with a fashion sense to die for, but even Aura found some of her guidance overbearing—especially when it came to guys. Harmony Kendall might hang on Cordy's every word, but not Aura. The Queen of Sunnydale High was a fine role model and companion, but Aura didn't need a second mother. When she saw Cordelia's features compose themselves into the familiar expression that promised a lecture, she rose without comment. She wiggled the fingers of her left hand in a parting gesture. Harmony noticed and waved back. Cordelia, focused intently on the world beyond their shared table, didn't seem to notice.

She never did, as far as Aura could tell. Cordy thought that it was her world, and everyone else just lived in it.

The Bronze was hopping, at least by weeknight standards. The table area and dance floor were crowded enough to make Aura's path zig and zag as she threaded through the other patrons. Most of them were familiar. A few times she paused to exchange niceties with other high school girls who weren't as pretty or as smart as she was. College girls were another matter; Aura eyed them warily, and they did the same to her. Aura knew that she was beautiful, and so did they, but competition was ugly.

She was looking for the sleepy-eyed stranger. Aura didn't care much for biker types, but something about this guy appealed to her, and she wanted to address the issue. Neither of her tablemates seemed poised to compete. Cordelia wasn't very quick on the draw lately; Aura had begun to wonder if she was seeing someone. And Harmony was sticking to the Queen of Sunnydale High like a blond shadow. But there were other girls aplenty in the Bronze tonight, and Aura didn't see any reason to let them have a chance.

The band started its second set as she glided past the bar. TDQYDJP was soon into a bluesy-salsa-reggae thing about good love gone wrong. In a world full of pairs, Aura's target stood at the dance floor's edge with his back to her.

"Hey!" she said, tapping his shoulder. Her prod met with pleasing resistance. Aura liked hard muscle.

He turned. Up close he looked even better. His eyes had a mesmerizing intensity. They burned, half hidden beneath drooping lids.

"Yeah?" the guy asked. It was less a word than a questioning grunt, but Aura didn't mind. She'd never been much for conversation.

"Looking for someone?" she asked. She smiled up at him.

"Yeah," the guy said. This time the grunt sounded a bit like "yes."

"Good," Aura said, her smile widening. "*I'm* someone."

And then they were off, their bodies moving in perfect rhythm.

Aura felt as if they'd taken flight together. The world seemed to fall away, and the throbbing beat carried them along, a perfect matching pair. Like two leaves on the wind, they swept across the dance floor, turning and spinning and spiraling in wild abandon.

She was making a bit of a spectacle of herself, she knew. Aura accepted her beauty as a fact of life, and she knew she looked good in motion. Some corner of her mind noticed that other Bronze patrons were watching them, and she noted their expressions. The guys were properly enthusiastic or amused; generally speaking, the girls seemed envious or scandalized. Aura didn't care. The night was young and so was she; the rest of the world could go to hell.

Their track carried them back to the dance floor's edge. The music faded as the band ended its first song and started the next. Aura took advantage of the moment to pause and catch her breath.

"Wow!" she said.

He smiled. Broad, sensuous lips pulled back over his movie-star teeth as he leaned in close. He didn't say anything, but words didn't seem very important just then.

"Yeah," Aura said, still drawing the club's smoky air into herself. As if of its own accord, her head titled back a bit, presenting her half-open mouth. She closed her eyes, readying herself for his kiss.

It never came.

After a too-long moment, Aura's eyes opened, darting from side to side in dismay. She was alone—not absolutely alone, but alone in a crowd. The dance floor was still crowded, but the only person who really mattered to Aura was gone. Her partner had vanished without a trace. She flushed in confusion and embarrassment and more than a little anger.

Ditched. She'd *never* been ditched before. It defied reason.

Standing nearby was another couple, the purple-haired girl and the bald fatty, who had evidently made their peace. The next song started, low and slow, and they moved out onto the dance floor again. Aura saw the girl shoot her a puzzled glance.

"Hey!" Aura said to her. The Goth was college age or older, and she certainly didn't look like anyone Aura wanted to meet, but that didn't matter right now. "Hey, you! Did you see where my partner went?"

"No," the purple-haired girl said over her date's shoulder. Her lips were black. "It was weird," she said, speaking loud in order to be heard over the band's increasing sound. "He, like, faded away or something."

CHAPTER THREE

Xander knew his school and its between-class traffic patterns well. In nice weather, like today, most students cut through Sunnydale High's central courtyard whenever possible. The courtyard route not only made the trip between school wings shorter, but it was also a nice change from the hallways' fluorescent lighting and institutional paint scheme. Xander too liked the moments of fresh air and sunshine.

Seconds after the school bell rang, he was standing outside with his back to one brick wall, about ten feet outside the entrance that led to the cafeteria. The surrounding courtyard sported little islands of landscaped greenery bounded by retaining walls, which served as impromptu gathering places. At this time of day they were empty. Xander purposely ignored the courtyard's bulletin board kiosk, the official posting place for announcements. He wanted his message received and read, not buried under other postings about garage sales, play tryouts, and policy changes.

"Here you go," Xander said as a sizeable segment of the student body surged past. He handed out the orange flyers as rapidly as he could. "Check it out. Something you will enjoy!"

He knew almost everyone's name but personally greeted only a few. He was there to pass out paper, not to make conversation, after all. If he tried to make things personal, with a greeting or even a nod of recognition, he was just giving the lucky guy or gal a chance to say no. But if he refrained even from making eye contact, there was a mighty good chance that the sheet of paper would leave his hand and find a new one. Speed was the secret.

"Take a look," Xander said. "Tell your friends."

Erik Morrison from the wrestling team accepted the flyer without even seeming to notice that it had been offered, and then he wadded it into a ball and let it fall to the walkway. Ralph Ellis, who'd been trying to recruit Xander for forensics competition, took one and tucked it in a pocket. Willow accepted one with a smile, then asked for more and tried to start a conversation before deciding that she really, really had to get to her next class because she hated being late. Jonathan Levenson accepted his without comment, but Jonathan never really said very much anyway. Harmony Kendall reached for one reflexively, then recoiled in horror when she realized that it was an offering from Xander. A teacher he didn't recognize—a substitute?—just shook her head in rejection and rolled her eyes. John Garcia took three, grabbing them up as if they were some kind of prize.

Friend, foe, and stranger alike, the tide of humanity moved on. In the five or so minutes when traffic was enough to make tarrying worthwhile, Xander managed to spread the good word about the drive-in festival to more than a hundred students. He'd need to get more flyers from his locker before trying again.

"Harris," said a familiar and disliked voice. "Just what do you think you're doing?"

Principal Snyder approached. He was a little man with rat-like features. The current joke about Snyder was that he had a face only a mother could love, but even his mother wasn't sure.

"Hello, Mr. Snyder, sir," Xander said. He came to attention, which was probably a mistake. It only made Snyder seem shorter. "Just—"

Snyder snatched one of the flyers. He read it quickly, or at least enough of it to know what he held. His narrow lips curved in an uneasy approximation of a smile. "A drive-in?" he asked. "In this day and age?"

Xander nodded. He hoped the confrontation would be brief: The between-class break was nearly over. "Yes, sir,

Mr. Snyder, sir," he said, feeling terribly alone. Most of the other students had made themselves scarce.

"Huh," Snyder said, returning his attention to the handbill. Finally, grudgingly, he nodded. "This is advertising," he said. "I shouldn't let you do this on school grounds."

Xander swallowed nervously. In his mind's eye he saw a house of cards collapse and a small bag with a dollar sign on its side sprout wings and fly away.

Snyder folded the sheet of paper neatly and slid it into his jacket pocket. "Go ahead," he said. "Just clean up after yourself. I don't like litter, Harris."

"Th-thank you, sir!" Xander said, relieved and surprised. Snyder never cut anyone any slack.

"I mean it. I'm holding you personally responsible," the rat-man said, then turned on one heel and strode away as Xander watched in disbelief.

Snyder had smiled. Snyder had actually smiled. That kind of thing just didn't happen. Clearly, the world had gone nuts.

"Whoops," Buffy said as her fingertips grazed her drink can. Even the glancing contact was enough to topple the container, and before she could right it, thick droplets of pink protein drink splashed from its open top. "Sorry."

"Buffy! Please!" Giles said.

Six massive books lay on the library table before her and Willow, each bound in what she sincerely hoped was leather. A rivulet of protein drink flowed toward one. The half-dozen volumes weren't from the school's state-issued collection, but from Giles's assets. With the protective instinct of a mother hen, he slid the endangered tome aside with one hand while he blotted the spilled drink with a handkerchief held in the other.

"I said I was sorry," Buffy said. She was, too, but not sorry enough to forgo her liquid lunch. Slaying burned a lot of calories.

"Yes, I can tell you're quite distraught," Giles said.

"See anything familiar yet, Buffy?" Willow asked, obviously eager to change the subject.

"Nope," the Slayer said. She shook her head emphatically and pointed at each of the books in turn. "No. Uh-uh. Nopers. That's a negatory, good buddy." With each rejection, she pointed at a different volume using the same hand that held her drink.

"Please, Buffy, if I could trouble you to be careful with your beverage," Giles said. He seemed physically uncomfortable. "That copy of the *Crimson Chronicles* is more than six hundred years old. It would be terribly difficult to replace."

She pulled the drink back, so that it was no longer above the open tome. Just in time, too: A drop of condensation trickled down its side and fell to the floor. "O-*kay,*" Buffy said. "But just because you ask so nice."

Giles had opened the half-dozen books, presenting illustrations for her review. The pictures varied wildly in style and execution, but each was of a wolf or wolflike creature. Some sported horns or forked tails or human eyes. One picture was an unsettling fusion of a human head and a wolf's body, precisely the opposite of what Buffy was looking for. Only the sixth image was even a slight match.

"This guy's in the neighborhood," Buffy said, pointing at the last open book.

Giles and Willow looked. The image she'd indicated was of a human figure with a canine head. The anonymous artist had rendered the portrait in awkward profile but with nice detail. The subject was bare-chested, was dressed in sandals and a loincloth, and carried a staff in one very human-looking hand.

"That's not a werewolf," Willow said. She sounded faintly dismayed. "That's Anubis, the god of the dead in ancient Egypt." When Giles and Buffy both looked at her in surprise, she continued more defensively, "Hey, I've been reading up on this stuff! I'm not just a computer geek!"

Giles lifted the open book. He made a great production of reading from the crabbed lettering. "It's an image of Anpu, actually," he said.

Willow rolled her eyes slightly. She said, "And Anpu is another name for . . . ?"

Giles sighed. "Anubis."

"It doesn't matter," Buffy said. "I don't care if it's Anubis or Andrew—"

"Anpu," Giles said softly.

"—or Anpu. That guy's not who I saw last night. He's just in the same general neighborhood," Buffy continued impatiently. "Human body with added wolfy badness."

"Anubis is a jackal deity, not wolf," Willow said.

"I. Don't. Care," Buffy said, emphasizing each word. "I want to know what he's doing in Sunnydale." She drained the last of her shake and thought back to wolf-man's absurd attire. "And I'd like to know what team he's playing for too, if that's not too much trouble."

Giles hadn't entirely believed her when she'd made her preliminary report. Convincing him proved difficult. Her story just felt too far outside his personal experience and research. He'd listened to her account of the evening's patrol but had actually tried to correct her on the details, which was ridiculous. While Buffy was prowling the cemetery and not kissing Angel, Giles must have been home sipping tea and watching BBC satellite feeds, or whatever it was he did with his evenings. That didn't seem to matter to Giles, though, not even when the Slayer pointed it out to him. Again and again he asked her if she was certain the wolf-man hadn't attacked her on all fours, or if she was sure that she hadn't used a silver bullet, or if the autumn moon might not actually have been full.

"I have some other texts," Giles said slowly, closing the Anubis book with great reluctance. "One in particular might be of use. We can consult it later."

"Later?" Willow asked. "Now is better, isn't it?"

"But I can't seem to find it at the moment."

That was a surprise. The Watcher was obsessively orderly. Not only did his books run according to a strict filing system that only he fully understood, but he kept his pens and pencils sorted according to type, color, age, and size. Both girls looked at him in plain disbelief.

"I'm certain it's just mis-shelved," Giles said.

"You never mis-shelve things, Giles," Buffy said incredulously.

He shook his head. "Not by me, then. Someone decided to explore the stacks earlier," Giles said. "Someone untidy."

"I thought the whole idea of your working on-site here was that you could keep your books in the library and no one would screw with them," Buffy said. "Hide in plain sight and all that. I mean, we're the only students who hang out here, right?"

"It wasn't a student," Giles replied. He looked even more uncomfortable.

"Oh? Spill!" Buffy said.

"Yes, Giles, make with the spillage," Willow agreed. "There's new faculty?"

"It would appear that the school secured the services of a new nurse," Giles said. He gathered up the other volumes and set them on a cart for reshelving. "I came upon her in the stacks. She was making herself at home and appears to have done some . . . rearranging."

"A new nurse?" Buffy asked. In a more ominous tone, she continued, "The name's not Ratched, is it?"

"No, no, not at all. Her name is Inga."

"Inga?" Willow asked.

"She's . . . Swedish," Giles said. The words came very slowly.

"Uh-huh," Buffy said. "Nurse Inga." She raised both hands

and made beckoning motions for him to be more forthcoming. "Swedish and . . ."

"Swedish and very attractive," Giles said. He cleared his throat and loosened his collar. "Blue-eyed and blond, quite tall, and very, um—"

"Giles!" Buffy said. She stamped her feet in delight. She always liked catching him in a human moment. "You *dog*! You sly, sly dog!"

"That's uncalled for," Giles said.

"Hallo, mister library man," Buffy said in her best bad Swedish accent. "Do you speak the Svensk?"

"Zee Alps, zey are very nice zis time of year!" Willow said, following suit. "Ve could go exploring, yah?" Her accent was even worse.

"No!" Giles said, clearly flustered. "It was nothing like that! I found her poking about and tried to direct her attentions elsewhere!"

Buffy planted her elbow and rested her chin on her hand, looking up at him. "I bet you did," she said, in tones that were soft and knowing. At her side Willow giggled.

"There's no way I can win this, is there?" Giles asked.

"Nope. None."

"Ahem," Giles said, and soldiered on. "Very well, then. She made a bit of a mess." He paused. "I was just reordering things when you two arrived, but—"

"Is anything missing?" Willow asked anxiously. "Some of your books are bad mojo."

"I'm not sure just yet, but I'm beginning to think so," Giles confessed. "Inga left empty-handed, though. That's why I wasn't particularly concerned until you asked for all my, um, 'werewolf goodies.'"

Buffy grinned. Her liquid lunch was done now and she dropped the empty can in a nearby wastepaper basket. Metal hit metal with a *clang* much too loud for the library's quiet confines. "Dashed inconvenient, that!" the Slayer said. She'd shifted to faux British. "Can me and the little miss give you a hand, guv'nor?"

Giles seemed to shudder. "I rather think not," he said.

"What happens if you can't find it?" Buffy asked. "Can I interrogate the nurse? Please, please?"

"I've got some questions for her," Willow said eagerly. "The hussy!"

"Please," Giles said. He put one hand to his forehead, massaging his temples as he shaded his eyes. "Oh, please. Let me do what I can first. And if I can't find it—"

Both Buffy and Willow looked at him brightly. They were eager to commence their investigation.

"If I can't find it by the end of the school day, we'll revisit the matter," Giles said. "I have some other works at home that may be of service. I'll review them this evening. Contact me before you go on patrol."

The sun was high in the midday sky, but the walls of Angel's lair sheltered him from its heat and menacing rays. He bolted the door against unwanted intrusion and dimmed the lights almost to the point of darkness, creating a private world of cool gloom. Alone with his thoughts, Angel lay on the bed and stared at the ceiling. Soon he was neither asleep nor awake, but in a tranquil state somewhere in between. Images and sensory impressions flitted though his mind like fish in the sea, each one bright and distinct and unique.

Being a vampire had its advantages. His enormous strength and stamina were beyond a human's dreams. He experienced the world through heightened senses. He could hide his thoughts from mind readers, and his image was invisible to mirrors. These were among the gifts of vampirism.

No.

They weren't gifts, not really. They were symptoms, part and parcel of his current state, like his thirst for blood or his vulnerability to direct sunlight. He would forfeit them all, strengths and weaknesses alike, for the chance to be human again. Even so, there was no denying that the traits of vampirism had their uses.

One of his most useful attributes was an eidetic memory, the ability to recall experiences in full quality and detail. Buffy called it "photographic," but the word was misleading. It was more than that, much more.

For Angel, with a bit of effort, the past could be as real as the present. Sight and sound, smell and taste, even touch—his mind recorded them in exacting fidelity. Angel had walked the world for nearly two and a half centuries, and he remembered clearly almost every moment of his existence.

Just now he recalled the events of the previous evening. The night was cool, the moon half-full. Crickets chirped and leaves rustled. Angel had been standing silently beneath a tree in the cemetery. He'd been alone, but was waiting to hear the familiar footsteps and heartbeat.

He slowly replayed the entire sequence of events in his mind. He walked again through the autumn night and heard anew the words he'd exchanged in low tones with Buffy. Once more he felt her breath on his cool skin. Then the wolf-man fell on them from above, and the battle began.

He considered the entire scene again and again. Like a dog might gnaw, he mulled over the memories, striving to extract every iota of information they held. Something about the night's adventure troubled him, even now. He had to know why.

The battle was nothing special, really; there'd been dozens of others like it. Recover from an enemy's attack, then counterattack. Defend Buffy and be defended by her, in turn. Triumph. The previous evening was like many before it, and like countless others to come.

Only one thing was unique: the monster himself. Angel was certain he'd seen the creature before, or one like it, but the memory was a faint one. Tantalizing and elusive, it hung at the very threshold of his ability to recall, defying his cognitive abilities. If he'd seen the wolf-man before, the encounter must have been a fleeting one, too brief and inconsequential to register in a vampire's memory. He might not have even seen the creature itself, he slowly realized; he might only have seen an image of the thing, a painting or drawing or photograph. . . .

When recognition came, it struck like a thunderbolt. Angel's eyes widened in surprise and his entire body tensed. He bolted upright in bed and shook his head in disbelief.

"No," he said softly. "That's ridiculous."

Buffy spun the dial and lifted the hasp. The mechanism made a *ka-chunk* sound, and her locker door swung open. She inspected its slightly chaotic interior. It held mostly teenage girly stuff; she didn't keep much Slayer paraphernalia at school, choosing to rely on Giles's resources instead. Dropping off two textbooks, she picked up a third, then used the mounted door mirror to make a quick hair-and-lipstick check. Everything was in order.

The walk from her fifth-period class to her sixth-period one typically took two minutes. Granted a five minute break, she had enough time to make a stop along the way. She smiled impishly. There was more than one kind of reconnaissance patrol.

"Knock, knock!" Buffy said a moment later, air-rapping her knuckles on the open door to the school nurse's station. "Hello? Anyone here?"

"Just a moment, dear!" came a woman's voice from the examination area. The privacy curtain whisked aside and a woman wearing a white uniform appeared. She was short and middle-aged and had curly brown hair that came from a perm and a dye bottle. Her smile was warm and friendly. "Why, Buffy Summers!" the woman said. She spoke with a musical Wisconsin lilt. "You never come calling. Is something wrong?"

"Nurse Forman?" Buffy asked, utterly nonplussed.

"Why, yes, dearie," she chirped. "You sound disappointed."

"Um, no, no, not at all," Buffy said. "Just surprised." She had expected to be greeted by the Norse goddess Giles had so reluctantly described.

The attending nurse cocked an eyebrow at her, and Buffy felt briefly ashamed of herself. Kitty Forman was motherly and sweet, with an endearing pixie-ish quality. Buffy knew that she should have been happy to see the familiar woman. "It's just—I heard there was a new nurse, and I wanted to meet and greet," Buffy continued. Even to her own ears the words sounded lame.

"New nurse? Was her name Ursula?" Forman asked.

"Inga," Buffy corrected.

Forman shook her head and laughed, a sound like silver bells. "No Inga here," she said. "Or Ursula, for that matter."

"But—"

"People have been asking about this Ursula or Inga or whoever person all day," Nurse Forman said. "I don't know what the world's coming to. Someone must be playing a prank." She shook her head. "A cruel, cruel prank."

Buffy wasn't so sure. Giles was a hard man to fool. If he'd

seen a Valkyrie in the library, there'd *been* a Valkyrie in the library.

A chime rang. Nurse Forman waved Buffy toward the hallway. "There's the warning bell," she said. "You'd better scat! Don't want to be late for class, dear!"

CHAPTER FOUR

The afternoon sun was bright. Cordelia lingered on one of the low retaining walls in the high school courtyard and luxuriated in the warmth. She needed a chance to unwind, and this was as good a place as any. There was a half-hour gap between the end of her classes and the beginning of cheerleading practice, and Cordelia intended to make the most of it. She tilted her head back, closed her eyes, and breathed deeply. The autumn air was scented with green, thanks to the ongoing work of the landscaping crew. The moment was worth savoring. It was like an afternoon at the day spa, except it was free, so it couldn't be as good.

A shadow fell across her and lingered. Someone was

blocking her sun. And she had a pretty good guess who it must be.

"Go away, you," she said without lifting her eyelids. "I'm busy."

"Good. I'd like to get busy too. Think you can help me with that?"

She was right. The voice was Xander's, filled with an easy familiarity that she found a bit presumptuous, even now. It was one thing to neck with a guy in a broom closet while vampires swarmed the hallways outside, and quite another to let him act like you were part of his life.

"Go away," she said again, but more gently this time, and with open eyes. Classes were done and witnesses were unlikely, so she favored him with a smile. It was brief but genuine.

"What's the matter, Cordy?" he asked as he stepped aside. "Not ready to be seen in public with me just yet?"

"'Just yet'?" She quoted his words back to him, but with a bit of a bantering tone. She didn't want them to sting too badly. "That implies ever."

She'd never tell anyone, but Cordelia had decided that there was a bit of long-term promise in the Harris boy. Xander's typical teen gawkiness was fading fast, and if he wasn't yet handsome, he had strong features and a good smile. Now that she'd gotten to know him better, much to her own surprise, she'd found that he could be sweet and warm.

Not that Cordelia spent much time telling him so.

"On your way to work?" she asked. She crossed her long legs. They were clad in designer jeans that fit like paint, and Xander's eyes followed the movement. Good. It was always good to know that a guy was still interested. More than once, it had seemed to Cordelia that Xander was on the brink of taking her for granted. She couldn't allow that to happen, no matter how weird it seemed to be with him.

"Huh? Oh yeah," he said, looking up again. His right hand held a thick sheaf of the orange handbills he'd been handing out to anybody who would take one. In his left hand was a staple gun. "Boss-man asked me to post some around town and stir up some interest among today's troubled teens."

"Seems kind of low-tech," Cordelia said.

"Boss-man's a bit low-tech himself," Xander replied. "What can I say? He likes the old ways."

Cordelia shrugged. She couldn't think of a response worth making.

Xander could, or thought he could. "You should check it out, Cordy," he said. "You'd have fun." He paused. "*We'd* have fun," he amended.

"You're still on that?" Cordelia asked. Without trying to be subtle about it, she looked at her wristwatch, a sterling silver wafer that her father had given her. Fifteen minutes had passed. She would need to report for drills soon.

Xander's answer was a silent nod.

"*Mysteries of Chainsaw Mansion*? Please." Cordelia grimaced. "Find someone else," she said. "Someone who's not a girl."

"Not even Willow?" Xander said.

"Especially not Willow," Cordelia said. "But especially, especially not me. I plan to be busy."

"Busy?" Xander sounded anxious. "Busy with someone? Someone else?"

"Not like that," Cordelia said, taking pity. "I'll likely be at the Bronze, watching Aura make a fool of herself again."

Without being invited or authorized, Xander sat down beside her. Cordelia decided to let it slide; after all, the courtyard was largely deserted. "Aura?" he said. "Fool? Again? It's sharing time."

Cordelia took a deep breath. There was that endearing goofiness again. She told Xander about the previous evening. Quickly she recounted her friend's sudden fascination with the mysterious stranger and how disappointed Aura had been when she returned to the table.

"He disappeared?" Xander asked. He listened to her attentively, which was always gratifying.

"That's what Aura said," Cordelia said. She corrected herself. "I mean, that's what Aura said the Goth girl said. I didn't see it myself."

Cordelia's world had been a reasonably clear-cut place before the weirdness that she associated with Buffy Summers had started to nibble at its edges.

"That can't be good," Xander said. "The disappearing thing, I mean."

"Guys have bailed on Aura before," Cordelia said. She looked at her watch. Another five minutes had passed.

"Bailed, not disappeared," Xander pointed out.

"That's if you trust someone with purple hair to get things right," Cordelia said tartly.

"A mysterious stranger disappears mysteriously in a town filled with mystery right on top of the Hellmouth? And you say there's no mystery about it?" Xander teased.

Cordelia rolled her eyes. She knew what his next words would be.

"Have you talked to Buffy about this?" he asked.

"No," she replied testily.

"I really think—"

"It wasn't like that," she said, interrupting. Her tone was sharper now. "I *told* you, Xander, guys have bailed on Aura before."

They sat together in a tense moment of silence. She was sure that Xander knew he'd erred. He had to. She'd told him enough times that invoking other girls to her wasn't a very good idea. Cordelia might get along with Buffy these days, but that didn't mean she wanted Xander to keep bringing up her name.

"I've seen some strangers in my day," he said finally, in a musing tone.

"I'm sure you have," she replied.

He surprised her then. “I’m sorry,” he said, changing the subject.

“Huh?” Cordelia asked, genuinely startled by his two words. Xander didn’t apologize very often. Usually he just protested that the world in general and women in particular didn’t make any sense. Then he would either storm off until the smoke settled or stay and try to wisecrack his way out of the situation. Either way, life would go on. It seemed out of character for him to apologize, especially so promptly and for such a minor slight.

“The Buffy thing,” he said again. “I shouldn’t tell you what to do.” He shrugged. “I’m just a typical teenage boy and I make mistakes. I really am sorry.”

Was he sorry that he’d brought up her name? Or was he just sorry that he’d suggested she report to Buffy, like some kind of flunky or minion? Either option seemed equally likely, so Cordelia gave him the benefit of the doubt.

“That’s okay,” she said. “No biggie.”

This time the shared silence was more comfortable. Though still relieved that they didn’t have an audience, Cordelia found she didn’t mind his company. For a second she actually considered going to the stupid drive-in with him.

But only for a second.

“Cordy?” Xander said slowly. “If they changed the school colors, I’d hear about it, wouldn’t I? I mean, I’d *know*, right?” He sounded even more confused than usual.

She blinked again in surprise. The question came out of nowhere. “They haven’t changed the colors, Xander,” she said with forced patience. “I should know. They just issued new uniforms, for the team and the squad. Why are you so interested in fashion?”

His answer was to point to the far end of the courtyard. A girl lounged in a shadowed fire exit. She seemed to be looking in their direction.

“That’s why,” Xander said.

At first Cordelia thought that he’d been dumb enough to raise the issue of another woman again. Then she realized that he was trying to make another point.

Xander’s finger-point morphed into a hand wave. “Hi, there!” he said a bit more loudly. The girl made no response.

Tall and curvy, she wasn’t a member of the student body; Cordelia was certain of that. She kept tabs on the competition and knew her rivals by sight, even at a distance. The stranger wasn’t a fellow student.

That wasn’t the only thing wrong. The girl wore a cheerleading uniform. It was a cut different from Cordelia’s, passé and unattractive, with a too-long skirt that did nothing for the poor thing’s legs. The style of the jersey was wrong too, but that wasn’t even the worst of it.

“Pink and white?” Cordelia asked, appalled. “Who wears pink and white?”

Xander shrugged. “Mary Kay Academy?” he asked. “Dixieland High? Peppermint Secondary?”

Cordelia sprang to her feet to investigate. She hardly noticed that Xander did the same. This was a matter of competition and territory, serious business for a person with Cordelia's social prominence.

"Hey! Hey, you!" she called. Her words carried the length of the nearly deserted courtyard and echoed from the surrounding walls. The girl came to sudden attention, startled.

The distance from the retaining wall to the mystery cheerleader was perhaps twenty yards. Cordelia didn't bother to run, but she strode briskly enough that the distance dwindled rapidly. "I want to talk to you!" she said loudly.

Xander kept pace. "Cordy," he said at her side, "is this really a good idea? I mean, I like a catfight as much as the next guy—"

"Hush," she told him. Boys could be so stupid.

Closer now, she could see the other girl better. The pink-and-white outfit wasn't the least of the stranger's offenses against good taste. She was blond, like Buffy, but wore her hair in a frizzy cloud that was years out of date and absolutely impractical for cheerleading work. Her makeup was wrong too, florid tones applied without blending or style. Cordelia wasn't very good with specific dates, but she knew passé when she saw it, and she was seeing it now.

What was the girl thinking?

"Okay, lady," Cordelia said, a mere ten steps away now. "You and me, we need to—*Hey!*"

The girl turned. She opened the door and darted through it, entering the school's interior without a backward glance. The door slammed shut behind her.

Cordelia and Xander quickly followed her inside, but she was nowhere to be seen. The locker-lined halls were empty. Not even distant telltale footsteps could be heard. The strange girl had simply disappeared.

"Well," Xander said. He looked completely baffled.

"Yeah, well," Cordelia agreed. Finally, reluctantly, she said what she knew he had to be thinking. "I guess I'd better have that chat with Buffy after all."

Willow's room was homier than Buffy's. Maybe it was because she spent more time at home and gave it a more lived-in look. Maybe it was just because the Rosenbergs had lived at their address in Sunnydale for so long. Tastefully decorated and tidy, this was actually Willow's home, in a way that the Summers house still wasn't Buffy's. The Slayer was still a new girl in town, relatively speaking, but Willow had lived in town all her life. She had roots here, and not in a gross, monster-plant kind of way.

Buffy, perched on the edge of Willow's neatly made bed, felt utterly out of her league as the other girl's hands moved along the keyboard of her laptop. They looked like tangoing spiders. Buffy stared at the monitor the same way Xander stared at girls: with complete fascination and focus. The keys seemed barely able to keep up with Willow's fingertips. Buffy understood just enough of what she was doing to realize that Willow had a genius for manipulating search engines, guessing passwords, and cracking encryption. The Internet world was Willow's oyster, even if she didn't eat shellfish.

The computer's speakers came to life, emitting demonic laughter that then resolved itself into Latin-sounding phrases. Willow had set the volume very low, so that her parents wouldn't hear, but the effect still startled. The screen, which Buffy could see over her friend's shoulder, filled with dancing skeletons. They were electric blue against a field of flames.

"I don't think that's what we want," Buffy said warily. "At least, I hope it's not."

"I don't think so either," Willow said. She studied her find. "What's 'German Dungeon Rock'?" she asked. "This guy really, really likes it."

"Don't know," Buffy said. "Don't want to." She picked up one of the stuffed animals that were part of Willow's room decor. She gazed into the stuffed bear's black button eyes. It seemed like a very long time since she'd had stuffed animals of her own, a long time and a world away. Part of her still missed them, though, especially Mr. Gordo, her beloved stuffed pig.

Willow entered some more commands. The skeletons faded away.

"Did you tell Giles about the nurse?" Willow asked without missing a keystroke, her eyes fixated on the screen. Her computer expertise extended to multitasking proficiency.

"Yeah," Buffy said. "He didn't quite believe me."

"Huh?" Willow said, surprised.

More than one of her previous reports had been met with

initial skepticism. Willow and Xander might accept Buffy's word as gospel. Even Cordelia, when pressed, might grant that the Slayer had a certain subject-matter expertise. But Giles could be a tougher nut to crack. Buffy told Willow how after her visit to the nurse's station she made a return to the library to tell Giles that Kitty Forman remained comfortably installed in the school administration. The only reasonable conclusion was that Inga had been a ringer and was probably up to no good. Giles said she might have been interviewing or maybe a temp of some sort. He promised to ask Principal Snyder.

"Well, it wasn't that bad," Buffy said. "It's not like she was a *giant* nurse with fangs or anything."

"He just wants to explore the Alps with Inga," Willow said, in a slight echo of her earlier bad accent. She continued typing.

"Ya," Buffy said, then set aside the toy bear. "Any luck?"

A pinky finger hit enter one final time. One last report filled the screen. Willow shook her head.

"Bubkes," she said, turning in her chair to face Buffy. "Same as with Giles's books. No hits of note on 'Sunnydale' plus 'drive-in' plus various hot-topic terms like 'mysterious death' or 'sacrifice' or 'brain weevil.' Drop 'drive-in' from the query string and hundreds of matches come up, running back centuries—"

"Well, the Hellmouth has been here a long time," Buffy said, interrupting.

"But 'drive-in' seems to be what you'd call an exclusionary

criterion," Willow said. The specialized words sounded a trifle odd coming from her; she usually just worked her computer magic without explaining how it worked. "It's right at the edge of the mouth too. The land might be clean."

"Huh," Buffy said, thinking. Outside, the sun had begun to set. She needed to leave soon. "That would be a nice change."

"Did your mom say anything else about the place?" Willow asked.

"Nope," Buffy said. "Some friend of hers said the place has a 'history of trouble.' Hereabouts that means someone got turned inside out or something."

"Not this time," Willow said. "I even accessed the crime reports. Not nothing at all, but nothing of note." She paused. "You're worried about Xander?"

"Not worried," Buffy said. "Concerned, maybe. The boy does have a history."

That was putting it lightly. For a civilian, even a civilian who ran with the Slayer, Xander had proved to be a lightning rod for trouble. Again and again the amiable teenager found himself up to his neck in the bad stuff, typically through no fault of his own.

Well, through *little* fault of his own, at least.

"Have you talked?" Willow asked. She closed out her search engines and pulled up a Word doc instead. Homework was pending.

"No," Buffy said slowly. "I don't want to unless there's

more to go on. And I don't want him getting the wrong idea. He's hell-bent on going to the movies, though." According to the ubiquitous handbills and Xander's eager accounts, the next night was the drive-in's grand reopening.

"You could go with him!" Willow said. "Keep an eye out!"

Buffy shook her head. "C'mon, Willow," she said. "I'd have to miss patrol. Besides, I don't want to give him the wrong idea."

Xander's attraction to Buffy had long since become a given in her life, and she didn't stop often to think about it. He was a good guy, and she trusted him with her life. Even so, there didn't seem to be much point in adding fuel to the fire. Alone with Xander, at the drive-in . . .

"I meant we could both go with him," Willow said, a bit plaintively. "*I* don't mind giving him the wrong idea."

"C'mon, Will," Buffy said. "Those things don't work that way."

"Don't worry about it, then," Willow said reluctantly. She toyed with the mouse. "He'll be fine without me—um, without us." She had known Xander Harris all her life. Although the two girls rarely talked about it, Buffy was quite aware that Willow had a bit of a crush on her childhood chum. "He's tough. I'd be more fretful about this Inga character."

"Huh?" Buffy asked. Her weapons bag sat on the floor next to her sensibly shod feet. She picked it up and glanced at the contents. She was carrying more blades than usual tonight. Better safe than sorry.

"Mysterious stranger plus missing book," Willow pointed out. "That can't be good news."

"Willow, she's a nurse," Buffy said, tossing her hair for emphasis.

"Nurses have needles!"

"I've got some kind of a werewolf to worry about. Werewolves are bad news," Buffy said. "If this even *is* a werewolf."

"I guess so," Willow said. "But I've met a scary nurse or two in my day, and there's still the missing book thing."

"Giles has plenty of books," Buffy said. She knew that Willow was right, but her mind was already on patrol. The nurse impostor was a mystery but not a pressing problem, at least not right now.

"Did you know Giles belongs to the Grimoire of the Month Club?"

"Can't say it surprises me," Buffy said. She shouldered her bag. "The wolves will be howling soon."

"I hope you're wrong about that," Willow said.

Buffy hoped so too.

Xander was working the blocks that flanked the east side of Main Street. It was a reasonably well-off and trafficked section of town, where franchises of national retail chains rubbed shoulders with locally owned restaurants, galleries, and shops. This was pretty far from Xander's usual haunts—no fast-food joints here—but today it worked well for him. Many of the men and women standing sentry behind cash registers were local entrepreneurs, ready to lend a sympathetic ear to his pitch.

"Thanks a million, Mr. Tate," he said to the man behind the soda fountain ice cream counter. "I really appreciate it."

"Hey, what's good for local business is good for me," Tate said. He was heavyset and completely bald. A spotless white apron was stretched tight across his sizeable stomach. He'd manned the old-fashioned soda fountain for as long as Xander could remember. "You'll have to make your own space, though," Tate said.

Xander took hasty inventory of the community bulletin board. The cork tiles were layered thick with postings. Moving quickly, he peeled away a dozen outdated band announcements, sales brochures, and missing-pet announcements. He wondered briefly if people in other towns lost as many dogs and cats, or if it was just part of life on the Hellmouth. Then he shook his head. There were happier things to think about.

Once he'd cleared enough space, and a healthy margin beyond, he positioned one of his handbills and stapled it in place. He wadded up the discarded documents and dropped them in a wastebasket.

"There," he said, making a great show of clapping his hands together as if to clean them. "A job well done is its own reward."

"Yeah, well, good luck to you all," Tate said as he wiped down the already immaculate countertop. "Most people use the Internet instead these days."

"Well, you know, that luck might be better if you'd let me leave a stack of these," Xander coaxed. He fanned the remaining handbills.

Tate shook his head. His soda shop was an old one, and he was quite experienced at saying no to teenagers. "You clear the space, you post, one post per event. No handouts. Them's the rules."

"Right you are, Mr. Tate!" Xander said. He didn't press the issue; he didn't want the owner to change his mind. Instead, he thanked the proprietor again and exited, the door's bell ringing as he re-emerged into the late afternoon sun.

It was time to start strategizing, he realized. So far he'd just been going door to door, but it was late enough in the day that at least some local operations would close their doors soon. It made sense to select the most likely options, in terms of both friendly management and likely clientele. Six doors down was a familiar storefront that promised both.

"Of course!" Xander said softly.

A moment later another door swung shut behind him, and another old-fashioned bell chimed. He took a deep breath, drawing in not the sweet goodness of ice cream and syrup, but something richer. Herbs and spices and incense filled the air.

"Welcome to the Magic Box," came a girl's voice. She didn't sound very enthusiastic. "Let me know if I can help you find something, but we close in, um, twelve minutes."

Perched halfway up a ladder was the latest in a long run

of Magic Box clerks, taking inventory of items on an upper shelf. She was dressed in black pants and a tank top and had purple hair. In one hand she held a clipboard, and in the other some kind of wizened root thing that looked like it had seen better days.

"I just wanted to see if I could post a notice," Xander said. The sight of purple hair stirred a memory. This had to be the girl Cordelia had mentioned, the girl who'd witnessed weird doings at the Bronze.

The girl sighed and set the items she held aside. She didn't so much descend the ladder as jump from it. Her booted feet thumped on the Magic Box's floor. "Gimme," she said, and took the proffered handbill. She stood near him as she read.

Close-up she was cute. She was older than Xander, but not by more than ten years. Under the pale makeup and dark lipstick, her features were elfin, and he could tell that she kept herself in shape. This had to be Aura's on-the-scene informant. Just below one shoulder a badge announced her name.

"You're Amanda?" he half-said, half-asked. He was interested now. As he'd told Cordelia earlier, he was a healthy teenage boy.

Still reading, the clerk grunted in acknowledgment. Unlike almost anyone else he'd spoken to, she seemed determined to read each word on the orange sheet. After what seemed like an eternity she wrinkled her nose and looked up from the page. "I dunno," she said.

The Goth girl had pretty eyes, he realized. They were hazel

and they sparkled, even in the shop's subdued lighting. Xander was really interested now. She had a certain eerie charm, but without any evidence of the supernatural strings that usually came attached to girls with wrong-colored hair.

"You don't know whether you're Amanda?" he joked.

"Yeah, I'm Amanda, and yeah, I'm new," she said. She was less preoccupied than he'd thought. She tapped the orange sheet. "I don't know about this," she said.

"The Magic Box has always been a good friend of Sunnydale High and the local business community," Xander said hopefully. "Band candy, yearbook ads, concert announcements, the whole schmear." He pointed at the window, where sun-faded remnants of older postings lingered.

Amanda was reading the drive-in announcement again. He wondered if she wanted to memorize it.

"Look," Xander said ingratiatingly. It was time to turn on the famous Harris charm. "This is a good spot. We're running a horror movie, and with the creepy-crawlies who come in here sometimes—"

Her head came up, as if on a string. Her hazel eyes flashed. He'd said the wrong thing.

"Sometimes," Xander repeated. "I said 'sometimes.' Some of my best friends shop here. Honest." He paused, trying to make up for lost ground. "Look, I can throw in a couple of passes, if you'd like."

He showed her the tickets. She plucked them from his fingers and read both sides carefully. Finally, grudgingly, Amanda nodded. "Okay, deal," she said. "And if the boss complains, it comes down."

"Fair enough," Xander said. "More than fair, really."

It took a few minutes to scrape an old posting of the same approximate size from the window's glass, but less time to tape his new one in place. While he worked, she set the door's lock and flipped the door's sign to SORRY, WE'RE CLOSED. She did it with remarkable speed and had already begun to count the day's receipts by the time he'd finished.

"You're done?" she asked, sorting bills. The hint wasn't very subtle. It was time for Sign-Posting Lad to vanish into the sunset.

"Yeah," Xander said. He watched her count for a moment. "Busy day?" he asked.

"I thought you were done," Amanda said. Coins clinked as she sorted them into the appropriate compartments. Clearly, she wasn't one for small talk.

"Can I ask you a question before I go?" Xander said slowly. He tried to choose his words carefully, but that kind of premeditation didn't come easily to him, especially not with girls.

"That's one already," she said. More coins clinked.

"Have you ever been to the Bronze?" There was a chance she could tell him more about what had happened the previous night.

The sound of coins being counted came to an abrupt halt. The purple-haired girl looked up from her work, dark lips parted in an amused grin. Xander knew instantly that he hadn't spoken carefully enough.

"You're wasting your time, townie," she said. "I don't date kids."

At the time of its original grand opening decades before, the drive-in had stood at the town's outermost fringes. Sunnydale had grown since then, but in other directions. Specifically, toward the new state highway and the connector roads to the federal interstate, so the open-air theater still lay outside its border. The distance and relative isolation helped save it from vandals and scavengers. Once the original management had reclaimed its projection and sound systems and stripped the concession stand bare, there simply hadn't been much left behind to attract visitors.

Angel had been one of the few visitors. His restless nature had led him to explore Sunnydale in some detail since coming there, and he knew the town better than most natives did. Now, in the dead of night, he stood on the hill overlooking the previously abandoned establishment and marveled at how much it had changed in such a short time.

Even at a distance he could tell it was ready to reopen. The parking area was weeded, reterraced, and strewn with fresh gravel. The speaker posts were gone, presumably superseded by broadcast sound. The screen's refurbished surface gleamed faintly under the autumn moon. A shiny new marquee was positioned near the box office.

"Very nice," Angel said to no one in particular. Like himself, the place was a reminder of a time gone by, even if its time was not as far past as his own. As an institution the drive-in had enjoyed its heyday in the 1950s, and some years of that tumultuous decade had been very good for Angel. Seeing the drive-in brought a smile to his pale face and made him think of Elvis and early rock and roll. As with most of Angel's smiles, however, it was faint and faded quickly.

With long, easy strides he made his way down the hill and to the theater's perimeter. Renovation extended to a hastily erected cyclone fence topped by razor wire, but neither posed any obstacle worth noting. A single leap carried Angel over the barrier, and he set about exploring in earnest.

Yet again the vampire's keen senses proved useful. He could see perfectly in the moonlit gloom. His touch and hearing were sensitive enough that he had no difficulty picking construction site padlocks or inspecting the newly installed projectors. As far as he could tell, there was nothing particularly sinister about the place. Certainly, there was no trace, however faint, of any kind of werewolf. Even the paperwork he found in the construction shack was in perfect order. Whoever Shadow Amusements, Inc. was, they managed their contractors well.

The phantom memory that Angel had dredged up earlier still pointed this way, but the thought was really an absurd one. The fact that it hadn't paid off didn't really surprise him.

The last structure he looked at was secure, relatively

speaking. It was the concession stand building, which also housed the operation's office behind a heavy door with a good lock. Angel needed nearly a minute to pick the locks on both doors, and then he let himself into the sparsely furnished space.

He started with a shelf anchored to the wall above the desk. It held a dozen thick catalogs with elaborate logos on each spine. The light inside the office was too faint for color, but judging from the images that Angel viewed in monochrome, the covers were impressively gaudy. He moved closer to the office's single window, hoping for enough moonlight to discern any more details.

They were booking catalogs used to arrange movie rentals. Angel flipped through one, uninterested and unimpressed. He was reaching for a second catalog when he heard the sound.

Outside, freshly strewn gravel crunched beneath one footstep, then another. Someone was approaching. Hastily he rammed the catalog back into place and cursed himself silently. He'd left the building's door ajar.

"I know someone's in there," said the person, presumably a guard. One of the files in the construction shack included a contract with a local security service. Angel said nothing.

"Let's do this the nice way," the man outside said. "I've already called the police, and I warn you, I'm armed."

Angel heard the *click-click* of a double action revolver's hammer. That was bad. Bullets couldn't hurt him, but they stung, and there was always the danger of ricochet. He didn't particularly want the guard to get hurt just for doing his job.

The vampire considered his options. One was the half-open door, with the armed guard on its far side. The other was the single window. It was old, and heavy beads of rust had welded the metal frame shut. The glass was thick and reinforced with embedded wires. He could break through easily enough.

Angel heard the door behind him start to swing open. He gripped the window's sash firmly. Metal shrieked as the corrosion of decades tore free. The opening was barely big enough to admit him, but he squeezed through, grimacing as his jacket caught a jagged edge and tore.

His feet had hardly cleared the window frame when the guard fired. Thunder roared and the night was lit brightly for a split second. Rock dust flew as a bullet buried itself in the parking lot's gravel.

A moment later the guard's head extended cautiously from the open window. He looked from side to side, then drew back. When he spoke again, it was in clear, businesslike tones. Angel could hear him perfectly from his hiding place.

"Ralph, this is Murray again," the guard said. Angel couldn't see inside the office, but it was easy to guess that the other man had a cell phone. "Yeah, Murray at the site. It's not an emergency. Looks like there was a break-in, but the perp is long gone." He paused. "Okay, I won't call them 'perps' anymore." He paused again, then lied. "No, I didn't fire my gun," he said. "I know better than that."

Finally Murray spoke again. He sounded both apologetic and exasperated. "Yeah, Ralph, yeah. I *know* false alarms are a pain. I'll come by tomorrow to help with the paperwork. Right, first thing."

There came a click as he closed his phone, breaking the connection. The guard poked his head out the window again and looked from side to side a second time.

"Huh," he said softly, speaking to himself. "No footprints at all. This place must be haunted."

Angel, watching him from the rooftop above, thought otherwise.

CHAPTER FIVE

Buffy sat slumped beneath the chestnut tree on the school campus. The day was very young, with only the earliest of early-bird students reporting for duty, but Buffy's eyes were already heavy-lidded and bloodshot. She leaned back against the tree's trunk, the open history book in her lap nearly forgotten. Next to her on the dew-damp grass was an unopened pint of orange juice and three chewy granola bars. She was too tired to eat.

"Good heavens, Buffy," Giles said with concern in his voice as he approached her. "You look dreadful."

"No wonder you're a bachelor," she said. Even her voice was colored with fatigue. "With patter like that, I mean."

"That's not what I meant," the master librarian said. Dropping his briefcase, he squatted beside her. She could tell that he didn't want to get grass stains on his tweed trousers. "Were you out all night?" he asked, plainly concerned.

She nodded. "Pretty much," she said, closing her history book. "Went home, did the dinner thing with Mom, pretended to go to bed. Slipped out later to go on patrol."

Giles nodded. It was a story he'd heard before.

"One thing led to another," Buffy continued. "By the time I realized the night was gone, the night was, well, gone. Went home, changed, and raided the fridge." She forced a smile. "And here I am, bright-eyed and bushy-tailed."

Giles picked up the orange juice carton and opened it. "Here," he said, "drink."

"In a minute," she said. "I want to tell you—"

"Drink," Giles said again. "Your stamina is remarkable and so is your dedication. Neither will suffer if you tend to your blood sugar."

Buffy drank. The OJ was still cool, and it admittedly felt good coursing down her throat. Almost immediately the world became a brighter place. "Um," she said. "Good."

Giles nodded. "Now," he said, "tell me what happened."

"That's just it, Giles," Buffy said. "Nothing happened."

He looked at her blankly. "Nothing?"

"Nothing at all," she said. "The night was dead. Not even a teensy-tiny vampire to be seen. I lugged twenty pounds of pointy weapons for nothing."

"You tarried on patrol all night because nothing happened?" Giles asked. Concern began to give way to annoyance. "Buffy, as I said, I admire your sense of duty, but—"

"You weren't out there, Giles," Buffy said. She looked in the direction of the parking lot. The first real wave of students began arriving. Xander might be among their number, she realized, and she tucked the granola bars safely into her pocket. "It felt like the whole world was holding its breath."

The words came to her without conscious thought, but they rang with absolute truth, even in her own ears. Once more the night air had been filled with an electric charge, but this time there had been no incident. For nearly seven hours she had patrolled the haunts and byways of Sunnydale, her nerves humming and her entire body tensed for action that never came. She was exhausted now, more tired than mere lack of sleep could have made her. Buffy felt like a sprinter who'd spent the entire meet on the starting line, without ever having a chance to run.

Giles stood and offered his hand. She waved him aside and rose in a single fluid motion, as if her body were a wave that had decided to flow uphill. It was Buffy's nerves that felt the worst of the night's fatigue, not her body.

"And Angel?" Giles asked. "Did he make an appearance?"

She shook her head. Her relationship with the vampire was one of trust and even love, but it was not without its mysteries. "No show," Buffy said. She tried not to sound wistful. "Business of his own, I guess. Happens sometimes."

They walked together toward the school entrance. Sitting had been a mistake; moving made her feel better. So did the companionship. The orange juice had probably helped too. She began to feel hungry and patted the granola bars in her pocket.

"You were supposed to contact me last night," Giles said in mild reproof. "Before patrol, I mean."

"Ouchie," she said. "I'm sorry. I forgot." She didn't tell him that she had visited Willow and researched the drive-in. Bad enough that she'd slighted him; it would make things worse to tell him that the effort she had undertaken instead had been fruitless. "Any luck in the home library?"

He gave a brief nod. "Possibly," he said. "Do you know what an *excursus* is, Buffy?"

"Something that used to be a curse?" she asked.

They were inside the school now, and the hallway was slowly filling with students. None seemed to give the mismatched pair a second glance. Even now, Buffy wasn't exactly Miss Popular, and his official role as school librarian often made Giles the next best thing to an invisible man.

He tut-tutted softly. "No, no," he said. "It's not an occult term but an academic one. It's a lengthy discussion of a specific topic, appended to another, larger work. Often they're published separately, after the 'parent' book."

"A super-footnote," Buffy said. "A footnote from the doomed planet Krypton."

He gave no sign of having heard her. "I keep certain excursuses at home, even when the parent volume resides in the collection here. They're very rare, very fragile, and—"

"And you don't want me spilling any orange juice on them," Buffy said. She paused in midstride. They were at the library entrance, which meant it was time for her to report to homeroom. Classes could be cut, if the procedure were executed right, but missing homeroom meant being marked absent, and she'd missed too many days already.

"Just so," Giles said. "I think they may be useful in the matter of the mis-shelved book."

"The missing book, you mean," Buffy said. She still had her doubts about that Inga character.

"The missing book," Giles said patiently. He made the three words sound like a great concession. "We should speak of it at length."

"I now call this meeting of the Secret Justice Club to order," Xander said. He stood at the head of the long table, hands at his hips, and drew himself up to his full height as he eyed the three seated girls. It was a very dramatic pose, and a good match for his portentous tone. "Thank you for convening here, in our secret citadel of justice, on such short notice."

Seated beside Willow, Buffy looked at him with hooded eyes. She was far more durable and resilient than even an Olympic athlete, but even so, fatigue from the long, stressful night left her irritable. Her friend's clowning wasn't helping things either. "Xander—," she started to say.

He gestured with one hand, waving her input aside. "No, no, Slayer Lass," he said with mock condescension. "I realize we all have hectic schedules, and I appreciate you all making time in your lives—"

"Put a sock in it, Xander," Cordelia said, speaking even more sharply than Buffy. She drummed perfectly manicured nails on the table's polished top. Whichever social event the gathering had taken her from, she wanted to get back to it even more than Buffy wanted to rest.

Xander flinched at the words. He looked at her, as he had at Buffy, but he didn't wave her words aside. He seemed confused and paralyzed by indecision, like a deer in headlights.

"Yes, Xander, put a sock in it," Giles said, suddenly behind him. Hearing the American colloquialism in his arch British tones made Willow giggle softly.

Xander shut up, taking the empty seat next to Cordelia. He shrugged and remained silent, but looked upward as if to say, "Why me?"

Ordinarily well groomed, Giles looked a bit rumpled now. He'd pushed up his sleeves and opened his collar. A lock of brown hair dangled onto his forehead, glued by perspiration. Without preamble he began, "I stayed here late last evening, conducting a total inventory of the occult holdings." He gently set three dusty volumes on the table. "It's a painstaking task and demands some concentration, as I'm sure you all understand."

"I'm sure we do," Willow said softly. Buffy elbowed her,

but the Rosenberg girl still smiled. Of the five gathered in the school library, she was the only one who seemed genuinely relaxed and happy.

Giles continued. "What I found was disturbing," he said. He glanced at Buffy. "You were right," he said. "The book that I thought might have been mis-shelved is missing."

The Slayer smiled broadly, pleased with herself.

"That's not good news, Buffy," Giles said.

Buffy's smile faded.

"The book is nowhere on the premises," Giles said. "I inspected the stacks as well."

"So Inga took it," Xander prodded. "So you complain to Snyder, or we go to the nurse's station—"

Buffy shook her head. "No," she said after Giles had nodded permission to interrupt. "I checked on that yesterday. We don't have a Nurse Inga."

"Well," Willow said. "She didn't last long."

"That's not what Buffy means," Giles said. "I confirmed it with the administration. Not only is Mrs. Forman still the school's attending nurse, she's very happy in her role. No one else has interviewed for her job, or even applied for it."

"Oh," Xander said. He blinked as the meaning of the words sank in. "Oh!"

Giles nodded. "It appears we've had an impostor," he said. "I can only assume that she was sent on some manner of reconnaissance mission. Now—"

"Not an impostor," Xander said, interrupting.

Cordelia nodded in instant agreement. "Impostor*s*," she said, emphasizing the plural.

At Giles's prompting, and in short, precise sentences, she told the assembled group about her and Xander's near encounter with the cheerleader in the courtyard. Being Cordelia, she emphasized points that the others didn't find nearly as interesting as she did: the disappearing cheerleader's outdated hairstyle and unfamiliar school colors. "Even after that, we checked some more," she continued. "She wasn't in any of the classrooms, or anywhere else she could have gotten to. I even checked the girls' locker room."

"I offered to," Xander pointed out.

This time it was Xander who got an elbow in the ribs, and not from Buffy. He winced and eyed the ceiling again.

"And you were going to tell us about this when?" Buffy asked.

"Now," Cordelia said in simple explanation.

"Well, in the future, in events of an occult nature—," Giles began.

"It was a cheerleader," Cordelia said, raising her voice. "Not a werewolf or a vampire or a hobgoblin. I had drills and homework, and, you know, it's not like I get to use any of my study periods to actually *study* anymore!"

No one had anything to say to the outburst. For a long moment the library was nearly silent, the only sound the *tap-tap* of Cordelia's fingertips, which she had begun drumming again.

"Yes, well," Giles said at last. He seated himself and reached for the first of his books. As he fanned the pages, dust billowed from between them and hung in the still air.

"A girl's got to have her priorities," Cordelia said. "And it's not like I can't hold my own against any girl from another squad."

"We agreed to tell you about it together," Xander said, sounding conciliatory. He smiled very slightly as Cordelia shot him a grateful glance. "And, like the lady said, we're talking cheerleader here, not creepy emissary from the outer darkness."

"There's where you may be in error," Giles said mildly, still paging through his book. His tone was mild, but he quickly moved into lecture mode. "Tell me, do any of you know what ectoplasm is?" he asked.

None of them answered. He shook his head sadly before continuing. "Ectoplasm is—"

"The visible but immaterial substance that makes up the physical composition of ghosts and similar occult manifestations," Buffy said, cutting him off. She spoke with the sing-song cadence of someone reciting from memory. She smirked.

"Very good," Giles said, impressed.

"There's another definition too," Buffy said. "For biologists. Outer part of a cell."

"That won't be necessary," Giles said, clearly a bit chagrined. "You've proved your point. You're up to date on your readings. Good show."

"So we're working with ghosts?" Willow asked. "Like, maybe Sunnydale High is built on an old nurse's cemetery, or Cordy's phantom cheerleader was from the class of fifty-two?"

"Believe me," Cordelia said, "those have *never* been the school colors." She spoke with great disdain. "I don't care *how* far back you go."

"Tell us about the books," Willow said eagerly. She liked books. "The ghosts and the books."

"I don't know that they're haunts," Giles said. He seated himself and steepled his fingers, considering how best to explain. "You must understand, many of the books that I've brought with me are from the Council archives, very old and difficult to replace. Even the least of them date back to a time when books were hand-bound and produced in very small number for highly demanding patrons."

"Yeah, yeah, yeah," Buffy said. "Written in human blood, bound in human skin—"

"No," Giles said forcefully. "Or, rather, not entirely. I refer more to much younger books, typeset rather than hand-scribed. The nature of the production process was such that it discouraged specialization. Books tended to be compendia, rather than focused works."

"Okay," Buffy said, and nodded. "Omnibi."

"Omnibuses," Willow corrected. The eyes of both Cordelia and Xander began to glaze, but neither said anything. Perhaps they didn't want to prolong the discussion.

"I won't trouble you with the titles," Giles said, "but someone seems to have absconded with four key works addressing the mechanics of what we now call psychic phenomena." He paused. "These were what passed for scientific works in their day. Sections deal with mind reading, mesmerism, transubstantiation of souls and base matter, spiritualism, psychoetherics, even phrenology." He glanced at Xander. "That's the study of head bumps," he said.

"I knew that," Xander said, but he didn't look like he expected anyone to believe him.

Giles resumed. "One thing that all four books have in common is that they have sections pertaining to ectoplasmic constructs."

"Ghosts," Buffy said.

"Or something similar," her Watcher agreed.

"The ghost of a werewolf?" Buffy asked skeptically.

"Not necessarily. It could be something more complex," Giles said. "And, at any rate, we cannot be certain that those sections are why the texts were taken. The commonality among the books *is* intriguing, though."

"You really know your stuff, Giles," Willow said, awestruck.

"Yeah, I mean, I can't even keep my comics straight," Xander said, only to receive a withering glance in return.

"I know the collection well, but I don't have them memorized," Giles said. "I do maintain an annotated catalog, though. That's how I was able to identify the missing works and get at least an approximate idea of their contents." He paused.

"They aren't particularly noteworthy volumes. Many books of greater rarity and importance were on the same shelves."

"But what does any of this have to do with the wolf-man?" Buffy asked.

"Possibly nothing. But it may have everything to do with him, with Nurse Inga, and with Cordelia's cheerleader."

"Hey, she's not mine," Cordelia said.

No one acknowledged the comment. After a long moment of silence Buffy bit the bullet and fed Giles the prompt. "Well?" she asked.

"I think our measure's being taken," Giles said. Even under his habitual reserve, his voice carried a concerned quality. Something that was not quite worry colored his words as he continued. "I think that, whoever our visitors are—whatever they are—they're here to investigate us and the extent of our knowledge." He looked at Buffy pointedly. "Perhaps of our strength, as well."

"So we're talking minions here, huh?" Xander asked.

Giles nodded.

"But—but why use something so, well, goofy?" Willow asked.

"Whatever do you mean?"

Willow fidgeted a bit. She traced an idle pattern on the tabletop as she chose her words. "I'm just saying it's funny," she said. "The details are all wrong. The wrong school colors, the wrong kind of werewolf. If they aren't haunts, why not get the details right?"

"I don't know," Giles said. "But as I explained to Buffy earlier, I have some additional materials at home that may provide some clarification. Until then, I urge you all to proceed with the utmost caution."

Jonathan was well aware of his place in the overall scheme of things. Fit but short, shy, timid, and studious-looking, he was not so much an also-ran in the Sunnydale High rat race as he was a spectator on the sidelines. The faculty and other students didn't particularly dislike him; they scarcely realized that he shared their world. He was as close to a nonentity as you could get. That accounted for his wary expression when Xander sat in the chair across from him at the cafeteria table.

"Hey, J," Xander said. He deployed his meal, arranging plates, bowls, and a drinking glass in front of himself before setting the plastic tray aside. "Anyone sitting here?"

"Um, no," Jonathan said. No one ever sat across from him.

"Mind if I join?" Xander had gotten three desserts and was arranging them in order of preference—banana pudding, chocolate cake, gelatin mold.

Jonathan watched without comment. Harris sure could eat. His own meal came from home and was much more modest: egg salad on rye toast, and barbecue-flavor potato chips.

"I don't mind," he finally said. Even to his own ears, his voice sounded nasal and reedy. He surprised himself by asking the obvious question. "Where's Buffy?"

"Huh?" Xander asked, pausing with a forkload of mystery meat halfway to his mouth.

"You usually hang with Buffy Summers," Jonathan said. Life on the fringes gave him a good vantage point for observation. "Her and Rosenberg. You guys are always together, and it's like you live in the library or something."

Jonathan refrained from mentioning Cordelia, even though he'd noticed Xander and her engaged in quiet conversation several times recently. Xander was higher on the social ladder than Jonathan was, but only by a few rungs. Cordelia Chase was at the top. The idea that Xander and Cordelia might spend time together was difficult to process.

"Ocupado, mi amigo," Xander said, mangling each word. He ate what appeared to be Salisbury steak. That was one thing he had in common with Buffy Summers: a healthy appetite. Maybe when they were in the library they researched recipes and swapped cooking tips.

"Ocupado?" Jonathan asked.

"Spanish for 'occupied,'" Xander said, with an air of imparting great wisdom. "That leaves you and me more time for manly-man talk, my friend."

Now Jonathan felt a twinge of worry. He had a passing acquaintance with Xander—less passing than with some other students, perhaps, but still only a passing acquaintance. They had their chance encounters on campus and ran into each other at the comic store and the movie rental place, but that was pretty much the extent of their interaction. Why had Xander joined him for lunch? More important, why was he calling him "my friend"?

Xander finished his entrée of overcooked steak patty with bad gravy, limp green beans, and runny mashed potatoes. He indicated Jonathan's food. "You going to eat those chips?" he asked.

"Of course I am," Jonathan said, and ate one to prove his point. It tasted good, so he ate another, then nibbled his sandwich again. He wondered if Xander would take the hint and go away. Xander clearly didn't want to eat alone, but Jonathan was used to it and didn't mind.

"Yep, manly-man talk," Xander said. He drank half his carton of milk with a single gulp. "The companionship of men. There's nothing like it, is there, my friend?"

"Buffy and Willow were too busy for lunch, huh?" Jonathan asked, trying to keep Xander on topic. He didn't ask how many others had been busy too. He knew that, socially speaking, the little Levenson boy was the court of last resort.

Xander nodded reluctantly. He said, "Dumb ol' girls." His generally clownish expression gave way to a halfhearted scowl. "I am just about tapped out on the ladies just now."

Jonathan sighed. It was time to take the bull by the horns. "What are you up to these days, Xander?" he asked, careful not to make the question a challenge. "What can I do for you?"

"Ask not what you can do for me," Xander said. "Ask, rather, what I can do for you."

Xander rummaged in a pocket and drew out a handbill. He

slid it across the table. He'd been distributing the sheets in the hallways and courtyard, even in the cafeteria line. Jonathan eyed the sheet warily. Clearly, Xander had forgotten that he'd already given him one.

Jonathan wasn't surprised.

"You *do* know what a drive-in is, right?" Xander asked. When Jonathan nodded, he continued. "Ever been to one?" he asked. "Want to?"

The elevator chime sounded: The cage had reached the penthouse level. Jim Thompson looked at his reflection in the gleaming metal doors one last time, verifying that his tie was straight and his hair neat. Word was that the gent in the penthouse was a heavy tipper, and Jim didn't want to give him any excuse not to live up to his reputation.

Everything looked fine. The wheeled cart's burden of covered dishes, utensils, and glasses rattled and clinked as he pushed it along the carpeted hallway. When he reached the appropriate door, he rapped on it once.

"Room service," Jim said.

"Enter," came the response. The voice was cultivated but strong enough to be heard clearly, even through the door. "It's not locked."

Jim obeyed. Wheeling the cart into the room, he got his first glimpse of the penthouse's occupant, who was seated at the small desk that matched the rest of the suite's furniture.

He looked pretty much how the hotel's day manager had

described him. He was lean and well dressed, wearing a dark shirt and linen trousers that reflected the easily elegant style of the very rich. He sat ramrod straight, with perfect posture. Four books lay on the desk before him. They looked old and were big, at least as thick as telephone books, and he closed the one he'd been reading as Jim entered. Even that simple movement the occupant made with a certain panache. Jim was impressed.

The only detail the day manager had gotten wrong was the color of the guest's hair. Jim had been told that it was white, but it was gray, not the gray of an old man but the gray of iron. Jim wondered fleetingly if he'd dyed it, then dismissed the thought. Who would color his hair gray?

"Your lunch order, Mr. Belasimo," Jim said.

"Balsamo," the man corrected him, standing.

Jim winced. "Sorry, sir," he said.

"That's quite all right," Balsamo said. His eyes twinkled. "It's not a common name in this part of the world, or in this day and age." He looked at the cart, waiting.

One by one Jim removed the covers and indicated individual courses. "She-crab soup," he said. "Caesar salad. Roast beef, center-cut, with asparagus and fresh bread. Mixed fruit."

"Capital," Balsamo said. He'd already lifted the wine bottle and was examining the label. He nodded in approval and returned it to its caddy. "You can put all of this on the dining table," he said. "Open the wine but leave the covers. I'm not quite ready to eat lunch yet."

Jim nodded. With quick, practiced motions, he arrayed the meal and utensils. As he opened the bottle, he asked, "Will there be anything else, sir?"

"Possibly," Balsamo said, eyeing him. "What's your name, young man?"

"Jim Thompson."

"Tell me, Jim, are you a native of Sunnydale?" he asked as he opened a wallet that was as limp as wet silk. He pulled a bill from it.

"Yes, sir," Jim said. "Born and bred."

"I understand that Sunnydale is a town where things happen," Balsamo said.

Jim knew what he meant. His own life (so far) had been straightforward and without incident, but you couldn't live in Sunnydale without hearing stuff. Jim heard a lot, much of which he preferred not to believe, but there was no way that at least some of the stories weren't true.

"Well, yes. Yes, sir, it is," Jim said.

"Put the meal on my bill," Balsamo said. He passed Jim a bill. "This is for you.

Jim sneaked a peek. His eyes widened. It was a fifty. "Thank you, sir!" he said.

"Not at all," Balsamo said warmly. "But tell me, Jim, what time does your shift end?"

"Um, three o'clock," Jim said. "Are you interested in a tour or something? The concierge prefers that guests make arrangements through his office." What the concierge really preferred was that the hotel staff not make extra money on the side.

"No, not at all," Balsamo said. "But I would like to speak with you some about your fair city and about the things that happen here; a native perspective would be especially useful." He smiled. "I'm quite prepared to compensate you for your time."

CHAPTER SIX

"Fine! Go! But if you get in trouble, it's on your mother's head!" Mr. Harris shouted as Xander ducked out the door, car keys grasped in one hand. "I'm warning you!" his father continued. "You only get one call at the police station, and it better not be to me!"

The door slammed shut behind him, muffling his dad's angry tirade but not blocking it out completely. Even worse, his mother joined in, and the two adults' voices rose in angry confrontation. Once outside, the specific words were hard to pick out, but words really didn't matter. The overall tone was plain: The Battling Harrises were at it again. Embarrassed and ashamed, Xander quickly made his way to the family car, hoping desperately that no one in the neighborhood would pick that minute to look outside and see him.

If he could still hear the rising argument, so could the neighbors. Xander wasn't in the mood for sympathetic glances.

The car started easily enough. Xander turned on the radio as he drove into the gathering dusk. He had plenty of time.

The drive-in's management had billed tonight's grand opening as a special sunset to sunrise show, but working on-site had taught him the truth behind the advertising lie. Sure, the projectors would come to life as soon as the sky got dark enough to serve as an outdoor theater, but the big screen would present nothing for an hour or so.

Xander stole a look in the rearview mirror. Already his family home had disappeared in the distance. If only all his troubles could be left behind so easily.

The Levensons lived fairly close, and he found their home without incident. Jonathan was already waiting for him at the curb. Xander pulled over and gestured for his classmate to get in.

"Hey," Jonathan said. He looked some fractional degree more at ease than Xander had ever seen him before. He was dressed more casually, too, in jeans and a jersey, with a light Windbreaker in case the night got cool. He carried a medium-size paper bag, spotted with oil, which he set between them as he buckled up.

"Sack?" Xander asked.

"Popcorn," Jonathan said.

"Sweet!" Xander said, surprised by the considerate gesture. He kept one hand on the wheel but used the other to scoop unearthed fluffy white kernels into his mouth. He chewed and swallowed, then continued. "Salty, I mean."

"Maybe we should stop somewhere and get sodas," Jonathan said.

"Nah, drinks are on the house," Xander said. He reached into the backseat and hoisted a small cooler, then set it down again. "Just like admission."

Some minutes and miles passed as they drove to the theater before Jonathan broke the silence.

"Y'know," he said, "at first I was surprised when you invited me to this."

"Mmmm?" Xander said. His mouth was full again.

"Uh-huh," Jonathan replied. He hadn't taken any of the popcorn but was staring raptly out the window. It was as if he thought the world's secret lay somewhere in the night beyond. "No one invites me anywhere, Xander. I figured the girls all turned you down."

"That's not true," Xander said, but he felt a pang of something like guilt nonetheless.

"S'okay," the shorter boy said. "And, the way I see it, there's one good thing about going to the movies with another guy."

"Oh?" Xander asked, suddenly vaguely nervous.

"Uh-huh. It's better than going by yourself."

A dozen thoughts flitted through Xander's mind, images

and sound bites summoned up from the depths of his memory. He thought of Cordelia's admonition against taking another girl to the movies, and he thought of how breezily Buffy had declined his overtures so many times during the preceding months. He remembered the smirk of dismissal he'd gotten from the Goth girl with the pretty eyes, and how readily he'd accepted it. For some reason he even recalled the plaintive way that Willow looked at him sometimes when she thought he couldn't see her.

"It's a melancholy truth you speak, my friend," he finally said. The words made him feel worldly-wise. "A melancholy truth, indeed."

TDQYDJP's gig was only through Thursday. Taking the stage tonight was another band, much worse and much louder. Their music sounded very much like the wailing of damned souls, and Cordelia could only understand every third word.

"What the frick is 'German Dungeon Rock'?" Harmony asked. Her barbed words cut through the fog of background noise that filled the Bronze between sets.

She wasn't looking for any real answer to her question, Cordelia knew. Queries like that were one of the many ways Harmony had of complaining.

"I don't know," Cordelia told her for what felt like the hundredth time. She wasn't enjoying herself. Harmony was well into petulant mode, and that was never fun. Most nights the other girl made an appropriately supportive audience, but not tonight. Part of the problem was that Aura hadn't shown, and Harmony was usually at her best in a group setting. Experienced one on one, as a central attraction rather than as part of an ensemble, she grated.

"I mean, it doesn't have a good beat," the blonde continued, as if she hadn't heard Cordelia. Maybe she hadn't; the background chatter was pretty loud, and the Bronze's DJ had picked some particularly obnoxious tunes for between-sets play.

No plain vanilla rock tonight, Cordelia realized as sounds like a cat being killed blared from the sound system.

Harmony was on a roll. "I mean, I don't think you can dance to this stuff," she said. She leaned forward and sipped from her glass's bent straw, then scowled. "Empty," she said, sounding like a very little girl having a very bad day. "This whole evening is a bust."

Cordelia continued to pay her as little attention as possible. Instead, trying not to be too obvious about it, she alternated between scoping out tonight's crowd and sneaking peeks at the Bronze's entrance. Tonight's crop of clubgoers was sparse; worse, most either repelled or bored her. Too many were known quantities, fixtures on the Sunnydale social scene, and the rest were unsavory types drawn by the evening's attraction.

That could change, though. Cordelia hoped it would. There was always a chance that someone new and interesting would arrive. She'd even be happy to see Buffy and the gang, provided that Xander played things cool. That wasn't going to happen, though, since Buffy was likely on patrol and Xander was sure to be at his stupid drive-in.

She wondered if he was having fun. She hoped so, as long as it wasn't *too much* fun.

"I just wish Aura would show," Harmony prattled on. "She hasn't been in school for two days now." Her eyes brightened. "Hey," she asked eagerly, "d'you think she, you know, ran off with that wild one from the other night?"

"Without telling us about it?" Cordelia asked tartly. "Don't be silly. Maybe she's sick."

There was a line at the ticket booth. Xander craned his head and tried to count the number of cars and trucks between the Harrismobile and the theater entrance. He gave up at twenty, partly because his neck got tired and partly because the line was moving with relative speed.

"You need money?" Jonathan asked.

He hadn't spoken much since being picked up, and Xander knew why. They really didn't have a whole lot to talk about. The realization was a humbling one, but nothing new.

"Nope, I told you," Xander said. "We're guests. The boss-man insisted."

The car moved forward in fits and starts as the patrons ahead of them paused to pay. That changed when they finally reached the box office and the ticket seller waved them through with a nod of recognition. Xander snuck a side glance to see if Jonathan was appropriately impressed, then guided the Harrismobile forward, negotiating the gravel bed of the parking lot easily. He was on familiar territory now.

The drive-in's basic shape was a bowl—a shallow one, lopsided and irregular. At the time of its birth, more than fifty years before, construction crews took advantage of a natural depression in the hills surrounding Sunnydale. With bulldozers and steam shovels they had deepened and customized it, terracing some two thirds of its curve to provide raked parking. Dead center in the remaining curve was the brick and steel-girder shell of the great screen, support for the lightweight, reflective curtain. Those two steps had constituted the major portion of the effort; the concession stand, projection shack, and other appurtenances had been minor in comparison. Everything that original crew had done, they'd done well.

Xander told Jonathan the story as he guided the car toward the reserved parking for staff and guests. "They built to last in those days," he said. Hanging around on the construction site earlier in the week had given him new appreciation for construction work and the men who did it. "The place closed down in the 1980s, but it has held together since then."

"Why'd it close?" Jonathan asked as they passed another rank of parked cars. Dusk was giving way to night, and it was hard to see into the other vehicles, but he seemed determined to give it a try.

"Don't know for sure," Xander said. Just in time he saw an opening in the line of cars and took advantage. Someone, somewhere, tooted a horn in greeting as he did. He chose to believe that the greeting was for him and made a vague wave in return. “Home video and rising gas prices conspired to—”

“That’s not what I mean,” Jonathan said, interrupting. That wasn’t something he did very often. “I looked it up online. You know what state still has the most drive-ins in operation?” he asked.

“Um,” Xander said, “I’d hazard a guess, but I think you’re about to tell me.”

“California,” Jonathan said with a nod.

Xander nodded. That made sense. California still had a fair amount of relatively open countryside, and Californians were remarkably tenacious in their love of driving.

“So why not here?” Jonathan asked, pressing the issue.

“Don’t know,” Xander said again.

He pulled the family car into an available slot, set the brake, and killed the engine. Before them stood the great curved screen that he’d watched a team of contractors reinforce and resurface. Just now its gleaming white exterior presented the image of a local car dealership.

“Sound?” Jonathan asked.

“Oh, right,” Xander said. He turned the dashboard radio on and set it to the appropriate frequency. The car’s interior filled with the voice of his favorite local DJ, extolling the virtues of a particular make of auto.

He grinned. The show was about to begin. This was going to be good.

• • •

The kettle whistled and Giles extinguished the stove burner, making the merry sound fade. He poured healthy measures of the boiling water into his teapot and teacup and returned the kettle to the stove top. Silently he counted to ten. Satisfied that the pot had warmed properly, he drained it, then put the loaded filter basket in place. He poured water again, through the tea leaves, and smiled as steam scented the small, tidy kitchen of his home with the rich, almost medicinal aroma of his preferred blend. Almost as an afterthought he emptied the china cup, also properly warmed now, and placed it on the service tray beside the pot. The entire ritual was oddly comforting, a reminder of his home, so far away.

He took the tray to his desk. As the tea continued to steep, he made a quick check of the effort's current status.

He'd only just begun, really. Three books lay open on the desktop with specific passages indicated by careful application of those insipid little yellow slips that the Americans had come up with. The books were secondary works, rare and desirable by some criteria but pedestrian by Watcher standards. The books' authors were not true adepts but disciples, dilettantes, and dabblers, with the good fortune to study more elevated tomes, if not to own them. They'd studied such works as the *Crimson Chronicles* and the *Pnakotic Manuscripts*, and then attempted to record the knowledge and processes in words of their own. A surprisingly high percentage had perished horribly under suspicious circumstances, but their derivative books had uses. They weren't essential to the work Giles did, but sometimes they served as what Willow might have termed "backups."

The excursuses were a different kettle of fish entirely. They were derivative too but were the products of superior minds, specialists in specific aspects of the occult. The four excursuses stacked at his left elbow were fragile and rare, so Giles stored them in Mylar sleeves that Xander had obtained for him at a local comic book shop.

Giles slid the first from its transparent envelope. Hand calligraphy, the letters and words elaborately intertwined, nearly filled every page. The document was made of some kind of thin leathery substance, and Giles knew from personal experience that it could not be photocopied. Any attempt to do so, with any machine, merely resulted in blank, wasted paper.

His tea was ready. Giles poured a cup, added a bit of sugar, and sipped. Perfect. He would have preferred a bit of brandy, but the night's work demanded his full attention and a clear mind.

Two of the excursuses were specific to the missing books. One was a treatise on ectoplasm; the other, a discussion of transmigration, the transfer of living souls between vessels. *The Book of Dorahm-Gorath* addressed many more topics, of course, but he had to work with what he had on hand. The idea was to cross-reference the excursuses with the secondary works and arrive at an approximation of the source document. He'd not be able to reconstruct all of the contents, but he had to start somewhere. It was a process akin to triangulation.

Giles read and made precise notes on the sheets of a yellow legal pad. He sipped his tea as he worked. The clock ticked as the hours slid by and the remaining tea turned cold.

He had just correlated an excursus reference with a passage in his well-worn copy of *Secrets of Alchemie and How to Profit Thereby* when someone knocked on his door.

"Odd," he said softly, after a glance at the clock. The hour was late and he hadn't been anticipating company. Perhaps it was Buffy dropping by while out on patrol?

Distracted, he started to gather books and work sheets into an orderly stack. Giles trusted himself to sip tea in an orderly manner, but he remembered all too well how casual the Slayer had been with her lunch shake.

Knuckles rapped on the door again.

"A moment, just a moment!" Giles called. Slightly irritated, he opened the door. "I do hope you realize the hour. It . . ."

His words trailed off as he saw his visitor. He blinked and laughed, a chuckle that sounded nervous even in his own ears. "Oh, my word. It can't possibly be Halloween yet," he said.

And then he said nothing else at all.

CHAPTER SEVEN

Sunnydale's warehouse district was quiet after sunset. Streetlights were few and far between, and the worn, weathered buildings loomed darkly against the night sky. Even the pale glow of the moon served only to accentuate the shadows.

Buffy liked to come here at least once a week, to look for signs of trouble or habitation. The nooks and crannies of the big old commercial buildings made good hiding places for vampire nests. Other times they served as way stations for the various occult artifacts that kept making their way into the city, and way stations for the people who traded in those artifacts.

She moved with easy grace though the night, not calling

attention to herself but not trying to hide, either. Her feet gritted audibly on the cracked and dirty pavement, and she didn't shirk the yellowish radiance of the one-per-block streetlights. One of many reasons that she'd made such a success of herself as the Slayer was that she looked like a victim: young and slight, with girlish features and bouncing blond hair. In an imagined vampire restaurant, "Today's Special" would have looked very much like her. Buffy's only real concession to the night's work was her weapons cache, hanging by cross-strap from one shoulder, like a paperboy's bag.

After the incident with the wolf-man, she wanted to keep her hands free.

Without trying to be too obvious about it, she eyed the surrounding darkness. Darkened doorways and darker alleys made good hunting stations for vampires, and right now, a plain ol' garden variety vamp would have been a relief. Though she'd never admit it, the past two nights had unnerved her, just a teensy-tiny bit. First there was the ambush by the surreal wolf-man, who fell so far outside of even Giles's knowledge and expertise. Then there was the persistent electric tension, the never-relieved sense that something terrible was going to happen. After two restless nights the easily recognized menace of fangs and bloodlust would be almost welcome. Sometimes familiar was good.

She managed a smile at the thought. Who would have believed that something like killing vampires could ever become routine? But that was precisely what had happened over the course of long months since she'd accepted, however reluctantly, the life of the Slayer.

For now, nothing seemed amiss. No vampires, no wolf-men, no demons—no nothing, really, except for the electric buzz of aging streetlights and that odd burnt smell that old buildings get. Even the sense of lurking menace that had gnawed at her for two nights now abated slightly.

Either that or she'd gotten used to it. Sooner or later, anything that persisted long enough became routine. Her own life had taught her that.

She paused for a moment, bathed in a streetlight's pale glow, and mulled over the possibility. It seemed unlikely, but still . . .

That was when she heard the roar of engines approaching.

On the huge screen's curved expanse was the gigantic image of a half-dozen men on chromed motorcycles, huge against a field of black asphalt and blue sky. They were big men, burly and strong, clad in ripped blue jeans and leather jackets or vests. Most let their hair and beards fly wildly in the wind, and only a few wore any kind of headgear at all. Those few looked very wrong: Rather than safety equipment with tinted visors, they wore German-style army helmets with broad, low rims. One had a spike on top. Guitar music blared, strident and emphatic.

"I thought the cheerleader thing came first," Jonathan said, but he didn't take his eyes from the screen. The image was bright enough that hints of color flickered across his face.

"Cheerleader last," Xander said. He spoke as if explaining the natural order of the universe to a novice. "Kung fu first."

"The marquee says—"

"Kung fu first," Xander said again. "Take the word of one who knows. Anyhow, this is just a coming attraction."

As if in response, a deep and booming voice thundered from the parked car's sound system, louder even than the guitars. *"They were the dark knights of the road and their horses were the two-wheeled, road-ripping, fuel-injected, rampaging machines they called 'hogs'! The highway was their hunting ground, and decent people were their prey!"*

Management had programmed the grand opening not just as a festival of vintage films but as a re-creation of the "authentic drive-in experience." Before and between movies there'd be coming attractions for action flicks of the past, chosen to appeal to modern audiences. Xander had spent an entire afternoon in the projection shack as it underwent renovation, chatting up the man who was running the films now. He'd taken a peek at the projection schedule, and thus had known for days what he could expect to see tonight.

The reality was different, though, and the difference was increasingly apparent as Xander munched and sipped his way through the preview for *Hellions on the Highway*. Images that seemed small and remote at home, even on the largest monitor, had new impact when blown up to fill the drive-in's screen.

They became so much larger than life, in more ways than one. Not only did they loom above their audience, but they took on a luminous quality as well. Xander had witnessed some remarkable things in his life, but when the preview zoomed so close that the lead biker's glaring eyes nearly filled the screen, even he was impressed.

"Yow," he said softly, then ate more popcorn.

"They're the kings of the road, and you'd better pray their *road doesn't lead to* your *town!"* the announcer warned.

The din started faintly in the distance, barely even a murmur at first. But the murmur became a rumble and the rumble became a roar, and then the roar gave way to a rolling thunder. It sounded like a thousand bombs being detonated all at once, and then, impossibly, detonated again and again and again. The thunder grew louder, becoming more intense.

It was the roar of motorcycle engines, and they were coming closer.

Buffy turned just in time to see the first headlight glare at her from the night's darkness. Almost instantly the single beacon was joined by five more like it, moving together in a formation that spanned the street and sidewalks alike. Looking past them, she could barely see chrome shining in the shadows beyond. The headlights' size and placement, the grumbling roar of high-power engines, and the hints of glinting chrome all added up to one thing.

A motorcycle gang was bearing down on her, moving

hard and fast. She didn't waste time wondering who or how or why.

With urgency but not fear Buffy looked from side to side, assessing the immediate terrain's strategic possibilities. A fire-escape ladder offered a potential avenue of retreat, but she'd need to turn her back on her pursuers. A narrow alley promised escape too, but it was thick with unexplored shadow. A loading dock to her left offered shelter and high ground and a wall for her back. It also offered the potential for being cornered, but right now it seemed like her best bet. She sprinted toward it.

The Slayer moved fast, but the leftmost motorcycle moved faster. With an engine snarl like the cry of a great cat, it raced into Buffy's path, obstructing her goal. The rider was a show-off, pulling his bike back and up into a wheelie as it rushed past her. Buffy caught a glimpse of torn jeans and a leather vest covering bare, hairy arms, thick with muscle. She saw a low-brimmed helmet and glaring eyes, and a lashing, whirling something that shone like silver even in the poor lighting.

It was a chain.

Buffy ducked back, nearly in time but not quite. The leading link of the lashing chain smashed into her shoulder. It hurt like a bullet, and she gave a gasp of pain.

The first biker roared past her, his job done. He'd delayed her just long enough for his fellow bikers to join him. With practiced ease, the five followers formed a circle with Buffy at its center. Even as she realized what they were doing, the first bike retraced its path and joined them. The now six bikes roared in a chrome-steel orbit, a whirling wall that blocked off any possible path of escape.

They'd surrounded her.

Buffy let her legs bend slightly and dropped into a half crouch, presenting a smaller target. She groped in her weapons bag and drew out her crossbow, with bolt already in place. Without looking, she cocked the weapon and set its release, then reached again into the store of weapons. Working by touch alone, she found her battle-axe. It was the only other instrument that might be suitable for distance work. With an axe in her left hand and a crossbow in her right, she looked warily from side to side, poised for battle. When the attack came, it would come quickly.

"Yee-haw!"

"Whoop-whoop-whoop!"

"Little lady want a ride?"

The shouts and mocking calls were loud enough to be heard over the bike engines, at least when they were this close. The six gaps between the six bikes narrowed, and the circle became smaller. In perfect coordination, they were closing in on her, like a sprung trap, or a closing noose.

When had this become her life?

At the barest edge of her vision, Buffy saw a liquid silver flash, the sheen of chrome steel rippling like water under the streetlight's glare. Another chain. With animal instinct she jumped straight up. Pavement chips flew as the chain struck where her feet had been. At the peak of her trajectory, in the perfect instant before gravity pulled her earthward again, Buffy took easy aim and squeezed the crossbow's release. The bolt flew.

One of Buffy's tormentors yelped in pain as the arrow stabbed him. Buffy's feet and the injured rider's bike struck pavement simultaneously. Sparks flew as the motorcycle, engine still roaring, spun on its side across the pavement.

"First blood!" one of her attackers yelled.

"Yeeeee-haaawwww!"

"Time to party!"

"Gonna getcha! Gonna getcha good!"

The circle of death grew tighter. Her crossbow was empty now, its bolt flown. She cast it aside. Even as she did, a third chain lashed at her, then a fourth. Buffy dodged them both, with an awkward twisting leap. If she fell, or if she drifted too far from the center of their circle, she'd be in serious trouble.

Yet another whiplash arc of steel whistled at her. But this attack arrived at chest height, offering an opening.

The axe's handle was a shaft of cured and seasoned wood that was a bit longer than her forearm, banded with reinforcing steel. She gripped it with both hands just beneath the axe's bladed head. She was running on automatic, executing moves that Giles had drilled into her during long hours of combat practice.

The axe came up, not to strike but to block. Buffy's two-handed grip tightened as she held it before her, precisely perpendicular to the whipping chain's trajectory and as far from her body as she could manage. Instinctively, she braced herself for impact.

It came like a thunderbolt. It raced through her arms and body, almost enough to tear the weapon from her hands.

Almost, but not quite.

She'd timed it just right. Night air whistled as the chain wound itself tightly around the axe handle, like fishing line on a reel. Buffy gritted her teeth and dropped back, yanking hard. The chain came with it, and the biker roared curses as she tore the lash from his grip and made it her own.

Buffy now held one end of the chain, spinning it rapidly above her head. She grinned. Numbers were still on her attackers' side, but her reach was as long as theirs now, and her strength was far greater.

"Somebody wanted to party?" Buffy shouted.

She braced herself and cast the chain in a sweeping, serpentine strike. As much by luck as by aim, it hit a biker and wrapped itself around one beefy arm. The man yelped in pain and lost control of his bike. More sparks flew as the second bike toppled and slid across the pavement, taking the biker with it.

Most of him, at least. Either Buffy's whiplash strike had been stronger than she realized, or her assailant's structure was physically weaker. His arm remained trapped in the chain's coils, torn free from his body. The grisly image lingered just long enough to register before the arm vanished into nothingness.

If she'd had any doubts that these guys were like the man-wolf of a few nights before, those doubts were gone now. The kid gloves could come off; they weren't human, probably not even alive.

"Okay!" Buffy shouted defiantly. "No more Ms. Nice Slayer!"

The remainder of the pack pulled back. She grinned, pleased with herself. She had them on the run. She spun the chain again.

That was when it happened. One second the captured chain was secure in her grip, reassuringly solid as its centrifugal force tried to pull it away from her. The next second, without warning, the seemingly solid metal evaporated to liquid, and then was gone.

Turning to her empty hand, she blinked. The bikers were like the wolf-man, but so were their weapons. *Could things get any worse?*

As if on cue, a figure dropped from the night sky.

A woman's voice, deep and throaty, purred from the car speakers. She had an accent that promised vague exoticism without suggesting a specific nation or language. Whoever she was, wherever she was from, she seemed very pleased to have found an audience.

"The Swedes have a word for it," she said. *"But doesn't everyone?"*

Jonathan's eyes widened a bit, and he sat more upright in his seat. He set his drink in its armrest caddy and pulled his other hand from the bag of popcorn, without taking any. His entire attention was fixed on the drive-in screen, where a very attractive blonde was winking at him and everyone else in the audience. She had cleanly drawn features and pursed lips that were as red as a fire engine. Her eyes were of the purest blue, and if her hairstyle and makeup were a bit old-fashioned, there was no doubt that they got the job done.

"Hel-lo," Xander said softly. He set his drink down too.

"Um?" Jonathan asked. Words seemed to come from somewhere deep inside him, slowly and with great reluctance. "Are we old enough to see this?" he asked.

"Why, yes, spoilsport, we are," Xander said dreamily.

"Are—are you sure?" Jonathan spoke with a mixture of relief and uncertainty.

"It's just the coming attraction," Xander told him. "The movie, now—"

The blond woman on the screen moved seductively as she made her way down a long hallway with many doors. She wore a white uniform and wheeled a cart loaded down with medical equipment. When a pudgy, balding man dressed in white approached from the opposite direction, she tickled his chin and kissed him on one cheek before whispering something in his ear. He blushed furiously, and Xander knew that no matter what language the blond woman spoke, he wanted very much to hear it.

Movie content had been the topic of more than one discussion during the previous week or so. Historically, drive-in films were known for their racy content and approach, but "racy" had meant different things over the years. According to Xander's supervisor, the new proprietor's fondness for the old-fashioned extended to a certain conservativeness in programming. This preview was as much of the movie as they were ever likely to see, at least at this venue.

"From a land of cold nights and hot passion comes a prescription for health and happiness," the announcer cooed. *"Really, it's* The Best Medicine."

As she spoke, the movie's title appeared on the screen in bold pink letters, then faded. Replacing them was another close-up of the pretty blond nurse, her lips pursed in an alluring smile.

As the screen faded to black, the announcer's voice sounded again. *"Report for treatment to this theater,"* she said. *"Ask for Nurse Inga."*

Xander sat bolt upright, not an easy thing to do in a car seat. "Inga?" he said sharply.

"Inga," Jonathan agreed. "That's what she said. Why?"

Xander didn't answer. Telling Jonathan about the phantom nurse on the Sunnydale High campus would have meant telling him entirely too much. Anyway, the matching names had to be a coincidence.

Didn't they?

• • •

Night air whistled in Angel's ears as he leaped from the warehouse rooftop.

As he fell, he changed. His perpetually youthful features shifted into something bestial and cruel. His brow dropped and his jaw thrust forward. His eyes receded into their sockets slightly and burned with animal fire, while picture-perfect teeth became ragged fangs. By the time he smacked into his target motorcyclist, he was in full-on vampire mode.

"Angel!" Buffy said.

He didn't answer. Instead, even as the big high-horsepower bike bucked and slewed, he wrenched the German-style helmet from the biker's head and threw it away.

"Hey! Wha—?" the biker yelled. "What's your problem, man?"

Hands that were inhumanly strong clamped on to either side of the rider's head. Angel gripped and wrenched. The biker roared in pain. He took both hands from the handlebars and tried to break the vampire's grip, but without success. The motorcycle broke ranks and went into a skid.

Angel expected to hear bones break, but instead he felt something tear. The biker gave a final yelp and then fell silent as his head came up and away from his shoulders, slightly more easily than Angel would have expected. He had only the briefest moment to consider the surprising development before the disconnected cranium evaporated, leaving nothing but empty space between his hands.

Then the rest of the biker melted away.

As did his motorcycle.

Angel found himself several feet above the ground, trying to ride a motorcycle that was no longer there. He dropped, bounced, and rolled. Returning to his feet, he threw himself back into the fray.

In some ways, the world moved in slow motion for a vampire. Angel's inhuman speed and fast reflexes made it easy to dart between two of the four motorcycles that remained, still circling his beloved. In seconds he was where he belonged, at Buffy's side.

"That was a surprise," the Slayer said. She'd reverted to a defensive stance, battle-axe in one hand and curved *boka* in the other.

"Pleasant one, I hope," he said.

"More the merrier," she responded.

She offered the machete-like blade to him, and he accepted it gratefully. The weapon's hilt felt good in his hand, reassuringly solid. Right now the sensation of substantiality was precisely what Angel wanted.

The four remaining bikes continued to circle. They too looked substantial—solid masses of muscle, bone, and metal. It was difficult to believe that mere physical force could turn them so swiftly from something that *was* into something that *wasn't*.

Angel's travels had exposed him to many religions and philosophies. A lesson from one drifted up from his subconscious. It was a Zen koan, a puzzle or question that was intended to teach and enlighten.

Where does a fist go when the hand opens?

Wherever it was, the vanished biker had gone there too. Angel had seen many things in his long years, but this specific phenomenon was something new.

He could worry about that later, though. It was time to finish the job.

Guitar chords blasted, fast, fat, and fuzzy. They echoed as the camera tracked down from the orange sun that filled the screen, sliding down along a yellow sky to seemingly endless sands that were the color of pale rust. Just watching it all made Xander feel hot and sweaty. It didn't make sense to start the car and run the air conditioner, so he retrieved a second soda out of the ice-filled cooler instead. It was the cheap stuff, supermarket-brand carbonated fruit punch, but it went down good.

On-screen, the desert sands seemed to stretch on forever. Where they met the yellow sky, something was increasingly visible. It was a man riding a horse.

"This is going to be good," Xander said. When he got no response, he glanced at Jonathan. The younger boy's eyelids were half-closed. "Hey!" Xander said sharply.

Jonathan sat up, startled. "Huh? What?"

"It's kind of early to doze off," Xander said. He would never admit it, but he had prepared for the evening by taking a nap after school.

"No, no," Jonathan said. "Just resting my eyes."

Xander had his doubts, but he allowed another abrupt guitar riff to command his attention back to the screen. Just in time, too: A jump cut eliminated the distance, and a man's face nearly filled the screen. Presumably, this was the distant rider shown a moment before.

He looked as though he'd been built out of beef jerky, as though the desert sun had sucked every molecule of moisture out of his body and turned his skin to leather, corrugated and rough. He had a Stetson hat pulled low over eyes that were little more than slits but that still burned with a fire all their own. A hand as leathery as the face raised a cheroot cigar to barely parted lips. The traveler took a puff and exhaled, and the swirls of smoke condensed into yet another movie title.

Reach for the Sky—and Die!

"They hardly make westerns anymore," Xander said helpfully. He drank more fruit soda. If he kept this up, he realized, he'd need to try out another part of the renovated open-air theater.

"Gee, I wonder why," Jonathan said. He'd opened a cooling beverage as well, but his choice was caffeinated cola.

"This one's Italian," Xander said, still trying to be helpful.

The guitar chords continued. The rider's face gave way to a rapid-fire sequence of images, some of them surprisingly violent. Having dismounted his horse, the man strode along the central street of a flyspeck western town. Storefronts, saloons, and plank sidewalks lined either side. He carried a sawed-off shotgun in one hand and a six-shooter in the other, and a bullwhip coiled around one serape-clad shoulder. In a series of tightly edited shots, he put all three weapons to extensive use.

The shotgun blasted twice, taking out the saloon's plate glass window. When townsfolk made their opposition known, booming shots from the six-gun silenced them . . . permanently. The bullwhip snaked out to impossible length, snared a rooftop sniper, and pulled him to the street. Interspersed between the frenetic scenes were glimpses of quieter moments, ones in which the characters exchange challenges, quips, and double entendres. When he spoke, the leathery-looking man's voice was as dry and raspy as stones sliding across one another. And because the film was dubbed from the original Italian, his lips never quite matched his words.

Reach for the Sky—and Die! the screen read again, and Xander grinned. Less than an hour into the festival, and he felt he'd already gotten an admission price's worth of entertainment—and he hadn't even had to pay.

Buffy and the others didn't know what they were missing.

Six against one had become four against two, now that Angel had joined the fray and stood at Buffy's back. The odds weren't great, she thought, but they were improving. Aside from inexplicably vanishing when their heads were torn off, their attackers hadn't manifested any other paranormal attributes to speak of. The biker-gang members seemed to be pretty close to baseline human—rambunctious and antisocial human, but human all the same, at least in terms of strength and durability.

Not to mention smarts, she realized as one of the bikes broke formation. Its rider had forfeited the advantage to try to strike at her with a length of chain doubled up like a club. The move was a mistake on the rider's part, and Buffy was more than willing to show him why.

"Watch this," Buffy said over her shoulder. There were moments when she liked showing off; besides, it was her turn. Angel had taken the last one.

The rider's spiraling track brought him close, then closer still. The chain lashed out as the biker swung his weapon in her direction. Buffy swung too, slashing the battle-axe in a short, perfectly timed arc. The steel head's razor-sharp edge intersected with the biker's arm just above the bend of his elbow. It passed through the arm as easily as it would have through flesh and bone. Forearm and chain spun away into the night.

The biker screamed a bad word. With his remaining hand, he twisted his handlebars hard and gunned the bike directly at her. The bike reared up. The rider screamed something at her, barely audible over the engine's roar but clearly very, very impolite. His eyes gleamed in the streetlight's yellow glow, and the chrome of his motorized steed flashed. Every muscle in Buffy's body tensed. Her mind was moving so quickly that the world around her seemed to have shifted into low gear.

She had to time things perfectly. Drop again into the barest beginnings of a crouch. Grip the battle-axe and get ready to swing. When the biker's close enough—too close to change course—spring to one side and chop at him again. The moves were simple stuff, things she'd practiced with Giles countless times, but the moment had to be just right.

The moment never came. As the motorcycle's front wheel raised and the big bike poised like a snake to strike, it began to fade. Adrenaline still pushed her senses into high-speed overdrive and slowed the world around her. For the first time Buffy saw what happened next not as an event but as a process. The outlines of both bike and biker wavered and softened. Their colors faded and what had been solid and real became misty and translucent, like a fading photographic image.

"Buffy, look out!" Angel shouted, from what seemed like a world away.

The bike's front wheel came down. The biker was trying to pin her between knobby tire and dirty pavement. She still had time to dodge, but she already knew that the need to do so was gone.

The biker's mouth was open, but no sound came out. He was fog now, and then less than fog. Looking up, she found that she could look *through* him and see the waxing moon beyond. Then he was gone completely.

"Wow," she said softly. "Wicked cool!"

The remaining bikers peeled off and beat a hasty retreat. As the last went, Angel hurled the blade she'd given him, aiming squarely at the last rider's leather-jacketed back. By the time it should have struck, the target had vanished.

"In the back?" she asked Angel, one eyebrow raised, as her world shifted back into normal gear. This wasn't the first time she'd experienced the time-dilation effect.

Her vampire paramour shrugged. The battle had come to an end, and as if to commemorate that fact, his features reverted to human-normal. As they softened and shifted, he said, "Seemed like a good idea at the time. I knew he wasn't human."

"I'm wondering if he was even alive," Buffy said.

"Ghost?"

It was Buffy's turn to shrug. "Dunno," she said. "Giles has a bug up his nose about spook stuff, though." With a few quick sentences she summarized the library briefing. By the time she finished, her breath and pulse were normal again.

They spent the next several minutes looking for evidence, but there was none. The only signs that the bikers had ever been there were secondary: tracks in the street's oil and dirt, and scrapes where the first, toppled bike had slid along the asphalt. There was no tire rubber, no metal trace or paint transfer, not even the scent of exhaust fumes. Once again it was as if their attackers had never existed.

"Busy night," Angel observed. He'd gone to retrieve the *boka* and was loping back to her now.

"Yeah," Buffy said. She almost smiled as she remembered her own complaints about the previous night, the long hours of wary tension and waiting for action. Someday, she thought, she'd need to count her blessings. "It was either that or go to the movies," she said.

"Movies?" Angel asked.

"Xander's thing," she reminded him.

He nodded as he fell into step with her, clearly intending to accompany her on the rest of her patrol. "I went out there," he said. "Did some looking around. If that place is a festering hellhole of occult evil, I can't see it."

But to Buffy's practiced ears he sounded like he had his doubts.

CHAPTER EIGHT

"*I'll always be a cheerleader in my heart,*" said the girl on the movie screen. She had long dark hair that fell to her shoulders like a waterfall. She pulled the handsome premed student closer to her for a kiss that was long and slow. When at last they came up for air, she continued, *"Always. But I'll never be lonely again!"*

The credits began to roll. Xander blinked and rubbed his eyes. He was only half awake. Eight hours of movie watching was a *lot*, and it seemed to him that the quadruple feature had stretched on even longer than the dashboard clock said.

Four features, uncounted coming attractions, a cartoon, and miscellaneous concession stand spots had filled their night at the drive-in. Xander had spent longer periods watching television at home, of course, but that was at home, sprawled on a well-worn couch with a remote control within easy reach. The marathon drive-in experience was something altogether different, even with the preparatory nap.

Xander's eyelids drooped and his muscles were sore. An insect or two had bitten him. Half a sack of popcorn and nearly a gallon of supermarket soda pop had left his mouth feeling mighty funky. He rubbed his eyes some more, then stretched and yawned, making each breath a deep one. Gradually full consciousness returned. With a tight grin he turned the key and started the engine

"Wow, what a great night!" he said softly.

He meant it too. Xander had enjoyed every minute, and even with the morning-after consequences, he logged the night solidly in the plus column. The film festival had been a nightlong peek into a world he'd missed by being born too late. The broadly drawn characters, the cartoonlike action, and the goofy plots struck a nerve with him. The drive-in was like a comic book come to life, just not a very good one. Asian men executing flying kicks, elderly aristocrats with chainsaws that roared, inmates rising up to free themselves—all of those were very neat things, indeed.

Sometimes the not-very-good comics were the best ones.

The car engine coughed once or twice, then came to life. Through the windshield the drive-in screen read GOOD NIGHT, FOLKS. DRIVE CAREFULLY! And beyond the screen, the dark bowl of the night sky displayed the barest streaks of pink. The morning sun approached. It was time to go home.

"What did you think, Jonathan?" he asked.

The only answer was a soft snore from the seat beside him. Levenson had conked out sometime during the closing credits for *Mysteries of Chainsaw Mansion*, the second movie. Xander had prodded him awake, only to lose him again during *Caged Blondes*. The poor little guy didn't get to see a single minute of *The Lonely Cheerleader*.

"So much for companionship," he said, backing the car out of its parking slot. He was one of the late-stayers; at least three-quarters of the massed cars had left an hour or more before. Even so, the Harrismobile wasn't the last car to roll slowly along the gravel-lined exit route. To his amusement, at least a dozen parked cars remained, their interiors dark and their occupants vague in the premorning gloom.

"Some people don't know when they've had enough of a good thing," Xander muttered, accelerating slightly. Gravel sprayed up from the roadbed and rattled against the car's undercarriage. "Hear that?" he asked in a louder voice. "That's the sound of horsepower, my friend!"

Jonathan snored some more.

Xander took his eyes from the road long enough to glance at his passenger. Jonathan was out like a light. He was slumped against the car door with head lolled back and mouth hanging open.

That wouldn't do, Xander decided. He reached across the

space between them and poked the other boy's shoulder, gently at first and then with more vigor. "Wake up, little Susie," he said.

No response.

"JONATHAN! WAKE UP!" Xander said again. This time he'd shouted loud enough in the closed confines to make even his own ears hurt.

"Grnk?" Jonathan said, startled. "Huh? Wha—?" He looked around himself, first at Xander and then at the predawn world as it rolled by outside. "We're going?" he asked.

"Uh-huh," Xander said. Some idiot had come to the event in an extralong SUV, and half the oversize vehicle extended from the parking slot, blocking Xander's path. He edged around it and tooted his horn in irritation. There was no response that he could see or hear.

What the heck were these people thinking? The show was over and it was time to go home.

"Cheerleader?" Jonathan asked.

"Very lonely," Xander said. "A masterpiece of the motion-picture art form."

It was only half true. Xander's own flirtation with drowsiness had come sometime during the fourth and final film—naturally, the one he'd wanted to see most, if only so that he could needle Cordelia about it. Even so, something about the flick had gnawed at him. Half awake, half asleep, he'd had a moment of insight about the events of the film. Now an insight about the movie bubbled somewhere just below the threshold of his conscious mind. It was like the answer to a question on a history pop quiz, the stray bit of knowledge that you knew wouldn't be available for use until long after you wanted it. The more he tried to dredge the thought up, the more it evaded him.

"Oh," Jonathan said. He sighed, but the sigh morphed into another snore.

He was still snoring when Xander pulled up in front of the Levenson house. This time Xander couldn't wake him. The best he could do was coax Jonathan halfway to awareness. With Xander guiding him, the kid moved like a sleepwalker as he opened his front door and tottered inside.

"Thanks for coming, J," Xander said.

"Grphl" was all he heard Jonathan say before the door slammed shut.

"Xander! Oh, my heavens, Xander!" Hands grabbed his shoulders and shook him. "Xander, wake up! Please wake up!"

"Huh? Wha—?" Xander said, his voice fuzzy from sleep. He struggled a bit, but something wrapped itself around him. Adrenaline rushed through him. Was he under some kind of attack?

"Wake up, please!" It was a woman's voice. It was probably a woman's hand that slapped his right cheek, barely enough to sting but hard enough to make a loud popping noise.

"He's probably drunk!" A man's voice, more distant but louder, boomed in his ears. "Out all night! I warned him!"

Xander's eyes opened. His hand came up, just in time to intercept a second slap. He blinked at the worried-looking woman leaning over his bed.

"Mom?" he said. He disentangled himself from the sheets and scooted back in his bed, partly to sit and partly in case another slap was coming. Slapping was a wake-up trick that played better in the movies than it did in real life.

"Oh, thank heavens," Mrs. Harris said. "I was so frightened!"

"Mom, what's wrong?" he asked.

"You were asleep and you wouldn't wake up—"

He was bleary-eyed but could see enough to read his clock radio's display. It was only nine a.m., he realized with a shock. "Mom," he said. "We talked about this! I was out all night! Of *course* I was sleeping late!"

"I know, I know," she said. "But I was so worried."

"Tell the boy I warned him!" his father boomed from somewhere down the hall. "He's lucky I don't come in there and tell him how lucky he is!"

His mother was near tears, and even his dad seemed pretty worked up about something. Suddenly, he had a bad feeling about the situation. "Mom, I'm fine," he said. "What's wrong? What's happened?"

"It's Jonathan Levenson," she said.

"Jonathan?" Xander asked. The bad feeling became a

really bad feeling. "I dropped him off on the way home."

"I know," Mrs. Harris said. "His parents called. They found him on the living room floor."

Saturday breakfast was eggs. Joyce had whipped up what she called a "sort of omelet," incorporating bits of ham and cheese with bits of leftover veggies from previous meals. As so often happened with such improvised dishes, the whole was more than the sum of its parts.

"This is delish," Buffy said, raising another forkful. She and her mother were seated in the breakfast nook, and the morning sun's rays streamed in through one of the large windows.

"Thank you, dear," Joyce said. The praise pleased, but it frustrated, too: She knew that she'd never be able to re-create the dish exactly.

"No, really," Buffy said, and favored her mother with a glance. "You've been watching PBS again, haven't you?" she asked in mock accusation. "All those cooking shows, with those French gigolos!"

Joyce shook her head. She ate some of her own serving and realized what Buffy meant. There was something vaguely exotic about the mélange of egg and oddment. For such a humble meal, it tasted surprisingly sophisticated. "Just some spices," she said, at a loss for any more detailed explanation.

Several textbooks sat in a tidy stack next to Buffy's elbow. Their presence at dinner would have been unacceptable, but in the morning, on a weekend day, they were welcome indicators of rare studiousness on Buffy's part. Joyce knew her daughter was a bright girl, and gifted in so many ways, but Buffy really hadn't seemed to have found her path in life just yet.

"What are your plans for today, dear?" Joyce asked.

"Study," Buffy said.

That certainly sounded like a fine idea to Joyce. "That's good," she said, offering up a bit of positive reinforcement before moving on to more challenging ground.

Buffy nodded. Her plate was almost clean, but one last slice of toast remained on the serving dish between them. She made a questioning glance in Joyce's direction and, after noting a nod of permission, took the piece of bread.

"Xander, Willow, and I are getting together," she said. "Maybe Cordelia."

The enthusiasm in Buffy's voice dropped a bit with the last words, but Joyce chose not to notice. When Buffy had first begun classes at Sunnydale High, she'd never wanted to talk much about her schoolmates. Cordelia Chase had been one of the exceptions, and the subject of regular grousing on Buffy's part. That seemed to be changing. Joyce didn't know how and she didn't know why, but to judge from some of Buffy's recent comments, there seemed to be the barest chance that the two girls were becoming friends, at least of a sort. As far as Joyce could tell, that pretty much had to be for the good; the Chases seemed to be a good family, and her daughter could always use a friend.

"You and Cordelia seem to be getting along well lately," Joyce said lightly.

"Things change," Buffy said, not quite as lightly. "But think of it as an armed truce. Or that détente thing."

"You're growing up," Joyce said hopefully.

"That's one way to look at things," Buffy said. Her expressive eyes took on a faraway look and she smiled, very faintly, as if at a joke that only she knew. A joke, or a kind of truth.

Buffy was hiding something, Joyce knew. Her own teenage years weren't so long gone that she couldn't remember the way things worked. Secrets were part and parcel of life, never more so than in the adolescent years. Whatever the secret, she could only hope that it wasn't too serious.

She soldiered on. "Maybe you could have Cordelia over for dinner sometime . . . ," Joyce started to say.

"Oh, yeah, like *that's* going to happen," Buffy replied with an air of absolute dismissal.

It was time to change the subject. Joyce took a breath, trying not to be obvious about it. "You were out late last night, weren't you?" Joyce asked. She made the question a gentle one.

Bite, chew, swallow, speak, then bite again: Buffy had it down to a precise system. Unfortunately for Joyce, her question had come at the beginning of the sequence, so she had to wait for an answer. That gave her daughter a chance to think things through before responding, Joyce knew, but there was nothing to be done for it.

Buffy swallowed. For good measure she lifted her glass and swallowed again, orange juice this time. At last she said, "Yeah, later than I'd planned. It wasn't a school night, and—"

"It's all right, Buffy," Joyce said. "I noticed, that's all." She liked to think that she noticed more than her daughter realized.

"Uh-huh," Buffy said.

"With Xander and the others?"

"Xander was at the movies," Buffy said. She finished her toast and drained the orange juice.

It was a nonanswer, but Joyce decided to let it pass. "What are you going to study, then?" she asked.

"What aren't I going to study?" Buffy asked, ungrammatically. She ticked items off on her fingertips one at a time. "History," she said. "Biology. Philosophy. And I promised Willow that I'd pretend to understand what she talks about."

"So you'll be at the Rosenbergs'?"

"Probably," Buffy said. She nodded but looked away, and Joyce knew that she was lying. No, not lying; more likely, she was shading the truth. That was part of being a teenager too, and the signs were obvious to a parent, if one knew how to look, and Joyce did. "For a while, at least. I'm supposed to drop by Giles's, too. He promised to loan me some research materials, from his personal collection."

"You're spending a lot of time with him, too," Joyce said. The function that the school librarian held in her daughter's life still loomed as a bit of a mystery. Well educated, soft spoken, and quite refined, he seemed every inch the proper gentleman. He was old enough to be Buffy's father. Despite that, he seemed to have settled into a role that was as much friend as mentor.

"Giles is okay," Buffy said. Coming from her, that was high praise for any adult. "For a stuffy ol' Brit, I mean."

"That's not nice," Joyce said. "He's doing you a favor."

"I meant it in a nice way," Buffy said mildly. There was no more food to be had, so she dropped her used utensils onto her empty plate and began to clear the table. "And, believe me, Giles just loves doing stuff like this. He's got books coming out of his ears, and he loves to show them off." She paused. "That sounds grosser than I meant."

"Call him before you go, then," Joyce said.

Buffy's response came in phases. First there was the clatter of plates and flatware being stowed in the dishwasher, followed by the *glug-glug-glug* of detergent being poured. Then, as the much-appreciated appliance hummed to life, Buffy picked up the kitchen phone and dialed.

Without meaning to pry, Joyce watched the transaction. She watched as Buffy looked first patient, then irritated, and, finally, worried. The expressions flowed one into another, like a plant blooming in time-lapse photography.

"That's funny," Buffy said, returning the receiver to its cradle. She didn't sound like she thought it was funny at all, though. "There's no answer."

•••

Gravel rattled against glass, a familiar sound. Willow set aside her computer mouse and went to the window. This really wasn't the time of day for such subterfuge. There was no reason why any visitor simply couldn't come to the front door and ring the doorbell like civilized folk, especially when her room was on the ground floor. She opened the window and said as much.

"I'm sorry," Xander called from the lawn. His words were apologetic but his tone was slightly irritable, and it was easy to see why. He looked very tired, with shadows under his eyes. "Old habits die hard."

They'd known each other most of their lives. That wasn't a terribly long span of time in absolute terms, but from Willow's viewpoint it was forever. She could remember sneak-watching Christmas specials on television with Xander, an interest that her parents didn't entirely approve of or even understand. She had a bit of a crush—more than a bit, really—on Xander, and had watched with increasing anxiety as he threw himself at one girl after another, never taking time out for her. Buffy was among the most recent targets of his unrequited affection, which had lent an interesting texture to their friendship of late.

"You could have called," she said, mildly chiding. Xander was a welcome guest at the Rosenberg home, but a girl liked to have a little warning.

"No, Will," Xander said sourly. He was sweating a bit in the late-morning sun, and Willow thought it made him look sexy. "No, I couldn't."

"Why not?" she asked.

"Because I'd need a phone to do that, and mine is dead right now," Xander said testily. His handsome features formed a half scowl. "And the MNN is on the air."

"M-N-N?" She pronounced each of the letters as if it were a word complete unto itself.

"Mommy News Network," Xander said. "Look, can I come in or not?"

Willow nodded and went to let him in. A moment later he dropped onto the edge of her bed as she seated herself once more at her computer.

Up close he looked worse, she decided. No, worse wasn't it, because you had to look bad before you could look worse, and Xander never looked bad to her. But sitting mere feet away from her, signs of fatigue were more clearly drawn. His eyes were bloodshot and his shoulders slumped as he gazed at her. He looked as if he'd aged a few years since the day before.

"How were the movies?" Willow asked.

Rather than answer, Xander asked a question of his own. "Did you hear the news?" he asked. "About Jonathan?"

"Jonathan?" Willow asked. She looked blank. That wasn't someone she thought about very often.

"He's asleep," Xander said. He gave her a quick rundown of the night before, of picking up Jonathan before the movies and dropping him off after. He got that awkward and abashed sound in his voice when he talked about the cheerleader movie and seemed honestly embarrassed to have fallen asleep during it.

"The next thing I knew, Mom was trying to shake me awake," Xander said. "Not that it took much effort. I'd only been out a couple hours."

"She could wake you," Willow said slowly.

Xander nodded.

"But Jonathan was dead to the world," she continued, and immediately regretted her choice of words. Just because she wasn't close to Jonathan didn't mean that she'd ever want anything bad to happen to him. She'd spent plenty of time on the fringes of school society, too much time not to have some sympathy for her low-key classmate.

"Yeah," Xander said. "My mom's ballistic. She's been on the phone all morning, and every time I try to catch some winks, she flips out." He made an expression that looked like a smile but wasn't, not really. "She's been on the phone all day and watching TV, and it's making her crazy. Threw a glass of water at me once," he said. "Dad really got a hoot out of that one. So I cut out."

"Oh," Willow said.

"Just in time, too. She was making noises about having me talk with the police, or public health people," Xander continued. "I don't think that's who needs to be told."

Willow thought again about the search she had run for Buffy into the background and history of the newly reopened drive-in. Was there anything in all those pages of reports that she'd missed? A chill of self-doubt swept through her.

Had she even asked the right questions?

Xander seemed to read her mind. He could do that sometimes. "I don't think it's the movie place, Will," he said. "Or, at least, not *just* the movie place. Mom talked to Aura's folks—"

"Your mother knows Aura's family?" Willow asked, startled. It was hard to think of those two bloodlines interacting, even on a social basis.

"I told you, she's calling *everyone*," Xander said. "But Aura wasn't at the opening."

"I haven't seen her in class lately," Willow said. She rummaged through her memory, looking for the few exchanges she'd had with Cordelia in the previous few days. "Cordy says she's been out of school since Thursday."

"That's because she's been in the hospital since Thursday morning," Xander said. "According to an exclusive report from MNN."

"Sleepy?" Willow asked. A small teddy bear rested on her desktop, next to the computer. Without conscious thought she picked up the stuffed animal and started to toy with it nervously.

"Very sleepy," Xander said.

"Maybe we should talk to Cordelia about this," Willow said.

"I'll tell you who we should really talk to," Xander said.

"Buffy?"

He nodded again. "And Giles. Cordy may know a lot about

penguins, but she's not the brains of the operation," he said. "Any chance I could use your phone?"

"Sure," Willow said. "It's just a matter of deciding who to call first."

She reached for the phone, but it rang before her fingers even made contact. Startled, Willow picked it up before the first ring completed. A brief exchange later, she passed the phone to Xander, who looked at her blankly.

"Buffy," she said. "She's looking for you."

He looked a lot happier when he took the phone and began talking.

CHAPTER NINE

Buffy had been to Giles's home many times before. When she knocked on his front door this time, its arched wood sounded precisely as it always had. Even the polished brass of the doorknob, warmed by the midday sun, was reassuringly familiar as she coiled her fingers around it.

Even so, something *felt* different.

She turned to the others lingering behind her. "No answer," she said. "Just like the phone."

That in itself was an ominous sign. Ten calls to Giles's number had produced responses numbering precisely zero. It was Saturday, and there was no reason to expect him to be at home, but Buffy was getting a bad feeling.

"Car's still here," Xander said. He took up position beside the little, low-powered vehicle. Cars as an institution engaged his attention, even when the example at hand failed to impress. He was a teenage boy, after all. He leaned to peer through one closed car window, shading his view with cupped hands. "Nothing here," he said.

"Here, either," Cordelia said, but she seemed to base her findings on only the most cursory inspection of the courtyard. It was Willow who was still taking the lay of the land, peering behind bushes and eyeing the cut grass.

"Stay out here, guys," Buffy said.

"Buff, you shouldn't go in there alone," Xander said. Cordelia and Willow nodded in agreement, but neither girl moved to join Buffy when he did.

"Down, boy," she said, waving him back again. "I need reinforcements on the outside." This time he obeyed and rejoined the others as Buffy knocked on the door one last time. "Hello?" she called loudly. "Giles, if you won't come out, I'm coming in."

Still no answer.

She repeated the command. "Stay out here, all of you. I'll let you know when the coast is clear." She continued more softly as she gripped the knob more tightly, "*If* the coast is clear."

She thought she'd need to break the lock. For someone with Buffy's strength, that kind of thing wasn't particularly difficult. This time, however, it wasn't even necessary. The knob turned easily, another ominous sign. It wasn't like Giles to leave the entrance to his home unsecured. Buffy pushed the door open.

"Hello?" she called. "Giles, it's me. Hello? Hello?"

With one final glance to make sure that the others didn't follow, she stepped into the shadowed interior of her Watcher's domicile. A minute or two later she re-emerged and gestured everyone inside.

"C'mon, guys," she said. "See if *you* can figure this out."

"Wow," Willow said less than a minute later, followed by echoes from Xander and Cordelia.

"You see my point?" Buffy said, and closed the front door behind them.

There was nothing wrong with the home, at least nothing that the naked eye could see. The windows were closed and unbroken, and the doors were similarly intact. The furniture had been recently dusted, and the books and magazines laid out on the low coffee table were in neat stacks. The place could have been a film set, or a model home, albeit one lavishly furnished with reading materials.

But Giles himself was nowhere to be found. She'd checked the other rooms. Worse, there was an odd feeling to the air, a faint reminder of the electricity she'd experienced while on patrol the previous nights.

Buffy felt vaguely as if she'd entered a haunted house.

Only one thing seemed overtly amiss: the desk's working surface. Next to open books, age-yellowed documents, and a legal pad, a tea service perched. It had been abandoned while still on the job, and that had clearly been a while ago. The water in the pot was room temperature, and the leaves in the basket filter were soggy and swollen from steeping far too long. Beside the pot sat a teacup on the same tray. The level of dark tea in it had dropped, leaving a ring to mark its original level, and Buffy could tell from the mark that much of the liquid loss had been to evaporation. The cup had been left unattended for some hours.

Giles had been sitting here, Buffy realized. He'd prepared himself a pot of tea to accompany his review of the books and excursuses.

Before he could finish, it had happened.

Whatever "it" was.

"Very *Marie Celeste*," Willow said. She inspected the tea service daintily and then lifted one of the open books. Her nose wrinkled as she leafed though it.

"Marie who?" Buffy asked her.

"Not a who, a what," Cordelia said, her back to the rest of them. She was busily inspecting a decorative wall hanging that clearly did not meet the elevated Chase family standards. "Crew disappeared, with meals waiting for them on the tables. It's a mystery that's never been solved."

The others stared at her for a silent moment. Xander broke it with a two-word question. "Book report?" he asked.

Cordelia shook her head. "Don't be silly. I saw a movie. That's what this is like, though."

"She's right," Willow said, sounding vaguely distracted. She had begun to read, and the words had drawn her in, but not so deeply that she couldn't kibitz. "It's one of the classic maritime mysteries, and it dates back to the 1870s. Very old school, and it's never been solved."

"This isn't good," Buffy said. "This isn't good at all."

Now Willow looked up from the book. "No," she said. She looked worried. "It isn't."

"What is it, Willow?" Buffy asked. "What did you find?"

"Just—just a story," the other girl said slowly. She tilted the worn book so that the others could see its title.

The worn gilt letters read *Secrets of Alchemie and How to Profit Thereby*, followed by a subtitle in smaller type too worn to be deciphered.

"You and Giles and your ancient secret texts," Cordelia said, then fell silent as Buffy shot her a glance.

Willow shook her head. "This isn't old," she said. "Not really. Only about a hundred years' vintage—"

"Sounds pretty old to me," Xander said from the kitchen. "Buff, there's tea fixin's laid out in here—you should take a look."

"Later, Xander," Buffy said but filed the information away in her head. It comported with what she'd already determined, that someone or something had taken Giles by surprise. "What's special about the book?" she asked Willow.

"Nothing, really," Willow said. "That's what's weird." When the others stared at her, she took a deep breath before continuing. "I mean, Giles has quite the library, you know. He's got books bound in demon-hide and printed on skin, and he's got books that I swear are older than people, even though I know that makes no sense at—"

"Willow," Buffy said. "Focus."

The red-haired girl nodded. She sat in the desk chair and set the book down, still open, as she continued. "This is nothing special," she said. "It's not very old, and—"

"A hundred years," Xander said again. He'd emerged from the kitchen and was standing in the doorway.

"Not very old by Giles's standards," Willow said, continuing on. "And this is a popular work." She paused. "Not best-seller popular, but aimed at a general audience."

"A *Reader's Digest* condensed occult text?" Buffy asked, feeling faintly boggled. What was next? A paperback edition of *The Crimson Chronicles*?

Willow nodded again. "Kinda," she said, turning pages. "More like an overview with pretty pictures. You could sell this down at the Magic Box and not worry about anyone losing his soul in the process. I'm surprised Giles even has something like this."

"He said he wanted to figure out what was in the missing books," Buffy said slowly. Her forehead wrinkled as she thought. "He wanted to extradite—"

"Extrapolate, probably," Willow said. She gave a faint smile. When Willow made corrections, she was far gentler about it than Cordelia.

"Extrapolate," Buffy said, more sharply than she'd intended. No matter who was doing it, she didn't like being corrected.

"Uh-huh," Willow said. She started to read. "Give me a minute. I've done enough research with Giles that I know his methods. Maybe I can figure out what he was working on." She paused again. "Specifically, I mean."

Buffy gave her the moment. To pass the time, she accepted Xander's invitation to inspect the kitchen. He'd been right. The work area was what she termed a tidy mess: kettle still half full, whistle top set aside. The tea-leaf tin was tightly closed but remained on the counter, rather than in the cupboard where she knew it belonged. An insulated pot holder lay beside it, along with the spring-loaded tongs that she'd seen Giles use to fill the teapot's basket filter.

Looking at the array made her feel worse. For some reason the tableau acted as a focus for the worry and presentiment she felt. She'd known Giles only a year or so, but that year had been filled with challenge and adventure. Though she'd have a hard time admitting it to anyone, he'd become more than a friend and a mentor. No one could ever fill the gap left by her absent father, but Giles's presence made the void somewhat less consuming.

And now someone or something had taken him from her.

"He was here," she said very softly. "He must have been working on the missing book thing." She tapped the work surface with one finger. "And they got him."

"Got him?" Xander said, still at her side. "I mean, are you

sure he didn't just pop off to the market or something?" But his question had the hopeful quality of someone grasping at straws.

Buffy shook her head. In her world there were no "rational explanations," no pat assemblies of fact and circumstance that could explain a situation like this. Even worst-case scenarios were almost never bad enough.

"And leave the door unlocked?" Buffy asked. Taking things in context, that seemed even more conclusive than the abandoned tea service. Giles spent countless hours impressing upon her the need for personal security. She couldn't imagine him not locking his own front door.

"No signs of a struggle," Xander said. He looked very worried now, more worried than she would have expected.

Perversely, though, she found some hope in his words. Xander had a keen grasp of the obvious, and sometimes obvious was good. There was, indeed, no sign of a struggle: no broken furniture, no spilled tea, no sign of damage to doors or windows. Best of all, no blood trace lingered. Wherever Giles had gone, he'd gone there uninjured.

That could change, of course, but for now, she clung to the hope.

"He boiled water and he brewed tea," she said slowly, thinking things through. She walked back into the living area and stood behind the desk, nodding at Willow before she continued. "He likes tea in the evenings. Says it helps him think clearly. He was working on the missing book thing."

Willow was buried in her review now, looking from open book to legal pad and back again. She offered not even a nod of acknowledgment in response.

"Uh-huh. And then someone knocked on the door," Buffy said. It was the only conclusion that made sense. Giles had gone to receive a visitor, only the visitor had received him instead. "Let's take another look outside."

Cordelia rolled her eyes slightly but accompanied Buffy and Xander outside. After the ominously empty interior of Giles's home, the afternoon sun felt good, and the air seemed fresh and clean. Even so, the open door and empty windows were haunting reminders that Giles had gone missing. Buffy tried to think of other things as she and the others took another, closer look for some indication of the night's events.

Xander hung close to Buffy after they'd exited. Even when Buffy told Cordelia that she was going to do a quick perimeter search, Xander fell in beside her, ignoring her suggestion that he inspect the driveway area a second time. Although the Slayer was accustomed to her friend's attentiveness, she was equally accustomed to being obeyed. His hovering struck her as being out of the norm.

"Xander," she said. "He's going to be all right."

"Huh?" Xander asked. The concern on his features was even more evident in the daylight.

"Giles," Buffy said. She forced herself to sound confident as they rounded the corner of the building. A small utility shed bordered on the courtyard, and she gave it a quick inspection. "He's pretty tough, really, and he knows how to fight. We didn't find any blood, so—"

"I'm not worried about Giles," Xander said.

"Why not?" Buffy asked sharply. The shed was securely locked. Xander's dismissal of Giles's situation irritated her.

"Not like that," he said, raising his hands as if to ward off an attack. "I like G just fine, you know that. But like you said, he's a pro. We'll find him and he'll be okay. Really. I'm sure."

"Then spill," Buffy said, still reconnoitering. The shrubbery that framed one window was intact and undisturbed.

"It's Jonathan," Xander said. "He went to the movies with me last night and he fell asleep."

"Well, c'mon, Xander," Buffy said. Genuine irritation cut through the generalized worry she felt. Her friend's priorities seemed a trifle misplaced. "They were just old movies."

"That's not what I mean, Buffy," Xander said. "I mean, he's *still* asleep—"

"Xander, you were out all night," Buffy interrupted. "I mean, you look beat even now, and—"

"No," he said forcefully. "His parents found him on the living room floor, sound asleep, and *they can't wake him up*."

Buffy paused in midstride. She looked at her friend. "Okay," she said. "I said it before and I'll say it again. Spill."

Xander spilled. In sentences that were surprisingly precise and succinct, he recounted for Buffy the previous night's adventures. He told her about borrowing his parents' car and picking up Jonathan. He offered summaries of the four movies they'd more-or-less watched and, remarkably, the summaries were short enough not to be annoying. He told her about the ride home and dropping Jonathan off at the Levenson house and going home himself.

"The next thing I know, Mom's flipping out," he said. "I scrammed. That's why I was with Willow when you called."

One thing that Buffy always liked about Xander was his overall good cheer, something that seemed intrinsic to his personality. Seeing him the way he was now, worried, fretful, and deeply, deeply concerned, was always jarring. She realized with a pang that she'd half-hoped he could provide her with reassurance, only to find the shoe on the other foot.

He wanted her to make things better, and Buffy knew that right now she couldn't.

"Xander," she said. "I'm sure everything's fine. He was out all night, he got sleepy—"

"Buffy, he's in the *hospital*," Xander said. "The doctors can't wake him up either. They're not calling it a coma, but there's something wrong with him, seriously wrong."

"It—it's not your fault," was all she could think to say. "You said that Aura was sick too, and—"

"I don't *care* about Aura," Xander interrupted again. He paused. "No, I don't mean that. It's just, Jonathan was with me—"

"Hey! There you are!" said Cordelia, sounding sharp and demanding as she came around a corner. Rather than continue, however, she eyed Buffy and Xander with what the Slayer could have sworn was suspicion.

Buffy sighed. Giles's absence was a more pressing issue than Jonathan Levenson's excessive drowsiness; Xander was just going to have to accept that. Besides, work was the best medicine sometimes. Once Xander got busy, he'd feel better.

"What is it *now*?" she asked.

Cordelia led them to her find. In a grassy patch, she knelt and pointed. "Look," she said.

Scarring the soft earth were a series of half-moon divots. Each was about the size of a large man's hand, and each dug deeply enough to tear grass aside and reveal the soil beneath. When she probed one cut with her index finger, Buffy could see that the gouge was mid-knuckle deep.

Buffy looked at her blankly. She couldn't find it in herself to be entirely pleased that Cordelia had made the discovery—any discovery.

"They're hoofprints," Cordelia said, as if it were the most obvious thing in the world.

"Oh," Buffy said, nonplussed. To her, hooves and hoofprints meant one thing. "You mean, like, hairy goat-legged demon hooves?"

"Don't be ridiculous," Cordelia said. She was looking closely at the prints, estimating the distance between them, busily demonstrating more expertise that was nearly as unwelcome as it was surprising. "These are *way* too big for a goat. These were made by a horse, a big one." She moved over to the walkway and pointed. "Here," she said. "Look."

More half-moon marks showed on the flagstones. They were bright scars on the gray stone, faint but undeniable. They were the marks that a horse's steel shoes would make on stone. Buffy eyed them. Clearly, Cordelia was right again.

Xander asked the question she wanted answered. "Cordy," he said, "what's with all the data points lately? You taking smart-girl pills or something?"

The taller girl shot him a withering glance. What Cordelia regarded as the famous Chase charm was in full bloom now. Most would have mistaken it for arrogance and hauteur, and Buffy wasn't at all sure they wouldn't have been right. Reluctantly, however, she decided that Cordelia had the right to be proud of herself.

For today, anyway.

"Don't be silly," snapped the Queen of Sunnydale High. "I told you before, I'm not stupid."

With that particular genius inherent in the human male, Xander dug the hole deeper. "But the *Marie Celeste* thing," he said. "And now this horse business—"

"Xander, hello!" Cordelia said, thoroughly peeved by the implied slight. The midday sun made her chestnut hair even more lustrous. "I'm not just not stupid. My family's rich, remember?"

"Uh, yeah," Xander said. "And your point is . . . ?"

"And what is it that rich families do at exclusive resorts?" Cordelia asked. "Some families, at some resorts, that is. Hint: We wear jodhpurs."

"Um," Xander said slowly. "Horseback riding?"

She nodded. Despite the unnerving situation, Buffy and Xander flashed brief smiles. There was something very satisfying about seeing Cordelia so thoroughly in her element.

"Okay," Buffy said. She massaged her temples, hoping to stimulate thought. "Someone got Giles and spirited him away on horseback. Maybe a cowboy."

"A . . . cowboy?" Xander said very slowly.

"Hey!" Willow called to them from the doorway. "I think I've found something!"

"—mysterious disorder that has claimed more than thirty local victims," the newscaster said. She was a youngish woman, no older than her early thirties, Asian, and with a good voice. She had skin the color of old ivory and her dark hair was short and neatly styled so that it looked like a tight black helmet. Joyce Summers had seen her work before, and knew that she was good at her job.

The newscaster continued, *"Earlier this hour we talked with a hospital spokesperson who offered a tentative theory on why some of our young people just won't wake up. Now, in response to those comments, I'd like welcome to our program a newcomer to our city, the proprietor of the newly reopened Sunnydale Drive-In."*

The camera pulled back into a two-shot, revealing the ballyhooed guest seated across the round table that was pretty much a standard fixture on local-market news and commentary programs. Even viewed through the camera's unblinking eye, the man had an immediacy and magnetism about him that Joyce found fascinating. He wore an Armani suit, and his iron-colored hair and beard were impeccably styled. His smile appeared to be directed at her and her alone. Joyce liked him instantly.

"Welcome to KRAD News at Noon, Mr. Belasimo," the newscaster said.

The guest winced very faintly at the sound of his name, and Joyce was certain that the newscaster had mispronounced it, but he didn't correct her. Instead, in a voice as warm and smooth as melted butter, he said, *"Thank you, Ms. Hasbro. I'm very happy to be here in this lovely city, and in the presence of such a charming hostess."*

Hasbro's professional demeanor broke, and she giggled. She waved one hand in dismissal and smiled again. *"The pleasure is all mine, I assure you, sir,"* she said. *"And please, it's Enola."* She became more businesslike as she addressed the camera. *"Mr. Belasimo is a newcomer to our community. The Sunnydale Drive-In ran its first programming in more than twenty years last night."*

"That's correct, Enola," Balsamo said genially. *"Although I feel constrained to point out that the movies we're running are at least that old themselves. For our inaugural exhibition, we chose to present a festival of vintage drive-in fare."*

Joyce, still watching, was suddenly all too aware that she was alone in the house and alone on the big sofa that offered the best view of the Summers family television. She spent a lot of time alone these days. She felt sudden envy for Hasbro, who had so much of her life ahead of her and whose work put her in close proximity to newsworthy movers and shakers. She knew that the emotion was absurd, but it was undeniable, too. She'd been alone so often lately, since Buffy's father had left, and Buffy's life had become so busy. Now, on such a beautiful day, she sat by herself and watched television.

Why was that? It wasn't the kind of question that Joyce allowed herself to ask very often.

Hasbro continued, *"We spoke in the last hour with Dr. Orloff, who's treating many of the victims of this sleeping sickness—"*

"So-called sleeping sickness," Balsamo said with an indulgent chuckle. It was an interruption, but the trim and attractive newscaster didn't seem to mind. *"I've been following the coverage, as you might imagine."*

"So-called sleeping sickness, then," Hasbro conceded with a smile. *"Dr. Orloff mentioned the fact that the majority of the thirty individuals currently being treated had attended the grand reopening last night of the Sunnydale Drive-In. He speculated that some form of food poisoning might be at work."*

Balsamo looked annoyed. Joyce sympathized. He was a businessman, after all, and had every right to be concerned about protecting his investment. *"I don't believe that Dr. Orloff's comments were appropriate,"* he said. *"At the very least, they were ill-considered. Representatives of my organization have been in contact with the hospital administration about this. Believe me, before reopening, the theater concession stand was thoroughly inspected. We comply fully with all health code standards."*

Joyce believed him. She believed him as thoroughly as she believed that the sun rose in the east and set in the west. Something about this gentleman commanded utter confidence in the words he spoke. Joyce hoped that Hasbro would just shut up and let the man speak.

Hasbro didn't. She persevered, with words that challenged, even if her tone of voice did not. *"But surely, Mr. Belasimo, the fact that twenty-seven of thirty victims have been verified as having attended—"*

"Precisely, Ms. Hasbro," Balsamo said. The use of her surname made the newscaster wince. *"At least three of the victims of this so-called illness have no connection whatsoever with my theater."* He smiled, and Joyce's world became a warmer, more welcoming place. *"Really, Enola, do I appear to be someone who would continue operations if there was the slightest chance that the innocent could come to harm?"*

Hasbro smiled ruefully, clearly impressed by the line of reasoning. *"No,"* she said. *"No, of course not."*

"Excellent," Balsamo said. His smile widened, and sparks seemed to dance in his eyes. *"In fact, I'd like to issue a special invitation. For tonight, and tonight only, the Sunnydale Drive-In will waive its quite reasonable admission charge."* The camera zoomed closer, until Balsamo's face nearly filled the screen. *"So, if any of your viewers are fans of classic drive-in fare, or if they simply enjoy a corking good yarn, I*

invite them to attend tonight. It's my treat. I think I can promise you an experience like no other."

The phone rang as Hasbro commenced her closing comments. Joyce let it ring a few times, waiting to answer it until she was sure that Balsamo would have nothing more to say. By the seventh ring Hasbro and her guest alike had been supplanted by an irritated-looking man in a white lab coat. A caption identified him as Dr. Orloff, presumably making some sort of rebuttal. She ignored him and lifted the receiver at last.

It was Barney.

"Oh, hello," Joyce said, once the bank official had identified himself. "No, no, I'm not busy at all." She paused and listened. "Are you sure that's a good idea?" she asked. Then, after another pause, she smiled. "No, Barney, I'm not busy tonight either," she said. "I think that's a nice idea. We could have fun."

"Do you all remember when Giles asked about ectoplasm?" Willow asked. Seated at the Watcher's desk, open books and notes at her fingertips, she waited for an answer. With Giles among the missing, Willow was pretty much the next best thing they had to a Watcher, since she'd assisted him so many times in his research. Now she was thoroughly in her element as the substitute fount of all knowledge. Dire as the situation might be, it was clear that she enjoyed the role fate had thrust upon her.

Cordelia, seated on the couch with the others, paid reasonable attention. She knew all too well that Willow was smarter than she was, or at least more knowledgeable. Recognizing that superiority was a tough pill to swallow; Cordelia consoled herself with the fact that the little brainiac's expertise ran to useless stuff like computer programming and ancient history. She didn't know a thing about basic fashion principles or what style might have made her stubby little legs look longer. No, the kinds of things that Willow knew were useful in high school and monster hunting, and Cordy fully intended to leave both behind after graduating.

"Cordy?" Willow asked. "We're waiting."

Cordelia checked to see if she'd raised her hand, by some dumb conditioned reflex. She hadn't, and said as much.

"Aw c'mon, Cordy, play along," Xander said on her left.

Without being invited, he had plopped himself on the center cushion of the couch, between Cordy and Buffy. No doubt Xander thought he'd nabbed the catbird seat, but all he'd really done was make it easy for Cordelia to give him a quick elbow in the ribs. She did so, and he gasped.

"I'd like this to be a demilitarized zone," he said weakly.

"I'll demilitarize you," she muttered from the corner of her mouth. More loudly, she continued, "It's what ghosts are made out of."

"Very good," Willow said with a smile and a nod. "You deserve a gold star, young lady! If I had any to give, that is."

"Willow," Buffy said. The edge in her voice made the name a warning.

"Um, yes," Willow said. "Well, ectoplasm is more than

that, really. It's uh, um, the underlying psycho-etheric constitutional substance of an individual's soul, spirit, or *atman*." She spoke the string of words in a singsong voice that suggested they were memorized, and recently memorized, at that. As if to confirm, she glanced at a sheet of Giles's notes. "Gold star for me, too," she said softly.

"Uh-huh." The two syllables could have come from any of the couch potatoes, or all of them. They were the kind of almost meaningless syllables so often used by students to indicate acknowledgment, if not understanding.

Cordelia could feel her eyes starting to glaze over. Giles was pretty nice for a guy who'd been around almost as long as fire, and she certainly wished him well, but life went on. She wondered who was playing at the Bronze tonight.

Not Willow, though. Such trivial issues were clearly long miles from the other girl's mind as she warmed to her subject. "Now, according to his notes, that's what Giles was researching," Willow said. "Or it's what the missing books were about. Ectoplasm and its practical applications." She held up another book, presenting its cover. The words read: *Psychic Humours and Their Uses.*

"A joke book?" Xander asked, then coughed as Cordelia elbowed him again.

"It's another word for 'fluid,'" Willow said. "There's bunches of terms for this stuff. Psycho-etheric fluxes, psychomatter, ectoplasm, and more."

"None of that sounds like magick, Will," Buffy said.

Willow nodded, looking genuinely and completely pleased for the first time in a while. Her happiness at Buffy's question pushed aside her worries about Giles, at least for the moment. "Very good, Buffy!" she said. "A gold—"

Buffy executed a short, emphatic shake of her head. Between that and the serious expression the Slayer wore, her message was clear. This was no time for role-playing or banter.

"It doesn't sound like magick because it's not," Willow said. She indicated once more the books that Giles had left behind. "Most of this stuff is what you'd call proto-science."

"Proto-science?" Cordelia asked. She gave voice to the question without conscious thought. Willow's term sounded so odd that it demanded explanation.

"Yeah," Willow said. She set the book aside and raised something else. It was some sort of plastic envelope, thick and rigid but transparent, so that its contents were revealed. Those contents seemed much more typical of Giles's Watcher archives. They were sheets of something that might have been paper, but which Cordelia knew intuitively was not. It seemed to wiggle slightly in the envelope, as if alive. Whatever the stuff was, it was browned and tattered by age, and covered with diagrams and runes that Cordelia knew she never could have read, not even if her life depended on it. That kind of stuff was Greek to her, and was likely Greek to the Greeks, too. Of course, if it was Greek to Greeks that would mean . . .

Cordelia tried to focus on Willow's mini-lecture.

"*This* is magick," Willow said. She tapped her finger on

the envelope, making a popping noise, then set it down. She gestured at the books. "These are proto-sciences. Alchemy, spiritualism, mesmerism, phrenology—well, that last one's more of a pseudo-science, really."

She went on to explain in more detail. According to Willow, magick was primarily an art, one that relied heavily on an individual's aptitudes and the invocation of superhuman entities such as gods and demons. Science worked differently. Scientists gathered data and built hypotheses that could be tested by experimentation, and relied on known physical forces and circumstances. Magick was as old as or older than mankind, depending on the definition. Science and the scientific method were much younger, dating back to about the Renaissance, filtering out into the general culture in the ensuing decades and centuries.

"That's the Cliff's Notes version, at least," she said. "It's messier than that."

"Science good, magick bad," Xander said, boiling it down further.

"No," Willow said. She picked up the plastic-clad document and shook her head. "No, not at all. They're different ways of dealing with the universe, and they overlapped for a while. They still have a lot in common. Why, some assembler language commands are an awful lot like incantations, and—"

"Cut to the chase, Willow, please," Buffy said. "What does *any* of this have to do with our kidnapping cowboy?"

"Cowboy?"

"I'll tell you later," the Slayer promised. "You said you think you found something. Tell us what."

"Two somethings, really," Willow said. She pointed at Giles's legal pad, the canary yellow sheets covered with notes in the Englishman's neat handwriting. "Giles uses a lot of abbreviations here and he wrote *around* a lot of stuff instead of *about* it, but as near as I can tell, he was zeroing in on the proto-sciences. Those were early mixtures of science and magic. Stuff like alchemy. That's the old version of chemistry, all mixed up with astrology and spiritualism and other stuff. Alchemists were heavy into the eternal mysteries—how to live forever, how to turn lead to gold, that kind of thing."

"I know about alchemy," Buffy said darkly. She'd seen a lot of things in her tenure as the Slayer. "It's not good stuff."

"Maybe not . . . but it's what Giles was looking into," Willow said.

She flipped through the notepad and found a particularly busy page, dense with occult-looking symbols and diagrams. Giles had made abbreviated sketches of the twelve signs of the zodiac, with arrows leading from one to another. Some lines of text were so small that even Cordelia's vision, excellent for distance, couldn't make them out completely. There were exceptions, though. Giles had made lists of terms. At their heads, in larger lettering, were words like "Ectoplasm," "Psycho-Etherics," "Astral Projection," and "Elemental Phases."

"So we're looking for an alchemist," Xander said.

"Maybe," Willow said.

Without asking permission, Xander half-stood and claimed one of the books, then settled back into his seat. He opened the volume and flipped through its pages. "Hey," he said, pleased. "This is in English! I can read this!" He paused. "Sort of."

Cordelia craned her neck and snuck a peek. She could see what he meant. Even setting issues of language aside, many of Giles's books were physically difficult to read, with ornate lettering and time-faded inks. This one, presumably because it was a much younger work, was a different matter. Its pages were worn and marked from handling, but only slightly yellowed with age. The text that adorned them was typeset rather than hand-illuminated, but the lines of type were uneven and had ragged margins. Worse, the text was in English, but only sort of. It seemed to Cordelia that every fifth word was misspelled or improperly capitalized.

"Jeezy-peezy," she said. "Didn't they ever hear of spell-check?"

Xander shrugged. Despite the urgency of the situation, he seemed oddly preoccupied, or even bored. He flipped though the pages more quickly, pausing only to eye illustrations, of which there were many. With each turned page, the musty aroma of old paper scented the air.

"You said you found two somethings, Willow," Buffy said. Her words were less a reminder than they were a prompt to continue, and her voice held a note of command that Cordelia had heard before. Willow might think that she was running the improvised lecture session, but it was the Slayer who was boss.

"Yeah," Willow said. She lifted the plastic-clad document she'd toyed with earlier. "These are excursuses," she said.

"Curses?!" Cordelia nearly yelped the word and pulled back the hand she'd reflexively extended.

"No, *ex*cursuses," Willow said. Without waiting to be asked, she provided the definition. "Detailed discussions of topics addressed in an academic work."

"Sort of a super-footnote, Cordy," Buffy said. "Giles and I talked about them earlier."

"What do they say, then?" Cordelia asked, still not accepting the proffered item. Something about the way the thing looked made her feel all squirmy.

"Well, as near as I can tell, this one's mostly about astral projection," Willow said. "I can't be sure, though, because it's in a dead language, and all I can puzzle out are some symbols. The second one's in some kind of debased Latin, and it's some kind of treatise on ectoplasm and spiritual regeneration. I can't make any sense out of the others, but none of them looks like good news."

Cordelia didn't like the sound of that. It was another thing she'd never admit to anyone who mattered, but she didn't like it at all when Willow expressed ignorance about things pertaining to slayage. Such comments were bad signs in the best of times, and made worse now by the absence of Giles. Her earlier boredom was completely gone now, and she waited to see what came next.

"Hey!" Xander said sharply. "Hey! I know this guy!"

He'd opened the alchemy book to an illustration. It was printed on paper better than the pages that flanked it, and looked to be some kind of steel-plate engraving, like the faces on currency. It showed an aristocratic-looking man in old-fashioned breeches and jacket. He had broad features, mutton-chop whiskers, and a powdered wig, resembling someone who might have stepped off a dollar bill. Cordelia took all of that in with a glance, but took little real notice. Her attention was drawn by the man's eyes.

Whoever the anonymous artist had been, he'd known his craft. The man's eyes were deep-set and shadowed, but, paradoxically, they seemed lit by an inner intensity. Even across the gulf of years, even filtered through an artist's sensibilities and the process of book production, Cordelia found them oddly compelling. They had magnetism that drew her attention and held it.

A caption identified the image as being of one Count Alessandro di Cagliostro.

"You don't know him," Willow said. "He's been dead for two hundred years."

"Oh, like *that's* a problem," Xander said. They'd met plenty of dead people in the previous year or so. "I'm sure of it. Here, I'll show you," he said, and drew a ballpoint from his pocket to amend the illustration.

There came a yelping sound as Willow protested. Rather than let him deface the book, she rooted though Giles's desk drawers and found a piece of tracing paper. Xander shook his head but complied. Positioning the sheet, he used quick, short pen strokes to add a beard to Cagliostro.

"There," Xander said. "Mr. Balsamo. You could put that on his driver's license."

"Balsamo?" Cordelia asked. She'd never heard the name before.

"Balsamo?" Willow said. "Are you serious, Xander?"

"Boss-man at the drive-in," Xander said. He closed the book angrily and turned to Buffy. "See?" he said. "I told you I got Jonathan into this. I told you it's my fault."

"Now, hold on," Buffy started. "There's more to this than—"

"Who's Balsamo?" Cordelia asked.

"Giuseppe Balsamo," Willow said, as if that explained everything.

It didn't, of course.

"Dammit, I know what I did," Xander said. His voice was thick, and the usual joking quality in his words was missing entirely. "I did it to him, and to Aura, and to all the rest. I was part of this, somehow."

"Aura?" Cordelia asked. She liked to think of herself as quick on her feet, conversation-wise, but the questions and answers were coming entirely too fast. She was getting lost. It seemed like everyone was talking at once, and about different things.

"Aura's in the hospital, Cordy," Buffy said with a sidelong glance. "So are a lot of people. Some kind of sleeping sickness."

"Cagliostro was some kind of supermojo alchemist back in the eighteenth century," Willow said. "Depending on who you talk to, Balsamo might have been his real name."

"Aura wasn't at the drive-in, was she?" Buffy asked Xander.

"Does the drive-in sound like Aura?" Xander responded.

"STOP IT! ALL OF YOU, STOP TALKING RIGHT NOW!" Cordelia shouted, as loud as the loudest cheer in the most contested football game. Her words were like thunder in the living room's confines.

The others were stunned, but complied. They fell silent and looked at her blankly. While they waited, she took a deep breath and gathered her thoughts. Finally, she continued. "You," she said, pointing at Xander. "Tell me what happened to Aura." She paused. "And Jonathan, I guess." She pointed at Buffy. "You tell me about this sleeping sickness," she said. "Willow gets Cagliostro."

Surprisingly, all three of them nodded obediently. Perhaps less surprisingly, they all began to speak at precisely the same time. Cordelia had to do some more shouting and issue some more orders before they fell into line and filled her in on their respective areas of (relative) expertise. When they finished, she took another deep breath and sorted through the flood of information.

"Okay," she said. "Aura's in the hospital and no one thought to tell me, thank you very much. There's, like, a whole bunch of people in town who won't wake up."

Buffy and Xander nodded again. Buffy, especially, seemed

bemused by the demands for information, but that was fine with Cordelia. It was about time someone started thinking about this stuff clearly.

"Most of those thirty were at the drive-in last night," Cordelia continued, "which is being run by some Penn and Teller type who died three hundred years ago. That doesn't sound very likely, does it?"

"Alchemist," Willow said meekly. "Those guys are illusionists, and he was an alchemist. And he only died about two hundred years ago. If it's him." She explained that Count Cagliostro was actually quite a shadowy figure, historically speaking. He'd used many names, and his death had been reported more than once. Even the identification of his real name as Giuseppe Balsamo seemed not to be certain.

"Close enough," Cordelia said. "Now, what do we do next?"

"We?" Buffy asked. "I'm heading out to the drive-in, and I'm going to turn this guy inside out and mail him to Antarctica."

Xander shook his head. He looked worried, worried enough that Cordelia felt concern. Certainly, even in her experience, Xander had involved himself in some pretty outrageous situations, but he rarely involved others. She knew that Xander was a lot more compassionate than most people realized, even if he didn't show it very often.

"That won't work," he said. "There's nothing out there in daylight. I don't know where the boss—where this guy hangs out in the daytime, but it's not there."

"Maybe we could find him," Willow said slowly. "Giles made some notes about tracking spells, and there's something about crystals—"

"Magick?" Buffy asked.

Willow nodded.

Buffy shook her head. "You've been a big help already," she said. "But I don't think you're ready to actually try a spell. Let's consider other options."

"There's always more research," Willow said. She looked thoughtful. "In fact, I'd like to look into this drive-in thing a bit more."

"Angel checked the place out," Buffy said. "So did you, for that matter."

"I don't think I asked the right questions, though," Willow said slowly. "This sleeping sickness business gives me an idea."

Buffy gestured at the crowded bookcases that lined much of Giles's living room. "Go wild," she said. "I'm sure Giles won't mind.

"Actually, the idea I have, I don't think these can help me with."

"There's more upstairs, and I might be able to figure out a way to get us into the school."

"No," Willow said. "I was thinking more like the public library. They have bound newspapers there."

"Okay, then," Buffy said. She stood. "Let's go."

"Not me, Buff," Xander said. His words were surprising. "I'm not going with you. Not right now, at least."

"Why not?" Buffy asked. Her tone was sharp, but she looked puzzled. Cordelia knew why. Given his head, Xander would spend most of his waking hours as Buffy's shadow. "You've got better plans? We really need your help, Xander."

He shrugged. "Not for this part. Willow can research rings around me," he said. "I want to go to the hospital and check up on Jonathan."

CHAPTER TEN

For Giles the world came back into focus very slowly. It was a far less pleasant world than the one he'd left behind. Gone were the cradling support of his desk chair and the welcome, musty scent of old books. Instead, he felt hard ceramic, cool and slick against his skin, and his nostrils flared with the astringent scent of cleaning compounds. Bright lights shone down on him from above, and the first thing he could see as his vision cleared was a network of white grout lines, separating squares of bright color that had been buffed to a high gloss.

He was on a foreign floor. His last memories were of opening his front door to a stranger.

With some effort he struggled to his feet. Reality resolved itself a bit more, and he realized that he was in a washroom. He tottered to the sink and ran water to splash on his face. The cold wetness felt good. Above the sink was a mirror. His glasses lay on the washstand. He donned them and returned his attention to the mirror, inspecting himself for damage.

He didn't find any. That in itself was worth noting. Giles had lived an interesting life—rather more interesting than most Watchers, actually—and he'd been knocked unconscious more than a few times over the years.

There was no blood, no bruising. Now that he was awake, he realized that there was no headache, either. Even the sour taste that usually accompanied knockout gas or chemical tranquilizers was lacking. The world had gone away, and then it had come back, without injury or incident between. He felt more as if he'd been turned off, like an electrical appliance, and then turned back on again.

It wasn't a good feeling. He didn't care for the idea that someone could do something like that.

Suddenly there came a gritting mechanical sound as a key entered a lock and turned, and then a *thunk* as a bolt slid back. Giles turned just in time to see the washroom door open.

"Awake, I see," said the man who stood framed in the doorway. "Good."

He looked vaguely familiar, enough so that Giles was certain he'd seen him before. The man was of average height and build, but his stance and posture suggested that he was very physically fit. His hair and beard were both neatly trimmed and styled, both the color of old iron, dark gray verging on black. In one hand was a paper sack that bore a familiar logo, and in the other was a glittering disk of crystal. He'd left the keys dangling in the lock.

"'Good' is not the word I would use," Giles said drily. He eyed the open doorway. "Who are you, and why have you done this?"

The man nodded and raised the disk. "Please, don't make any attempt at escape," he said. "I assure you, it would be futile."

Trying not to be obvious, Giles studied the piece of crystal. From a distance it seemed perfectly transparent, its surface ground and polished to a smooth curve. A ring of brass surrounded it, plain under the man's fingertips. It was evident from how he handled it that the disk was some manner of weapon, or an object of power.

No, Giles realized suddenly, it wasn't a disk. It was a lens.

"Here you are," the man said, and handed Giles the paper sack. "A late lunch. I know what it's like to be hungry."

Giles didn't think he could eat, but when he opened the bag, the aroma of fried food rushed out and he realized that he was famished. Even so, he set the fast-food meal on the washstand without further examination.

"It's perfectly wholesome," the familiar-looking man said. "Wholesome by colonial standards, at least." He paused. "I owe you an apology, I suppose. Perhaps several."

"Well, never let it be said that I'm not a forgiving sort," Giles said. "If I can just trouble you for a ride back to my residence—"

The man shook his head. "It's not that simple, I'm afraid," he said. There was nothing of menace in his voice, and he spoke with great culture and style. Perversely, Giles found himself warming to the man. He seemed immensely likeable. "It's too late for that. But if I'd realized that this city was home to a Watcher, I might well have pursued other opportunities, or undertaken things here differently. It's too late for that, however."

He knew about Watchers, and presumably about the Slayer, as well. As such things went, the Watchers Council, its reason for being and its operations, weren't terribly secret, but neither were they common knowledge. The fact that his host knew of them said something of the man's nature, and of the circles in which he likely moved.

"Do I know you?" Giles asked. Sometimes it was best to be direct. The sense of familiarity still gnawed.

"No," the man said with a head shake. "You may know *of* me, however. We're colleagues, of a sort."

"You seem like the civilized type," Giles said. "This is terribly awkward. Could I at least have your name?"

His host laughed. Like his voice, the sound was warm and rich. "I think not," he said, still chuckling. "We both know that giving one's name is to give power over one's self."

"That's true in only a limited, technical sense," Giles said dismissively. It was curiously refreshing to speak with someone who knew of such things and was willing to treat them seriously. "On a personal level—"

"If I give you my name, you'll know who I am," the man said. He didn't laugh this time, but he smiled, revealing perfect teeth. His eyes twinkled. "That's more power than I care to give you, Mr. Giles."

"Oh," the Watcher responded. "Of course." With slight chagrin he reminded himself that this was a captor-captive situation, however politely staged, and not a discussion between learned colleagues. The man's personal magnetism was undeniable, however, and it took conscious effort to resist. "What comes next, then?"

"You'll stay here for a bit," the man said. "After that I'm not sure."

"Hostage?" Giles asked. "I warn you. Experience is that I don't make a very good one."

"Perhaps not," came the reply. "But I've always found it wise to deprive an enemy army of its general. I rather fancy that your Slayer will be less inclined to interfere, absent your guidance."

Giles managed a laugh. It echoed hollowly against the washroom's hard surfaces. One thing he knew with grim certainty was that Buffy would never hesitate to act in his absence. Whether she would act wisely or not was another question altogether. Buffy was, in so many ways, completely unlike any other Slayer who had come before her.

"I'll have to tell her you said that," Giles said. "She'll be quite amused."

That netted him another nod. "I'm going to leave you here for now," his host said. "Forgive the accommodations, but security, in this instance, is a more pressing concern than comfort. I'm sure you understand."

"Quite."

"Eat or don't eat," the man said. "It matters not to me. But attempt to escape or send for help in any manner, and I assure you, you'll be stopped. These quarters are quite secure, and I've taken other safeguards beyond walls and locks."

The door closed and the bolt slid home again. Giles made a quick inspection of the washroom and learned approximately what he had expected: The door was heavy and the walls were thick, and there was no window. The entire place was quite solid, however, clean and in excellent repair; presumably, it had been built or renovated only recently. The only way out was through the door, and going through the door meant going through the presumed guard outside as well. Without a weapon of any sort, he was at an extreme disadvantage.

For lack of anything better to do, he perched on the washstand and took inventory of the food bag. It looked beastly: deep-fried trash food of the sort that Americans devoured with such gusto. Even so, his own words to Buffy about blood sugar applied to him as well, so he selected the least of available evils. It was an ominous-looking thing that purported to be a fish sandwich. He began to eat. It was with his third bite that Giles remembered where he'd seen his captor's face before.

It had been in the pages of a book.

Sunnydale had a history; there had been settlements on its site for hundreds of years. It was an old city, by California standards, and the public library's holdings were impressive evidence of the long years that it had been in operation. The aboveground levels of the library were modern, nicely designed and brightly lit, but the lower levels were darker and more claustrophobic. That was where management stored the old books, the ones that almost no one ever asked for, but that were worth keeping for their historical or archival value. It was also where the bound periodical collection lived, thick volumes of aging paper that bowed the shelves. Each pseudo-leather spine was labeled in stenciled gilt letters, presenting title and dates, and volume and issue numbers.

Buffy and Willow were there now, the sole occupants of a reading room. After Willow's fifth request for old newspapers, the librarian on duty had given up. She had led them to the long-term storage area—usually off-limits to browsers—explained how the file system worked, and left them to their own devices.

"See?" Willow asked. Her hair was mussed and her skin shiny with perspiration, but she seemed quite pleased with herself. "There's plenty of stuff that's not online. It never will be, either, most likely. It takes time to scan this stuff in."

"And time is money, yeah, yeah, yeah," Buffy said. With

a sound like a thunderclap, she dropped another two volumes of bound newspapers onto the sturdy table. The librarian had provided them with a wheeled cart, but Buffy found it easier just to lug the huge tomes from point to point.

And huge they were, each with a page size slightly larger than a modern newspaper, each five inches thick or more, and each bound with thick boards that Buffy was sure could serve as armor in a pinch. These once had been the morgue copies of the local newspaper, and of the newspapers that had preceded it. Print started dying a long time ago, really, and as the morning and afternoon dailies ceased operations, they ceded their histories and files to the papers that succeeded them, or to the library. The bound periodical collection was a treasure trove, if you thought of stuff like this as treasure.

Buffy didn't, not really. She didn't even find the papers particularly interesting. Newsprint aged badly, becoming brittle and brown and issuing a telltale acidic miasma that made her eyes sting and her nose run. She recognized the historical value of such repositories but didn't think they held any particular charm.

Willow was different, Buffy realized yet again. The other girl had a mind like a sponge, that absorbed information greedily and connected data points in ways that Buffy could only dream of. She had a lot of data to deal with too. Willow was a voracious omnivore when it came to information. Her interests were diverse and far-ranging, and she had the kind of mind that seemed equally at home soaking up info on science or mysticism, with many stops in between. Buffy knew that she herself was bright, but she knew Willow was something more than that.

Even better, Willow was an expert researcher. She'd started with generalized requests, but in the hours since they'd been there, her search had become more focused as she found and followed leads. She had brought Giles's legal pad with her and already filled more than half its remaining pages with notes of her own.

"Isn't this *fun*?" she asked.

"Yeah, loads," Buffy said. She inspected her nails. One had broken against a shelf's support bracket. "What next?"

"*Box Office Reports by Region* for 1922, 1923, and 1924," Willow said. "If they have 'em."

"Why wouldn't they?" Buffy asked. "They've got everything else down here, don't they?"

"Yup," Willow said with an enthusiasm that bordered on outright cheerfulness. "Hollywood's been in California for a long time."

The librarian had provided them with a diagram of the lower-level stacks. Entertainment publications were on the far end of the floor, beyond the central elevator shafts and near the maintenance access tunnels. The shelving units here were particularly closely spaced, and Buffy, focused on the job at hand, hardly noticed the shadowed spaces between them.

She noticed when one of the shadows moved in her direction, though, and the blot of darkness resolved itself into something solid and real.

"Hey," Angel said. He had a book tucked under one arm.

"Hey, yourself," Buffy said, startled.

He had the most amazing way of sneaking up on a person, really, and not just in the literal sense. It was difficult sometimes for Buffy to believe that she'd known him for such a relatively short time, during which she'd seen him only intermittently. He'd become so much a part of her life that it seemed she'd always known him.

She wondered if he felt the same.

"What brings you here?" she asked. It was daylight outside, probably late afternoon. Buffy would have liked very much to be outdoors now, away from the dust and shadow, perhaps taking an afternoon stroll. But even a brief excursion into the direct rays of the sun would reduce Angel to ash.

"Tunnels," the soft-spoken vampire said. He gestured at a nearby metal door. "Plumbing and electrical are through there, and they communicate with the storm sewers. I get around."

She nodded. "Let me put that another way," she said. "Why are you here?"

"Research," he said.

"Yes, Willow," Buffy replied, with sarcasm that was mild and gentle.

"No, really," he said. He showed her his book: *Cheap Thrills: A History of Offbeat Entertainment*. The dust jacket was a lurid illustration of a gigantic dinosaur-like beast locked in combat with an oversize gorilla.

"Don't you get enough of that kind of thing in real life?" she asked. The shelves she needed were another ten units over; she gestured for him to follow as she looked for Willow's books.

"Too much, really," Angel said.

"That doesn't look like part of the bound periodical collection to me," Buffy said. She eyed the shelves. The library's collection of *Box Office Reports by Region* was incomplete. The volumes for 1922 and 1923 were where they were supposed to be, but then the sequence skipped ahead to 1926. Buffy shrugged and pulled the two target books, with the next one for good measure. Willow would let her know if she'd made the wrong decision.

"I was upstairs," Angel said. "I was just leaving when I heard your voices."

He didn't say anything as they walked together back to the reading room where Willow waited. For an absurd moment Buffy thought he might offer to carry her books, like a student after school, but the offer never came. That was just as well, maybe; she wasn't sure how she'd respond.

Buffy's status as the Slayer made such niceties effectively superfluous. She might lack a vampire's enhanced senses, but she was at least as strong as Angel. She was quite capable of bearing her own burdens, physically at least, and her personal preference for independent action predisposed her to do so.

Still, a girl liked to be asked.

"Hey, look who I found," Buffy said as she re-entered the workroom.

Willow looked up from her notes, startled, and then she grinned. "Angel!" she said. "Using the night depository?"

"Not just yet, Willow," Angel said as Buffy set the bound magazines in front of her. He looked around at the stacks of aging newspapers and magazines, and at Willow's copious notes. "What is all this?"

"Research," both girls said brightly.

"Have you heard about this sleeping sickness thing?" Buffy asked.

Angel looked at her. Very slowly, he said, "No, I haven't."

Buffy filled him in about the mysterious disorder that had struck so many of Sunnydale's youth. When she finished her summary, she added, "That's where Xander and Cordelia are now, at the hospital."

Angel nodded. "I was wondering," he said. "Buffy, this could be very serious. I've heard of things like this before. In Europe in the 1860s—"

"And in Harrisonburg, Virginia, in 1953," Willow said.

Buffy and Angel looked at her but said nothing.

Willow continued, referring to her notes, "Forty-seven students in the local college fell asleep and didn't wake up for three weeks. Ten didn't wake up at all, ever. They fell asleep and they kept sleeping."

Certain that she had their attention now, she continued. Springfield and Arlen, Pottersville and Bug Tussle, the location names were mostly obscure and picturesque, scattered across the United States and Canada. The dates she listed were similarly dispersed, following no cycle that was especially evident. One thing linked them all, though. After every paired date and location, Willow told them how many locals had fallen asleep and how many hadn't woken up.

"And something else," Willow said, concluding. "That's why I wanted the box office magazines. It looks to me like every one of these incidents happened in conjunction with a new drive-in theater, or with new management at an existing one."

"Wow," Buffy said softly. "That's quite a pattern. Why didn't anyone catch it before?"

Willow shrugged. "It's hard to see, really," she said. "They happened so far apart, and over such a long time—"

"What about here?" Buffy demanded. "What about the 'something bad' that happened years ago, that everyone keeps talking about?"

"Don't think so. There's no report of anything like this happening here, ever," Willow said. "At least, not before today." She paused. "That's where we made our mistake. Sunnydale and the drive-in weren't part of the pattern; at least, they weren't until now."

"So no prior 'something bad'?" Buffy asked. "Something Angel missed?"

He shot her a reproachful look.

"He didn't miss anything," Willow said. "Drive-ins are

where this stuff happens. They're the context, not the cause."

"Oh." Buffy loved Willow, but there were times when she hated how her friend talked.

"That explains it, then," Angel said. "Here."

He set his book on the table, opening it for their benefit. He pointed at a grainy photograph. "Look familiar?" he asked Buffy.

The image was eerily familiar. It was a werewolf, or a sort of werewolf. It was an unsettling fusion of man and beast, basically a human build but with animal-like head and claws. It wore a lettered varsity jacket.

"Anubis?" Willow said softly. That was the Egyptian god of the dead she'd mentioned days before, in the school library.

"No," Buffy said slowly. "But there sure is a resemblance. This is the critter Angel and I saw the other night." She looked to her vampire paramour. "You said you'd never seen anything like that before," she continued, half-accusing.

"I didn't remember," Angel said.

She looked at him doubtfully. Vampires were notorious for having good memories. They could carry grudges for hundreds of years.

He explained, "I must have caught a glimpse of a movie still, or an advertisement a long time ago. Not enough to register consciously, but enough to make some kind of impression. I had to work to dredge it up."

"Wow," she said again softly, with renewed respect. To remember an experience or an enemy across the long years was impressive enough. That he could recall something barely glimpsed reminded her just how different a kind of guy she had.

"It says here that *Varsity Werewolf* was a 1958 Skull Features release," Willow said. "You guys ran into a refugee from a drive-in movie." She turned some pages, then squealed in surprise. "Hey! Look!"

The book had a signature of color pages bound into its middle. One image was a sad-looking girl clad in pink and white. A caption identified her as the star of *The Lonely Cheerleader.*

"Uh-oh," Buffy said.

Willow kept turning pages. Familiar-sounding titles leaped out at them from the book, scattered through it like chocolate chips in a cookie: *Double Drunken Dragon Kung Fu Fight*, *Mysteries of Chainsaw Mansion*, *Caged Blondes*. They were the component elements of the handbill Xander had distributed so eagerly.

Willow kept skimming the pages. She paused as another still caught her eye. It was from something called *The Best Medicine*, and featured a strikingly attractive blond woman in a nurse's uniform. "Hello, Inga," she said, looking at the nurse who had ransacked Giles's holdings.

"How is this possible?" Buffy demanded, once she and Willow had explained to Angel the reason for their surprise.

"I don't know," he said, taking the book back. "Look." He pointed at yet another captured image. It was of six burly gents riding motorcycles that were bigger than some cars. "Look familiar?" he asked.

She nodded. She knew what he meant. Together, they'd spent a fair piece of time the night before clobbering a set of bikers who could have ridden right off this printed page.

"You said there was something like this in Europe," Willow said. Her fingertips were black with newsprint smudges. "Something like the sleeping sickness. But that was before there were movies, right?"

"Right, a long time before," Angel agreed. He paused. "But there were pup—" His words trailed off into silence.

They both looked at him expectantly.

"Well, I heard something about monks in one village fighting giant puppets," Angel said slowly. "Punch and Judy puppets."

They looked at him, united in an utter lack of understanding. Who the heck were Punch and Judy?

"Puppets?" Buffy asked.

"Punch and Judy puppets," Angel said. "Marionette shows, about a husband and wife team. All the rage, back in the day." When comprehension declined to dawn, he sighed. "I really wish Giles were here," he said. "It's a European thing."

"So do we," Buffy said. "But since he isn't—"

He took the hint. "Punch and Judy shows were blood-and-thunder stuff, entertainment for the masses. They drank and they cursed and they hit each other a lot. With clubs," he said. "And axes."

Buffy ran her fingers through her blond locks, thinking. "Sounds pretty un-PC," she said.

"Entertainment for the masses," he said again. "Cheap thrills. The shows moved from town to town."

"Giant puppets fighting monks, you say?" Buffy said.

"Life-size, anyway," Angel said. "That was the rumor, at least." He smiled, faintly and sadly. "I've been around a long time, Buffy. I hear a lot of things."

"It sounds familiar," Willow said. "I mean, marionettes are kind of like movie characters, aren't they? And you said that there were sleeping-sickness outbreaks in the 1860s, but that was a long time after Cagliostro—"

"Cagliostro?" Angel demanded sharply, interrupting.

"That's right," Willow said. "You guys were contemporaries. You know about him?"

"About him?" Angel repeated, with a short, sharp laugh. "I knew him. I used to go out drinking with him." He paused again. "Or, I guess you could say, Angelus did."

Buffy felt as if something cold had just run its fingers along her spine. Angelus was Angel minus the soul that gave him compassion and so much more. Angelus was the vampire Angel had been more than a century before, when he'd painted much of Europe red with fire and blood.

If this was the same Cagliostro who had been Angelus's drinking buddy back in the day, Sunnydale was in serious trouble.

• • •

"Really, ma'am, I can't suggest any specific medical or therapeutic treatment," Amanda said to the worried-looking lady on the other side of the counter. The words were a legal disclaimer, and she'd learned them by rote. The owner had been very clear on such things. The Magic Box wasn't a pharmacy or licensed health-services provider, and if Amanda ever said or did anything to suggest the contrary, she'd be out on her rear.

If it had been up to her, though, she'd have made her suggestions, taken the money, and let the woman have her powdered wolfsbane or dried goblin root or whatever nostrum sounded like it might do the job.

"Don't you have some kind of incense or something?" the customer asked yet again. She was plump and curly haired, a little long in the tooth for typical walk-in traffic, and her wardrobe ran to faded tie-dyes. Amanda had pretty much decided that she was some kind of over-the-hill hippie. Amanda hated hippies, but she felt a vague sympathy nonetheless. Experience with her grandparents had given her a crash course in how difficult medical challenges could be.

"You might try the Good Luck Tea," she said. "It's supposed to bring good fortune. That might help. It comes in a mint and berry blend."

She'd tried the Good Luck Tea herself. It was sour and gave her gas.

"No," the chubby lady said. "That won't work. How can I get him to drink tea when he won't wake up?"

"Huh," Amanda said. It was a reasonable question and she didn't have an answer.

"But incense, now—"

The phone rang. Amanda gestured in a mute request for patience and lifted the handset. "Thank you for calling the Magic Box," she said. Those words were rote too. "Proud provider of wondrous things to Sunnydale and surrounding environs."

"Hey," a voice said, husky and familiar. It was the heavyset guy she'd met at the teeny club earlier in the week. His name was Otto, but he preferred being called Skull.

"One moment, please," Amanda said. She covered the mouthpiece. "Incense is on the left wall, next to the candles," she told the lady with the sleepy kid. As the woman went to inspect the stock, Amanda whispered into the phone. "I'm not supposed to take personal calls, Otto." She took pains to use his real name.

"Yeah," he said. He could be a real mouth-breather. "Doing anything tonight?"

"Maybe," Amanda said slowly. Otto wasn't much, but he was more than nothing, and if she spent another night in her grandparents' house, she was going to pop like a blister. "Is there a band?"

"I was thinking movies," Otto said. "At the drive-in."

Amanda rolled her eyes. Bad enough that the townie kid had tried to pick her up, but if Otto was going to climb on the drive-in bandwagon—

Otto continued, "It's free."

"Free?" It wasn't much of a selling point, especially since Amanda had her own set of passes, but she was curious as to how Otto might have swung such a deal. She asked.

"Guy on TV," Otto said. "I saw him on the news. Belasco, or something like that."

Reflexively, Amanda corrected him. "Bal-sa-mo," she said, giving the name the rolling power that she remembered so well from the chance encounter of a few days before.

"Uh-huh," Otto said. "Really. Seemed like a nice guy. Liked him."

"He is," Amanda said. Long silence greeted her response, and she could almost hear the gears in Otto's head working, or trying to work. He was asking himself how she knew the theater owner. *She* was asking herself if she might get to see the guy again. It might be kind of nice.

"Yeah," she finally said. "I'll go to the drive-in with you, Otto."

CHAPTER ELEVEN

It was late in the day when they came for Giles. There were no windows in the washroom and he wasn't wearing a timepiece, but the air filling the enclosed space had become hot and muggy, and then had slowly cooled a bit. That meant the sun had passed its peak and was descending now. He'd been held prisoner at least half a day, maybe more.

Giles tried to use the time wisely. He ate the meal that his jailer had provided, drank plenty of water, and even performed a few exercises in an attempt to keep himself limber and aware. If any opportunity were to present itself, Giles wanted very much to be ready to take advantage. Even so, he'd become bored somewhere along the line.

That was the worst part of confinement, really: the mind-numbing monotony. A man could review the facts he held in his mind only so many times before they ran together, crying out for new information, new data, new contexts. So he was actually a bit relieved when the lock mechanism clicked and the washroom door swung back.

"Howdy, pardner," said a lean man with a wide-brimmed hat pulled low over his grizzled features. He was clad in worn black breeches and a soiled work shirt, with a Mexican serape draped across his shoulders. There was a cheroot cigar in one corner of his mouth and an antique army repeating pistol in his right hand. Another, bulkier figure stood just behind him.

Giles had seen the lean man before, twice. Once when the man abducted him, and once on the television, when he'd chanced upon a western movie, vintage 1960s.

"Here's how we're goin' to do it," the gunfighter said. Curiously, the movement of his lips didn't quite match the words he spoke. "You're goin' to be a good boy, and I'm not goin' to put a hole in you. Leastways, not just yet."

"Pop him one, Pops," the gunfighter's companion said. He was a motorcyclist by the looks of him, unshaved and unwashed, and wearing a scuffed leather vest and trousers. He made a fist with his right hand and drove it into his left, to make a meaty sound that echoed in Giles's Spartan quarters. "Pop him one, and show him who's boss."

"Kids these days," the westerner said, still in a dry, whispering drawl. He stepped back a bit and gestured for Giles to emerge. "Don't know how to treat a classy gent like you, do they?"

"No, they don't," Giles said, obeying. "But I hardly think you're the one to provide him with guidance. Why don't you introduce yourself?"

The lean man snickered. "Boss told me that you were a bug for names," he said. "I'd give you mine, but I ain't got one."

"The proverbial man with no name, eh?" Giles asked.

The response was a nod and a gestured command for him to raise his hands. Again, Giles obeyed. "Now, my friend's goin' to lead the way, but I won't be far behind. You try anythin'—you even think of trying anythin'—and you'll get a bullet in the back."

"No Spell of Entrancement this time?" Giles asked. That was most likely how they'd taken him from his home, he'd decided. He had only the vaguest of memories of that encounter, phantom images of these men and his host wielding a lens or an amulet of some sort.

"Nope," the gunfighter agreed. "It was handy, when I came and got ya, but don't need it this time. This time there's no one local to hear."

They fell into line, the biker, then Giles, then the man with no name. Viewed from behind, the motorcyclist was remarkably simian in appearance, with stooped shoulders and a slouching gait, his head dropped low. He was silent as he led the strange trio from the improvised cell toward their destination. Giles made no move to escape as he followed the human gorilla, but he did take careful note of their surroundings.

They were about as he'd expected. The washroom was part of a building that housed a theater concession stand. A popcorn kettle, soft drink dispensers, hot dog racks, and other aluminum-clad appliances glistened. The three men walked past the appliances and outside onto a concrete walkway and then into a gravel-strewn parking area. The late afternoon sun made Giles's eyes sting and water, but he kept his hands elevated.

To his right was the curved shield of a drive-in screen. He recognized it instantly from the handbill.

"Over there, pardner," the westerner said. "On the left."

Giles turned left, keeping pace with the others as the biker led them to another structure. This one was smaller than the refreshment stand, with a low slanting roof and slitlike windows. The biker opened the door and went inside, into a smallish chamber housing projection equipment and racks that held reels of film. Giles followed, then blinked as the leather-clad ruffian passed from view.

No, not passed—vanished. He disappeared as utterly and swiftly as light did when a lamp was turned off. One moment he was there, and the next he was not.

"Very impressive," Giles said.

"I thought you would appreciate it," came the response.

Seeing his host again, Giles realized that he was correct. The man who'd brought him his fast-food luncheon had the same face as the man in his alchemy book. Differences in clothing and facial hair obscured only slightly the strong resemblance between his host and the archival image. This, indeed, was Giuseppe Balsamo, Count Cagliostro.

The motorcyclist had departed, but two other underlings remained. They scurried about the projection shack, presumably in the service of Cagliostro. One fellow wore an overcoat and a fedora, despite the heat outside. The other was the Anubis-like wolf-man Buffy had described before. Giles rather wished now that he'd given more credence to her account.

"You're something of a film aficionado, I gather," Giles said.

Cagliostro smiled. "Films are the only art form of any value that this misbegotten nation has created," he said. He pointed at his underlings and identified each in turn. "Dick Shamus, private eye," he said. "And the varsity werewolf. Behind you—"

"Is a man with no name," Giles said. "From the old American West, by way of Italy, I think."

The booth held two film projectors, each taller than a tall man. Moving in perfect coordination, the detective and the wolf-man tended to the mechanisms. Dick Shamus swung open the round door of a film-reel cover and stepped aside as the werewolf wrestled a loaded reel into place. After locking it, the detective fed a length of footage from it into the projector's inner workings and set about guiding past gears, spindles, and the bulb. Were it not for his situation, Giles would have found the spectacle laughable. As it was, the entire sequence of events seemed more than ominous.

"Sit," Cagliostro commanded. His beard and hair were black as night now, and the twinkle in his eyes was now a fire. Gone was the amused and indulgent aristocrat, and in his place was someone vastly less pleasant.

"I'm fine, thank you," Giles said.

The wolf-man growled, and Giles sat. The chair that Cagliostro had indicated was uncomfortable and without ornament, but sturdy. Giles knew better than to complain or resist as the gunfighter bound his wrists to the chair arms with a length of rope he took from his belt.

"And does your fondness for the cinema extend to desiring an audience?" Giles asked, honestly curious.

Cagliostro shook his head. He dropped into another chair and eyed Giles. "Not at all," he said. "But we'll open for business shortly, and it seemed wise to move you from your cell. The locals will have need of the facilities. Besides, I know all too well how unpleasant such accommodations can be to a man of learning."

"You flatter me," Giles said. "But the attention, really, is unnecessary."

Cagliostro shrugged. "I hadn't planned on finding a Watcher here," he said. "I hadn't expected anything other than a sleepy California town. Really, all I'd hoped to do was visit, exhibit some motion pictures, refresh myself, and then move on. Nothing out of the ordinary, I assure you. Business as usual, I think the Americans say." He paused. "But Sunnydale has proved itself to be a most surprising place."

The words sounded odd, coming from a man with a werewolf at his beck and call.

"I discovered a curious establishment called the Magic Box," Cagliostro continued. "I had expected to find it stocked with nothing more than inexpensive novelties, and instead I found something remarkable: a matched set of Latverian soul crystals. Imagine that, Mr. Giles. A matched set! I had to destroy them, of course. Imagine how useful such a complement could be to one who knew their uses, as a weapon or a means of detection."

Giles didn't need to imagine. The owner of the Magic Box had excellent suppliers, a fine eye for value, and a remarkable attentiveness to the needs of his clientele. More than once Giles had found unexpected treasures there.

"How is it that you're in America, Count?" Giles asked bluntly. "You look remarkably well, for a dead man."

"Ah," Cagliostro said. Still seated, he tipped his head in a mocking half bow. "I'm honored that my humble story has come to the attention of the Watchers Council."

"Only obliquely," Giles said frankly. In popular literature, Cagliostro was a towering figure, legendary in stature; alchemist, occultist, and Italian nobleman, he had founded quasi-religious orders that stood the test of time, and he had performed unexplainable feats of mysticism. Supposedly, he had spearheaded the French Revolution and been plagiarized by Napoleon Bonaparte. In the annals of the Watchers, however, he was little more than a footnote, written off as a con artist and minor political schemer.

Under the circumstances, however, it seemed likely that the popular literature had the right of things.

"I came to these fair shores following the War Between the States," Cagliostro said, answering the question. "Then, as now, this was a rude nation, rough and unrefined, but it offered great promise and opportunity. It has been my home in the long years since."

"Most sources have you as deceased, circa 1795," Giles said slowly. The details were coming back to him now. "Rome tried you for heresy, magick, and conjuring and imprisoned you for life in Montefeltro."

"If it were truly for life, I would be there still, my friend," Cagliostro said. "But no. I have led many lives. I've used many names. They fall from me as the years pass, like leaves from a tree. They fall away, but I endure."

The werewolf was moving film reels from rack to rack. He dropped one, and he yelped in pain as it struck his foot. Cagliostro murmured a word that Giles couldn't quite hear, and the man-beast dissipated. Without waiting for instruction, the gunfighter picked up the dropped reel and took his fellow's place at the storage rack.

"You have no idea how pleased I am to have made your acquaintance, Mr. Giles. You seem to be an educated man, well versed in matters worth knowing," Cagliostro said. "As you can see, my current associates are less erudite. They're little more than extensions of my own will, really, and the patrons of my little enterprise are scarcely better." He paused. "I look forward to many conversations with you."

"They'll be one-sided," Giles said.

"I think not," Cagliostro said. "I have many interesting means of persuasion."

"He wasn't such a bad guy, really," Angel said. "A bit pompous. He liked to talk and he liked to drink, and he liked playing host. I don't think I paid for a single drink in the entire time I knew him. Liked to wager, too."

"This is Count Cagliostro we're talking about, right?" Willow asked. She looked skeptical. "The master alchemist played the ponies?"

The vampire nodded. They were still in the library, still in the quiet confines of the lower-level research room. Angel, however, was now at least partly in the past, wandering the labyrinth of his long and convoluted memory.

"You won't say things like that when you're older, Willow," he said. Angel was still in human mode, wearing his eternally youthful features, but his eyes looked suddenly old.

"I don't think I'll ever be as old as you," Willow said. "Um. No offense."

The vampire shook his head. "I know what you mean," he said. "But that's not what *I* mean. You'll get older. You'll see things differently. You'll see that people are more alike than they are different. They want food, drink, and companionship. Entertainment. The simple things are what make them feel human, even when they aren't."

It was the simple things that made him suffer, as well. The pleasures that most took from food and drink had been replaced by the driving need for blood, and the soul that was his curse made him an outcast among his own kind. He could enjoy existence, at least on a momentary basis, but true contentment and joy were denied to him.

"He was more than an alchemist, though. He was into many disciplines, and he was a bit of a schemer, too," Angel said. "Got drunk in a tavern one night and told me that he'd been born of common blood and spent his entire life and wits trying to rise above it. I kept telling him that all blood is pretty much the same, but he was so busy talking that he wouldn't listen."

"Wait a minute," Buffy said. "You. Knew. Cagliostro?" She paused briefly between each word, dragging out the question, clearly still having difficulty with it.

Angel knew why. In her relatively brief tenure as Slayer, she'd encountered demons and vampires by the dozen, and had somehow managed to remain in many ways a typical teenage girl, well grounded in the here and now. That was something he loved about her, one thing among many. But even though she knew full well who he was, what he was, his own apparent youth made it easier for her to look past that unpleasant truth. The comment about Cagliostro had served as a reminder.

Angel nodded. "He was a popular guy," he said. "He was sort of a doctor, too."

"A doctor?" Buffy asked, unbelieving.

"It's like the proto-science thing," Willow said. "Stuff hadn't gotten sorted out all the way just yet."

Angel nodded. "He treated Benjamin Franklin for a headache once. That was in Paris. Never let anyone hear the end of it either." Even two hundred years after the fact, he sounded annoyed. "What a blowhard."

"How dangerous is he, then?" Buffy asked. "If this is him, I mean."

"I don't know," Angel said after a moment's thought. "The Cagliostro I knew was a charmer and a showman more than anything else. He talked a lot about transmutation and raising demons, but I never saw him do either."

"That could have been a cover," Willow said. She'd apparently finished her research and was closing the bound volumes and stacking them neatly for a return to the shelves. They made a sizeable pile. "Like in Poe's 'The Purloined Letter,' when everyone's looking for something that's been hidden in plain sight."

That made sense, Angel thought. Willow's comment cast a new light on things, making him consider them from a new perspective. Indeed, the Cagliostro of his memory had demonstrated at least one gift, even if he'd not consciously realized it at the time. He'd been an immensely likeable man, with a magnetism that defied easy description, but which could not be denied.

It wasn't easy to charm a vampire, after all.

"Is there anything else we should know?" Buffy asked.

"He was fascinated with the idea of vampirism," Angel said, remembering more and more of his late-night chats with the egotistical European. "I think that's why we got along so well. What I was—what I *am* interested him."

"He wanted to be turned?" Buffy asked. "Yecch."

Angel shook his head. "No, nothing like that. It was the metaphysical end of things that he liked. He wanted to run tests and do experiments," he said. Again he smiled. "But I knew better than that."

"Oh," Buffy said.

"We lost touch after the French Revolution, of course," Angel said.

"Of course," Willow said.

"That's about it," Angel said, returning to the present again. "But you believe he's running the drive-in?"

"Well, that's what Xander was telling us," Buffy said. "You didn't see anything suspicious out there?"

"Nothing," he said. "Just a nervous security guard. But, Buffy, the place wasn't open for business yet."

Buffy sighed. Xander wasn't there to see it, but he got his wish. "I guess we're going to the movies, then," she said.

CHAPTER TWELVE

The phone on the nightstand buzzed. The sound wasn't loud, but it was enough to rouse Xander from his light, uncomfortable sleep. He blinked in surprise as vague dreams fled his conscious mind, leaving behind phantom images of reporting for a biology final while clad only in his gym shorts. He rubbed his eyes, momentarily disoriented, and then reality reasserted itself. He was still in the white-finished hospital room, and nothing seemed to have changed much since his last waking moment. Jonathan remained still beneath the bedsheets, his eyes moving beneath their lids. The bedside monitor continued its work, and the air was thick with that wonderful hospital scent, the smell of sick people and medicine.

The phone buzzed again. He stood and went to answer it. The catnap had helped, but he was still tired, and a bit stiff from sitting in the chair for however long it had been. He had a bad taste in his mouth and his lips were dry; he licked them before answering.

"Xander?" Buffy's familiar voice asked.

"Yeah," he answered. There was a pitcher of water on the nightstand and a pair of drinking glasses. He eyed them thirstily. "What's up, Buff?"

"You're still there?" she asked. "Your mom said she didn't know where you were, but I thought you'd have gone home by now."

How late was it? He looked for a clock but didn't see one. From the looks of the sky outside, however, visible through the room's window, it was very late afternoon at the earliest. The sky had begun to darken, just a bit.

"What time is it?" he asked. Then, after she told him, he whistled softly. He'd been asleep for hours. He must have been more fatigued than he'd thought. Jonathan's still-slumbering form was a reminder that another explanation might apply, but Xander chose to hold on to the mundane. He'd been up all night, after all.

"Sorry," he said. "Yeah, I'm still here. What's up?"

As Buffy told him what she and Willow had learned, and about Angel's contribution, Xander drank some water. It was rude, he knew, but he couldn't help himself. Buffy's account was rapid and precise, but curiously uninvolving. Usually he found these things fascinating, but not now. Maybe it was because he was hearing them in the worrisome context of the hospital room, but her words simply didn't draw him in.

"That's great, Buff," he said, trying hard to be sincere. "I mean, not great, but—"

"I know what you mean," she said.

"Do you want me to come with?" he asked. Even to him the offer sounded unenthusiastic. Maybe it was that famed Buffy focus on all things Slayerish, but she hadn't asked how he was, or if there'd been any change in Jonathan's situation. She hadn't even asked if he had spoken to any of the doctors. Ordinarily, such oversights were business as usual and perfectly understandable, but right now, in the last of his sleep hangover, the oversight rankled slightly.

She must have heard it in his voice. Even over the phone her sigh was audible. "You're worried about them, aren't you?" she asked, more gently now. "All of them, I mean."

"Yeah." There wasn't much more to say.

"Look, Xander, we know that this character can send minions out, to do his work. Maybe you'd better stay there, keep an eye out," she said. "You know?"

"Yeah," he said again, but this time more gratefully. Deliberately or not, she'd said just the thing he needed to hear. Now he could stay without feeling guilty.

"Is Cordy there?" Buffy asked.

"I haven't seen her." The idea that the Queen of Sunnydale High would spend her Saturday afternoon in a hospital visiting sick friends seemed unlikely. Cordelia had shown surprising depths to Xander in some of their private moments, but he didn't think she'd come that far, not just yet.

"Her dad says she went out," Buffy said.

Xander felt a pang of worry. "It's early for the Bronze," he said.

"He said she went out hours ago," Buffy replied. A moment's silence stretched between them before she continued. "I'm sure she's fine, Xander. Cordy can take care of herself. But I'll keep an eye out."

He told her he'd do the same, and then, at her prompting, told her as much as he could about the drive-in itself. Before being banished to handbill duty, Xander had undertaken many chores on the site, most of them somewhat demeaning. According to Buffy, Angel had taken a quick look-see too, but Xander knew the place better. He was able to provide reasonable details about what went where, who to go to, and what to see.

"Good," she said. "That'll help." She paused. "Xander, this really isn't your fault, you know."

Jonathan's beside monitor chirped again, another reminder. Xander eyed it and then his sleeping classmate. Jonathan seemed unchanged, but Xander couldn't be certain. Sometimes staring at something too long blinded you to its details.

"Isn't it?" he said, not quite bitterly.

"No, it's not," Buffy said. Now her words were nearly a command. "Look, think about it. We know something like this has been going on for at least two hundred years. Jonathan was just in the wrong place at the wrong time."

"Emphasis on *wrong*," Xander said. "And because I put him there."

"Yeah, like you put Aura there?" Buffy said.

"But Aura wasn't—Oh," Xander said, realizing what she meant. "The others were," he said.

"Not all of them," Buffy told him. "Look, we can talk about this later, but there's no reason to tear yourself up. You didn't do anything wrong and you're helping now."

"Yeah," Xander said. "Helping."

"Take care of yourself, Xander," Buffy said. "That way, you can take care of the rest of us."

She ended the conversation on that oddly philosophical note. Xander shrugged and replaced the handset. He glanced at Jonathan, then at the monitor, and then out the window at the darkening sky.

There wasn't much else to do, really.

"Am I getting old?" Buffy asked, hanging up the phone.

"Huh?" Willow asked. She could not have looked more confused had Buffy sprouted a second head. The question threw her for a loop.

"Don't be silly," Angel chimed in. "You're just growing up. That was pretty mature advice you gave him at the end there."

"No, it's not that," Buffy said. She sounded half amused,

half confused. "It's just, Xander doesn't want to go to the drive-in with me. I must be losing my girlish good looks."

They were in her room at the Summers house. Joyce was nowhere in sight, and the note she'd left just said that she'd gone out with a friend. That was just as well. Buffy had preparations to make and didn't want to have to provide excuses for Angel's presence in her room.

Some of those preparations were prosaic enough: a quick shower and a change into something stylish but durable, since there was almost certain to be some violence in the offing. That violence was also why she and the others were taking quick inventory of her personal arsenal, choosing what was likely to come in handy.

"These things Cagliostro has are bad news," she told Willow. "And they don't hold to the usual rules, to judge from that wolf-guy. I'm guessing that the traditional crosses and such won't be much use."

"If they're made out of ectoplasm, you're probably right," Willow said. She set the crosses and holy water aside to make space for more pragmatic tools, being careful not to wave the blessed items in Angel's direction. Rules were rules, after all, and Angel very definitely was a vampire, no matter how good a guy he was. "It's funny," she continued. "Alchemy's bound up in the kabbalah."

"Kabbalah?"

"Ancient Jewish sorcery," Willow said. "I wish I knew more about it. Maybe I could help with some kind of hoodoo—"

"I don't think that's a good idea, Willow," Angel said. "Magicks are bad news, unless you know what you're doing, and dabbling in a new discipline is especially bad. Besides, old Giuseppe may be an alchemist, but that doesn't mean this is alchemy proper that we're talking about."

Buffy knew what he meant. They'd talked about it on the way home from the library. This was more of the hide-in-plain-sight stuff; Angel had suggested that, even back in the day, Cagliostro might have used expertise in one field to divert attention from others. Everything she'd heard so far suggested that Cagliostro had pursued many lines of inquiry into the workings of the universe, and this was no time to try to second-guess him. It was better to stick with what she knew worked.

That meant knives. Knives and axes and swords, and other edged things that could slice pieces off the conjurer's cat's-paw agents. A dozen deadly implements lay arrayed on Buffy's chenille bedspread, incongruous-looking on the frilly thing. "Take your pick," she told the others.

Angel went for the largest implement of death, of course. He was a guy, after all, even if an undead one. He picked a Roman-style short sword, thick and solid but honed to a razor edge. The air whistled as he test-swung it, and he nodded in approval. "I'm ready," he said.

"This one's pretty," Willow said. She selected a wavy-bladed dagger with a red stone set in its hilt, and banded decorations that bore cryptic runes.

"You're sure about this, Willow?" Buffy asked. She wasn't. Xander, by his absence, had reminded her yet again that taking civilians into battle wasn't always the best strategy. Willow was smart and brave, but there were things in life that simply weren't meant for non-Slayers.

"Hey! You're not leaving me behind," Willow said. She was very pretty, in an impish sort of way, but also very good at showing irritation. "I've been through a lot lately, you know."

"Okay," Buffy said, resigned. This was an argument she never seemed to win. "In that case, ditch the pretty knife. Take this instead."

She handed Willow a battle-axe, like the one she'd used the night before, but smaller and lighter; Willow didn't have Slayer strength, after all. "Chop with it," she said. "Stabbing holes in these things doesn't do much good, but cutting pieces off does."

"So it's an issue of structural integrity, hey?" Willow said. She hefted the weapon and tried to make a snarl, but she was just too cute to make the effect work.

"Just hang back and follow our lead," Buffy told her. "Let Angel and me handle the heavy lifting. Don't be afraid to run if we tell you to."

Willow nodded.

Coins rattled in the machine's inner workings, and numbers lit next to the slot. She fed it two dollars in quarters, which was all she could find in the depths of her handbag. As she considered her snack choices, Cordelia wondered when the modern world would make its way to Sunnydale. If this thing were able to read credit cards, like they could in civilized places, she'd be able to buy it out.

After a bit of mix-and-match, she settled on Twizzlers and a bag of those baked potato chip things, the former for their durability and the latter out of consideration for her figure. Either had to be much better than the cafeteria's grim fare, which ran to salted fat. At least they were prepared by national manufacturers. She stooped to claim her purchases from the machine's chute.

"You *are* here," Xander said.

She whirled, startled. He stood behind her, framed in the doorway of the alcove that held the snack machines.

"I thought I saw you walk by," he continued. He looked bad—not bad ugly, but bad tired and bad worried.

"Huh? What? Yeah," Cordelia said.

"How long?" he asked.

"A while," she said. The next words didn't come as easily as she would have liked them to. "I was worried about Aura," she said. "I didn't want her to be alone."

"Yeah, I know," Xander said sympathetically. "But everyone's doing what they can, and the doctors say there's nothing anyone can do. Jonathan's signs are all good, except for this pesky sleep thing."

Cordelia tried to muster some sympathy for Xander's

little friend, but with only the slightest success. She had other things on her mind.

"Aura's been here for days, Xander," she said. "She was the first, and they say she's getting weaker."

"I don't think they're telling us everything, Cordy," Xander said seriously. "In fact, I know they aren't. I heard the doctors talking. The longer this thing lasts, the less likely it is that they'll wake up." He paused. "Wake up ever, I mean."

"Why would they hide something like that?" she asked.

He shrugged. "Worried about a panic, I guess," he said. He sounded worried.

Without asking, he fell in beside her as she left the vending-machine room. The hospital was only lightly staffed, for whatever reason, and no one seemed to take note of them as they paced down the corridor toward the patient rooms.

"Buffy called," Xander said. "She asked after you."

"How sweet," Cordelia said without particular sincerity. "Any news on the Giles front?"

"Yeah, Willow thinks she's figured it out," Xander said. "Whoops. Here's my stop."

Cordelia followed him into Jonathan's room. Remarkably, the place had an unoccupied bed. Again without any conscious coordination, they sat on it, side by side, but with a reasonable distance between them.

Even so, Cordy had a feeling about where things were headed.

"Twizzler?" she asked, only to have him decline. That was

a surprise. Xander nearly never turned down food, and the ropy candy strands qualified as food, at least on a technicality.

Rather than accept the proffered sugary treat, he gave her a quick rundown on what Buffy had told him about Willow's research and about their plans for a run to the open-air theater. It was a lot to take in, but Cordelia managed.

"Well, to be honest, that sounds pretty logical to me," she said. "I'm not sure about Willow, but Buffy and Angel are the right choice for that kind of thing." Buffy and Angel had enhanced capabilities, and each could do things that Cordelia even now found amazing.

"Yeah," Xander said. "It's just—I feel so helpless."

"I know," Cordelia said. She'd never seen him like this before. Xander could be irritating and a bit of a buffoon, but he never seemed to lack self-confidence. Clearly, he had hidden depths.

"What about you?" he asked.

"Nothing better to do," she lied, biting into her cherry red candy.

They sat together in effective silence for another minute or two, Cordelia eating and Xander watching her eat. The air seemed thick with apprehension, apprehension concerning their friends who were in the hospital and those who weren't.

Then something remarkable happened. Xander managed a smile. "Cordy," he said, "I changed my mind. I think I will have some of that."

He kissed her, hard, and she kissed him back. He pulled

her to him and she pulled too, until they fell back on the bed in a mutual embrace.

What the heck. It beat necking in a broom closet.

Traffic was bad; everyone in town seemed to have picked tonight to go to the movies. The road that led out of Sunnydale was heavily trafficked with cars and vans, pickup trucks and SUVs. The procession looked like it included a pretty good sampling of town society, and Buffy had a bad feeling about that. Even now, even with the sun beneath the horizon, the caravan continued. Parking would be at a premium tonight.

"This is going to take forever," Angel said. He was seated behind the steering wheel of Giles's little car, which they had commandeered for the evening. Buffy had called shotgun, leaving the backseat for Willow.

"Do the best you can," the Slayer said. Eyeing the seemingly endless procession that stretched before them, she worried that even Angel's best wouldn't be good enough.

"Everyone buckled up?" he asked.

"I am," Willow said.

"Buffy?"

"Oh, all right," she said, and pulled the woven belt into place and clicked the buckle shut.

He grinned wolfishly at her. "Thanks," he said.

"Don't you think you're being a little—*Yow!*"

The next twenty minutes or so were as frightening as any in Buffy's young life. Angel drove the little car with unrelenting aggression and the skill of someone who could combine superhuman reflexes with lessons learned through decades of experience. Immediately they were darting in and out among the other vehicles. The compact's engine coughed and stuttered but never failed as Angel called on all of its strength. He snapped the wheel from side to side, exploiting every opportunity to gain even a few car lengths' distance. He swerved on and off the road, spraying gravel as he used the roadbed shoulder to pass illegally on the right. By the time they'd arrived at the drive-in and Angel had forced his way into the front of the line, Buffy was very nearly carsick.

The ticket seller was an older man, balding and portly and dressed in black. "It's free tonight," he said affably. "But we're running out of spaces." He leaned down from the booth opening, as if to say something more. As he did, Buffy realized something odd: He was wearing a priest's collar.

That should have been her first clue.

"Hey," the man said, "aren't you Angelus?"

"Huh?" Angel said, more perplexed than alarmed by the use of his old name.

"DIE, VAMPIRE!" the ticket-selling priest screamed, stabbing at him with a wooden stake.

CHAPTER THIRTEEN

"I see that we have visitors," Cagliostro said in tones that were free of his earlier bombast. He sounded eerily calm, even detached, and his voice seemed to come from a distance. "The Slayer and her pet vampire. You really must explain that situation to me, when we have the time."

"If you survive," Giles said. He tested his bonds again, but they remained secure.

Cagliostro didn't seem to notice Giles's actions or his words. Still facing Giles from his own chair near the big projectors, he seemed absolutely unconcerned with any challenge that Giles might offer. His gaze was trained in Giles's direction but seemed focused on something else entirely. The effect was disconcerting. It was as if he were looking not *at* the Watcher but *through* him. The confines of the projection booth were filled by the clatter of the running projector, but his placid tones cut through the noise with remarkable clarity. They were nearly alone in the place; only the nameless gunfighter shared it with them as he tended the equipment.

"You'll talk to me later, Rupert," Cagliostro said. His lips twitched as he used Giles's first name for the first time, but the hint of a smile faded almost instantly. "There's much you'll have to explain to me, once I've taken my leave of this remarkable settlement. I've long been curious about the inner workings of the Council."

Giles said nothing. There was no point. He'd never permit Cagliostro—never permit anyone—to extract such knowledge from him, but displays of defiance would do him no good. Better to allow events to play out and wait for an opportunity.

"This land must offer great frustrations to a man with a Watcher's education," Cagliostro said dreamily. "So much ignorance—"

"So much vigor," Giles said in correction. He certainly had issues with the so-called New World—what Americans did to food bordered on the barbarous—but the bonds he'd made here were strong and ran deep. There was no point in countenancing insults.

"Ignorant cattle," Cagliostro said, still speaking with a distracted air. "Peasants who don't know that they are peasants. Like sheep without a shepherd."

That was the second time he'd used animals as a metaphor. Were they simply the first insults that came to mind, or had the alchemist inadvertently revealed something of himself? Did he think of people as a means of sustenance? That thought, coupled with his host's longevity, hinted at an unpleasant possibility.

"There's something of the vampire in you, isn't there?" Giles asked.

Cagliostro actually laughed at that. "Quite the contrary," he said. "Rather, there is something of me in at least some vam—*Uh!*"

He flinched. As Giles watched, fascinated, Cagliostro slumped slightly. The smooth composure of his features broke again, and an expression of pain flickered across his face, almost too quickly to be seen. He bit his lower lip and murmured, "Well struck, Slayer. First blood."

He was speaking of Buffy, Giles realized—perhaps even *to* her.

How could that be?

Angel was fast but not quite fast enough. He gave a gasp of pain as the stake penetrated his chest. His evasive maneuver hadn't failed completely, though: The spear of wood stabbed into him just below the collarbone and into the joint of his shoulder. It missed his heart entirely.

Buffy's speed served them both even better. She drew the *boka* and swung it in a short arc that passed through the priestly ticket seller's wrist. The hand that had held the stake separated instantly, and the remainder of their adversary vanished nearly as fast.

"Th-thanks," Angel said. He pulled the wooden stake from his shoulder with a wet tearing noise. "Took me by surprise."

"You okay?" Buffy asked.

"I'll live," Angel said. He moved his injured joint tentatively. "Hurts," he said. "Hurts, but it works."

"End of the line. Everyone out," Buffy snapped, kicking open her door. "Now!"

"We can't just leave the car—," Willow started to say.

"Now!" Buffy said. Her earlier misgivings about Willow's presence belatedly reasserted themselves, but what was done, was done. The here and now were what mattered.

Horns honked as they scrambled from the car, and other drivers shouted, making their displeasure known. The line behind them was long and couldn't move now, with the path blocked. That was to the good, Buffy decided. According to Angel and Xander both, this was the establishment's only entryway. That meant there'd be fewer bystanders to worry about.

Not that there weren't plenty, she thought as she viewed the entirety of the drive-in for the first time. With the parking area lit by the screen's reflected radiance, Buffy could see the place was nearly full. There were scores of vehicles—perhaps hundreds. No one went to the movies alone; if there were even two people in each car . . .

"We've got to get moving," she said. She pointed to a distant building, squat and low. A beam of light spilled from one window. "There. I'm thinking, the projection booth. If we're talking magick movies, that's where we need to be."

She took the lead, in part because of her own anxiety and in part to give Angel a moment to recover. Moving quickly, they followed her along an improvised path that snaked between parked cars. *Boka* in one hand, a simple machete in the other, she did her best to use the terrain to her advantage, darting between parked cars to block prying eyes, however briefly.

The priest's greeting still rang in her ears. For the vampire it had been a threat; to her it had meant something else, or two somethings.

They'd come to the right place. If ever she'd doubted that, she was certain now.

And Cagliostro was ready for them.

"Coffee?" Barney asked. He offered his thermos, and when Joyce nodded, he topped off her cup.

Now that they'd arrived at the open-air theater, Joyce felt a little silly for having accepted his invitation. These were hardly the kind of movies for a grown woman to watch. Her tastes ran more to love stories and art films, but she couldn't image them running in a place like this.

And if she felt silly, it wasn't a bad feeling. Being silly reminded her of being young. There was an electric excitement in the air that helped her momentarily forget that she was a middle-aged woman out on a lark with a man who was more of a friendly acquaintance than anything else.

"I remember this one," Barney said as the image of a grizzled, world-weary man in western garb filled the screen.

Joyce did too. She'd seen *Reach for the Sky—and Die!* with Buffy's father on its first run, in a conventional theater, back when the world was younger. She'd been younger too, of course, but her memory wasn't gone yet. She reviewed the handbill. Black letters on orange were hard to read in the reflected light, but she managed. "It's not on the list," she said, puzzled.

"Coming attractions," Barney said, staring raptly at the screen's display. "Man, this was so—Hey!"

The gunfighter was gone. In a convulsive wrench, its image had given way to something else. Cheap-sounding music, made up mostly of chimes and woodwinds, spilled from the car speakers, and the title frame of a movie appeared on the screen. It was for some kind of martial arts film, Joyce realized, annoyed. Movies ran on twinned projectors, she knew, switching off between them as films ended. Someone had botched the changeover and transitioned from the previews to the main program.

"We can rent it sometime, if you want," she told Barney, trying to console him. "The western, I mean. It might be fun to see at home."

• • •

"Well struck, Slayer. First blood," Cagliostro said.

Even as Cagliostro's brief expression of discomfort faded, the gunfighter moved to act as Giles watched carefully. One leathery hand grasped a lever extending from the first projector, and one booted foot came down on a pedal connected to the other. Hand and foot acted simultaneously, and the pitch of projector motors abruptly shifted. One unit was shutting down, Giles realized, and the other was coming to life.

Something else was happening too.

It wasn't natural light but a different kind of light that was emerging from the second lens. It didn't follow a conventional radiance's straight path, but it looped and curled. Like a serpent's tongue or a demon's tentacle, it writhed and undulated as it extended itself into the open area between Giles and Cagliostro. One end remained securely anchored to the projector lens, while the other did a delicate dance in the electricity-charged air, as if on a quest. Once, the latter end came ominously close to Giles's eyes, and Cagliostro chucked softly.

"How odd. The lens likes you," he said. His tone was still distant and cool, as if he spoke from the depths of a dream. "It doesn't like everyone. But it likes me more."

As if drawn by the tranquil voice, the glowing tendril shifted in midair. It had moved slowly before, but now, almost too swiftly for the eye to follow, it darted in Cagliostro's direction. It darted, struck, and buried itself in his chest. The alchemist gave another gasp, a sound that could have been pleasure or pain. Almost instantly the tendril began to pulse and throb.

"There. That's much better," the gunfighter said.

He spoke with Cagliostro's voice.

Buffy was leading the others past one real behemoth of an SUV when the wolf-man dropped on her from above. She felt rather than saw or heard his presence, spinning just in time to see his dark form against the darker sky.

"You again," she said, and swung her machete. The wolf-man's head went flying with gratifying speed, and his body disappeared, dissipating into the night air. Willow gave a squeal of surprise, and Buffy realized that she'd never seen the effect. She glanced in her friend's direction and said, "See? Like a light turning off."

"Buffy, look out!" Angel shouted.

It was happening again: same SUV, same varsity werewolf, like instant replay or a summer rerun. Buffy chopped at the doppelgänger quickly, but not fast enough. He had taken her unawares. Her slash went off course and the beast hit her. The impact sent her tumbling to the ground, with the monster crouched on top of her. She raised both weapons to defend herself, but like an expert wrestler the wolf-man's clawing hands clamped down on her wrists, blocking both of her strikes. Forcing her arms apart to give himself easier access, the creature lowered his jaws to her throat.

• • •

"Mmmm," Cordelia said, then broke the kiss and came up for air. "You've got your failings, mister, but you're a good kisser."

"Yeah?" Xander said. He swallowed the last of the candy. "What's that thing in English grammar?" he asked. "Nominative, comparative—"

"Huh?" Cordelia asked. The non sequitur made no sense.

"I don't want to be good," Xander said, but it wasn't a complaint. He said with a smile, "I don't want to be better, either. Let me show you that I'm the best."

He locked lips with her again, and pulled her even closer. They were still rolling around on the unassigned bed, but Cordelia didn't intend to let things go any further.

Some small corner of her mind was still filled with surprise with herself for the unscheduled make-out session. This was different from the other times, somehow richer and more textured. She knew that there was still danger afoot, but there was something more. There was Jonathan and there was Aura, and the mysterious malady they shared. The mysterious illness was what her English teacher termed "an intimation of mortality"—a reminder of how fleeting life could be, and Cordelia enjoyed life very much.

Xander was coming in for another pass when something caught Cordelia's eye. Over his shoulder she could see something moving.

"Ooomp!" she said, pushing him back.

"Ooomp?" he asked, baffled.

"L-look," she said, pointing. "Look at Jonathan!"

That did it. He gave up trying and turned to look at his slumbering classmate. Jonathan was still asleep, still . . . still. He lay unmoving, as if frozen in time, but something was different.

A glowing line of something had drifted in through the window. It traced a lazy, meandering track to Jonathan's chest and attached itself to him directly above the heart. In the room's bright lights it was difficult to see clearly, but as Cordelia and Xander watched, that changed. The line thickened and resolved itself, until it looked solid and real. Then it began to pulse, with a rhythm that Cordelia found unnervingly familiar.

It was like the beating of a human heart.

Buffy felt the beast's hot breath on the skin of her neck and tried to push him back and up to free herself. The effort was futile. He had leverage and she didn't. The wolf-man's bared fangs came closer and closer. Saliva dripped onto her face, hot and disgusting.

There was a sound of impact. Something solid slammed into the wolf-man from behind. The varsity werewolf instantly blurred and faded, and then the thing was gone.

"Take that, foul beast of darkness," Willow said. She still held the edged weapon and seemed remarkably pleased with herself. Buffy didn't blame her: It had been a good strike. Willow would have made a fine avenging fury, if avenging furies came in a Jewish pixie variety.

Buffy glanced at Angel. He opened his hands and shrugged, as if to excuse himself for not coming to her aid first. "I'm faster, but she was closer," he said.

"Yeah, yeah, yeah," Buffy said, catching her breath and leading them forward. "I—for gosh sakes. Will you look at that?"

They'd rounded the SUV's sheltering bulk now and could see the bowl-like parking area of the drive-in. The view was much like what they had seen before, with an awe-inducing difference. The cars and trucks and vans remained where they were, but now lines of pale fire emerged from half of them. Narrow and faint, the tracks the lines followed were fluid and undulating, like vines blowing in the wind.

"Wow," Willow said.

"Yeah, wow," Buffy said, struck by the mysterious tableau. It was strangely beautiful. The silvery tendrils branched and converged, bent and doubled and looped. In school, Buffy had seen documentary footage shot underwater, films of jellyfish trailing tendrils in subsea splendor. What she saw now reminded her of those films. Each had one thing in common: One end led to a parked vehicle and the other led to the projection shack.

"What is it?" Willow asked. Buffy could tell that her friend was desperately trying to make sense of it. "It looks—it looks like some kind of fiber-optic network."

"No," Angel said. "Those are silver cords," he said.

"Huh?"

"I told you, Cagliostro was a dabbler. He followed a lot of belief systems," Angel said. "He told me once about spiritualism, and about out-of-body experiences." He paused. "The silver cord is what ties the spirit to the body. He pulled their souls to him. He's feeding on them."

CHAPTER FOURTEEN

It's easier here," Cagliostro said. "I imagine I have your Hellmouth to thank for that. I can do more than I could ever do before."

He was still speaking through the gunslinger, but his voice had a curious echoing quality now. It was somewhat like hearing a stereo broadcast with the channels out of phase, and the effect varied as the gunslinger paced back and forth.

"It's hardly *my* Hellmouth," Giles said. He knew the meaning behind the alchemist's words, though. Sunnydale sat atop the Hellmouth, a portal that led to nearly every imaginable evil. Most texts characterized the Hellmouth as a mere gateway, but that was simply a concrete image intended to make things more easily understood. Certainly, the Hellmouth was a hole that led to various hells and such, but it was a cauldron, too, seething with endless dark power. He knew that the drive-in was outside the town limits, but it perched at the very rim of the Hellmouth. Here, now, with someone like Cagliostro in command, surely enough stray energies drifted up from its depths to make a difference.

"You can't imagine how it feels," Cagliostro said. The gunfighter's body paced steadily, as if to expend nervous energies. "I can do so much more now. I'm in so many different places, so many different forms—"

The gunfighter's outlines shifted. He became shorter, squatter. His serape lengthened into an overcoat and his hat restyled itself. "See what I mean?" he asked. "I developed the ability to field agents like this centuries ago, and to direct them to act on my behalf. But it's only since coming here that I could extend myself into them, and exercise my other abilities through them." He was Dick Shamus now.

Yet again Giles tested his bonds, in the vain hope that the rope might have vanished along with the gunslinger who had brought it. No luck. The ropes indeed were gone, but steel handcuffs had taken their place. Even Cagliostro's props had made the transition from one identity to the next. "You really do like the movies," Giles continued.

Dick Shamus nodded. "The images, the color, the verve—vastly more impressive than mere puppetry. Mr. Edison was quite a fellow. I had dinner with him once, you know."

"I hadn't," Giles said drily.

"I was in the magick lantern business then," Cagliostro mused. "Stage shows, with projected images. A transitional form. Better than puppet shows too. It served my purposes well enough."

"And before that?"

Dick Shamus reverted to the gunslinger. "Minstrel shows. Before that, puppet shows. Punch and Judy, and that rot. Any mass entertainment that draws crowds," he said. "Anything that brings the cattle to me, so that I may connect with them. They come, I drain their spirit-force, and I add it to my own. In olden times, I had to do it directly, but now, here—"

"You have these—these proxies," Giles prompted.

Cagliostro nodded. "Extensions of myself, made from the stuff of souls. Mere puppets anywhere else, but here, they are extensions of myself," he said again. "I can use them to—"

"Prey on anyone unfortunate enough to make their acquaintance," Giles said.

"*Harvest* is a more appropriate word, I think," Cagliostro said. "And not *anyone*. It varies by population. I've found more here who are susceptible to the charm than anywhere else. I don't know why, really. It must be the Hellmouth, either strengthening me or weakening them. The numbers rise by the minute." He paused. "Isn't it odd? I'd sent the wolf and the others out merely to get the lay of the land, and instead, they've fed me."

"You're a monster," Giles said.

The gunfighter laughed, a stereo chuckle that was deep and complex. When he spoke, the seated Cagliostro's lips moved too, and words emerged from both mouths. "I'm but a dabbler and an explorer," he said. "In all my journeys I've never pretended to be more. But I think that when the time comes to leave this pleasant community, I may well be something more." Two heads tilted, and four eyes gazed at Giles. "I might be something like a god."

Booted feet gritted on gravel. The sound made Buffy turn just in time to see someone or something emerge from the darkness between two parked panel vans. She saw a figure in black leather with skin that was as white as bone and hair that showed as purple even in the poor light. Reflexively, the Slayer raised her machete and swung.

"Hey!" The voice was girlish and angry. Cardboard containers of popcorn and soda flew, scattering their contents as Buffy's target tried to dodge.

It was a civilian on her way back from the concession stand. Just in time, Buffy pulled back and changed the path of her blade. There was a tearing *thump* as the machete slammed into one of the panel vans, embedding itself deeply in the metal.

"What is your problem, witch?" the Goth girl asked. She made a great show of brushing popcorn from the front of her outfit. "You made me drop my stuff!"

"Sorry," Buffy said. An apology certainly seemed in order, but her heart wasn't in it.

"Otto is going to kill me!" the girl said.

Heaven might know who Otto was, but Buffy didn't. "Really, I'm sorry," she said.

"You're going to pay for that," the Goth girl said, but then her mouth opened in a silent O of surprise. She'd seen Buffy's machete and *boka*, and realized the Slayer's companions carried weapons too. "Hey," she said, turning even paler, "I don't want any trouble."

"You won't get any," Buffy said, brushing past her. Calling back over her shoulder she said, "And get out of here if you can. Walk out if the entrance is still blocked."

She'd just finished speaking when the next wave of attack came.

Xander was being stupid again, Cordelia realized as she re-entered the hospital room. She was out of breath from her hasty patrol of the corridor, but she managed to draw enough air into her lungs to shape the words. "Get away from that!" she commanded.

He tore his gaze from the thread of light. It was much thicker now and flared where it met Jonathan's chest. Xander's fingertips were inches from the gleaming line.

"Huh?" he asked, startled. The sudden movement almost brought him into contact with the tendril, and Cordelia gasped in concern. "Okay, okay," he said, drawing back. "It's just—it doesn't look like much."

"Neither do the others," Cordelia said. She was relieved,

but she still watched carefully in case Xander did something that was, well, Xander-like.

"Others?"

She nodded. "I checked every room I could find without getting caught. Everyone I could find who's like—like him, has one of those things coming out of their chests," she told him.

According to news reports, the hospital held thirty victims of the mysterious sleeping sickness. Cordelia had found only half that number, but they had all been much alike. Friends or strangers, teenage or adult, they all lay unmoving beneath white sheets, with silvery luminances sprouting from their chests like some strange plant.

Worst of all was Aura. The sight of her had nearly made Cordelia weep. Her friend's skin had paled further, and the heart monitor's panel suggested that she was at the lower margin of safety. She'd thumbed the call button but left Aura's room before anyone had arrived.

"All of them, huh?" Xander said. He leaned closer to the strand and eyed it suspiciously. "It doesn't look like much."

"Maybe not one, but I assure you, seeing more than a dozen of those things will give you the creeps," Cordelia said.

"Huh." Xander was repeating himself. "I wonder what it is?"

"So do I," Cordy said. "And once Buffy gets back from the drive-in, I'm sure that she and Giles will tell us all about it."

"I wonder how it connects up?" Xander asked, speaking more to himself than to her. He brought his fingers close to it again. "I bet I could tear it loose."

"Xander!" She nearly screamed his name, but she was too late.

He'd already touched it.

After a certain point the process became monotonous. Dodge, hack, then dodge or strike again. There were nights when slaying had a certain rhythm to it, like an elaborate dance of strike and counterstrike, but not tonight. This was extermination, pure and simple.

Another wolf-man leaped at her, so she swung one blade to remove his head and the threat. Hollywood's idea of a vampire—presumably from the same movie that had given form to the ticket-selling priest—lunged with fangs bared, then died as she lopped off an arm with a lucky swing. In real life, that wouldn't have worked, but Buffy didn't have time to be thankful for her relative good fortune. Inga was coming at her with a chainsaw and needed to be put down. Buffy dispatched her, only to have to do it again as another kill-crazy Swedish nurse materialized out of nowhere.

"How're you holding up, Buffy?" Angel called out to her. He was busily decapitating a biker brute but whirled just in time to fend off another priest and then a cheerleader.

"Could be better," she said, panting. "Could be worse."

She was serious. The sheer number of assailants was daunting, but they were vulnerable individually. Now that they knew how to destroy the phantasms, it was just a matter of being wary and strong. Even Willow was keeping pace, thanks in part to protective cover from Slayer and vampire. For whatever reason, the movie afterimages were concentrating on vampire and Slayer, and not on their little friend. They were making progress. It was slow, hard work, but the distance between them and their goal dwindled gradually.

Allowing Willow to come along had been a mistake, though. More and more, Buffy was sure of that. The farther they went, the greater the resistance became, and that worried Buffy. Sooner or later, she could be worn down. So could Angel. If either of them was struck down, the balance would tip from their favor and all would fall. They had to reach Cagliostro before that happened.

Three bikers attacked, whipping chains. Buffy sliced at them, first the chains and then the goons who wielded them. As she swung and spun, Angel extinguished a kung fu fighter in midkick. He was in full vampire mode now, and the grin he flashed at her was both bestial and reassuring.

It was good to have a boyfriend who appreciated your profession.

The projection shack neared. The attacks came more furiously, increasing in number and intensity. Buffy swung and cut and swung some more, then called out, "Willow!"

"Yeah?" came the answer. Willow took another slice at some guy wearing an overcoat and a slouch hat.

"This is where you get off," Buffy said.

"No!"

"Yes!" She made it a command. They were mere yards

from the doorway now, and Buffy could no longer spare her friend the protective attention she needed. "Break and take cover. I mean it!"

"I won't leave you!" Willow said, but her voice was failing. She was wearing down. It was amazing that she'd made it this far, really.

"Now!" Buffy repeated. "It's time for the professionals to take over."

Xander felt as if he'd gripped a live wire, fully charged with high-voltage electricity. He managed a grunt of surprise as the hammering force swept through him, a grunt that became a yelp of pain and then silence as his voice fled him.

He tried to pull himself free, but couldn't. His body was in revolt, the muscles refusing to obey his commands. He could not speak or move, and even the beating of his heart seemed to have stilled. The world seemed poised to go away.

"Xander!" Cordy screamed.

And then he was somewhere else. Somewhere else, and *someone* else.

Or many someones.

"Remarkable. Your champions are making progress," Cagliostro said from his chair. His voice still echoed slightly, but the gunslinger had fallen silent. Evidently, the battle that Giles could hear raging outside was commanding more and more of the alchemist's attention. "You've trained her well," he told the Watcher. "You've given her a kind of greatness."

Giles allowed himself to shake his head. "No," he said with complete honesty. "Any greatness Buffy has is of her own making."

Cagliostro didn't believe him and said so. "I'd entertained fantasies of taking her alive," he said. "I've long wanted to study the inner workings of the Slayer. The blood, the nerves, the elemental tissues—they really must be most remarkable."

"You'll never take her alive," Giles said.

"Defiance?"

"Not defiance," Giles said. "Simple fact."

Scarcely had he spoken the words when the booth door flew off its hinges. It bounced and spun as it flew, freed by one savage kick from a nicely booted foot. Startled, both men turned to face the opening, and in it, the trim outline of a girl. Behind her was darkness, filled with half-seen images of battle and thick with the sounds of combat.

"All right, mister," Buffy said. "Fun's fun, but the show's over. I need my librarian back."

Giles had never been so happy to see her in all his life, and his joy was dimmed only slightly when the nameless gunslinger pressed a loaded pistol against the back of his head.

Willow dropped to her knees. No one seemed to notice—not Buffy, not Angel, not any of the spectral horde who defended the projection booth. She half-crawled, half-walked, and let the tide of battle sweep over her, unmindful and uncaring.

They were focused entirely on Buffy and Angel. Whoever or whatever commanded them must have decided that she didn't matter. Whether deliberately or by utter lack of concern, she was being allowed to retreat.

She hated that. She hated being useless, being the weak link. Most of all, she hated retreating, but there was nothing she could do.

Then she realized that there *was*.

Cagliostro stood. Still connected to the projector via the glowing umbilical cord, he bowed politely, a complete bow, and smiled at Buffy. "Well played," he said. "The trap is sprung."

"Trap?" Buffy said. "You've got to be kidding. This wasn't a trap." She raised the two blades.

"Oh?" he asked.

"I've read up on you," she said. "I've asked around. You're just a blowhard trying to make the best of a bad situation. I figure, you didn't think I'd come running, at least not quite as fast." She paused. "Giles, you okay?"

"I'm fine, Buffy," came the Watcher's response.

"That could change," Cagliostro said ominously.

Every muscle in Buffy's body was vibrating with tension. "I wouldn't advise it," she said. "Now, tell the cowboy to put down his gun, and we can end this easy."

"I think not," Cagliostro said. Without the slightest show of concern, he continued. "You'll put down your weapons.

Surrender to me, and I'll grant your Watcher his life, though not his freedom. If not . . ." He shrugged.

Buffy scarcely looked as she threw the *boka*. The casual toss was dead on target, though, and felled the phantom gunslinger. "There," the Slayer said. "We'll do it the hard way, then."

"The *very* hard way," Cagliostro said as even more agents materialized: the six bikers who had given her and Angel such a hard time the night before. They arranged themselves between her and the alchemist.

"He dies, you die," Buffy promised. The odds were terrible, but she knew she could beat them. Only one question made her pause.

Would she be freeing Giles, or ensuring his death?

It was as if Xander were everywhere at once, or nowhere at all. He seemed to be seeing the world from a thousand different angles, all at the same time, and his hearing was even worse. The overwhelming rush of information seemed like enough to make his head explode, only he didn't seem to have a head anymore. He didn't seem to have anything but his thoughts and his senses, all of which worked with what had to be superhuman clarity.

He saw Principal Snyder, alone in the Snydermobile, watching *Double Drunken Dragon Kung Fu Fight* and chuckling as he nibbled a corn dog.

He saw Joyce Summers shake the shoulder of her sleeping

escort, and he heard her worried voice ask, "Barney? Are you all right, Barney?"

He saw the girl with purple hair lead her fatso boyfriend toward the drive-in exit, and heard her angrily telling him about her encounter with some uppity blond chick with an axe. If he could have, Xander would have nodded. The Magic Box girl had to be talking about Buffy.

He saw Willow, moving fast in a half crouch, crawl between parked cars and approach the projection booth from its blind side, where the long cables that powered the place hung low.

And then he heard a familiar voice say the kind of words he'd heard so many times before: "He dies, you die."

"Buffy?" he heard himself ask.

The bikers had been approaching, but now they froze in place. So did the replacement gunslinger who had suddenly materialized behind Giles. Even Cagliostro seemed locked in place, but his paralysis was less complete. Where the others were frozen like a video still frame, Cagliostro had merely paused. An expression of absolute confusion formed on his aristocratic features, and he licked his lips as he looked from side to side.

"Buffy?" he said. "Giles? What's going on here?"

Buffy blinked, completely dumbfounded. The centuries-old master mage, philosopher, and politician had spoken in a different voice, the voice of a confused teenager.

"Xander?" she asked.

"Buffy, what's—"

Giles interrupted. "The projector, Buffy. It's the projector. That's the secret of his power."

"Of course," Buffy said.

"No," Cagliostro said, speaking in his own voice again. "No, you—"

Willow had watched Buffy enter the projection booth. Angel stood with his back to the door, serving as rear guard, fighting off an army of apparitions that sought to follow the Slayer inside. Willow watched as Angel's arms rose and fell in merciless, killing strokes. Heads and arms and other body parts flew, then faded into nothingness. It was like seeing Horatio at the bridge, or the last stand at the Alamo. With his back covered, the vampire could make his stand and hold it for a very long time.

At least long enough for Willow to be of some help.

She still held the petite axe, and she kept it at the ready to defend herself, but there was no need. No one and nothing tried to stop her as she made her way to the rear wall of the projection building. Heavy cables entered the structure through fixtures on the blind wall. Willow eyed them. Her own words came back to her: "It looks like some kind of fiber-optic network," she'd told Buffy as they'd noticed the silver cords that led to the projector's rays.

Whatever the system Cagliostro used, the projection equipment was part of it. Projection equipment needed power.

Actually slicing the cables with her axe would be dangerous, even fatal, but if she could *throw* the weapon . . .

Willow raised the axe and took aim.

Buffy's machete really wasn't well balanced for throwing, but she made do. Only one of the paired projectors was running, which made her choice of target easy. She cast the machete like a dagger, fast and hard. Heavy tempered steel, honed to a razor edge, buried itself with gratifying effect into the projector's switch box.

Lightning struck. Long, liquid sparks sprayed and splashed as the machine's housing sundered. They were nothing like the pale tendrils that Buffy had seen outdoors, but savage, searing bolts that split the air and burned it with their passage. The projection shack filled with the stink of ozone as the projector shuddered to a halt and died.

Cagliostro died too.

He died screaming, with the accumulated fury and frustration of a life that had gone on for entirely too long. Haloed in electrical fire, he shook and convulsed, and then seemed to collapse into himself in obedience of some strange geometry. As Buffy watched, he dwindled and twisted in ways that made her eyes hurt. It was as if he were falling away from her in all directions at once, only to be lost in an infinite distance.

She tore her gaze from where he'd been and turned to Giles. They were alone in the small room now; the bikers and gunfighter had vanished as thoroughly as their creator, albeit with less spectacle. Dark spots danced in her vision as she reached to untie his bonds, and it took her a moment to realize that they were gone too.

"They belonged to the cowboy," Giles told her as he stood.

"Gunslinger," Buffy corrected him, but she hugged the Watcher, hard enough to make him gasp. "You're safe? He didn't hurt you?"

"I'm fine," Giles said, wriggling free. "But what on earth is that cacophony?"

It sounded like a hundred car horns were blaring, and when Buffy and Giles stepped outside, the reason was obvious. The screen had gone black. Angel, certain now that the war was over, offered an explanation. "I think they want their money back," he said.

"But—but—everyone got in free!" Buffy said slowly.

EPILOGUE

That's when the screen went dark," Willow said. She seemed disappointed. "Before I could even throw the axe, I mean."

"Don't worry, Will," Buffy said. "It was the right idea. You just weren't the only one to have it."

"Well, sure, but—"

"Next time, you can save the day," Buffy said. "Really, I promise."

Willow beamed.

They were back in the school library, seated again at the table. Giles was watching nervously as Xander examined the lens that Giles had retrieved from the ruined projector. Perhaps three inches across, it was thick and convex on both sides. It was heavy, too—much heavier than ordinary optical glass. Whatever it had been crafted of, the substance didn't seem to bend light—an odd property for a projector lens.

"So that's the little toy that caused so much trouble," Xander said. He plucked the bit of crystal from the velvet-lined box where Giles was keeping it. "Doesn't look like much," he said.

"It's only a tool," Giles said, still watching Xander carefully. "Think, Xander. How much use would a lens be at a puppet show, or in the days before magick lanterns? Balsamo's basic abilities were his own, I think, though we may never know how he gained them. The lens was but a means to focus and direct them."

"I thought he said the Hellmouth—"

"I said, *basic* abilities," Giles reminded him. "The lens gave him focus, but the Hellmouth made him stronger." He paused. "Even so, be careful with that. I want very much to study it, which means I don't want you to damage it."

"Yeah, yeah, yeah," Xander said. "Anyone ever tell you that you worry too much, G-man?"

"Maybe it's diamond?" Cordelia asked. It was like her to ignore the most interesting aspect and focus instead on the most materialistic one.

Giles shook his head. "A form of crystal, I think. Possibly Latverian."

"Where do you think he got it?" Willow asked.

"I suspect he made it," Giles said. He claimed the stone and eyed its rim. Minute symbols were etched there in an undecipherable language. "Latverian crystals are sensitive to astral energies, and he probably began with one of those."

It was Monday. Sunday had been a day of recovery and happiness. The news had spread that all thirty of the sleepers had awakened, and that no more had been found. News media were speculating that it was some form of food poisoning and had turned their attention to the mysterious doings at the drive-in. Oddly, no one seemed to draw a connection between the two events; the team consensus was that Cagliostro's charming disclaimer had endured past his death.

"How is your mother, Buffy?" Giles asked.

"Mom? Fine. Just embarrassed about falling asleep at the movies," Buffy said. "I'm surprised she was there at all, after all this Barney character's talk about 'something bad' happening years ago." She looked disgusted. "Turns out that 'something bad' in grown-up talk means 'losing your investment capital.' But everyone is fine. Mom, Jonathan, Aura, everyone. There's some bellhop who says he's going to write a book about the whole thing."

"What about you, Xander?" Giles asked. "That must have been quite an experience."

"Oh, yeah," Xander said. He mock shuddered. "Kind of creepy, really. Going to be a while before I sleep well. Not that I'm complaining."

"I'd like to discuss it with you at length. You actually

stepped outside your body without the years of training that such things require," Giles said.

Willow offered up a theory of what had happened, elaborating on what she'd discussed before: Cagliostro's web of sorcery was something very much like an astral Internet. As long as his was the only waking mind online, he ruled the network.

"But when Xander put himself online, it was like adding a second file server without the right trafficking protocols," she said. "The network locked up and the system crashed, at least for a moment."

"Of course," Giles said.

"You didn't understand a word of that, did you?" Buffy asked him.

Giles didn't answer directly. "All that matters is that it gave you the opening you needed," he said. "And whatever it was that Xander did, it was astoundingly dangerous." He placed the lens in its box. "I'm certainly glad that Cordelia thought to use a pillow for insulation when she pulled you free."

"Well, it's like she keeps telling us—," Xander began to say.

"I'm not stupid," Cordelia interrupted.

ABOUT THE AUTHORS

Christopher Golden is the award-winning, bestselling author of such novels as *Of Saints and Shadows*, *The Myth Hunters*, and *Soulless*. A lifelong fan of the "team-up," Golden frequently collaborates with other writers on books, comic books, and scripts. During his tenure with Buffy the Vampire Slayer, he wrote or cowrote more than a dozen novels, several nonfiction companion books, dozens of comics (including the comics-writing debuts of Amber Benson and James Marsters), and both Buffy video games. Golden was born and raised in Massachusetts, where he still lives with his family. His original novels have been published in more than fourteen languages in countries around the world. Please visit him at www.christophergolden.com.

Nancy Holder has published more than seventy-eight books and more than two hundred short stories. She has received four Bram Stoker awards for her supernatural fiction. Among her books for Simon Pulse, she is the coauthor of the *New York Times* bestselling Wicked series and the Once upon a Time novels *The Rose Bride* and *Spirited.* She lives in San Diego with her daughter, Belle, their two cats, and their two Corgis. Visit her at www.nancyholder.com.

Diana G. Gallagher has written young adult and adult novels in several series: Buffy the Vampire Slayer; Charmed; Smallville; Sabrina, the Teenage Witch; and others. She lives in Florida with her husband, five dogs, three cats, and a cranky parrot. Her hobbies include gardening, politics, and grandchildren.

Pierce Askegren was born in Pennsylvania. At various points in his so-called career, Pierce was a convenience store clerk, bookstore manager, technical editor, logistics analyst, and writer for business proposals and industrial instruction materials. At one point he knew an alarming amount about wireless communications protocols. Pierce also wrote extensively for Marvel Comics characters, having authored or coauthored five novels featuring Spider-Man, the Fantastic Four, the Hulk, and the rest of the gang.

THE VAMPIRES LIVE ON. . . .

BUFFY THE VAMPIRE SLAYER 3

CARNIVAL OF SOULS

BY NANCY HOLDER

ONE THING OR YOUR MOTHER

BY KIRSTEN BEYER

BLOODED

BY CHRISTOPHER GOLDEN AND NANCY HOLDER

Turn the page for a sneak peek . . .

The vampires live on. . . .

Buffy the Vampire Slayer 3

Carnival of Souls

By Nancy Holder

One Thing or Your Mother

By Kirsten Beyer

Blooded

By Christopher Golden and Nancy Holder

Turn the page for a sneak peek . . .

It was Tuesday.

After nightfall.

In Sunnydale.

And Buffy Summers the Vampire Slayer was out on patrol instead of at the Bronze with Willow and Xander (and hopefully Angel) because Giles had figured out that tonight was the Rising.

The Rising of what, Buffy's Watcher did not know, but it was easy to guess that it probably meant vampires. Maybe zombies. Something that rose from graves, anyway.

Something that kept her from the fun other sixteen-year-olds were having.

Sighing, Buffy trailed her fingers over the lowered head

of a weeping cherub statue and waved her flashlight in an arc.

"Here, rising guys," she called plaintively. "Ready to play when you are."

She had on her black knitted cap and Angel's black leather jacket, but she was still a little chilly. Maybe it was just because she was walking through Blessed Memories, the cemetery that contained the du Lac tomb, famed in the annals of Buffy's diary as the cemetery out of which Spike and Dru had stolen a fancy decoding cross called, amazingly enough, the du Lac Cross. They had used it to nearly kill Angel. Since then, it was not her favorite cemetery ever.

Blessed Memories also contained a pet cemetery, a little square of plots with miniature headstones that tugged at Buffy's heart. TOBY MY PUP RIP 1898. R KITTIE LUCY 1931. She had no time for pets, not even zombie cats freshly risen from the grave. She had hardly any time for anything, what with the slayage and the studying, okay, not the studying; but still and all, it was Sunnydale that was the problem, with all its death and monsters and standard normal-teenage-girl pressures, like having friends and not getting kicked out of school. . . .

If my best buds and I could be anywhere but here, that would be . . . She thought for a moment. She and Willow were really good at that game. Anywhere But Here was created for high school kids, especially those who had to live in Sunnydale.

. . . in Maui, with Angel. . . . Okay, not. Too much sun for a boyfriend who would burst into flames if he stepped into the tropical rays. So . . .

. . . in Paris, with Angel . . . and Willow could be with James Spader—I officially give him to her because I'm with Angel now—and we're so not eating snails, but oh, I know! French pastries. And we are shopping . . .

. . . for rings . . .

Buffy stopped and cocked her head. Did she just hear something? Snap of a twig, maybe? A cough?

She listened eagerly for a replay so she could head toward it. She waited. Waited yet more. Heard nothing. Turned off her flashlight. More waiting.

Behold the sounds of silence.

She tried to pick up the Paris thread again. French pastries, okay, maybe too early in the relationship to shop for rings, then for shoes. . . . Truth was, she really *would* be happy to be just about anywhere but here. If only she could just run away, join in the fun-having of other kids her age. Join the circus, even.

Except she didn't like circuses. Never had. What was with those clowns, anyway? She shivered. She was with Xander on that one: They gave her a wiggins.

Send in the clowns.

Six miles away, just past the outbuildings of Crest College, the trees shivered. The clouds fled and the moon trailed after them, desperate to hide.

Sunnydale, loaded with souls ripe for the plucking . . .

Five miles away.

The clowns materialized first, big feet flapping, overstuffed bottoms wiggling, in polka dots and rainbow stripes, and white gloves hiding fingers that no one should ever see.

A jag of lightning:

A parade of trucks, wagons, lorries. A maroon wagon, its panels festooned with golden Harlequins and bird women plucking lyres, shimmered and stayed solid. Behind it, a Gypsy cart with a Conestoga-style bonnet jangled with painted cowbells, and beneath the overhanging roof, black-and-silver ribbons swayed. Behind the wagon, a forties-era freight truck blew diesel exhaust into the velvet layers of moonlight. A jagged line, creaking back into shadows, disappearing. Maybe the entire apparition was just a dream.

Thunder rolled, and they reappeared.

Maybe they were just a nightmare.

Spectral horses whinnied and chuffed; it began to rain, and through the murky veil of downpour and fog, the horses' heads were skulls; their heads were . . . heads. They breathed fire; they didn't breathe at all.

They began to rot in slow motion.

The clowns ran up and down the advancing line, applauding and laughing at the flicker-show, the black magick lantern extravaganza.

Skeletons and corpses hunkered inside truck and wagon cabs and buckboard seats. Whipcracks sparked. Eyes lolled. Mouths hung open, snapped shut. Teeth fell out. Eyes bobbed from optic nerves.

Things . . . reassembled.

A creak, and then nothing.

Two ebony steeds pulled the last vehicle—the thirteenth wagon in the cortege. It was an old Victorian traveling-medicine-show wagon, maybe something that had crisscrossed the prairies and the badlands, promising remedies for rheumatism and the gout when the only ingredients in the jug were castor oil, a dead rattlesnake, and wood alcohol.

Where their hooves touched, the earth smoked. Black feathers bobbing in their harnesses, black feathers waving from the four corners of the ornate ebony wagon, the horses were skeletons were horse flesh were demon stallions ridden by misshapen, leathery creatures with sagging shoulder blades, flared ears, and pencil-stub fingers. And as the moon shied away from the grotesquerie, the angle of light revealed words emblazoned on each of the thirteen vehicles that snuck toward Sunnydale, home to hundreds of thousands of souls determined to ignore the peril they were in:

PROFESSOR CALIGARI'S TRAVELING CARNIVAL

The wind howled through the trees—or was it the ghostly dirge of a calliope?

Too soon to tell.

Too late to do anything about it.

When Aura's boyfriend dies, she is devastated.
But it's hard to say good-bye to someone who is not really gone. . . .

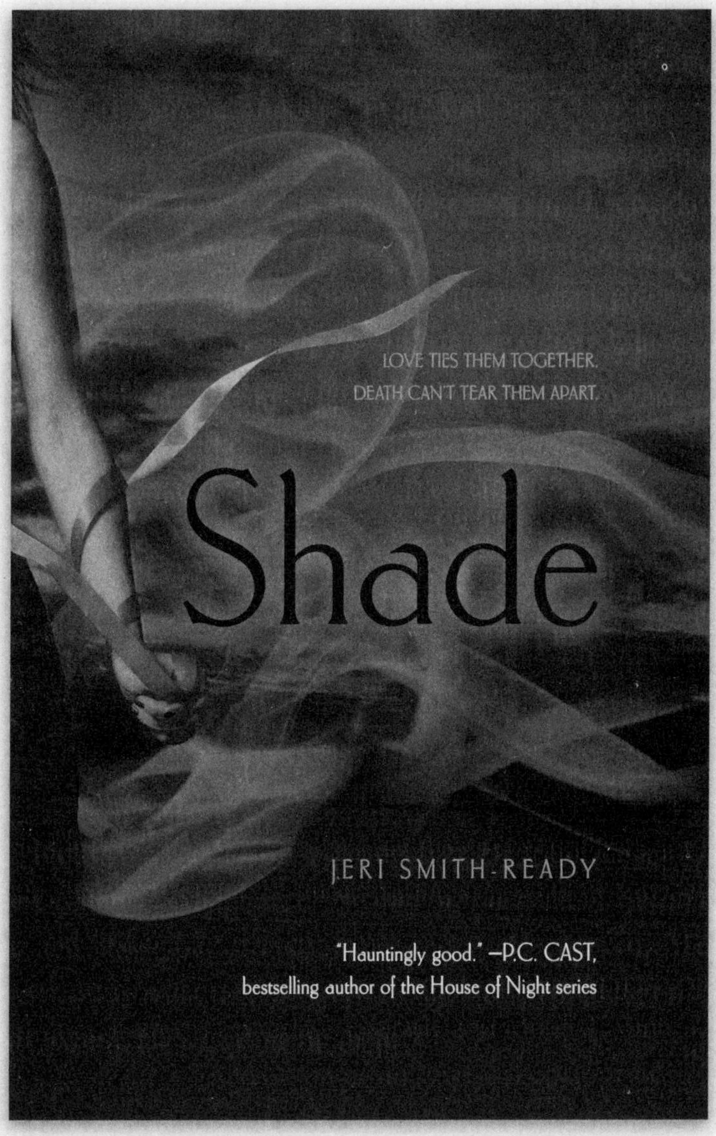